DRAGON BRIDE

The Lightbearer Series

Iman Christians

CONTENTS

Pronunciation Guide

Characters

Asha Osei — *AH-sha OH-say*

   Adriel — *AY-dree-el*

   Kwasi — *KWAH-see*

   Nayeli — *Nye-ELL-ee*

   Kitchi — *KEE-chee*

   Ashkii — *ASH-kee*

   Enapay — *EN-ah-pay*

   Ekon — *EH-kon*

   Iná — *EE-nah*

   Miren — MEER-en

   Kadir — kuh-DEER

   Cane — KAYN

Dragons

Drakkar — *DRAH-kar*
   Mwana — MWAH-nuh
   Igbo — EE-boh
   Ala — AH-lah
   Zyphur — *ZYE-fur*

Kingdoms & Places

Ujuima — *Oo-JEE-mah*
   Wiyotak — *WHY-oh-tak*
   Firepeak — *FIRE-peek*
   Entioch — *EN-tee-ock*
   Wyrmwood — *WIRM-wood*
   Saeleria — *SAY-lair-ee-ah*
   Ifambe — ee-FAHM-bay

CONTENT WARNING

Dragon Bride contains content that may be distressing to some readers. Please be advised of the following:

Sexual violence and assault (including references to past trauma)

Domestic abuse and intimate partner violence

Child abuse and neglect

Graphic violence and torture

Misogyny and gender-based violence

Captivity and imprisonment

Power imbalance and coercion

Generational trauma

Mental and emotional manipulation

Bodily harm

This book also contains explicit sexual content and is intended for readers 18 and older.

If any of these topics are sensitive for you personally, please take care of yourself first.

ACKNOWLEDGEMENTS

To my husband, thank you for listening to every delusion and wild idea.

To my parents, thank you for teaching me I could have them. Mom and Dad... maybe skip this one.

To the woman who carries a dragon inside her.
May you stop shrinking yourself for rooms that fear your fire.
Unfurl your wings. The sky was never too small for you.

PROLOGUE

It is a given that dragons are safer than men. Dragons are stubborn and slow to trust, but that is a vast improvement over men, who cannot be trusted at all.

Still, there was a man once. He was the last person I should trust and yet, for the first time, I wondered if one day I would.

Chapter One

Elan

There was something about having a woman's hand around your dick. It was a pleasure only surpassed by soft pouty lips. Normally, I'd be enjoying the sensation. The woman in question was one of my best, but tonight, despite her enthusiastic efforts, I could not rally. I had not been able to since the burning. No number of women, men, or combination of the two could rouse me. Even the wine that fell from my drooping lips tasted bitter. I flung the gold chalice, and the woman flinched but did not dare stop her efforts, instead doubling them, loud moans coming from her throat as she increased her rhythm. This is the type of devotion I had come to admire her for, but tonight it just annoyed me. I fisted my hand in her hair until I reached her scalp and pulled.

She gasped, terror in her dark brown eyes as her back arched. "Please, Your Holiness. I can do better. The scarring…"

My other hand closed around her throat, tightening until her words dissolved into a thin whimper.

"What did you say?"

A knock at my chamber door brought our moment to a halt.

"Go away," I snapped.

There was a moment of quiet, before another knock sounded. I sighed deeply before shoving the woman to the floor.

"Stay there," I said, pulling my trousers up as I stood at full height over her cowering form. "You may enter."

Something rustled behind the door as if there was a disagreement on who would enter first. Ekon pushed the door open, followed by two other dragonlords. It only seemed fair to promote Ekon, as he was the only one with the courage to protect his emperor. I needed another one after I executed the failed ones anyway.

"What is it?"

Ekon bowed, revealing his carefully cropped hair before saying, "There is someone here to see you."

I tapped my foot impatiently. "Tell them to go away. I am not seeing visitors."

"That is what we said, Your Holiness, but..." He paused, pulling a scroll from behind his dracite armor. "He would not leave. He asked that you read this. It has a royal seal."

I tore it from his outstretched hand, breaking the seal. As I read through the scroll, my foul mood shifted. "Well, well, well..." I chuckled, shoving the scroll back to him to read.

His eyes scanned the parchment, and his brows arched as he found the signature. "Nightborne?" he asked.

"It seems not all the royals are useless after all," I mused. "Ready our horses, Dragonlord. I want the whole army to accompany us."

"That might take some time, Your Holiness. At least two weeks to get everyone armed and the dragons fed and ready."

"No," I barked. "You have three days. Don't tell me you can't do it. I will just find someone who can."

Ekon lifted his gaze slowly before giving one final bow. "Of course. Where will the army go?"

I was so gleeful, I did not even mind that I could not smile properly. "To pay my dear sister a visit."

When the door closed behind them, I turned back to the woman, still kneeling where I had left her. Power crackled beneath my skin, alive and impatient. "Close your mouth, darling, and show me your skin. I have something else in mind for us tonight."

She trembled before me, struggling to unclasp her dress. And for the first time, arousal stirred.

CHAPTER TWO

Adriel

It was strange to be home in Empira Palace and find as little of it as I remembered. I supposed years away would do that. It had taken that long to grind down my brother's army, bolstered by the emperor, but we'd successfully reclaimed our kingdom piece by piece.

I stepped into the afin—the grand hall where my brother once ruled. Where ivory and copper ornaments had stood, gold and silver from Ujuima now gleamed. The floors had been replaced with dracite, a precaution against dragon attacks.

Only the throne remained unchanged. It was the same seat our father had used, built from sapele and copper, shaped to endure. Standing beside it, I realized how much larger it had seemed in my memory. Raised on its steps, it still projected authority, though the illusion faded up close.

I opened my hand and summoned the quiet blue fire of my battlemage. It flared to life as it always had, unchanged by the years I had spent without my abilities. I had always believed the throne would make one feel regal. Instead, all I felt was empty.

"What took you so long, my dear?"

My lip turned upward. "Iná Nayeli," I said as she walked slowly into the room. Her reliance on her cane was greater than normal. The war had not been kind to her. I stood, trying to embrace her, but she batted me away.

"I did not mean to interrupt your victory," she said with disapproval.

"What victory?" I said. The words tasted bitter. "Enapay has escaped."

Nayeli nodded with caution. "He was always an elusive one, but not very bright."

"If I can't catch him, then what does that make me?"

She frowned as she peered at my face. I turned away, uneasy under the scrutiny. "These years have been hard on you." It wasn't a question.

"War is hard on everyone."

She tutted. "That is not what I was speaking about."

Not wanting to continue the conversation, I asked, "You wouldn't happen to have any idea of where my dear brother is?"

"How things have changed between you," she continued without acknowledgment of my words. "You're harder. Colder."

"I am a war chief. That is how it must be."

"No," she said firmly. "You are a king, a better one than your brother, I hope."

I shook my head. "I don't intend to rule. I came to free my people."

"They are not free if they have no one to rule them," she said, patting my cheek. "And no one to hold the letter of the law. Without a king, Wiyotak will descend into darkness. Allowing Enapay to destroy the thing would have been best if you didn't have intentions to rule."

I grimaced. "I plan to set up a military state until a new ruler is chosen."

She chuckled. "A smart ruler would make sure you don't live. They won't want the competition."

The doors of the hall burst open as Chato and Moki dragged a familiar face into the room. They dropped him at the bottom of the steps.

I smiled as I saw Winnow's weary frame. "I never thought we would meet again, War Chief," I said with open disdain.

Winnow met my eye. From the floor I could only imagine what he saw, tall and broad, hardened muscle from years of war and a battle that never seemed to end. His eyes filled with defiance, malice even, but there was the unmistakable thread of fear.

"What's the matter? Don't have anything to say?"

"Just get on with it," he grunted. "I am prepared to die."

"Die? Who said anything about dying?" I asked with mock surprise. "I want you to live, Winnow, I just want you to earn it."

"What is this?" he asked warily. "Do not play with me. End it!"

"You see, you have two choices, Winnow," I continued. "You can tell me now where your king has gone, or I can have my Guardians take you back and beat the information out of you."

He spat on the ground. "I will never betray my King."

I looked behind him and motioned. Kitchi stepped forward and punched him in the face. He fell over, and she kicked him in the ribcage, a distinct *crack* filling the room.

"Come now, Winnow. We both know you know where he is, so stop pretending."

"You son of a—"

He wasn't able to finish because Chato punched him in the jaw. His head snapped back and he spat out what looked like several teeth.

I smirked. "I hope you don't tell me, because I am going to enjoy beating it out of you."

"Fine," Winnow gasped. "Disappear me. Take your brother's throne. You won't have it for long," he said between swollen lids. Still, I could see the barest hint of his eye as he looked at me. "Not with that dragon bitch flying around. What happened, by the way? I thought the great war chief would have been able to tame that whor—"

He didn't get a chance to finish. His next breath was a scream as his entire body erupted in the blue fire of my battlemage. It took seconds before Winnow was a heap of ash at my feet. Kitchi gasped as my other men watched me with unease. I closed my eyes, trying to shut out the voice in my head as I reached for the cool metal in my hand. I clung to it, like it was the singular force that could ground me. Only Nayeli dared approach. She warmly brushed the sweat from my brow.

"Vengeance will not make it better, my boy."

I closed my eyes. "No. But it feels so damn good."

CHAPTER THREE

Asha

Two years in Firepeak and I still had not come across a single Lightbearer. I sat cross-legged on the floor, my hand outstretched to the man across from me. I picked up a handful of ash and sprinkled it over the man's hand for good measure. Ash was a part of life in Firepeak, just as sand was in Ujuima.

The man's other hand sat drumming against his pants legs like he was trying to drown out his impatience. Dust curled between us, smoky at first, then arduously bitter in the end, as if it knew something I didn't.

"Your energy is strong," I said, letting my fingertips graze his palm. I'd read his aura several minutes ago, but I found small drops of information to appear more realistic when doing these readings. It also allowed me to pry very little. Most men who came to see me for my aura reading abilities wanted to hear about fortune and a better life—most would never see it. He was no different.

"Ambition suits you. Though it has a cost."

His fingers made a distinct *pop*, as if he curled them to seize the fortune as we spoke. "Ambition always costs something. Tell me what it gets me."

His aura pressed at the edge of my senses. He worked with metals; that much I'd worked out. He helped forge many of the weapons in the small town of Pyhrral, fondly called Nis. I steadied my breath and pretended to reach deeper.

"You'll rise, but not without consequence. There are riches that await you, but you must foster patience." I paused. "And humility."

He laughed. "My wife says the same thing. Only she doesn't sound as pretty saying it."

My hands stilled at his words. "Your wife?"

"Too soft for this world," he said, waving the thought away. "She should thank me for keeping her fed. Go on—what else do you see?"

The ash in the room thickened on my tongue. Without meaning to, I reached further into his aura until I saw her.

She was young, too young, with round cherub cheeks marred by a cut on her face and a purple bruise under her eye. A cup shattered as she grabbed beneath her dress to rub her collarbone, which was also bruised. Cruel laughter met my ears as she trembled, watching him enter the room. My jaw clenched as I tried to keep my own memories at bay.

I dropped his hand, bile rising in my throat. "I don't see anything else."

He leaned forward, the humor in his voice gone. "Nothing? Really. You don't stop when it gets interesting. Finish it."

"I'm done," I said, rising slowly.

He scoffed. "You charge me half a day's wages and stop halfway through? I gave you a chance because you are the best-looking palm reader I've come across. Dark skin, and that hair—"

I pulled at my blue tresses as if to protect them from his gaze.

"Turns out you're just a useless woman," he continued, "the least you could do is rub my—"

"Leave." I bristled.

His voice sharpened as he stood, towering over me. "Or what? How dare you treat me this way? Do you think I'm going to pay you for this shit?"

"I don't care what you do as long as you leave. You think you are the first asshole I've come across today? You're not even the most interesting. GET. OUT."

He lunged—fast, reckless. I felt the motion before it reached me, the surge of his battlemage flickering like lightning. I let instinct take over. My own battlemage rose through me, bright and sharp as the air crackled between us.

He froze mid-strike as his force dampened. His body locked in place as I held tightly to his aura. "You know what I love about men like you?" I asked through gritted teeth. "You are all so unimaginative," I said as I flipped through his thoughts, most of which had me beaten and bruised at his hands, and I instilled a few of my own. "I don't need a dragon to deal with you. This *useless woman* is enough."

He screamed as if his body was on fire. I relented only when I heard a familiar voice from behind me. He hit the ground hard, chest heaving, his face contorted between pain and disbelief.

I stood still, pulse steady. "I told you to leave."

"Alright," he gasped, as his feet dragged slowly across the floor.

As he climbed down the stairs, I said, "And if I ever hear about you hitting another woman, especially your wife, I will find you. Believe that."

"I...won't," he stammered, footsteps hitting the ground as he ran away.

"Ada?" Miren, my roommate, spoke, her voice cutting through the silence. "Should I even ask?"

"No need," I said, lowering my hand. "He got what was coming to him."

Miren clicked her tongue. "You could have just used the code word. I was nearby."

I shook my head. "I wanted to hurt him," I admitted. "That is wrong of me, isn't it?"

"It is dark," she said with a slight air of disapproval.

Miren was practical at her core. Barely a year older than me, already running her own booth out of the entertainment caravan. Firepeak was one of the strictest kingdoms—cards, dancing, even most reading was forbidden. Which, naturally, meant there was always a market for it.

Miren was a bone dancer, performing and teaching the forgotten art. It was intimate, the couples dancing skin to skin. From what I'd gathered, it was a far cry from the disciplined movement I grew up with.

The caravan served as the perfect cover while I searched for Lightbearers—people born like me with the ability to bond with dragons, a trait the emperor had tried to stamp out. First my father, then my brother for as long as I could remember.

"It's a good thing I've never been scared of the dark," I said with a smile.

Miren groaned. "You are going to get us kicked out."

"I'll be more careful," I promised.

She sighed as if she didn't believe me. She shouldn't. My grift brought about a lot of unsavory men, but no Lightbearers.

"Are you alright, Little One?"

I glanced behind me as if Drakkar would be there, but of course he wasn't. *"Yes,"* I said down the bond, the invisible thread that connected us. *"Nothing I can't handle."*

"I don't like your being there," he grumbled.

"Not now. I'll find you soon," I said, walking after Miren.

By nightfall, I joined Miren and a few others from our caravan circle. Mabel, a seamstress, stirred something thick over the fire—probably stew scavenged from Lisdal a week ago. Her daughter, Lacey, handed out bowls while I crushed herbs for flavor.

"I hope you're hungry," Mabel called.

"I'm not eating that," Miren scoffed. Lacey gagged beside her.

"You'll eat if you plan to go gallivanting with that boy tonight," Mabel retorted. "You don't know how good you have it. Ada never complains—she knows what it's like to go without."

My head jerked up at the name I'd adopted after joining the troupe.

"Who would she complain to? She's an unseer," Miren said, pointing out the obvious.

My fork fell from my hand onto the floor, and I cursed. "Sorry."

"I've got it," Lacey said as she knelt to pick it up for me. "It takes very little to be nice," she said with an air of maturity that belied her thirteen years of age.

"You are so rude, Miren. And don't use that—word. It's impolite," Mabel scolded.

"It's okay, Mabel," I said.

"I'm done talking about this," Mabel said. "Now what's this I hear about you having trouble during one of your readings today?"

"Why do you have a portrait of yourself on your back?" Miren asked, undeterred. "It is odd."

My mouth hung open for a moment. I was at a loss for words. That was one question I had not prepped for. I had gone back and forth about removing it, but it was one of the few reminders I had of Adriel. Without it, did our time together even exist?

"There's a portrait on my back?" I asked, feigning surprise.

Lacey fell into a giggling fit.

Miren, unamused, tapped her hand on the table. "No, I'd really like to know. Who did it?"

Mabel pursed her lips. "Look at the girl. She is blushing. It was obviously a boy, a talented one by the sound of it."

I'd tried so hard to run from the memories of him, but even here, Adriel was everywhere. I remembered everything, the rough line of his jaw beneath my palm, the curtain of his chestnut hair falling forward when he bent over my back to etch the design into my skin, the cool blue of his aura that only warmed when his defenses fell. Every time I caught a glimpse of the tattoo, even in my dreams, I couldn't escape him.

The tattoo had been his idea, a mark inked in hope and passion to cover the scars my brother had left behind. Now it burned like a brand. I hated it some days, needed it on others. It reminded me that I'd once had deep feelings for another. It felt wrong to forget that.

"It was a very long time ago," I relented.

"You should have it removed if it makes you uncomfortable," Miren offered sympathetically.

"No!" Lacey lamented to my surprise. "It is so beautiful." Had everyone seen it then? It appeared I'd have to take more care when dressing.

"Eat!" Mabel barked as we all sat down. Mabel said a prayer wishing health to the emperor, and I did my best not to sigh too loudly. "Where is this boy taking you again, Miren?" Mabel asked between mouthfuls.

"I told you. He's taking me to a prayer meeting, and then we'll probably get spiced apricots after."

"Hmm," she said. "Lacey's father used to take me for spiced apricots. Out she popped nine months later."

Lacey gagged beside me. "Mama!"

"I'm just saying, perhaps Miren should skip the spiced apricots."

"Don't worry," Miren groaned. "You've ensured I will never eat one again."

"Never say never," Mabel teased. "I still think they are a strange lot. I saw one the other day. Did you know their blood turns silver when they join?"

"It is temporary," Miren said. "A part of the process."

"I just think that is a lot to go through to join a club. I miss the old gods. All we had to do was bring an offering and sing a few hymns."

Miren sighed. "Can we change the subject?"

"Perhaps you could take Lacey. She loves spiced apricots, and it might be good to have a third party."

"No," Miren said quickly.

"And why not?" Mabel challenged.

"Ada is coming with me."

That stopped both Mabel and me in our tracks. "Oh, is she?" Mabel asked.

"Uh"—I schooled my expression, feeling a swift kick to my shins—"yes, I am."

"Can I come too?" Lacey asked.

"Absolutely not. Four would be a crowd," Miren chided.

Lacey's pout was palpable across the table. "It's not fair!"

"But Ada," Mabel began, "won't you be conspicuous leaving? What if others notice your condition?"

"That is the best part," Miren said. "The Shadows welcome all."

I stiffened, knowing exactly who the Shadows were—a faction who had been quietly infiltrating the Five Kingdoms for years, recruiting and concentrating power. They were searching for us, searching for me, but I had no intention of being recaptured. Flashes of their masked faces still sent shivers down my spine. The dragons had been warning for months about how they'd begun to infiltrate the kingdoms, scooping up and recruiting people to their side en masse. Could they also be searching for Lightbearers?

"I'll be careful," I said.

"*You are not going,*" a voice boomed in my head. I'd had enough practice at this point not to react when Drakkar used the bond.

"*This could be our chance to find Lightbearers.*"

"*It's too dangerous,*" he chastised.

"*Nothing else has worked. They seemed to be adept at finding others like me. Maybe we can learn something.*"

He grumbled loud enough that I worried the others would hear, but the continued chatter about spiced apricots told me they didn't.

"Fine," he said, "*but I'm coming with you.*"

CHAPTER FOUR

Asha

What's harder than being blind in a world that did not want me in it? Pretending to be.

Pretending, when I could see through my dragon's eyes—like slipping on a pair of glasses to view the world in a different light. It only worked when outside, walls and enclosed spaces cutting the connection like severed thread.

I stumbled once or twice on purpose as I followed behind Miren and her boyfriend, Cane. He doted on her openly and was friendly enough to me, which somehow made my deception feel worse.

"Where is this meeting?" I asked, steadying myself with my staff.

"At the old library," Miren said. "Since the book burnings, few people use it for much these days, but it's a big enough space to gather."

Libraries that were open to the public had long disappeared sometime during my father, Emperor Idris's reign. Only royal libraries remained, leaving the others abandoned and barely standing. "What have you heard about these Shadows?" I asked.

She hesitated, cracking her fingers. "It's hard to explain. They possess wisdom from before the Five Kingdoms were formed. They're loving. Accepting." She gave a small, uncertain smile. "And there's always good music."

"And food, apparently," I said.

"Oh yes," she said. "They always have the best food."

"It is curious," I began. "Who has extra food to spare these days?"

"It is what initially drew me to them," Cane boasted. "I've gotten quite fat off their shaved meats and dried jerky. But they believe a full belly opens the ears and the soul."

The library was not what I expected. It wasn't a hall at all, but an open amphitheater, its stone steps arranged in a wide semicircle descending toward the center stage.

"Good," Drakkar said. *"I'll be able to keep my eyes on you."*

"Oh, let me help you," Cane offered as we got to the steps. I took his hand, allowing him to guide me down. As we descended, broken stone brushed the edges of my awareness—disfigured faces of Orúnmìlà and Èṣù, gods of wisdom and consequence, cracked and eroded, as if even they saw no point in this place.

There was commotion below as nearly a hundred people gathered. I recognized the baker from next door to Mabel, not by sight but by the tenor in his voice, and the healer, who had a slight trill to her cadence.

At the bottom of the steps, tables overflowed with food. Several figures dressed in black distributed plates and small bags of provisions. Miren's eyes lit up as she pointed out each dish, delight dancing in her voice.

I hung back, studying the servers. Each of them wore white masks, featureless and still.

"Good evening," one of them said. I was surprised to hear a young voice greet me. "Welcome. Please take as much as you'd like. We have plenty. Is this your first meeting?"

"Uh, yes. Yes, it is."

"We are so glad you are here. We hope that you enjoy the message tonight."

"I hope so too," I said, forcing a smile. I walked away with the food but no appetite for it.

Cane chattered eagerly beside me, recounting the teachings he'd learned and the ones he still hoped to master. His enthusiasm grated; it felt like being trapped in someone else's fever dream. I was relieved when the music began. Everyone stood and began to sing.

Cane and Miren both seemed to know the lyrics. Everyone did. They sang it with a reverence that gave me chills, not in a good way. The melody was simple enough, deceptively so. I found myself mouthing the words before I knew it, a feeling of dread sweeping through my body until I forced myself to stop.

I used my staff to stand.

"This is strange," I called to Drakkar, but I was only met with silence. *"Drakkar?"* That was unlike him, especially since he seemed so adamant a moment ago. The bond felt muffled, like I was speaking from underwater.

We followed the others to the lower floor, forming a wide ring and joining hands. The person to my left gripped me tightly, their pulse throbbing with either excitement or fear—I could not discern. When the music began, low drums threaded with something metallic before five people were called into the center.

"These brave souls have chosen to join our ranks," one of the Shadows announced..

Cheers erupted around us. They were loud and immediate, like they had been waiting for this exact moment.

"You, too, may join," he offered. "All it takes is the oath. In return, you will be gifted a text from Nightborne, and a community who will provide for you."

He turned to the first in line. "Repeat after me."

The initiate swallowed.

"I," they said, voice trembling.

"State your name."

"Phakiso."

The Shadow continued. "In the presence of the Shadows, I swear my allegiance to the sacred principles of the Shadowcasters. I release my former ties and offer my will to this family. Should I betray this vow, may my name be erased and my fate claimed by the Shadow."

The others followed, each voice steadier than the last.

A chill ran through me as they did. I'd heard countless oaths made by dragonlords, clergy, and servants—but this one felt different. This oath felt older, like no matter how learned you were about such things, the oathtaker would never fully understand the weight of these words.

Our circle began to move, first in one direction, then the other. Slow at first, then faster. The rhythm pulled at my lungs. Hands rose, fell, and then lifted again.

Miren spun easily in Cane's arms, her bone-dancer training making her movements fluid and precise. I stumbled more than once, for their benefit.

The five in the center began to fall to the ground. One dropped to their knees. Then another. One was on the ground convulsing.

"What's happening?" I asked, my voice sharp with alarm.

"They're changing," Cane said, grinning. "The stronger the display, the more powerful the transformation. Isn't it glorious?"

My stomach twisted as thin, silver veins crept along the recruit's arms and throats, branching like frost. Their eyes flared, glowing faintly.

"But are they okay?" I pressed.

"Of course," he said easily. "Their souls are being freed from the weight of this world."

"Drakkar?" I called quietly, panic curling in my chest.

No one answered.

The music cut off abruptly. The movement stopped. We stood panting, sweat slick on our palms.

One by one, the initiates were helped to their feet. They looked unsteady, slightly off, as though the room no longer aligned with them, but otherwise unharmed. Each was given a white mask and a thin, dark-bound book.

Applause filled the chamber as they took their places among the others lining the walls.

"You have all witnessed something sacred tonight," the Shadow said. "This, too, could be yours."

As we made our way back toward our seats, something snagged my attention about the person speaking. Not his face—he was cloaked in black like the others, a smooth white mask hiding every feature—but his aura.

I stopped short.

It was a bright, unmistakable yellow. Familiar. Too familiar. I had only ever sensed that particular warmth once before.

My breath caught as my gaze followed him.

He did not look at me. Instead, he stepped forward, lifting his hands to address the crowd. "Please return to your seats," he said calmly. "I hope you have taken enough food."

The crowd responded in appreciation, their plates full in their laps.

"Come on," Miren whispered.

"I—do you know that man's name?" I asked, following behind her to sit.

"That is Shadow Vne'l. He runs this meeting every week."

Every week? I'd been here for months, and Ashkii had been here the whole time, right under my nose.

"*Asha!*" Drakkar called.

"*There you are! I've been waiting—*"

"*Asha, we have a problem. I need you to get up and leave right now.*"

"*I can't just leave. What about—*"

"*NOW!*"

The alarm in his voice forced me to stand. Cane and Miren looked at me in confusion.

"I think that stew is wreaking havoc," I whispered.

"What? Are you leaving?" she asked in disappointment.

"I must."

"We can walk you home," Cane offered.

"No, enjoy your night together. I know the way back."

"Ada, you might be found out. We can't—" Miren began.

"I can take care of myself, really." I held my stomach to make my point. "You don't want to see me like this."

"Okay, but we will be along shortly, so just stop on the road if you need help to get home."

I nodded before grabbing my staff to go.

CHAPTER FIVE

Asha

Eyes darted toward me as I made my way up the stairs. People seemed to note my status as an unseer, but no one made any move toward me. It was a strange feeling, particularly in Firepeak, where the rules of fitness were so strict.

One Shadow reached out to assist, but I waved her off. She nodded somewhat reluctantly, retreating into the line of cloaked figures, but not before saying, "You don't have to leave. Unseers are welcome here."

I wanted to ask her how many unseers she had come across and where they were, but Drakkar's urgency stopped me. "Thank you, but I really must go," I said, pushing past her.

As I turned a corner, she said, "May your light bring you back to us."

What the fire and ash did that mean?

Once I was at the top of the steps and away from the crowd, I called to Drakkar. My vision blurred as I saw flashes of copper. Was there another dragon nearby?

"Drakkar?"

My vision dissolved as Drakkar flew out of range. I moved quickly toward the caravan, so that when it returned, I would hopefully be walking in the right direction. It was a good thing I did because within seconds, my vision left me entirely. My head rose to the sky as I waited for it to come back, but there was nothing.

"Incoming!" Drakkar yelled as he finally came into view, and he wasn't alone.

"Zephyr?"

Zephyr's scales glistened in the moonlight as the two of them flew through the sky in the direction I'd just come from. My heart lurched as I took it in.

Dragons couldn't fly. None but Drakkar. The dracite that Ujuima used to control the dragons had seen to that generations ago. I'd not seen another dragon fly, until now.

"Drakkar? What is happening? Zephyr is flying."

"Yes," he said breathlessly. *"I think... I think his Lightbearer is near."*

No sooner had the thought settled than cries erupted below. My vision flickered back just in time for me to circle back and watch as Zephyr landed in the open theater with a growl. Everyone in the crowd began to scream and run as a stream of fire flew through the air. Drakkar landed on the other side of him and let out his own growl. Drakkar was twice the size of Zephyr and higher in rank. Zephyr should have backed down, but he didn't.

Drakkar began to circle, tail lashing, and his growl a low, rolling thunder that rippled through the mob. I wanted to cry out and tell them that they had nothing to fear, but my voice was lost in the shouts of the crowd. As I neared, the throng of people pushed me until I was finally knocked over. Drakkar turned then. *"Little One,"* he cried frantically. *"Stand up!"*

"I'm trying!" I cried, curling in a ball as people continued to step over me. I gasped as a boot landed on my ribs. Drakkar roared again and took to the air, the downdraft of his wings sending dust and screams swirling through the crowd. But his approach only made the panic worse. People surged like water edging off a cliff.

He wasn't going to reach me in time.

Just as my vision began to fade—heat and bodies pressing in—a hand shot through the chaos and yanked me upward. My feet left the ground. I was suddenly in the arms of one of the Shadows. I recognized his aura before I was able to look up.

"Ashkii?" I breathed, his mask long gone.

He did not spare me a glance as he pushed through the press of bodies. This was not the young, gentle boy I remembered. He was older now, his face shadowed with facial hair, his locs grown long and untamed. The slight frame I once knew had broadened into strong shoulders and a solid chest.

"Ashkii!" I called again. This time he looked down at me, only there was nothing familiar in his expression. He looked different, not just physically. His aura felt different too.

I held up my hand to touch it, but he struck my hand away. "Don't!" he said.

My eyes felt heavy as the word landed, the sting settling in my chest.

By this time, Drakkar was circling downward. His eyes narrowed as Ashkii held me tighter against him. *"Drakkar, no! It is Ashkii."*

"He does not smell right."

I spun around in a daze. "Why haven't you gone to Adriel? What's happened?"

He looked away as if the question itself felt like hellfire.

When he finally spoke, his tone was low—hoarse even. "I can't," he said. Then, softer— "I have to go." He turned as if to walk away.

I grabbed his hand. "Wait! Is that it? You are going to pretend we don't know each other?" He kept walking. "Ashkii!" I yelled.

He paused, but did not turn. "You should not be here, Ash. Leave this place while you still can."

"We have to go!" Drakkar warned, watching Zephyr jump in the air again.

I took one last glance at Ashkii, but he was already melting into the shadows.

CHAPTER SIX

Asha

I was finally safe enough to breathe, sitting on Drakkar's back. My mind was anything but calm. I had so many questions about what I'd seen. Ashkii was a Shadow. The thought felt like a blade slowly twisting in my gut. Something was definitely wrong there, but instead of going down that line of thinking, I launched into a series of questions as I turned toward Zephyr.

"What was that?" I asked in Dragontongue.

His eyes remained a bit wild, yet the frantic edge appeared to decrease somewhat. "They were there," Zephyr said quietly. "I felt them."

"Who?" I asked, trying to piece it together. "You don't mean—"

He turned his head away, chomping his jaw in frustration. "My Lightbearer."

"Take it easy," Drakkar warned. *"He is unsettled already. We need to get him back to Saeleria."*

"He could have been killed."

"You were almost killed," he shot back. *"I will never understand how you continue to put yourself in such danger."*

"You called, and I answered."

"Next time," he grumbled, *"answer with self-preservation in mind."*

I rolled my eyes skyward, but I could not drum up any anger. *"Finally."* I smiled. *"Another Lightbearer. Did you see him? Who is he?"* I asked Drakkar.

"No, Zephyr will feel compelled to go out and find him again. We will know soon enough."

"All these months," I murmured. *"And there was one right under my nose. And Zephyr is flying!"*

"Yes," he sighed. *"Unfortunately."*

I patted his neck. *"Does it make you feel less special?"*

"Hardly," he scoffed. *"I am in a league that cannot be matched."*

I smiled, but it didn't quite reach my eyes as my mind once again drifted to Ashkii, and what his presence with the Shadowcasters meant. Was he truly one of them?

Firepeak was the closest kingdom to Saeleria, so it took little time for us to make it to the Saelerian Mountains, the one and only haven for dragons not in the emperor's custody.

Once I had thought dragons were better off being cared for by humans, but I'd learned differently once I'd bonded with Drakkar and spent time in Saeleria.

As we touched down in the field near the Pyrethra, the dragons' palace I considered home these days, I stretched my limbs. Riding had gotten much easier, but we'd been on the road with the caravan for weeks. I was ready for a long soak in the heated pool, but before I could say anything, thunderous footsteps approached. I turned my head and saw flashes of blue and indigo scales barreling toward me—two of them, identical at a distance except for the dark birthmark beneath Igbo's chin.

"You are here!" they said in unison as they tackled me to the ground. I giggled as two young dragons nuzzled my neck, their scales smooth and cool against my skin as they gripped my cloak in their teeth.

"Igbo, Ala!" I squealed. "You are getting much too big to be pouncing on me like this."

I remembered the moment I'd seen their tiny, trembling bodies that barely fit in the palm of my hands. Now I was lucky if I could hold them, as they were the size of a medium canine.

"Why were you gone so long?" Igbo demanded.

"We missed you, Iyla."

I rolled my eyes at the pet name they'd given me that meant *aunt* in Dragontongue. "Where is Mwana?" I asked, searching beyond them.

"She's coming," Ala answered. "She is so slow!"

I frowned, looking down the hill, as Mwana struggled and was failing to climb up it. I put my hands on my waist as I watched. "And you left her behind?"

The two boys had the sense to look slightly embarrassed. "We will go get her," Igbo offered.

"I will get her first!" Ala called as they raced after her. I smiled, thinking of how much they reminded me of Seraphina, down to their blue scales and graceful necks. That smile quickly faded as I looked back at Drakkar. He'd turned away, purposefully avoiding the sight of his brood. He'd been like this since they were born, unable to connect.

"Will you join us, Drakkar?" I asked, though I knew the answer.

He faced me, pain laced in his eyes. *"Er, no. Mattias calls, and I must see after Zephyr."*

I sighed, deciding not to push him. *"Very well. I will see you soon."*

"Thank you, and…" he began. *"Have someone look at your injuries. You look like death."*

I shook my head. *"Thanks."*

He leaned down to nuzzle my cheek. *"We are all each other needs. Don't forget that."*

My heart clenched at his words. He knew the pallor of my skin had nothing to do with my injuries but the fact that I had a brush with someone connected to Adriel. There was a time when I thought differently, that I could allow someone else into my heart. I closed my eyes, pushing that fantasy away. I'd worked so hard to erase all memory of him.

Drakkar pulled back and gazed at me knowingly. "Maybe we should pay the mortal a visit."

I turned away, staring down at the three young dragons jostling each other down the hill. "If he desired to see me, he would. You have your limits, and I have mine," I said, patting his chin before following after the hatchlings below.

The dragons coaxed me down to the watering hole, where the springs merged, and the dragons could swim and dive to their heart's content.

"Why won't you go in, Mwana?" I asked as she lay beside me in the sun.

"I'm not a good swimmer," she mumbled. "The others will make fun."

I watched as she waved the wing that was slightly smaller than the other. She lifted the appendage and gave it a weak flap. The uneven movement tugged at my heart.

"It is not easy, but you can't let it stop you from living."

"Easy for you to say," she grumbled. "You have no idea what it is like for me," she said, covering her eyes with her claws.

I smiled, taking one of them in my hand. "Look at me, Mwana." She turned her head, but I was insistent. "Look at me."

She tentatively lifted her head.

"It may be hard to imagine because you've only experienced Saeleria, but where I am from, I am different. Remember when I said that I lack sight once I leave the mountains?" I said, running my hands along the wing. "This is the only place I have it. Everywhere else I am referred to as an unseer."

Her brow furrowed in confusion. "But you have Drakkar. Surely your people must revere you."

I shook my head. "I am loathed by my own people, hated more because I was born of royalty. A condition like mine usually comes with a death sentence. I am lucky that Drakkar found me, and that the Great Dragon allowed me to reside here."

"At least you have a place to go."

"That is true," I acknowledged, "but do you know I would never have made it here if I had not accepted the beauty in my power?"

"Beauty?" she asked doubtfully.

"Yes." An image of Adriel running out of the basin with a handkerchief around his eyes flashed in my vision. I willed it away. "I realized my lack of sight was not a curse, but a gift. I never would have been able to access a power without accepting that." I looked toward the watering hole, watching as the other dragons splashed within. "I would never have gotten the three of you here."

She followed my line of sight, watching her brothers play wistfully. "I think I understand now."

I inhaled slowly. "You do?"

She stood, and a rare grin adorned her mouth. Her tiny, pointed teeth reflected in the light. "I must learn to fly, just like Drakkar!"

My eyebrows shot up. "Well, that's not exactly..."

Mwana sprang forward and nuzzled my neck. "Thanks, Iyla!" she called as she sprinted away.

I sighed, rubbing my hand over my face. Some role model I'd turned out to be.

"You should not encourage such behavior," a familiar voice called. I looked up and spotted Carinth looking down from her perch. Her deep emerald eyes matched the dark green of her scales.

I crossed my arms. "And what behavior is that?"

Carinth growled under her breath. "The child will never fly. You should be ashamed of even putting that in her head."

"You don't know that," I challenged.

"You have to admit it is unlikely," a dragon with auburn scales added. I believe her name was Kissy.

"We have no idea what she is capable of," I pushed. "We should not make any assumptions. She is young still."

"Not so young," Carinth admonished. "She is not like her brothers—strong, healthy."

"She is none of your concern," I said, rising angrily. "And last I checked, none of you can fly."

"That's not the point!"

"I would hate to tell the Great Dragon how you speak about his grandling."

That quieted Carinth. She huffed before stalking off.

"Now you've done it." I jerked my head back and smiled as I saw the familiar gentle eyes of Baquar. He was my attendant and friend. He reminded me so much of Khaliya—steady, and far too good at reading me. "You shouldn't antagonize someone who can strike you down in a breath."

"Mwana has enough to overcome without Carinth getting in her ear. Where have you been? I thought I would have seen you as soon as we got back."

He looked away. "With you away, I took a holiday."

"Dragons take holidays?"

He smiled. "Are you saying mortals don't?"

"Okay, where does a dragon go when on holiday?" I asked.

"Anywhere we want," he said teasingly. "The Saelerian Mountains are sparse, and I rarely get to fully enjoy their beauty."

"You should take me next time."

"I'd love to."

We watched Mwana flapping her wings, furiously trying to lift herself above the water. Igbo used the rock to dive in, which caused water to rise and ruin her efforts. "The Great Dragon would like to see you and Drakkar. I thought bringing the grandlings might help soften the wrath he will have for you both." It was a statement, but I heard the question in it.

"What did we do?" I moaned.

"Besides endangering all of Saeleria by letting mortals know there is not just one but two flying dragons?"

I sighed. "I'll call them over, but they'll be disappointed to leave."

"What do you mean? Uye Baquar is plenty of fun." I rolled my eyes at that.

"What could he want with me?"

Baquar shook his head. "He would not say."

I'd long grown accustomed to the dragon palace, made more for dragon comfort than for their riders. Massive steps had been built to accommodate the dragons' size, particularly since they could no longer fly. I pushed open the golden doors to the Great Dragon Mattias's study. He was bent over a table, his silver scales reflecting the firelight, with a smoldering log clamped idly between his teeth the way a man might chew a toothpick. He squinted at the papers on his desk, each one weighed down by stones to keep them from scattering.

"Where are my grandlings?" he asked, continuing to peer at whatever was on his desk.

I clasped my fingers together impatiently. "They are on their way. Baquar is gathering them from the watering hole."

His teeth flashed in the firelight as he frowned, as much as a dragon can. "They are not with Drakkar then?"

I turned away. Drakkar was my bonded dragon, and I would say nothing ill of him, even if he was making a mistake by not having a relationship with his brood. "He is looking after Zephyr," I said, trying to hide the defensiveness in my voice.

This time Mattias's eyes met mine, and they were filled with unbridled rage. "That is unacceptable," he seethed. "I'll have him dragged back here at once."

I clenched my teeth together and knotted my hands at my thighs before saying, "Perhaps, Great Dragon, he is still mourning his mate." *Your daughter.* "I am no expert on grief, but I have experienced it. I was not myself for a long time after my mother's death."

"Doesn't he know we are all grieving? You don't see me shirking my responsibilities, and she was my daughter. His duty is to his brood, and that is final. There is no excuse."

Seeing that I was not going to change his mind, I dropped it, spying the parchment on his desk. "Is that a map of the Five Kingdoms?" I asked.

He shuddered as if forcing himself to come out of a rage-filled trance. "It is a map that predates the formation of the Five Kingdoms. Before Ujuima began its rule, the Lightbearers and dragons called it Maa'ndara."

I stared at the map more closely, gently splaying my hands over the delicate material, as if it would disintegrate at any moment. The continent was devoid of the defining lines of each of the kingdoms I had come to know—Wiyotak, Firepeak, Entioch, Wyrmwood, and Ujuima in the center. On the edge, bordering Wiyotak and Wyrmwood, were the Saelerian Mountains.

"It looks so different," I said. "When was this map drawn?"

"Approximately one hundred and sixty-eight years ago."

My hands trailed to Entioch, into the Caan Sea. There were several landmasses there. Islands?

"I don't think I've ever seen these on a map."

The Great Dragon tilted his head to look closer. "Those are the Ifambe Islands?"

My fingers traced the cluster of islands. "Why have I not seen these before?"

"Probably because they are underwater now."

"Really? Does the tide never recede?"

He lifted his shoulder in a manner that I'd attributed to a shrug for mortals. "I have not heard of it doing so." He pulled another paper with an opened brown seal out of his desk. "The maps are not what I called you in here for," he said, handing me the envelope.

My heart constricted. It took everything I had to hold my hands steady as I took the letter from him. "Who sent it?"

He seemed to consider me carefully. "It is from your brother."

For some reason I could not explain, my heart fell. I could hardly hide my disappointment when I saw the seal was indeed not from Wiyotak.

"You seem disappointed," he noted.

"Not at all," I said. I had not seen Kwasi since I'd left Adriel's camp. I'd sent him a message to let him know I was alright, but there had been no correspondence since.

"What is in the letter?" I asked.

"It's best I let you read it."

As I opened the envelope, I found a neatly folded letter, just one page in Elliarb.

Dear Sister,

I have missed you dearly, and I'll try not to take it personally that you have not called on me of late. I hope you are well. I have been spending time in the central libraries, and I believe I have found something. It is too delicate to put in this letter. I must see you. I will eagerly await your response..

Kwasi

"Typical Kwasi," I sighed. "He says nothing and everything all at once."

"Will you go?" Mattias asked.

"I suppose I have to eventually, but not right now. We've found another Lightbearer."

Mattias growled. "Yes, I wanted to speak to you about that. Could you have been more reckless?"

I averted my gaze. "You're the one who told me I needed to find more. I plan to go after him."

"I thought as much," he said darkly. "Then what? Then there are two of you? How are you going to take down the Shadowcasters with only two Lightbearers? And that's supposing you aren't captured and killed."

"I don't know. I'll figure it out." I ran my hands through my hair, trying to calm myself.

"What if Elan catches you? They may have a trap set for you."

"It's been two years. What if this is the only lead we have? We cannot wait any longer." I exhaled sharply. "The Shadowcasters grow stronger. They're infiltrating Firepeak as we speak. Maybe they've infiltrated other kingdoms already. I get the feeling that our time is short. It is worth the risk, and Zephyr will have to return."

My back relaxed as I sat in a chair by the fire, contemplating what to do next. It was silent between us for a while, that is, until we heard Mwana's high-pitched scream sounding just outside the open door. My eyes snapped to the Great Dragon's, but he was already barreling toward her. "Mwana!" he called. "Where are you, children?"

I followed behind him. Screams were unusual for Mwana. We'd barely made it to the outside steps when a copper speck caught the corner of my eye as I looked up toward the sky. *Drakkar?*

"He has my brood on his back!" Drakkar roared as he flew after him.

My eyes widened as I noted the panic in his voice. "Well, don't scare him. We don't want him to lose control."

Drakkar seemed to ignore me as he flew toward Zephyr with claws and teeth, black scales against copper, like a copper kettle blackened by fire. Zephyr ducked down and began a slow spiral descent to the ground. "He doesn't know how to land," I said.

Mattias and I sprinted for the field just as Zephyr came crashing down. His feet struck the ground awkwardly, his weight pitching left as he lost his balance. The hatchlings clung to him at first, but when the momentum finally carried them forward, they tumbled loose.

I lunged, catching Igbo as he fell. Mattias reached for Ala and Mwana. I searched Igbo for broken bones or any sign of a concussion, but instead, he dissolved into laughter in my arms. His brother and sister quickly followed, and the air filled with squeals of delight, shattering the silence. "Again, Uya Zephyr! Again!" Ala cried.

Zephyr found his footing but looked slightly off balance. The ground rumbled as Drakkar landed in front of him, teeth bared. Zephyr ducked to the ground right before fire streamed where he had stood just moments before.

"Drakkar!" I called in warning, but he ignored me as he ran toward the other dragon. Their heads locked as they held onto each other. I set Igbo on the ground and attempted to intervene.

"Stop!" I turned in frustration to the Great Dragon as he stared down at me with disapproval. "They will hurt each other."

He turned back to the altercation. They were swiping at one another with claws and teeth. Other dragons began to form around them in a semicircle, looking on with curiosity.

"They will not," the Great Dragon explained. "Lightbearers do not interfere in the business of dragons. They must settle this on their own."

I watched in horror as they continued. Zephyr had moved far enough away that his jaw was opening to release fire. Drakkar anticipated it and leapt into the sky above him, landing on Zephyr's back. Zephyr yelped, rolling violently and striking with his spiked tail. The blow caught Drakkar across the shoulder, and he grunted in pain, loosening his grip just enough for Zephyr to twist free. Audible gasps fell from onlookers as they watched Drakkar hasten after only the second dragon to be able to fly in years.

After a few more breaths, the Great Dragon moved forward and grunted with command into the sky. The dragons on the ground all bowed their heads in deference. I kneeled as well in respect, inviting the hatchlings to do the same. They filed toward me before lowering themselves to their grandfather, their king.

To my relief, Drakkar and Zephyr began their descent in our direction. As they landed, they lowered their heads. My eyes raked over Drakkar's torso, scanning for any severe injuries, but all I saw were minor scrapes. Zephyr looked a little worse for wear, but as Mattias invited them closer, Zephyr and Drakkar looked at each other as if they respected one another.

"It seems we have much to talk about," Mattias barked, but as I peered closer, I saw the hint of a smile on his lips. I also felt a glimmer of hope.

CHAPTER SEVEN

Asha

Zephyr did not reveal much to Mattias, except that he had to return. Something in his demeanor had changed. It reminded me of my father's hunting dogs—once they caught a scent, they could not rest until they found their mark. Mattias quickly gave up and cautioned him to be careful now that we'd been spotted.

I sighed at the thought of the bath I'd be missing and the playful chaos of the hatchlings. They whined at my departure, and I had to promise to bring back persimmons, their favorite, upon my return. I'd barely gotten a few hours of rest before we needed to depart.

As we took flight, Zephyr soared beside us. Another dragon could fly. It was no longer just Drakkar. The other dragons had taken interest too, speculating that another dragon had chosen its rider. Zephyr had insisted on going with us, seeming to feel the pull.

"If you keep staring at him like that," Drakkar noted, *"I may get a little jealous."*

I rolled my eyes before leaning down to wrap my arms around his body in an embrace. It was difficult in the clothes I wore. Firepeak was much more conservative than its neighboring kingdoms, particularly in the capital Cynthar. At least the material was light and airy; otherwise, I'd never have survived the heat. *"Just because you are not the only flying dragon does not mean I don't still adore you."*

He grumbled in response. *"I don't need platitudes. I need a better plan than the one you've thought up. It feels careless."*

"We have no choice. Aren't you curious about this Lightbearer?"

"I'm more interested in keeping you safe."

"I will be," I assured him.

"I hate to break it to you, Little One. Your word is rubbish when it comes to keeping promises."

He was right. I wouldn't trust me either.

I rehearsed the story I'd planned for Miren and others as we neared the caravan. Drakkar had to leave me half a mile out. As I approached the caravan, I was surprised to see that the lights were dimmed. It was nearing dusk, peak time for Nis.

My room was empty. I tripped over an item as I entered and grew more alarmed as my feet caught on more and more things on the ground. As I moved throughout the room, I realized it had been ransacked. All our things were scattered on the ground, making it difficult to navigate. Where was Miren?

I left quickly, fearing whoever did this might still be lurking.

"Drakkar," I called. *"I need your eyes."*

"What is wrong?" he asked in alarm. *"I'm coming."*

"I'm okay; I just want to be cautious. Miren is missing, I think."

"Get out of there."

"Not yet. Give me a minute. Maybe she is with Mabel and Lacey."

My vision flickered as he neared, the world warping as light fractured. For a moment, everything blurred into a painful shimmer behind my eyes. I waited until I had consistent sight before I made the familiar trek to Mabel and Lacey's dwelling.

I sighed with relief as I saw the two of them standing outside. That quickly faded as Mabel's eyes widened in horror once she saw me. Lacey appeared confused. Something had happened.

"Are you okay?" I asked them.

"I told them it wasn't true, Ada!" Lacey called, attempting to move closer. Mabel stopped her in her tracks. I stopped as well.

"What is going on, Mabel?" I asked.

She looked at me and then back toward Lacey. "Go inside, please. I need to speak to Ada alone."

"But Mom…"

"I will not tell you again, Lacey Pyre. Get inside." Her words did not invite any argument. Lacey's shoulders drooped as she glanced toward me before turning to go.

Once the door was shut behind her, Mabel turned to me. "You know I don't care that you are an unseer, right? But…"

Dread filled my heart as I waited for her to divulge the rest.

"The soldiers, they say you rode away on a dragon."

Soldiers? "Soldiers came looking for me?" I asked in alarm.

"Not long ago," she said quietly. "They questioned us, threatened to take Lacey from me. They say you are—that you are not who you say you are."

My heart pounded in my ears as I opened my mouth to tell her the truth. "I am—"

"Don't say anything else. We don't need to know," Mabel said quickly. "But you need to get out of here before the soldiers come back."

My mind flickered to Zephyr. He wouldn't want to leave without his Lightbearer. We'd have to come up with a different plan.

"Okay, I will go," I said. "Is Miren okay? She wasn't in our dwelling."

Mabel's eyes flickered. "I think so. I wouldn't worry. She is a strong one. I will look in on her."

There was something in Mabel's words that made me wary. "Perhaps I should wait for her."

Mabel put her hand on my shoulder, her eyes full of something, pity? "I'm telling you, she is okay. You will not be if you stay here." She glanced back at the window where Lacey was peering through the curtains. "I'm sorry. I have to go," she said.

Tears brimmed, and it took everything in me to hold them back. "No need to apologize. I am sorry for putting you in danger."

Mabel stopped on the steps. "Take care, sweet girl," she said before shutting the door behind her.

I inhaled sharply. They were in danger because of me. I'd done this. I took another shuddering breath before I turned to meet Drakkar.

I halted my footsteps and relied on my walking stick as my vision began to fade once more. I called to Drakkar, wondering what was happening. Had he flown out of range?

"Psst!"

I turned to the sound but did not see an aura.

"Psst! Look up."

I lifted my head and was surprised to see Miren's aura above me. By the sounds nearby, she was on the backstairs of the inn travelers stayed in when they were staying the weekend. "What are you doing up there, Miren?"

"Come. I'll throw down the ladder."

Stiff rope hitting the soft grass met my ears. I hesitated. "I can't," I said. "I need to go, but I'm relieved that you are okay after—"

"Oh, come on, Ada," she interrupted. "Just for a moment. You can see everything from up here!"

I bit my lip. I shouldn't. Something in her tone made me uneasy. Still, if she was in danger, I couldn't just walk away.

I fastened my staff to my waist before reaching for the rope. The coarse hemp scraped my palms as I climbed. Years of mounting Drakkar had hardened my muscles; what once would have left me trembling now came as easily as breathing.

"Careful," Miren said above me.

By the time I reached the balcony, Miren's hand shot out, gripping my forearm to pull me the rest of the way up.

"I just came from Mabel's," I began. "She said the soldiers questioned her. I think they ransacked our place as well. I will need to leave, but I wanted to make sure you were okay first."

"Is that why you were walking out of town?" she asked, the barest bit of hurt in her voice.

"I wasn't sure where to find you. Mabel wouldn't say where you were."

Miren gave a short laugh that didn't sound like her. "Good old Mabel has her secrets, doesn't she? You know how she worries."

I frowned. "She's right to worry. The soldiers were threatening her."

"Were they?" she said, voice rising just a little too brightly. "Well, that's to be expected, isn't it? You've gotten quite the reputation lately."

Something in her tone made me stiffen. I felt her aura shift. There was a hard edge underneath it.

"I just came to see that you are alright. It appears that you are, so I will be going now."

"Wait!" she said sharply. "I'm sorry. I'm just... I'm not sure what to say. I watched you on a dragon, Ada. The way that you moved, like you were so comfortable with them, was jarring."

So she had seen. "I'm sorry. I didn't want you to find out this way."

"That your name isn't really Ada?"

The tenor of her voice was unnerving. I called out to Drakkar once more to see if he was close. Still nothing.

"I never meant to hurt anyone."

"All I wanted was a soft life," she said quietly. "To find someone to settle down with, so I wouldn't have to dance for coins to eat."

"You can still do that. Cane—"

Miren gripped my hand. "Cane is gone."

"What?" I asked in alarm. "What's happened?"

"Haven't you been listening? The soldiers have him. They took him as leverage." Her hand tightened around my wrist.

"What do you mean? Where have they taken him?"

"To the palace, to the dungeons. I don't know!" she gasped. "The look he had on his face when he realized he was being taken because of me. Because I'd been foolish enough to pity an unseer."

"Let me go," I said calmly, though I felt anything but. "We can find him, release him. Together."

"Yes. He will be released once I turn you in," she said, pulling me forward. The sky cracked with lightning, and we both jumped at the sound.

She was trying to turn me in. That's what this was. I should have been angry, but all I could feel was pity. "Miren, what are you doing?"

"Turning you in. Maybe then he will forgive me," she cried.

"What is there to forgive? This isn't your fault." This was my fault. All my fault. "Let me help you."

"Help?" she said, stepping back. "Helping you got us into this."

"Miren, you will never see him again if you hand me over. They will imprison you and try you for treason. Do you know what the penalty is for treason?"

"Apparently you do," she gritted out.

"You're right. I do." I took a breath before saying, "You are practical. You know the best chance is to try to find him and get him out. Now where would they keep him?"

"The dungeons. I don't know how to get there; I just know they are on the lowest level."

"You can find a way."

"Not with all the soldiers looking for you."

"I just need to blend in, is all. Can you get me one of your bone skirts? No one is looking for a dancer."

"Yes, I have something back at the dwelling that might fit. I will go back to get it. Stay here."

"I can go—"

"No, I'm taking enough risk as it is," she said, dropping the rope. "Stay here. I will return."

I nodded. "You are right. I will wait here."

She untied something from her clothing and placed it over my head. The beads clicked together as she secured it over my face.

"This is your hyun veil. What are you doing?"

"Helping you blend in just in case you are spotted." Seeming satisfied, Miren began to climb down the rope. She stopped midway. "I could just turn you in, you know."

"I know," I whispered. "But you won't."

As Miren walked away, I was left wondering if I'd just made a grave mistake.

CHAPTER EIGHT

Asha

As I waited, the noise from the inn swelled with raucous laughter and the clinking of glasses. There had to be a large party within. The auras that spilled out onto the balcony were the wrong color—too many, too bright. Not Miren. My pulse jumped as I pressed myself against the wall, realizing it was already too late to hide.

"There you are," a voice called.

I froze.

"We are the entertainment tonight," a female said from behind me. "We don't know where to go." By the scent of the women's body oil, a mixture of rosewater and myrrh, I could tell what kind of entertainment she meant.

"I—I don't know if I can help you," I said.

The woman huffed, clearly unsatisfied with my answer. "Well of course you can help us. Are they through that door?" Before I could stop her, she grabbed my arm and pushed me forward until my hand brushed a brass knob I hadn't realized was there. My stomach twisted. Why hadn't Miren told me there were other entrances?

"Open it up and announce that the female entertainment is here. Go on! I'm not losing any money over this."

Before I could make an excuse, the door beside me flew open. "I thought I heard you. You're late," a man barked with impatience. "Hurry. They are waiting."

"Of course, sir. We are coming."

The woman brushed past me as the entourage went inside. I attempted to slink away when the man at the door grabbed my hand. "Where do you think you're going?" He put a pitcher in my hand. "You think this is appropriate attire?" he said, grasping the linen of my dress.

"Sir, I—"

"It wasn't a question. Come."

I thought about my options. I could refuse and bring about suspicion, or I could go inside and hide against the wall. Potentially, I could sneak away once the entertainment got going. Where was Drakkar?

"Yes, of course," I said.

Inside, I was greeted with the clinking sounds of plates and silverware as the guests were being served. Very quickly, the music began to play—a mix of the kora and ngoni, followed by the mellow sounds of the djembe. This was a kind of private dining room. I'd heard there were private rooms reserved for the elites that visited Nis.

I followed the man's aura and prayed I could find a corner deep enough to hide my lack of sight. "Wrap this around you," he said, pressing a sheer fabric into my hand. It was light, scented faintly of incense and smoke, threaded with tiny golden coins that clinked together with every movement.

I did as he said, tying it around my waist with trembling fingers. The metallic chime of the coins betrayed every shift of my body.

"Stand here until you're called," he instructed, already moving away to scold another woman for the strength of her perfume. I could actually feel sweat pooling down my back as I waited to be found out.

I listened intently, trying to locate a window to climb out of until I heard a voice that made me nearly melt into the floor. My mouth dried as I heard the familiar cadence and turned to see the midnight blue aura.

Adriel. He was here. How could that be? Had he seen me come in?

I quickly scanned around him to see if I could pick up any other Guardians—Kitchi, Moki, Chato—but there were none. Were they here because of Ashkii? Had they come to bring him home? It seemed unlikely as Ashkii appeared to be a willing participant with the Shadowcasters.

I leaned in, eager to hear Adriel's voice. It had been so long, I'd nearly forgotten what it sounded like. It was quiet and commanding in a way that made everyone else lower their voices to match his.

"It is quite impressive what you did in Wiyotak," a man at the table noted. "Any news from that brother of yours?"

"No," he said smoothly. "But we will capture him soon enough."

So, Adriel had taken Wiyotak. The war had been brutal from all accounts, but I was glad to hear the Guardians had taken back the kingdom. If Wiyotak had fallen, the balance between the Five Kingdoms would alter.

"Have you thought about what comes next?" another asked. "Will you take the throne?"

"There is time enough to decide all of that. Right now, I'm focused on finding my brother and restoring order in my kingdom."

There was a murmur of agreement followed by the clinking of chalices. "Messy business, family wars."

A chime rang, and everyone stopped moving, including the dancers.

"I want to welcome everyone here to my court today. King Fourie Heloc from Wyrmwood, Prince Zaib Otum of Entioch, and soon-to-be King of Wiyotak, Prince Adriel Foxtrail."

My heart stuttered. Kings? I had stumbled into a room full of the most powerful men in the Five Kingdoms. The only man missing was Elan. Why was that and why were they all gathered in the heart of Nis?

"If I may," a voice interrupted.

"I'd prefer you didn't, Fourie," the speaker said.

The room grew tense until a soft voice cut in, followed by small feet padding across the floor.

"I apologize, gentlemen." The room quieted as the female voice entered. "I apologize for my late arrival. I wanted to look perfect this evening."

"And who are you?"

"As I was saying, Dija," Fourie cut in. "This is my daughter, Princess Celia, future Queen of Wiyotak. Celia, this is our host, King Dija."

My chest tightened. Future queen of Wiyotak?

"Come, daughter, so the prince can have a look at you."

Something heavy clinked behind Celia as she walked, precious stones perhaps.

"I was not told of this," Dija said sharply.

"I'm newly out in society," she offered, though it was clear that was not what he meant. "I am honored to be a guest in your kingdom."

"We did not give clearance to bring daughters," Dija chastised. He snapped his fingers, and the auras of the women began to leave their perches to line up against the walls.

Celia's aura, a deep green, began to swirl around the room. It wound and spun, until it damn near took over the entire room.

"Please forgive me, Your Majesty. I wanted to meet my betrothed while he is here."

The words were sweet, but there was an understated power beneath them.

The king relented, but he was not happy about it. "If you must. My opinion of things clearly doesn't matter if these alliances are being made behind my back."

"You sound so cynical, Dija," Fourie cut in. "I have a beautiful daughter in need of a husband, and Adriel is an unwed heir to his realm—"

"Who needs a steady supply of soldiers to finish Enapay off?" Dija finished.

I could not focus on their words because my attention swayed to Adriel. I desperately wanted to know what he was thinking. I had no claim on him. I'd left in the most savage way I now realized. Of course, he had to move on and do what was best for Wiyotak.

Celia's aura lowered as she bowed before Adriel. Lips meeting skin met my ears. He'd kissed her hand, as was custom in royal circles but only if the two were familiar.

"I hope I look pleasing to you, Your Highness," she said in the most saccharine tone I'd ever heard.

"I am very lucky indeed, Princess."

The way he said 'Princess' felt like a slap. I must have audibly recoiled because they stopped speaking.

Dija laughed. "It appears you are making my dancers swoon, Adriel. Now let us end this so that we men can get down to business."

"I very much look forward to your calling on me soon, Your Highness," she said.

"Call me Adriel."

I turned away then, unable to listen to the rest. I needed to get out of here.

Once Celia departed, Dija continued as if he'd never been interrupted. "We are called here to discuss a certain mad emperor."

That caught my attention. So, the other rulers knew my brother was unhinged. "The reign of the Oseis was lucrative for as long as it lasted—"

"Lucrative for whom?" This was a new voice.

"For all of us, Zaib," Dija pressed.

"Not all of us," Adriel interjected. "You've enjoyed a relationship with the Oseis that none of us have had."

The tension in the room began to rise.

"Okay, gentlemen," Fourie said. "We can spend all day measuring whose dick is bigger, but I want to know what we are going to do about Elan."

"It's simple," Dija said, chewing something from his platter. "We must kill him, of course. He and that bitch sister of his are responsible for my boy Atar's death. Atar was meant to rule, and now I have to settle for a second son as my heir."

The patrons in the room began to shuffle uncomfortably at his words. Drakkar had killed Prince Atar during our first meeting when Enapay and Elan conspired to release me into the bridegroom ceremony. I did not feel a drop of sadness at his death. A marriage between us would have surely ended in my death. Drakkar just got to him first.

"We continue to be very mournful for your loss," King Fourie said.

"My only solace over these years was that the bitch who did it had died."

I panned over to Adriel's aura to see if it had changed. It had expanded slightly but remained the same color.

"However," he continued, "it has come to my attention that there was a recent sighting of her." Short inhalations cascaded through the room.

"Quiet!" Dija said, banging his hand on the table. All the people in the room cowered in their corners.

"Is that why you called this meeting today without the emperor's blessing?" Prince Zaib asked boldly.

"He has lied to us every step of the way. We cannot trust him to handle this matter. He is far too close to it."

"I have seen how he treats the princess," Adriel began. "I do not think he carries any warm regard for her. Perhaps she could be useful to us."

A sharp noise, like a knife being embedded into a table, sounded. "Nonsense!" Dija began. "You are lucky you are even at this table."

Again, the room grew eerily quiet. Adriel's aura shifted and expanded to the size of half the room. He was using his battle magic, I realized, as I felt tendrils of heat. "If you have something to say, Your Majesty," he began in a bone-chilling tone, "let's hear it. I'm sure the skin grafts you will need to repair your body won't be too painful."

Dija's chair screeched across the floor as he stood. "How dare you," he said between clenched teeth. "You don't scare me. Between your family interfering with the dracite supply and you running off with her, and worse, losing her, I have a mind to cut you down right here."

There was movement in the room, and I realized this would be the perfect opportunity for me to leave, but something held me there. I felt protective of Adriel, even now after all this time. I held my breath, planted where I stood in my corner.

"We are missing the point of our gathering!" King Fourie reminded everyone, trying to lower the tension. "We are here to discuss what to do about Elan, and Adriel is right. The princess could help us cement our rule. The people fear her, but not as much as they fear him. Elan's policies have driven all our kingdoms into poverty, as did his father before him. He needs to be stopped."

"But how?" Dija asked. "With all of his dragons, we would be cut down immediately."

"Through marriage." Everyone's auras seemed to swivel at Zaib's suggestion.

"What do you mean?" Adriel asked.

"The way to build alliances is through marriage," he said. "It is the obvious choice."

Dija barked with laughter. "Are you proposing to marry Elan?"

Zaib did not miss a beat. "I think you are smart enough to know I mean the princess, the girl with the dragon."

I would have been shocked by the layered insult if I weren't so astonished by what he suggested. Marriage?

"The princess who is to be killed on sight?" Dija howled.

"Wait, he is right. Think about it," Fourie offered. "What if we gave her the opportunity to join our realms? You have to admit, Dija, she is more valuable to us alive than dead."

"Never," Dija said in quiet disdain.

"We must be rational," Fourie persisted. "We cannot go on this way with the emperor. Our people will turn on us. If she can be reasoned with and courted properly..."

"We've tried this before and my son died."

"We tried under Elan's orders," Fourie corrected. "He set up the game that got your son killed. We have to be smarter."

"And how do we know she won't just have her dragons cut us down?" Dija asked.

"We give her what she wants. The rumor is she is looking for something. We offer whatever it is."

"And which one of us will marry her?" Dija asked. "And more importantly, once that marriage is secured, does that continue the emperorship?"

"We are trying to dismantle it," Fourie reminded him. "Each kingdom will rule on its own."

"But how do we know that the moment this marriage happens, that will be honored? Whoever it is can just take the throne."

Zaib sighed as if the conversation bored him. "The answer once again is marriage. King Fourie, you are widowed and eligible to court the princess, but you also have a daughter that soon will be on the Wiyotakin throne. Dija, your heir is of marrying age." He continued despite Dija's protests. "My cousin Balyn will be of marrying age soon."

"She's thirteen," Adriel said.

"We will have to wait a few years, of course," he amended.

"And that conveniently leaves you to marry Princess Asha," Adriel said.

My skin burned at the way he said my name.

"Well, naturally, I cannot marry my own cousin."

"You don't have to marry anyone at all," Dija interjected. "My son can marry the princess."

"So could Adriel. He is not married yet," Zaib pointed out.

"Now let's not be hasty," Fourie said.

"This will never work," Adriel huffed. "She won't come out of hiding, not for this."

"Perhaps I can help on that front," Dija offered.

"Forcing her to do things is why Elan lost her in the first place," Adriel argued.

Damn straight.

"Perhaps we give her a choice in whom she marries," Fourie suggested. "With any luck, she will agree and we will be able to divvy up Ujuima."

"And the dragons?" Dija asked.

"We dispose of them."

"Seems a waste," Zaib lamented.

"And," Fourie cut in, "the only way to ensure none of us has more power over the other."

"I thought we were here to talk about the Shadows," Adriel growled, deftly changing the subject. "I saw you have a large infestation of them here, Your Majesty. I'm sure it is the same in Wyrmwood and Entioch."

"It is quite unsettling," Prince Zaib said. "They rile up my people. Suddenly they feel free to ask for higher wages and time to worship," he scoffed. "Can you believe that?"

"They cut down my men in the field like they were nothing," Adriel said. "Men like that cannot continue. They are our biggest threat, not Elan."

"I disagree," Dija said. "Our attention should be on Elan. He will end us if he gets wind that we are even meeting without him."

"Perhaps we can work on both fronts," Fourie offered. "Adriel, you have been quite effective at bringing down Enapay. Perhaps you could look more into these Shadows? Find their weakness."

"And risk my own Guardians and deplete my forces? No."

There was quiet again in the room. "Very well," Fourie said. "I will pledge my ninth regiment, a force of 200 soldiers. And I'm sure the others will give as well."

No one spoke.

The fire popped somewhere in the room, the sound unnaturally loud in the stillness that followed. I could hear the faint scrape of fabric as someone shifted their weight, the slow exhale of breath being held too long.

"I will pledge the same number of men, but I want my son to be the only one to court the princess," Dija said.

"That is hardly fair," Zaib began.

"You cannot even pledge forces, boy. Don't you need to go home to daddy and get approval?"

Zaib inhaled sharply. "I have been given authority to negotiate on his behalf. I will give twice what you have given, and I want to meet the princess first."

There continued to be bickering among the men, and I felt sick hearing how they discussed me and my marriage like it was a product in the market. I had no plans of meeting any of these men. I needed to get out and to get out quickly. I made sure my veil was in place before moving to the door Celia had exited.

Unfortunately, I ran into a cart of food in the process. This caused the men to stir.

"You have a clumsy one, don't you?" Zaib noted. "First day?"

"Indeed," King Dija said disapprovingly.

"How do we know our discussions are safe?" Adriel queried.

"We have a memory mage at the door."

I swallowed. That meant the moment I left, I would forget everything that was said here. I had to find another way out.

"Are we in agreement, men? Zaib will take his forces to find the girl, and Adriel will start peeling off the Shadowcasters."

The men all spoke in agreement before clinking their glasses in a toast. Dija clapped his hands.

"Now that we have settled it, let's bring in the musicians and dancers. Girl, pour us some wine!" Dija called.

A man nearby pushed a pitcher into my hand and suddenly I was being shuffled toward them. My heart raced. This was bad. Very bad. I had lived without sight most of my life and had gotten really good at pretending to have it, but pouring wine into a tiny glass was a step too far. Perhaps there were windows I could escape through.

"Girl! Are you simple? I said pour these men some wine."

"Drakkar," I begged. *"I need your eyes. Can you find me?"*

Silence, just like before. It had to be because of Zephyr.

I approached the auras, deciding to start with Adriel's. He was the least likely to cut me if I misstepped, but the most likely to recognize me. At least I hoped, as I secured the veil around my face. It was strange being near him, and he not knowing it was me. I wondered how he'd changed since I'd been gone. Did he have a woman that warmed his bed? With his elevated station, it would make sense. Did he ever think of me?

"Would you like some wine?" I whispered, afraid he'd recognize my voice if I spoke any louder.

"Yes, fine," he said tersely.

Damn it to hell. I reached out to gather his glass and nearly knocked it over. He grabbed my hand to stop me, and the moment our hands touched, I felt an electric current flow through me, down to my bones. Did he feel it too?

"What is going on down there?" Dija called.

I was sweating profusely. I was going to have to run. I started to pull away, but Adriel held me there firmly. "Just admiring the girl. You are a fortunate man indeed to have such beauty as this."

I would have blushed, except I knew he was just being kind. With one word, he could have me beaten for spilling his drink or worse.

"How can you tell? She's got her veil on," he said between bites of food. "You can have her tonight if you like. That is if your future father-in-law will allow it."

"He is not married yet," Fourie replied with a low chuckle.

My heart stuttered at the exchange, caught somewhere between dread and a shameful flutter of warmth. I hated myself for it. He brought the hand he was still holding to his lips and kissed it.

I inhaled sharply, and I could tell he noticed. He dropped it slowly and took the wine to pour it himself. "That is very generous, Your Majesty. But I will need to leave very early tomorrow. I do not have time for such dalliances."

I sighed. He didn't recognize me.

"You are overly kind," one of the dancers crooned. "Of course he doesn't want her in his bed. He is to be the King of Wiyotak." Her voice drew nearer. "I had hoped we could take a turn around your bedroom. I want to hear all about your heroic efforts on the battlefield. A man with your... prowess is bound to have provoking stories to tell."

"I am afraid I am needed elsewhere," he said, handing the pitcher to me. "Another time."

"Another time soon, I hope," she giggled, but there was unmistakable disappointment there.

I clenched my fingers tightly, trying to get a hold of the anger I felt. It was ridiculous. This man did not belong to me. I'd left him, in the worst way possible. I needed to get out of this room somehow with my memories intact.

"Drakkar! Where are you?"

I inhaled sharply as I felt him. *"We have a problem. Zephyr has set his sights on someone. You will need to be ready to run. They will ring the alarm in seconds."*

"Well, I, for one, want to know what this beauty you speak of looks like," Zaib said, leaning toward me. "Lift your veil, darling. Let's see if there is anything there."

Chapter Nine

Asha

I just needed to know how many paces to the door. If I could just get an ounce of sight back, I might have a chance.

"Girl!" Dija shouted. "His Highness has given you a command. I don't care how tight your little cunt is, you will obey when given an order. Lift your veil."

My breathing quickened. Drakkar said it would be seconds, but the threat was here now. If I lifted my veil, Adriel would certainly realize who I was, and potentially King Fourie, who I'd met when I was a child. But they were all present for the last ball, where Elan had made sure people noticed me. Would they remember? Would Adriel turn me in?

So, I did the only thing that came to mind—I stalled.

I shifted my weight, letting my hips sway gently to the rhythm of the sultry music still hanging in the air. The stones stitched into the sheer veil and the coins at my waist clinked faintly.

"Ah," Fourie said with an exhalation. "She's a performer, Dija. Give her a moment. The tease is part of it."

Dija huffed but leaned back, irritation wrestling with curiosity. "She'd better tease my cock when she is done. I've waited long enough."

I shuddered, taking one slow step forward, keeping my head bowed. I needed to avoid him at all costs. My pulse thudded so loudly I could barely hear the music. I turned toward Prince Zaib, feeling his aura flare in lazy amusement as I drew a careful circle before him. I brushed past him lightly, and he grasped my hip momentarily in appreciation. I sighed in relief when he released me, and I quickly moved away, bumping into the foot of a chair, which sent me tumbling backwards into someone's lap—Adriel's lap, I realized in horror.

"She's pretty enough," Zaib said. "Not much of a dancer."

I made to stand but to my complete and utter shock, Adriel pulled me back, one hand around my stomach and the other arm just below my chin until I sat flush against his chest. I froze. What was he doing?

Even through the veil, I could feel his attention shift. His aura burned, pulsing in a rhythm that matched the beat of my own heart.

For a fraction of a second, he exhaled slowly. I almost lost my composure.

I tried to pull out of his grasp, but he only held me tighter. "Stop. Moving," he whispered against my ear, and to my amazement, I did. "I hope you are a better actress than you are a dancer. Because you are going to put on a show like your life depends on it because it does. Can you do that?"

I had no idea what he meant, but I nodded anyway.

"Good girl. I need you to turn your head and run your hands through my hair, then down my body. Make it believable."

I licked my lips. My mouth had gone dry. Every breath I took trembled against him.

Adriel's tone was low enough that only I could hear.

"Now," he murmured.

I did as he said, turning slightly so my veil brushed his cheek. My fingers moved through his hair, loosening the plaits of his braid, until it ran free. Images of our last night together flashed through my head. I was like a starving woman, desperate for sustenance. I couldn't stop. Slowly, I traced the line of his jaw. He tilted his head just enough to sell the illusion. To everyone else in the room, it looked like seduction. To me, it felt like life, like I would die if I did not have this moment.

"Good," he whispered. Though I was taking great liberties with his body, he sat patiently, keeping his hands to himself.

The room erupted in laughter and crude commentary, all eyes undoubtedly fixed on us.

Adriel shifted beneath me, reaching for his goblet with a showman's grin. "Gentlemen," he said lazily, "you keep such company in this city, I might never want to leave."

The men roared their approval, their conversation mercifully sliding toward their vices and away from me as I trembled in his lap.

Just as my heart started to slow, Adriel pressed at my ear. "On my word," he said under his breath, "you're going to stand, bow, and walk toward the door. Don't look back."

"What—"

"Trust me."

He lifted his goblet high. "To the future of our four kingdoms!" he said.

Zaib and Fourie toasted jovially, but Dija grunted in disapproval. "I am still waiting to see your face, girl. Do not make me drag you off his lap to get you to obey."

Fuck.

"Just do what he says," Adriel whispered calmly. "Let me help," he said, grabbing the edges of the veil.

I was frozen, unable to do anything as he lifted the first layer. The rulers in the room yelled in delight. My heart raced as Adriel lifted the second. "It's okay," he soothed, placing his hands on my shaking body. He thought I was just nervous. He couldn't know the truth. I couldn't let him.

As he grasped the edge of the last layer, I did the only thing I knew to do. I bent down and kissed him. Now it was his turn to be in shock. His hands fell and the veil never lifted.

The room erupted in jeers and hollers and despite myself, I leaned into him in search of the remnants of the night we'd shared. For a moment he didn't respond, and I almost pulled back in fear.

His breath shuddered against mine, and to my surprise his hand went underneath the veil to cradle my face and pull me closer. The kiss deepened, slow at first, uncertain—like a language we'd both sworn we'd forgotten.

The heat of him, the scent of his skin, the shape of the mouth I'd tried to erase from my memory. It all came rushing back now with cruel clarity.

For a few stolen seconds, nothing else existed. I had almost forgotten that I needed to escape.

A chair scraping sharply against the floor and yells from inside the room broke the spell. The world came rushing back in all its noise and peril, and I remembered, I wasn't supposed to be here.

I tore myself away, breathless; my veil remained intact as I pushed away from him. He grabbed my wrist almost desperately. "Wait," he whispered.

Before I could respond, people flooded the room in a hurry. I turned away quickly, pretending to get out of the way.

"What is the meaning of this?" Dija roared.

"The dragons are back. We believe they are the same two as before."

My head turned abruptly.

"Have we spotted the princess?" Adriel asked suddenly.

"There is a woman who fits her description that has been sighted, War Chief." My heart danced at Chato's voice. It felt so good to hear it again.

There was a pause before Adriel said, "Let's go."

I sighed with relief. Adriel had been so close to figuring it out. As people clambered past me, I made my way to the door.

"Not so fast, girl. What is your name?" an attendant asked. "I want to make sure you go through the memory mage and that you never serve His Majesty again."

"I am Lena," I lied. "I'm really not feeling well. I must go."

"We don't have a Lena who works at the inn. Who are you?" he asked suspiciously.

As he reached for my veil, I touched his aura and peered into it. He wasn't a bad man, just one who put his ambitions above everyone else. His aura was open, and I pulled hard enough that he collapsed to his knees. He hit the floor before he could release a cry that would give me away. I had seconds.

Before his consciousness faded completely, I'd caught a flash through his aura—an imprint of the space around us. There was a door that was unguarded to my right behind a curtain. I moved. Wood creaked beneath my hand, then the cool night air. I could see once more, and what I was seeing, I would have never believed.

Miren was crouched on the ground in a defensive stance. The look of terror on her face was uncharacteristic but warranted with Zephyr staring her down. I shuddered as my sight returned. I knew exactly where they were. I traveled as quickly as I could, avoiding the soldiers now filling the streets. They were by the trees Drakkar and I often met at after dark.

I stepped out into the alley and didn't stop moving. The road beyond the tavern was chaos, with people shouting, hooves striking dirt, people pouring from their homes to see the source of the commotion. The smell of smoke stung my lungs.

I pulled my veil lower and pressed forward, guided only by Drakkar's faint echo in my mind, like a heartbeat in the distance. My sight was hazy, pulsing in and out with every step, but I knew the way. Past the market square, through the shattered arch where the old wall met the forest path.

Every shout made me flinch. Twice, soldiers brushed so close I could feel the heat from their torches, but none stopped me.

By the time I reached the edge of the city, the air smelled of pine and rain instead of smoke. My legs ached.

And then I saw a clearing bathed in silver light.

"Easy, Zephyr," Drakkar called. He was still in the sky. *"You don't have long, Little One. Mortals are near. I will try to draw the mortals away. They need your help."*

Right. I moved closer, calling out to Zephyr gently. His eyes were fixed on Miren.

"Zephyr, you are scaring her," I said, cautiously moving closer. "She has never been so near a dragon. Perhaps take a step back."

Miren's eyes darted to mine. "Ada? What is going on?" she asked, looking between me and the dragon.

"It is okay," I told her. "He's not going to hurt you."

"How do you know? He's been trailing me since the moment I left you." I took a breath. "I know. Because he is your dragon. I have one too. You saw him two days ago."

She looked at me as if I had lost my mind. That was a fair response. "I knew it!" she seethed. "I knew this had something to do with you.

Can you see him, Ada? Can you see me? When will I meet the end of your lies?"

"I am not Ada," I said carefully. "I am Princess Asha Osei." It felt good to use my real name for once.

Miren did not look at all surprised as she shook her head. "I knew it. I should have turned you in when I had the chance."

"We have to go, Miren," Zephyr implored.

Miren put her hands over her ears as if the dragon was screaming at her. Zephyr, seeing her distress, drew closer.

"Zephyr, don't!"

"We don't have time."

I ran to Miren to grab her arm. She shook me off. "Get back. Both of you!"

Zephyr opened his jaw, and I felt the heat emanating from him. He turned his head sideways. Before us, guards steadily approached but stopped when the dragon turned his sights on them.

They pulled out their swords, but it was too late. A stream of fire licked the air and lit up the dozen or so of them. Screams permeated the night, but they were not coming from the guards falling over and succumbing to the flames. They were coming from Miren.

"What has happened? I can't see!"

"It's going to be okay," I said, wrapping my arms around her. "I will help you; just trust me."

Tears streamed down her face, but I could not spare a second further as I helped her climb Zephyr. It wasn't easy amidst her full panic attack.

"Deep breaths, Miren."

Zephyr lifted us into the air, and I could almost feel the tension in his muscles begin to relax. Drakkar joined us shortly, and together we flew north.

"My eyes," Miren whimpered.

I gripped Miren's waist tightly. "I know you're scared," I began. "The blindness, it is part of the bond with Zephyr. You can open your eyes now."

"They are open," she whispered.

I leaned around her and saw that they indeed were.

"Why can't she see?" I asked Drakkar.

"I'm not sure. Perhaps it doesn't work the same way with every bonded. We will figure it out when we are back in Saeleria."

"Will she be allowed into Saeleria?"

"I don't know. The Great Dragon will tell us."

For Miren's sake, I hoped an exception could be made. She looked like death. "Hold on, Miren."

CHAPTER TEN

The press of her lips still lingered like the hush left after a name is spoken. It was not the kiss itself that unsettled me, but the way my body responded before my thoughts could catch up, as if something old and buried had been stirred awake.

At first, I thought I'd imagined it. A sip of wine, a moment of confusion. But as I stood outside in the courtyard hours later, the memory refused to fade. The scent of jasmine clung to me, stubborn and sweet, the same fragrance that had haunted every dream since the night Asha disappeared..

My heart clenched as I looked skyward. Drakkar, her dragon, cut through the clouds in wide, deliberate circles. "Do you see her?" Kitchi asked, running toward me.

"No, we've been watching him, but I don't see her. She has to be near. He wouldn't leave her here."

"You don't think Dija has her locked away, do you?"

That had occurred to me, but it didn't seem logical based on the conversation we had. "Dija looked just as surprised as the rest of us."

"What is she up to? Do you think she's found another Lightbearer?"

"War Chief!" Moki, my chief trainer, called.

"What is it?" I barked.

"Another dragon," he panted. "The same one spotted the other day. He cut down a dozen of Dija's men."

My pulse quickened. "Where?"

"He's gone now, sir. But they said he had two riders—one with blue hair."

The ache in my chest, the one I'd buried with every memory of her, split wide open. "Asha." Saying her name out loud hurt more than I expected.

It had felt strange, the way the others spoke of her earlier, as if she were not a person but a bargaining piece in the endless games of kings. I'd kept my composure; the only thing steadying me was that poor dancer who'd nearly spilled wine at my table. She clearly wasn't a dancer. Her clumsiness made me doubt she was even an attendant.

Dija would have had her flogged for spilling the wine. It had cost me nothing to intervene. She'd seemed so disoriented and fearful. When I reached out to steady her, something about her body's reaction was so familiar. Then there was that kiss. It was unexpected. I hadn't realized until that moment how I craved to feel something, anything. Somehow, I had.

I turned back to the sky.

"Where is the dragon now?" I asked.

"We lost him, sir."

My eyes trained back on Drakkar. He was circling at the top of the castle. Servants and townspeople ducked into their homes in fear. This wasn't good. People in all the kingdoms were growing restless. This would drive more of them to the Shadowcasters. We could not have that.

Suddenly Drakkar rose higher and began to head away from the castle. "Where are you going?" I whispered.

As if in answer, he banked hard, veering toward a second dragon—copper-scaled, smaller, the same one reported earlier. The two rose together, wing to wing, before disappearing into the clouds.

Once the chaos had abated, Dija brought us back to the room.

"It's true," Zaib breathed. "The dragons really can fly."

"Of course they are real!" Dija bellowed. "What do they want?"

"You say there were two riders?" Fourie asked.

"There's more of them! Is there going to be a whole fleet?" Dija growled. "What are we going to do about this?"

"We already have a plan," I offered carefully. "We will convince her to join us. That is what we agreed to, is it not?"

Dija's glare could have cut stone. "Everything has changed. She has entered my kingdom twice without permission and has now killed not only my son—but my men. That cannot be forgiven."

I tilted my head, schooling my expression into cool indifference. Every lesson my father taught me whispered that men like Dija only respected two things—fear and power. "That's it then," I said with nonchalance. "You're out. Feel free to get back in bed with Elan. We'll see how long your kingdom lasts."

Dija paled, sinking slowly into his chair. "No," he muttered, shaking his head. "That is over."

I narrowed my eyes. "What did he do? What finally cost him your loyalty?"

Dija was quiet for a moment. He looked up at the sky. I thought he wasn't going to answer, but then he whispered, "He hurt my son "Not Atar, though had he not commanded him to go after the girl he might still be alive." The pain was evident in his voice, but he quickly got it under control. "Elan is drunk on his own power and doesn't care about alliances or loyalty. If you come across him on the wrong day, he will cut you down. His father, at least, understood the importance of allies."

"Do you?" I asked, letting the challenge sharpen. "We forged an alliance hours ago, and you're already wavering at the first sign of danger."

His scowl deepened, but he had no answer.

"Elan is going to hear of what happened today," he muttered darkly.

"Good," I said. "Make sure he hears our version. That we tried to capture the princess and narrowly missed. But we won't miss again. We can send some of our troops in the opposite direction looking for her while we focus on bringing her into the fold."

"I can send my men after her," Dija offered.

"She won't trust you," Fourie replied.

"I can go," Zaib offered.

Fourie turned his gaze to me. "I think young Adriel should go. You have a history, do you not?"

"I'm focused on the Shadows. Plus, we agreed that Zaib would go."

Fourie didn't like it, but after a long pause, he yielded with a quiet nod.

"I will send my best men with you," he said to Zaib.

"You will start in the mountains," Dija said, "then head for Wyrm-wood. Bring the dragon girl back. No one—no one—is to speak a word of this." His gaze pinned Zaib, icy and unblinking.

Finally, Fourie rose, surveying each of us. "Will you keep your pledges?"

Zaib and I answered without hesitation.

Dija stared at the floor, jaw clenched.

"...Aye," he said at last.

But every man present knew that an oath given could be easily broken.

CHAPTER ELEVEN

By the time we got to the basin, a small group of dragons was waiting for us.

"What is happening?" Drakkar asked.

They exchanged uneasy glances, each silently urging the other to speak. At last, the ivy-scaled dragon stepped forward, his voice low. "Oxu is no longer guarding the mountain."

A chill rolled through me. Oxu was an ancient creature that served as a gatekeeper for those trying to access Saeleria. Both Adriel and I had been forced to face her illusion. As a master deceiver, it felt impossible that she could just... abandon her post.

"Gone where?" I asked.

A look of uneasiness crossed their faces as they communicated silently through eye contact. Finally, Drakkar said, "You may speak. She is mine."

It was hard to describe the thrill that went through me at Drakkar's claim on me. It felt like the love I'd always wanted from my own father.

"We are unsure where," the ivy dragon said finally. "But her absence means there is no one to guard outsiders from entering, and more importantly, it means that the magic that protects this place is weakening."

I turned to Miren, who had fainted at some point during our travels and still lay unconscious. The only thing that kept me from landing was Zephyr's assurances that she was okay.

"What does that mean for her?" I said, pointing to Miren.

The dragon bristled. "Well, she cannot enter."

"There is no one to test her. That is not her fault," I challenged.

"No one enters without being tested."

"Says who? Who made that rule?"

The dragon looked at me as if I had two heads. "It has never been done."

"Look, Zephyr is flying. She is a Lightbearer. What other test could be more important?"

"Lightbearers are not the only beings that can bond with dragons."

That piece of information gave me pause. "Shadowcasters? Are you saying this rule is to keep away Shadowcasters?"

The dragon did not answer, but the shift in her expression was confirmation enough.

Zephyr finally spoke, voice ringing with quiet certainty. "She is mine—and under my protection."

A hush fell over the basin. Even Drakkar's wings lowered in stunned silence. I looked at each of the dragons and then at Zephyr. Something important had just happened, but I did not understand what.

"Under your protection? What does that mean?" I asked.

"It means," Drakkar began, "that if she causes harm in any way to any of our kind, he has to pay the ultimate price."

I looked at Zephyr. He nodded in confirmation. "Oh. We don't have to, Zephyr. We can wait until Oxu returns."

"We aren't sure how long that will be," he stated. "She needs to rest. Let's get moving. I want her to be comfortable when she wakes."

He looked at her as if she were the most precious thing he had ever beheld. Did Drakkar look at me that way? We locked eyes, and Drakkar tilted his head at an impossible angle.

"It is the same for me," he confirmed.

It always caught me off guard when he seemed to know what I was thinking before I'd even sent it down the bond. *"Really? Sometimes I think I annoy you. Well... not sometimes, but all the time."*

"You do," he said, nuzzling my hair, *"but in the most adorable way possible."*

"What is the meaning of this?" Mattias thundered, his tail slamming against the stone, sending smaller dragons scurrying back.

Drakkar instinctively stepped in front of me, placing himself between Mattias and Zephyr, wings beginning to rise in defense. I reached out and pressed my palm to his scales. *"I can handle this,"* I sent through the bond. *"If you speak for me every time, he will never see me as capable."*

Drakkar bristled. *"Then tell him who he's dealing with."*

"Are you even listening?" Mattias fumed.

I inhaled deeply. "I did exactly what you told me to do."

Mattias gave an incredulous look.

"You told me to bring back Lightbearers," I continued. "I have finally found one. Why are you upset now that I have done exactly what you've told me to do?"

Mattias turned away as if betrayed by his own words. "We lack certainty about her being a Lightbearer. She didn't go under the mountain."

"Did you see the way Zephyr looks at her? There is no doubt."

"She could be the enemy!" he seethed.

"I don't believe that," I said. "I've been living with her for months. She can't be."

Mattias hissed. "Yeah, well you would have said the same about your friend."

I winced, realizing he was speaking of Ashkii. The sweet boy I remembered was now rising through the ranks of the Shadowcasters.

"Paw Paw!" Igbo squealed.

I turned just in time to see the small forms barreling toward us. Soon the room was filled with the three young dragons. I marveled at how fast they were growing these days. It did not seem long ago that they could fit in the palm of my hand.

"Paw Paw," Mwana called. "Don't yell at Iyla. She has brought us a new friend."

"Stay away from that girl," Mattias scolded.

"But she is nice," Ala lamented. "She told us all about her homeland and where she learned to dance."

My eyes rose. "She is awake then?"

"Yes," Ala said. "She kept looking at us like we were the strange ones. She is the one who is afraid of her own dragon."

I stood abruptly, ready to go to her.

"I did not release you," Mattias seethed. I squared my shoulders.

"If she is awake, I must go to her. She has to be terrified."

"Paw Paw, we want a story! You promised," the three dragons cried.

Mattias's gaze flickered to them, and for just a moment his eyes softened. "She is to stay in her quarters. No exceptions. Am I understood?"

I swallowed at the intensity of his stare. It wasn't the ferocity in his voice that disturbed me. It was the fear in his eyes, though he hid it well.

I bowed. "Yes, Great Dragon. We will take every precaution."

When I was out of the room, Drakkar darted in front of me.

"Before you go to see the girl, I need you to heed my warning." When I kept walking, he butted his head against me until I stopped again.

"What?"

"The way Zephyr is with her is as it should be. He will do anything, give his life, or even sacrifice yours to keep her safe."

My face scrunched. *"Well, I'm not going to hurt her."*

"You say that, but we do not know what she is. If she is a Shadowcaster..."

"She is not!"

Drakkar continued as if I had not spoken. *"It is me, Asha, not Mattias. If she is, he will follow her into the darkness and light up anyone who tries to stop her. Keep one eye open at all times."*

His words were unsettling, but I heeded them. *"Did you see how big the hatchlings are getting? I swear they doubled in size in just a couple of days."*

"Puberty," Drakkar groaned. *"They will be insufferable soon."*

I smiled. *"You think everyone is insufferable."*

I knocked softly on Miren's door, half-hoping she'd answer, half-dreading what state I'd find her in. When nothing came, I lifted my hand again and knocked harder.

"Go away!" Miren yelled.

"Miren, it's me."

There was shuffling inside before the door creaked open. Relief flickered through me when I saw a hint of color had returned to her cheeks, but it vanished just as quickly. Her pupils didn't track me. She was still blind. The stiffness around her mouth told me she was scared and trying to hide it.

Saeleria was unique in that it was the only place I'd encountered that allowed me to see without relying on Drakkar. I'd asked Mattias and the other dragons about it, but none would speak of why. Not even Drakkar. Not knowing how the magic worked, I'd assumed Miren would regain her sight as soon as she'd arrived in Saeleria.

"And who are you today?" she asked impatiently. "Ada, Asha, or the liar?"

I winced but was slightly relieved she had left the door open before she walked back into her room.

"Ouch!" she yelled as she walked into a stone bench.

"I can help you—"

She flinched as I neared, holding her hand up in warning. "Don't touch me. You're as bad as that one over there."

She pointed in the general direction of Zephyr, who was curled on the ground in a fetal position. He looked beaten down, not the regal dragon I'd come to know.

I looked around the room and was surprised to see the sheets missing from the bed of flowers she was meant to sleep on. I turned to Zephyr in question, following his shame-filled glances toward the balcony until I saw them. The sheets were knotted together, dangling uselessly into the night air.

"You know there are not enough sheets in this whole castle that will get you anywhere close to the ground."

"Stupid dragon," Miren hissed.

Zephyr turned away, curling further into himself.

"Don't talk to him like that. You two are bonded. His connection to you is deep."

"I never asked for this! How did you do it? How did you make me into this?" she accused, clawing at her eyes. "I can never go back," she whispered. "They'll never take me back. All I wanted was to meet a nice boy and live a simple life." She turned to me, a single tear falling from her eye. "Cane is probably dead by now, and it is all because of you!"

A fragile beat passed between us. "And what now?" I asked quietly. "You were willing to climb out of a balcony window? If you're trying to escape, at least use Zephyr. He can fly you out of here safely."

"I'm never riding that—that thing again."

Zephyr roared, his heartbreak visible in his features. He rose, dragged himself to the balcony, and with a powerful beat of his wings, hurled himself into the sky, the knotted sheets clutched defiantly in his talons.

I sighed, looking toward Drakkar. *"Go after him. I'll stay with Miren. And make sure he brings up new sheets, preferably silk ones, so she doesn't try that again."*

Drakkar looked uneasy, his gaze moving between us.

"Go on," I pressed. *"He needs you."*

Without a word, he reluctantly flew off the balcony toward Zephyr.

Miren ducked onto the floor. "Damn it to hell! There's another one in here."

"There's something blocking your bond," I said, crouching to her level. "We need to find out what it is quickly. You should be able to see in Saeleria."

"I should be able to see always."

"Something is not working right. If you allow me to use my battlemage, I may be able to see what is happening."

"I said, don't you dare touch me!"

I moved onto the bench beside her. "Fine. But I am not going to help you get to Cane until you do. So, whether it is now or in three days makes no difference to me."

Her eyes widened. "You wouldn't dare."

"I don't want to," I said sadly. "You don't know how long I've been waiting for you. I was starting to think I was the only one."

"The only what?" she asked in confusion.

"The only Lightbearer." I quieted for a moment, letting the word seep in before saying, "We are descendants of dragon riders, basically driven to extinction. I'm the first that I know of to come into my power. You are the second."

"I didn't ask for this," she hissed, putting her face into her hands.

"I know," I said emphatically. "Neither did I, and yet we are here."

We sat in silence for seconds, minutes, and what felt like hours before she finally said, "Tell me more. Why do we ride dragons?"

"Do you remember the Shadows, the religious group you meet with? They are called Shadowcasters. They live to bleed all the light from the world—at least, that is what I've read. The dragons are not very forthcoming."

"Where do these Lightbearers come in?" she asked.

"We are the light. We keep things in balance."

"How?" she demanded.

I was at a loss. "I don't know."

"So, you know nothing."

I laughed. "I guess not. But I do know that what you are experiencing with Zephyr is not normal."

Miren seemed to turn my words over in her head. Then with a swish of her auburn hair, she said, "Fine. Do what you have to do."

Finally. I rubbed my hands together, warming them. "I'm just going to touch your aura if that is alright."

She scrunched her nose. "Aura? What the hell is that?"

"It is easier to show you than tell you. It won't hurt," I said, leaning toward her.

"That is exactly what people say when something is going to hurt," she protested.

I lightly grazed her aura before she could change her mind. I moved around cautiously, pulling gently on the strands. I inhaled sharply as I saw flashes of dark corridors and bodies pressed together. Cane and Miren had been using the Shadow meetings to have sex. I saw that while she enjoyed his company, she loved her life on the road more. More flashes of his dead body discarded in a field. She was afraid he was already dead.

"Can you hurry up with whatever you're doing?" she said.

"Just a moment longer."

I paused when I got to the memories of her first meeting with Zephyr. He was sharing his elation at finally finding her. But she had been frozen with terror, unable to hear him beyond her own panic.

I pulled back.

"And? What did you see?"

I stood, pacing in the room.

"Asha, you are scaring me."

I looked up at the use of my given name. "I—I think you hurt his feelings. It has severed the bond?"

"What?"

"Maybe not severed but frayed it. You are going to have to accept him as yours if you want your eyesight back."

She scoffed. "Meeting him is how I lost my damned eyesight."

I shook my head. "No, the loss of sight is part of the process. It is a wonder it hadn't happened to you sooner. Mine occurred after I was nearly killed by my brother."

She seemed surprised by my words. "The emperor?"

"No, it was Kwasi, though my father and eldest brother encouraged it."

She sighed. "And I thought I had a strange family."

"I believe it will come back in time."

"Cane doesn't have time," she gritted out.

"I know. But I think I have an idea of how to get him back."

CHAPTER TWELVE

Asha

"*W*hy do your plans always center on your putting yourself *in harm's way?*" Drakkar groaned, scratching his back against the stone column like an alley cat. No matter how long I lived among dragons, I would never grow accustomed to their peculiar habits.

"*The Great Dragon wants her out; she wants to leave. What is the problem?*" I asked.

He snorted smoke. "*Must I state the obvious? Those rulers wouldn't hesitate to kill you the moment you're in reach—plan or no plan. You cannot trust them.*"

"Except they want something more than my death," I countered. "*They want power. And they believe I'm the key to getting it.*"

His tail lashed. "*Why do we care about this mortal? And a male, no less.*" He gagged dramatically. "*You and your attachments.*"

I folded my arms. "*Funny. I seem to recall your having a brood. They weren't spawned from solitude.*"

Drakkar paused. It was so slight anyone else would have missed it, but I wasn't anyone else. I was his. Guilt struck instantly. *"I didn't mean to—"*

"It is not your fault this man is captured," he interrupted. *"It is likely he is already dead."*

"Just think of this as an opportunity," I said.

"An opportunity for what?"

"For Miren, the second Lightbearer. Maybe the only one we will ever find."

"I doubt that," he grumbled. *"And what will you do? Marry one of them?"*

Before I could respond, Mattias entered the room along with several of his court. You could always tell royal attendants from others because of the braided manes. I'd once asked Drakkar why he did not have one. He told me that only a mate could braid a dragon's hair once paired. The way his gaze drifted after he spoke told me he was recalling something. I desperately wanted him to have more good memories than bad, to take away the hurt in his eyes.

Mattias didn't bother with greetings. "It will give her an excuse to see the mortal again," he said.

My eyebrows puckered. "That is not what this is. He doesn't want to see me. Trust in that."

"You mortals are so peculiar," he said, tilting his head. "The way you lie to yourself would be comical if not so sad."

"This is not helping," I bristled, turning away.

"Well, I have a gift for you, anyway."

I scoffed. "The marriage will be in name only. I plan to come back."

"Yes," he said, unwrapping the bundle. "This will ensure it. You are a fan of elixirs, are you not?"

"You want me to poison a king?"

"No. This is for you." He met my gaze steadily. "I promised you a favor long ago, and I intend to keep it."

Inside the cloth lay a small metal case. When I opened it, I frowned. Nestled within was what looked like a shard of blue gem, no larger than my smallest finger, set into a thin chain.

"What is this?" I asked.

"I promised you a favor years ago, and I am here to deliver." He grinned. "Sourced from the Phoenix of Tears, our most coveted resource. The only place we are able to hatch our young. Do you know why that is?"

"You know I don't. None of you will tell me anything about it."

"It is forbidden," he acknowledged. "But you have proven yourself loyal. The Phoenix of Tears is protective. The gem you hold is forged from years of pressure of the rock and heat, infused with unique properties."

I blinked. "You aren't making sense."

"Open it," he instructed.

I ran my hand over the smooth gem, confused about what he was asking. My fingers stopped on a small crease, and I paused. I used my fingernails to push into the crease until it opened, revealing a small vial of liquid within.

"What is this?"

"Rhyphren," he said, "sourced from a local plant. One drop and you will incapacitate anyone it touches, whether king, dragon, or War Chief."

I turned the tiny gem in my hand, marveling at how the liquid moved. "What do you mean incapacitate? Like they won't be able to see me?" I asked.

"Precisely, long enough that should you need to escape, you can. There is only enough for one attempt, so use it wisely."

"Why not give me more?"

His brow lifted. "You have no idea the lengths we went to create this for you, and you have the nerve to be ungrateful by asking for more?"

"No," I said quickly, "I just—"

"Good." He cut me off with a satisfied nod. "Once I heard you had seen Adriel again, it was only a matter of time before you did something foolish. You are mortal. It is in your nature. This," he gestured to the gem, "could be your salvation."

"She won't need an exit because she is not leaving," Drakkar said firmly.

"Leaving where?" Mwana questioned as she walked into the room. Even she had grown. It would be a stretch to think I could lift her anymore. "You are not leaving again, Iyla? You just got back."

"It won't be for long," I said softly. "You'll hardly notice I'm gone."

Her wings drooped. "Can I come with you?" she asked, eyes bright with hope that made my throat tighten.

I didn't answer. Instead, I fastened the chain around my neck and pointed to the object tucked beneath her wing. "What do you have there?"

Mwana grinned. "A message for you!" she said, jumping in the air. "Who do you think it is from?"

I looked at the seal. "My brother again," I said, ripping it open.

I was relieved to see that he was not in danger.

"How old is this?" I asked.

"It came the day you left," Mattias said.

Just a couple days. A second request for us to meet. I quickly scribbled a reply—I will come as soon as I am able.

I had things to do.

CHAPTER THIRTEEN

Adriel

We'd rounded up as many Shadows as we could find in the city, but the moment they realized we were detaining them for information about their leaders, they scattered. There was nothing more to be gained in Halal, so we set our course for Sharam, the small border town where Firepeak and Wyrmwood meet. From there, we would continue to Locburn, Wyrmwood's capital, to convene with the other rulers. And presumably, Asha would be with them.

"This feels familiar," Kitchi said with a bright smile. She had been far too excited ever since I explained the mission, talking endlessly about how she knew we'd cross paths with Asha again. "Now she has two dragons! She gets to have all the fun."

Her constant chatter grated on my nerves, but I kept my mouth shut. Kitchi didn't deserve the sharpness simmering at the back of my throat; none of this was her fault.

"Hm," I managed, the sound coming out dull and useless.

She raised a brow, smoothing a hand over her newly cropped hair. "Do you think the eggs hatched?"

"I wouldn't know."

"They have to have, right? Oh, what I would give to have seen them hatch."

My mind flashed to Asha cradling the eggs against her chest, humming to them, guarding them as fiercely as any mother dragon. "I hope they all made it," I said quietly, thinking of the smallest one—Mwana. Had she survived?

Before the ache settled too deeply, a commotion stirred behind us. I turned just in time to see Moki stop his horse, blocking the path of Dija's son, Prince Kadir. "I need to speak to Foxtrail. Kindly move out of my way."

"You must get permission," he said flatly.

None of us had wanted Kadir to accompany us, but he had insisted. I saw it for the power move that it was. Dija did not trust me, and he'd sent his son to monitor our moves. Did he really think I'd go running to Elan of all people?

"Let him through," I said.

Moki stood down, motioning the prince to proceed.

"What is it now, Kadir?" There was a bristle in my throat that I failed at hiding.

"All your men are like feral animals. I see why you keep the woman there by your side."

Kitchi bared her teeth as if to keep back the brash reply she had for him. Kadir startled at the deep growl that came from her. The surrounding soldiers snickered behind their hands, even the ones serving Firepeak.

"What can I help you with?" I asked impatiently.

"I want to know why we cannot stop in Truin tonight." He swatted at a horsefly near his neck. "It has been a long journey. Don't we deserve a night of rest away from the wilderness?"

Kitchi snorted behind me. I shot her a glare.

"I'm sorry. I think I'm feral after all," she said as she trotted off. Thankfully, several others began to follow.

"We aren't stopping," I said. "We will barely make it to Locburn on time as it is."

"But surely the Shadows you are looking for are also in Truin." He swung at another fly unsuccessfully. "We want to look refreshed when we arrive, do we not? Both for my bride-to-be and yours."

I inhaled slowly, the grip on my temper hanging on by a delicate thread. "Truin has a population of less than a thousand, not enough to waste our time with. And let me remind you that the only reason you are here is because Dija and Fourie insisted. I will not slow down for you."

"Well, we don't plan to go any further," he challenged, looking to his party. "Do not forget that without us, there is no deal."

I pushed my horse forward, leaning my head as close to Kadir as I could to see the whites of his eyes. "It works both ways. So, tell me, should we turn around and go home to Wiyotak?"

The soldiers behind us went silent. Kadir swallowed, but before I could press the point further, a firm hand settled on my shoulder. Moki. His eyes held a silent warning.

Are you really going to start a war with a child?

He didn't say it aloud, but the meaning was clear in the hard set of his jaw and the pointed dip of his chin.

I exhaled slowly and eased back, letting my horse shift beneath me.

"Fine," I said, keeping my voice steady. "We ride like hell, and we should arrive by dusk. Only one night, Kadir."

I turned around as Moki passed down the order.

We moved at a brutal pace. I stayed clear of the prince after our exchange. If he'd so much as looked my way, I would have punched him in the face. I took in the pitiful inn Kadir had fought to secure for us, its walls sagging beneath the weight of neglect. The townspeople watched as we passed—silent, hollow-eyed. There were twice as many soldiers as civilians.

Over half of the villagers were children. Many of them were barefoot and clothed in rags. Some held out their hands to the soldiers, hoping for coins or morsels of food. Elan was starving his own people into obedience. I would have given them every scrap of food we carried if I could have.

"Get back!" someone yelled from behind. I turned and watched as Kadir threw his baton at the children.

"Don't do it," Moki warned.

"We really should," Chato grimaced. "I can't believe this is the man who will replace Dija."

"Which is exactly why we shouldn't make an enemy of him," Moki said. "Let's break for the day."

"Wait," I said, watching the swarm of children running as the Firepeak soldiers brought out their whips.

"What is it?" Chato asked curiously.

I shook my head. I couldn't put into words what I thought I saw. "Nothing," I said, turning away. I really needed to rest.

"Tell them to stop."

As Chato and Moki broke away to carry out my orders, my horse suddenly reared beneath me. I barely had time to brace myself before she lurched sideways, forcing me to wrench the reins and steer her clear of the scattering villagers.

"Easy," I muttered, fighting to steady her. "Easy. Beast!" I gritted between my teeth, but she wasn't having it. "Beast, calm down. Nothing is here to hurt you."

The horse took off despite my calls to her. I'd never experienced this behavior with her ever. She'd always followed my commands... with one exception.

She stopped suddenly, and the force unseated me. I flew forward onto my stomach. As I spat dirt from my mouth and moved to sit up, my hand grasped leather. I looked up suddenly, reaching for my sword as I realized it was a pair of boots.

In my efforts, I fell backwards just as I locked onto a face I thought I'd never see again.

"Hello, War Chief," Asha said.

Before I could form a single word, Beast surged past me, hooves pounding the earth. The big mare skidded to Asha's side and pressed her broad head against Asha's shoulder, snorting as she nudged her insistently.

Asha let out a soft laugh, stroking Beast's neck. "I missed you too, Candy."

CHAPTER FOURTEEN

Asha

Candy shoved her nose against my chest again, nearly knocking me off balance. I laughed and buried my face in her mane, inhaling the familiar scent of dust, sweat, and the faintest hint of dates. It was strange being among the Guardians again, like walking into a room you used to know well and realizing everything is still where you left it. Kitchi pulled me into a warm hug the moment she spotted me, squeezing as if she would never let go.

Chato gave me an exaggerated wink and leaned in. "Couldn't stay away from me, could you?"

And Moki prowled around me, eyes assessing as if looking for battle scars. "You've been training," he said with approval. "We will have to see what you've got in the ring later."

Before I could answer, Chato slung an arm over my shoulder and guided me through the camp. "Did you see how mad Adriel was?" he asked. Then, realizing his words, he winced and corrected himself. "Well—I guess you can't. Or... can you?"

"That's not funny," Kitchi interrupted, kicking his boot.

"Oh, don't be sore. The War Chief likes me better," he said. "You are still his favorite lieutenant ... for now. You just need better manners."

Tears welled up in my eyes before I could stop them. Kitchi paused in her retort. "Are you alright? Are you hurt?" she asked, looking me over.

"It is just so nice to see you all again."

The three of them hesitated, then respectfully turned away to give me space. Tears were considered unsightly in the Five Kingdoms—signs of weakness, shame. I felt none of that. But for their sake, I wiped the tears away anyway.

"So you can see us then?" Chato asked again. "You have a lot to fill us in on. Where's your dragon?"

"Not too far away," I answered, looking upward.

"I heard you have two," Moki said excitedly. "That is impressive."

I thought about correcting him, but I decided to keep the detail of Miren to myself. It seemed safer for her to stay back until she had a better grip on her bond with Zephyr. She wasn't happy about it, but with her inability to bond, she was more of a liability than a help.

Chato offered me a choice of accommodations at either the inn, which looked like it had seen better days, or the tents that the soldiers were erecting. I held up my hand. "No need for that. I won't be staying long."

The three Guardians exchanged glances as if they knew differently. Drakkar and I had already decided. I would travel in my own company. It was better that way.

"I only require speaking with Adriel once he is recovered from his fall."

"That might be a minute," Chato chortled. "He ate the ground pretty hard."

I was acutely aware. Every muscle in my body had wanted to reach out to him and make sure he was okay, but then I remembered the princess with long blonde tresses and a slender face that he was betrothed to.

"We need to set up a patrol. Are you all right if we leave you by the campfire for an hour or two? I can return afterwards."

I smiled. "I'd really like that."

"How long is he going to make you wait?" Drakkar called down the bond.

The day had quickly descended into nightfall, and no one but the inn attendants had come by, offering ladles of stew and bread that had to be days old.

Feeling restless, I pulled a meal I'd prepped for the journey and began to heat it in the makeshift fire. Once properly heated, I wrapped it in a cloth and walked through the camp. Guardians in conversation paused and gawked at me as I walked by. Not all were Guardians. Some of the soldiers wore the green and blue of Entioch and the red and black of Firepeak.

The look on their faces was much more concerning. It was not admiration or respect, but fear and maybe even disgust. I needed to find Adriel quickly so I could leave this place. I stood to search for any traces of Chato and the others. I stopped as I felt tiny hands at my belt.

I gripped the hand as the figure struggled to run away. The boy froze as my battlemage flared instinctively. His mouth parted, eyes going wide as I brushed against the edges of his aura. Eleven, maybe. Thin. Hungry. One of many mouths in his home and not the first to go without.

Images struck me like blows, him digging through pig slop for scraps, stopping himself from eating even the salvageable bits, saving them instead for younger siblings whose ribs pressed against their skin. There was something there, something I had not seen before. His eyes weren't looking at me but off in the distance.

I pulled back in fear or excitement; I wasn't sure. "Are you an unseer?" I asked.

His eyes widened further. "No! Of course not," he said.

But I could feel it clearly now in his aura. There was no denying it.

"Let me go!" he barked and swung his tiny fist in an act of desperation rather than anger.

"Hold on," I said, reaching into my bag. "Is this what you were after?"

I pulled out nearly everything I had—bread, dried fruit, and a handful of salted meat.

His stomach growled in answer before he could speak.

"One question," I said softly. "Answer it, and the food is yours."

He stopped struggling just as I released him. "What... what is it?" he asked skeptically.

"Were you born an unseer or did you lose your sight at some point?"

He paused as if he had not anticipated that question at all. "I don't rightly know, Miss," he said, shaking his head. "I've been this way as long as I can remember." My heart sank. "But I don't remember much from before hittin' my head. Fell out of a cart when I was eight."

My head lifted abruptly, the smallest bits of hope beginning to flourish. "Surely your parents know," I said.

He frowned, ducking his head. "They are both gone, Miss. It is just me and the little ones now."

An overwhelming sense of sadness took hold as I looked at his collarbone that seemed to protrude from his chest and the gaunt face where round cheeks should have been.

"I'm sorry," I whispered. And I meant it. "Here. Take it all."

I offered him coin as well, but he shook his head, gently closing my fingers around it.

"It'll get stolen. Best you keep it."

"What's your name?"

"Jondrey."

"Jondrey," I said, "find me tomorrow. I'll make sure you have enough for your family before we leave."

His features lit up. "Thank you, ma'am. Truly."

I watched him leave without issue as if he knew the area very well. He did not even bother with a walking staff.

I had barely shaken off the encounter by the time I'd arrived at the inn. Men and women were congregated outside, dancing and laughing as the villagers filled their cups with foul-smelling ale. I pinched my nose, wondering how in fire and ash they could drink it.

Near the entrance, Moki and Chato appeared deep in conversation. They broke apart when I approached.

Chato smirked, though it didn't reach his eyes. "Asha. You can never stay put, can you?"

"I'm ready to see him. I've waited long enough."

Moki stepped forward. "It's not a good time. Give him another hour. We will bring him to you."

"No," I said with a shake of my head. "I will see him now."

Chato crossed his arms. "Unfortunately for you, Princess, we do not follow your orders."

I tapped my foot impatiently. "Is that your final decision then?"

They looked at each other as if trying to understand my meaning. "Yes."

"Very well then." I turned around, giving them my back, but instead of leaving, I called on the bond.

In seconds, Drakkar appeared in the sky, preparing his descent. Gasps and shouts followed as people ran in all directions to take cover and hide from the dragon. I could not blame them. Drakkar remained the biggest dragon I had ever seen, even bigger than Mattias.

The ground shook as he landed, and he bared his teeth as smoke swirled around his nostrils. Moki leapt aside; Chato wasn't as quick. Drakkar snatched his cloak in his talons, lifting him effortlessly before dropping him in the dirt.

I took that moment to sneak into the inn. My nose scrunched at the acrid smell of dirty floors and foul-smelling ale. The space felt narrow as I used my staff to find the closest wall, a hallway, I realized. It was surprisingly quiet inside except for hushed voices. I felt along the wall until my fingers found a curtain where a door should have been. I leaned closer, the fabric muffling the sound, but I could still hear the voices beyond. Though my sight had left me and I could not make them out, I knew one aura belonged to Adriel.

It appeared Adriel was having a heated conversation with another man.

"You've already gone back on your word. I was supposed to meet her in Wyrmwood."

"I couldn't have predicted she'd show up on the road, Kadir. What would you have me do? Tell her she is to go back to the mountains so that you could meet her there?" There was a muddiness in Adriel's voice that I had not heard before.

"This is unacceptable. I'm not even in my lapel coat and high tops. She is to be mine, and you have ruined it for me!"

Adriel laughed. It was the kind of laugh that took your breath away because it was laced with a threat. "Why don't you tell her that? She's listening by the door."

My heart stalled. I'd been caught. I took a bold step forward toward Adriel and Kadir's voices. The room fell silent as I approached.

"Princess," Kadir said. "Please forgive our crass conversation. We were just, that is—"

"I need to speak to the War Chief," I demanded.

Kadir stepped closer. "Well, that wouldn't be proper. As your future... that is, I am the heir apparent to Firepeak. Whatever you have to say to him, you can also say to me."

"I know who you are," I said coolly. "And I am not here for you. I am here to talk to him."

A sharp breath escaped him. "Not here for me?" he repeated, as though the words themselves offended him. "You cannot simply refuse—"

"She just did," Adriel cut in dryly.

What was wrong with him?

"Run along, Prince," he continued. "I will call upon you when the princess and I are done."

A low growl erupted from Kadir, but he didn't take a step toward Adriel. He stood his ground as if deep in thought. I wondered who he was angry at—Adriel who mocked him, or the woman who rejected him. He seemed to quell whatever emotion he nearly unleashed and took a bow. "Very well, Princess Asha. I will be upstairs in my room. But I should like to meet you properly when you have a moment."

I nodded politely but made no such promise.

Once Kadir ascended the stairway, the room quieted. A light *thump* sounded as Adriel patted the seat next to him. "Come, have a drink," he said. "I have plenty."

It was odd being alone with this man again. I'd certainly never experienced him when he wasn't completely in control. I shivered as I felt his gaze upon me. My mouth ran dry as I recalled how his hungry hands had touched me and how his mouth...

"I brought you soup. I thought it might help restore you after your injury," I said, reaching into my pouch and stopping when nothing was there.

"Where is it?" he asked.

I sighed. "I gave it away."

"You gave my soup away," he chuckled. "How?"

"There was a young boy, never mind. Here, at least have a sip of water," I said, handing over my canteen. When our hands brushed for the briefest of seconds, my heart flipped, and my body tingled. I stepped back immediately.

"Do you really think I would have eaten anything that you've prepared?" he asked with genuine amusement. "After you've poisoned me, more than once, I might add."

"Are you drunk?" I asked incredulously.

I heard a bottle tip back and liquid being poured. "What of it, Princess?"

My breath stumbled at the way he used my title. "I thought we established you may use my given name."

The chairs scraped and his boots shifted as he moved.

I felt the heat drawing closer, and instinct urged me to step back—not out of fear of him, but fear of myself. Of what I might say. What I might want.

"You've said a lot of things, Princess. I don't suppose you remember the night you told me I could call you by your name." The smokiness of the whiskey on his breath flared in my nostrils. "What were we doing when you made that request?"

I swallowed but refused to back away. "I hoped you'd be a bit more... alert this evening, but what I have to say cannot wait."

We stood there just inches away, breathing the same air. If I moved toward him in the slightest, we'd be touching. "What do you want from me then?"

"I want—" I said, breathlessly. "I want a man who has been taken into custody by King Dija."

That seemed to surprise him. "And why do you want this man? Is he your lover?"

"That is not your concern. The only thing I need you to know is that I need him freed."

He stood tall but didn't move away. "And why would you ask me?"

"I seem to recall you once saying that you would burn the world down for me."

A humorless laugh escaped him, and he lifted my chin with two fingers, angling my face toward his. His touch was deceptively gentle, but his next words were not.

"Funny," he said, tilting my head up to face his, "I believe you were naked in my bed when I said that. I would have said anything."

I flinched, moving away. That hurt, and he'd meant it to. "I am not here to litigate the past or explain myself," I said.

"Then why are you here?"

"I know what you and the other rulers are planning. I know that you want to use me to get to Elan."

Wood splintered. He was holding something in his hands tightly, perhaps a cup. "And who told you that?" He strode over and grasped my hand. I tried to take it back, but he held it firmly, running a thumb on the underside. "Wait!"

"What are you doing?" I asked in a panic.

He lifted me then, my legs finding his hips to keep balance. "Put me down!"

"As you wish, Princess," he said.

But instead of lowering me to my feet, he sat down and set me so that I straddled his lap. He ran a hand through my hair until he cupped my face. All I had to do was tilt my lips slightly, and my mouth would be upon his.

"These hands," he breathed, clasping mine in his. "I never give you enough credit, Princess. Though there is one more thing I need to do to make certain."

I was silent, trying to keep my head from losing all sense of myself. "I think the ale has addled your brain. I don't know what this is about," I managed.

"You've always been a terrible liar," he mused. "And now you want me to break out this man you have some history with. A man you refuse to elaborate on. I thought you were better than that."

The words struck too close. My pulse stuttered because now it was my turn to hurt. "Says the man who is engaged for power," I said coolly.

"At least she won't leave me in the middle of the night," he said, pulling me closer.

I put my hand against his chest to push him back. "Give her time."

That was the exact moment Kitchi cleared her throat. I stood abruptly, extracting myself from Adriel's grasp. "So... Asha, does that mean you are coming with us?" I turned to watch as her, Chato's, and Moki's auras entered. I sighed heavily, realizing they must have watched the entire encounter.

I shrugged. "It is up to your War Chief."

Silence fell upon the room as we awaited Adriel's response. "What is it you are not telling me?"

It continued to catch me off guard how well he was able to read me. "I would like help to find more Lightbearers. Yours and the other rulers'. That is my price for my cooperation."

"They'll never agree to it."

"They will if you convince them. You know as well as I do how dangerous the Shadowcasters are. We are living on borrowed time. They are growing stronger every day."

"We know," Chato said. "We've been tracking them closely for months."

"Then you also know Ashkii is now one of them."

"Yes," Moki confirmed. "We've made several attempts to retrieve him, but he has refused to come with us."

"Why?"

"He does not talk to us, other than to tell us to leave him be. We do not know why. Has he spoken to you?" Moki said.

I shook my head. "He told me the same thing."

"We have heard similar from other families who have lost their loved ones to the Shadows," Kitchi added. "Usually young men, but some women as well. It begins the same. They attend these meetings, which are held in areas where the emperor's famine has hit the hardest. These young people leave their families behind to recruit more."

Silence settled over the room before Adriel spoke. "Then why come to us?" he asked. "Why not go directly to Dija?"

"Because I doubt my presence would be welcomed," I said evenly. "I need someone who can negotiate on my behalf."

"And what exactly are you asking for?" he asked.

I drew a slow breath. "The immediate release of Cane. Safe passage for him—and for me. And your cooperation in finding the Lightbearers."

His gaze sharpened. "And in exchange?"

"My name," I said. "My hand, if that's what it takes."

A pause. Then, "You mean marriage."

"Yes."

He studied me for a long moment before exhaling. "I will consider it. But I won't make such a decision tonight." He straightened, already turning away. "You'll have my answer at sunrise."

And with that, he left—as though the matter were already settled.

Chapter Fifteen

Asha

I woke to the sound of breath that was not my own. My eyes snapped open to find a massive golden eye peering down at me, unblinking.

"Drakkar," I groaned, rubbing my face as I pushed myself upright.

"The day has begun, Little One," he rumbled.

I swung my legs over the side of the bed, the cool air biting at my skin. My body ached with the kind of exhaustion that sleep didn't touch. I hadn't truly rested—not with my thoughts gnawing at me all night.

"I was asleep," I muttered. "Or trying to be."

He tilted his head, smoke curling lazily from his nostrils. "You were restless. You dreamed."

I ignored him and reached for my cloak. The truth was, I hadn't slept at all—not really. Every time I closed my eyes, I saw him. The way he'd held me, in his arms, on his lap. The way his voice had wrapped around my title because he refused to say my name.

For various reasons, I hadn't intended to stay in the camp. Drakkar was a large dragon, and very few tents were big enough to accommodate him. Even then, half of Drakkar's body hung outside.

I hadn't intended to see Adriel at all, just follow at a distance until I could make my own deal with the rulers in exchange for Cane. Everything stopped when I saw him again.

"I see the mortal did not find his way into your bed last night," Drakkar observed. "Your meeting with him must have gone badly."

"Leave, Drakkar. It is too early," I grumbled.

He watched me for a long moment, ancient eyes seeing far more than I wished. "Then why does your heart still sound like it's running?" he asked, ignoring my temper.

"I am here for Miren. It is the only way that she will trust me, the only way she will bond with Zephyr."

"They will find their way," he said. "Just like we did."

"I am not having this conversation anymore," I said as I stepped out of the tent.

An arm came over my shoulder, pressing me into an armpit. "Chato!" I squealed.

He held his stomach as he laughed. "I wish you could see your face. You are such a princess."

I brushed my hair back into place, pushing him away as he drew near in fake apology. "Careful. Drakkar is watching."

Chato's laughter halted immediately as he took in the dragon, likely remembering the attack from last night. Drakkar bared his teeth for good measure. Chato flinched but did not retreat. "At least you're not sad anymore," he observed.

"You're right. Now I can direct all the fury I feel this morning at you instead of Drakkar."

He rolled his eyes, mumbling something about taking all the punches for others. "I'm here to escort you."

"I don't need a babysitter, and definitely not without some assurance from Adriel," I said.

"Ah, about that. We are changing our route to head straight to Wyrmwood, where you can ask King Dija himself for this man you are looking for."

My eyes widened. "Really? He is going to help me?"

Chato dug his foot into the dirt before saying, "He will get you there. Whether he will help you once you are there, I am uncertain. Come, I will bring you to your horse."

"Is this truly necessary? I have my own transportation," I said.

"The War Chief believes you would be better received on horseback. Drakkar might feel like a threat."

Drakkar growled in response, and though Chato watched him warily, he stood his ground.

"It is fine, Drakkar," I said, turning back to Chato. "I will ride the horse. But why is the War Chief unable to relay this message himself?"

Chato winced. "I know I give our War Chief shit, but go easy on him. Your leaving did something to him. He is not the same."

Was that why he'd been drinking? "And you're saying it is my fault."

"Calm down, dragon woman," he said, bumping my shoulder with his fist. "I'm saying he was doing better—until last night. I'm trying to avoid more nights like that."

Before I could answer, Candy came galloping toward me, ears perked, tail flicking with excitement. I offered apple slices in my palm. She nuzzled into them eagerly. "She's yours for the journey," Chato explained.

My head swiveled as I looked over in Adriel's direction, but he had his back to me. "Why?"

"Something about the horse not being trustworthy when you're around. I am guessing our War Chief doesn't want to be thrashed again in front of his men."

"*Again*, that is not my fault."

Chato winked. "Come on. Let's get her saddled."

As he led Candy forward, movement caught my attention. Near the edge of the encampment stood Jondrey—his three little sisters clustered behind him, a small brother clinging to his shirt. All of them thin. All of them were hungry. Too young to carry the weight they were carrying.

I approached, pulling a satchel from my pack. I handed it to Jondrey. He stared at it as if it were treasure.

"Would you consider coming with us, Jondrey?" I asked gently. "All of you."

His brows knit together. "Leave here?"

"It seems... there isn't much here for you all."

He shook his head, clutching the satchel. "I appreciate the offer, miss, but this is our home. Being poor here or being poor somewhere else... it makes no difference."

I wanted to argue. To tell him it made a difference to me. That safety, and food, and warmth could be obtained elsewhere. But then his stomach growled loudly, breaking the moment.

I smiled softly. "Enjoy this. There's bread and honey inside. A treat."

His eyes brightened. It was just a flicker, but enough before he ushered his siblings away.

CHAPTER SIXTEEN

Miren

"Watch me fly!" Mwana squealed as she jumped from Zephyr's back. A dull thunk hit the ground beside me, followed by an indignant grunt. Zephyr exhaled hard, the warm gust ruffling my hair.

"You're kind of boring today," Igbo complained.

"You are so rude," Mwana cried. "Can't you see he is heartbroken because Miren can't ride him?"

"That's not true. She rode him here."

"Actually, it was Iyla, right, Miren?"

"Enough!" Zephyr barked. "Leave Miren alone."

"Miren can speak for herself," I said with annoyance. The dragons had been kind enough to use my common tongue to communicate, a skill that Asha had helped them with apparently. Though on days like this, I wished I didn't understand them. I just wanted to pretend this wasn't happening.

There was movement in the corner of the room as Zephyr began to move. My heart raced as I realized he was moving closer to me. The heat brushed along my cheek, his breath rolling over the back of my neck in warning waves.

He would never hurt me. Zephyr claimed the bond made such a thing impossible. I knew that, and yet I feared I'd never grow used to being near such beasts.

"What's it going to take, Miren?" he growled. "What do I have to do for you not to hate me?"

I was startled by the question. I was used to sad Zephyr, and stubborn Zephyr, and even desperate Zephyr. But not this. He was angry, really angry.

"You could give me space," I snapped.

"That's all I have done!" he roared. "No more!"

Before I could so much as inhale, movement rushed toward me and Zephyr seized the collar of my blouse. My feet left the ground as he hoisted me up like it was nothing.

"Zephyr!" I sputtered, gripping his hide instinctively. "Put me down!"

"No!" he snarled.

His breath blasted across my face as he held me aloft, trembling not with violence, but with something far more unsteady.

Panic clawed at my ribs. Air rustled through my hair, and my heart stopped. "Get me away from the window. Don't let me fall. Let me go!"

"As you wish," he said, opening his jaw. He'd dropped me out of the window. Screams ripped from my throat as I continued to fall with no landing in sight. I grabbed wildly, trying to find something to latch onto. When there was nothing, my screams grew louder as tears trailed down my face. "Zephyr!" I called.

As soon as I called, he was right underneath me. I clung to his scales as if they were life as he flew so high my ears began to pop.

"I'd never let you fall—I would never leave you. Don't you see that?"

When I didn't respond, he cried into the night sky. I assumed it was night, but there was no way for me to know because my sight had not returned. I was stuck in this place with him when all I wanted was to go back to my life.

When he landed back in our room, I slid off his back into a puddle on the floor. There, I rocked and cried myself to sleep.

CHAPTER SEVENTEEN

Elan

Pain had a rhythm if you were paying attention. It moved in waves, swelling, receding—only to return like a fire that refused to die down.

I enjoyed the pleading, especially when it was wet and frantic. I reveled in the way people would bargain. I don't care what anyone says, men and women differ in how they beg. Men always broke first, which made it a challenge to make their pain last. I always knew I was close when they began to cry out to their mother, as this one did now.

"Don't worry, she is next."

The way the man cried let me know my words had the desired effect. I ramped up my battlemage until the flesh around his nipples sizzled.

Yet no matter how much I lived for these moments, there was something missing.

Asha.

She had always been the one who resisted longest. Others broke under my methods, always pleading, bargaining, begging for mercy, but she never gave me that satisfaction. Even when fear etched itself into her breath, her mind remained stubbornly intact. That defiance only sharpened my interest.

My father had intervened once—beating me within an inch of my life when he discovered what I'd done. He said it was unbecoming. I knew better. He hated her more than I did, but he feared my methods if left unchecked even more. That made the moments I could corner her all the sweeter. After our last encounter, I now knew why. She had a battlemage after all and with our father out of the way, I could whittle away at it piece by piece. No one would steal her from me again.

The messenger, bowed on his knees in front of me, had reached that final stage. His head lolled forward, chin slick with blood and spit. One eye had swollen shut. He knew what was coming.

I stood before him, hands clasped behind my back, my cloak falling in neat folds. The chamber was cool, but not overly so. They were the perfect conditions to see the steam rise off the skin. If I closed my eyes, I could almost pretend it was Asha I burned, that it was her fear coating the air.

"Again," I said softly.

The man flinched. Not from my voice, but from the knowledge of what it summoned. I pressed my battlemage to the man's shoulder. Flesh hissed. The smell rose, thick and immediate.

I groaned at the knock on the door. "A message for you," Ekon said with a bow.

Ekon did not hesitate. He never did. He was good at that—at moving when others would question, at obeying when others would weigh and doubt. He crossed the chamber with measured steps to hand it to me.

I smiled. "Another message from our dear Nightborne. How helpful he has been to us."

"What are your orders, Your Holiness?" Ekon asked.

I threw the letter into the fire. "Do you know why I promoted you?" I asked.

Ekon straightened. "Because I protected you," he said carefully. "Because I am loyal."

"Yes," I said, and then smiled as if granting him a gift. "And because you are not sentimental."

Ekon's face tightened.

"You are able to do what must be done," I continued, voice low. "Even when it offends softer men."

Ekon held my gaze. "Yes, Your Holiness."

I nodded once, satisfied. "I am going to send you on a task soon, and I will need it carried out without question."

His eyes widened, but he did not question further. "Yes, Your Holiness."

When the chamber finally fell silent again, I stood alone. Asha was alive, and soon she would be mine again.

CHAPTER EIGHTEEN

Asha

"You seem on edge," Kitchi said as she rode beside me.

"I'm marching directly into another marriage," I muttered. "How would you feel?"

"That's fair, I suppose. At least this time you get to choose. Aren't you just a little happy to be back with us again? You aren't tied up this time, although with the right partner, I hear that can be fun," she said with a wink.

Instead of responding, I asked, "How long has Adriel been engaged?"

Kitchi looked down at her hands as they tightened on the reins. "Not long, though talks have been going on for at least a year. It was the boost we needed to bring down Elan's army in Wiyotak."

Her words solidified what I'd suspected and what King Dija had said a few nights ago. "What do you know about her?"

"She's royal and rich," Kitchi shrugged. "What else is there to know? All royals are about the same to me."

"Hey!"

She put a hand dramatically to her chest. "Not you, obviously."

I needed to let the subject drop, but the next question forced its way past my lips anyway. "Does he plan to go through with it?"

Kitchi looked off into the distance, as if debating on answering. "Have you considered that I may not be the best person to ask that of? You could ask him yourself."

I wasn't sure I wanted to know, nor was it my business. Adriel could do whatever he wanted. I'd left the relationship and given a second chance, I would make the same decision—I think.

Refusing to allow my thoughts to go any further, I asked, "Where is Tazbah?"

Kitchi's face fell instantly. She shut her eyes as if bracing against a memory. "She left Wiyotak because of the war. We were writing to each other, but I am not sure where she resides now. We lost contact."

"Well, why don't you find out? There can't be too many libraries. Surely, she is still working in one."

"She knows how to find me," Kitchi said quietly. "And she hasn't. I think that speaks for itself."

"Perhaps, but it seems worth it to find out for sure."

"Do you really want to talk about love lives, because if so, I have my own questions for you?"

I shook my head. "No. I don't."

Kitchi and I were quiet after that. We continued through the countryside at a snail's pace compared to how quickly I could have flown on Drakkar.

Moki used our breaks as interrogation sessions to learn more about my training and to devise a tailored regimen that would keep me strong for riding Drakkar and fighting if necessary. Chato volunteered to be my training partner despite my objections.

"We have to make up for lost time," Moki admonished. "What you've been able to do on your own is amazing, but with your ability to channel your dragon's sight, we need to adjust strategy."

The training began with footwork, positioning, then drills, lots of them. Sweat gathered quickly at my temples as he corrected my stance, moving my elbow into place. My muscles burned in protest, but beneath the strain I felt relief, relief to be doing something other than fretting about Wyrmwood, Miren and Zephyr, the Shadowcasters, and yes, Adriel.

"You favor your left," Chato noted. "Good for balance but bad for unpredictability."

I gritted my teeth and adjusted. We moved again. Faster this time. Chato came at me without warning, forcing me to react on instinct alone. I ducked, pivoted, but Chato was ready for me. I gasped as he knocked me on my back.

"Again," Moki ordered.

We'd only begun when Kadir called out to me. "What on earth are you doing?" he asked in horror. "I was told you weren't raised in the court, but this is... highly improper. You won't need these skills as a queen, and certainly not as an empress."

I bit my tongue until it bled. "I don't intend to be a helpless empress."

He laughed as if humoring a child. "If you choose the right man to be by your side, you won't need to fight."

Kitchi appeared behind him like a shadow. "And what if the danger is the man she chooses?" she asked sweetly. "Or someone in her own court?"

Kadir stiffened. Chato stepped in quickly, clearing his throat. "Our rest break is almost over, anyway. We will give you some privacy, won't we, Kitchi?" He formed it into a question, but it was clearly a warning.

"Of course, Your Highness," Kitchi said before stalking away.

Once we were alone, Kadir flipped his cloak in distaste. "You have to learn how to talk to these people. If you don't assert your rank, they will walk all over you."

I gathered my horse, giving her a treat before mounting her. Kadir followed behind on his own. "I thought I'd travel with you a bit so we can get to know each other."

"I appreciate you taking the time, but it wouldn't be fair to the other suitors."

His eyebrows raised as if he had not expected that response. "We can break a few rules. I won't tell anyone."

"If I am going to be a different ruler than my brother, I can't start off with a lie. You understand." He gave me a look that indicated he didn't. "Have a good day, Your Highness," I said before fleeing as quickly as I could to catch up with the others. Thankfully, he did not follow.

Adriel had set a grueling pace, and my thighs throbbed with every shift in the saddle. Riding Drakkar wasn't easy, but I could adjust my posture as much as I liked while in the air, and we could move from place to place much quicker. Traveling with the Guardians was painfully slow. I sat on a rock by the fire with Kitchi, catching up with all that I missed.

The war Adriel waged had been long and brutal. So many had died, though more of Enapay and Elan's soldiers than anyone else.

"Why didn't you write?" Kitchi asked suddenly.

I looked up from my hair that I was in the process of plaiting. "Huh?"

"You disappeared. I can understand why you left, but I thought we were friends. We didn't even know if you were alive."

Chato and Moki suddenly got very busy skinning the rabbits that were going into our dinner, leaving us in a pocket of uncomfortable quiet.

"I suppose because it was too hard. I was afraid I'd give in and return."

"Would that have been so bad?" Kitchi challenged. "For us to continue our friendship? It sounds like an excuse to me. I shared so much with you."

I looked down. She had. She'd opened up to me about Tazbah and her fears regarding that relationship. And I'd just left.

"I guess I did not know you would care so much. I was a prisoner before all of that."

"We were your friends," she said defensively.

I met her eyes directly. "Friends don't lie to each other."

The hurt in her demeanor was instant and I immediately regretted my words. It was unfair, and I knew it. "Kitchi," I began, but she stood abruptly and walked away.

I made to follow her, guilt twisting beneath my ribs, but a firm hand settled on my shoulder. Chato.

"I'll talk to her," he said gently. "We are glad to have you back." He gave my shoulder one last squeeze before moving to Kitchi's side.

That left Moki and me alone by the fire, the quiet settling between us like a blanket. "Do you hate me for leaving too?" I asked.

"There is a time to stand and face what's in front of you… and a time to strategize and recuperate. I like to believe you chose the latter." He poked at the fire, sending sparks upward. "It doesn't warrant anger. It just is."

I exhaled, frustrated. "You never answer a question directly."

"I've never found direct answers to be all that useful."

I resisted the urge to glare at him. He would just ignore it.

"I am more interested in this new rider. Miren, you said her name is? How is she doing?"

"I'm not sure. She's reluctant. She does not embrace being a Lightbearer like I have."

"Not surprising."

"Why do you say that?"

"I don't know this Miren, but I know you," he said. "Your life was bleak before Drakkar came into it. Being a Lightbearer has only enriched it. Miren was likely content with the life she had."

He was right. She'd had a lover, a vocation that she loved, friends—roots. A life she'd chosen. A life I'd disrupted simply by existing within it. "But it is who she is. I don't know how you can reject a part of yourself."

Moki's knife stilled over the rabbit. His dark eyes lifted to mine, steady and searching. "You'd be surprised what people will reject if it means holding onto comfort. Truth isn't a gift in these cases—it is a burden."

I frowned, twisting the loosened strands of my hair around my finger. "But once you know, you can't un-know. Doesn't she feel it? The pull of the bond, the fire in her chest?"

"She probably does." He sliced cleanly through the rest of the rabbit's hide and dropped it beside the fire. "But some will chain themselves to the familiar rather than be swept away by the new. It is fear. And fear is stronger than you realize."

I leaned back against the rock, the flames flickering over my face. His words gnawed at me, because hadn't I done the same? Hidden myself away instead of facing my father, my brother Elan?

The sharp beat of wings cracked overhead. My head snapped upward, heart jolting as Drakkar's silhouette passed low across the treetops. But the dragon's cry wasn't one of greeting—it was warning. The Guardians moved, unsure of how to respond.

"What is wrong?" I sent through the bond.

"Someone is coming. Prepare yourself."

I tried to see what Drakkar was seeing, but there was nothing, as if he was blocking me out. Before I could ask, shouts came from behind. "Move! He needs medical attention." It was Adriel, clearing the way. He and another Guardian carried a limp figure through the sea of people. I recognized the crinkled forehead and the black aura surrounding the figure immediately.

"Kwasi! Move, that's my brother," I shouted, following them into the tent. My sight left me, and I had to follow the auras to the medical cot.

"I need a shaman!" Adriel called.

I barely had time to clasp Kwasi's hand before I was asked to step back. "Please, Your Highness. I need to examine him."

"I'm not leaving him," I snapped. The words were filled with a rawness and fury. I did not care.

There was a brief silence... then a warm hand settled over mine. Adriel's. "You don't have to leave," he said softly, so low I almost could not hear it. "You can stay right here. Let's just give the healer a moment. The more we interfere, the longer he is not being assessed. I'll stand here with you."

Reluctantly, I stepped back, dropping his hand. Letting go of Kwasi felt like letting go of a cliff's edge, hoping and praying that someone would catch me. Adriel kept his firmly atop my other hand. At some point he must have realized because he snatched it back as if it burned.

"Tell me," I whispered. "What does he look like? What are they doing?"

"He appears to be unconscious but breathing," he said carefully. "The shaman has lifted his tunic. There don't seem to be any visible wounds."

No visible wounds. "Could he be dehydrated? Is his battlemage spent?"

"Let's wait," he said calmly.

I didn't want to wait. I wanted answers, solutions, certainty. I wanted anything but this crushing helplessness, but I forced myself still. After what felt like hours trapped inside a single shallow breath, the shaman exhaled deeply. "I am not certain what has happened, but it does seem to be a magic wound. The best thing for him is to allow him to rest. His magic will eventually be restored."

"Perhaps I can touch his aura and see what happened."

"I would advise against that, Your Highness," she cautioned. "Aura work expends energy, and Kwasi has very little at the moment. It is best to allow him to wake naturally."

I pulled my hand back. "Can I sit with him?"

"Of course," the shaman answered. "He is not responsive, but hearing your voice might help with his recovery."

I sat with Kwasi, pulling out the last letter he'd sent me. He'd wanted to see me, to tell me something. If I'd gone to him sooner, would he be lying here now?

"This is not your fault, Little One."

"It feels like it is," I responded..

Adriel sat in the room with us for a time. Eventually he whispered something about checking the perimeter, and Kitchi took his place. She took me in her arms, and the hurtful words we'd said to one another seemed to melt away.

"Thank you for sitting with me, Kitchi."

"You won't be thanking me for long."

"Whatever it is, it can't be any worse than this," I said, turning towards Kwasi.

Kitchi took a deep breath before saying, "We need to keep moving. Whoever did this to Kwasi could be nearby."

I turned my head. "No. He is very fragile. The shaman said…"

"That he is safe here. Adriel has ordered the medical cot to be assembled for carrying him. The sooner we get to Wyrmwood, the more medical attention he can receive."

I reached for Kwasi's hand again, threading my fingers through his. His skin was cool, too cool to the touch.

"I won't let anything happen to you," I murmured, unsure whether I was promising it to myself… or daring the gods to try me.

Chapter Nineteen

Miren

Finding my way through the castle without sight wasn't easy, but the hatchlings found it entertaining to help guide me through the halls.

"Come!" Igbo called. "There is something we want to show you!"

"You know, whatever it is, I won't be able to see it, right?" All three cackled at my response. "What are you up to?"

"We can't tell you!" Ala teased.

"I'm not even supposed to leave my room," I said warily.

"Everyone is in the council room. They won't even know you left," Mwana said. So that is where Zephyr went. He rarely left me alone, not even to eat, but he slipped away as soon as the summons came. We hadn't spoken much after his flying spree.

Still, the dragons nudged insistently at my ankles and tugged at my sleeves like overeager children. It had been so strange living among the dragons and learning their ways of life. I'd never been so well fed or cared for. But there was always a stabbing guilt within me. My heart ached at what had befallen Cane. I needed to convince Zephyr to find him somehow. I could not wait for Asha any longer.

"We are almost there," Mwana called. "Watch your step."

I leaned on her just before I stumbled on the uneven stone floor. When I raised my head, my jaw fell open. There was light all around me. It was like looking at beautiful patterns of colors through glass.

I could see everything. It was jarring after two weeks of darkness. The room was lit by a sphere at the center of the room that cast light throughout. There were crystals hanging from the ceiling. The room was round, with archways that led outside. I neared a window to see the night air, but as soon as I did, my sight vanished.

"You will have to stay in the dome if you want to see," Mwana said.

I turned and looked at her. Her maroon scales glimmered in the light. She was much bigger than I'd imagined. They all were. Igbo and Ala were both dark blue. Only their voices helped me tell them apart at first.

"What do you think?" Ala asked.

Tears streamed down my face as I looked around the room. "Did you know I'd be able to see up here?"

"Of course," Mwana said. "I read about aura crystals in one of Iyla's books," handing it to me.

"This is a journal," I said with surprise.

"A journal from Wiyotak! Iyla said she'd take me there someday."

"She said maybe," Igbo corrected.

"Iyla always keeps her promises," Mwana said before sticking out her black tongue. It coiled not like a snake, but like a helix vine.

I snorted, then held my hands to my face. "Sorry. I just wasn't expecting that."

"Expecting what?" Ala asked. "What does your tongue look like?"

"Ala," Mwana scolded. "That is rude to ask. Mortals are embarrassed by their tongues."

"I'm not," I giggled. "At least, I don't think so. I've never thought about it."

"Why do you hide it then?" Ala asked, sticking out his tongue once more. Igbo did the same.

"I don't know."

"Show us," Igbo insisted.

I shook my head at first but eventually acquiesced. The hatchlings tilted their heads in perfect unison.

"Why is it like that?" Ala asked first, horrified and fascinated all at once. "It's so short."

"And the wrong color," Igbo added gravely. "Is that normal? Are you ill?"

Mwana gasped softly. "Is your tongue... broken?"

I burst out laughing. "No. This is what all mortal tongues look like."

They put their claws to their mouths like they didn't believe me. "Can that happen to us?" Igbo asked.

This time I burst into laughter so full, I nearly shed a tear. It felt good. The dragons seemed to light up at my enjoyment and joined in. I turned my head when the orb in the middle of the room began to flash. It changed colors from bright yellow, to red, then to a dull gray.

"What is that?" I asked.

Mwana's laughter cut off first, her black tongue retracting. She stared at the orb, the glow reflecting in her golden eyes. "It is the Hearthstone, but it's never done that."

"What does it do?" I asked, approaching to look closer.

"It allows Pawpaw to monitor the border. Though dragons are monitoring it themselves now."

"Yes, I remember them saying that something was no longer protecting it."

"Oxu. The divine mother. She protects the mountains," Igbo offered.

I looked into the orb, surprised to see dragons on guard. They were crouched like sentries ready to fight if necessary. "What are they looking at?" I asked.

There was no time to answer because the pound of footsteps sounded down the hall. "Pawpaw Mattias!" the hatchlings whispered in unison.

Ala nudged me away. "We need to hide. He will be angry if he finds us here. Hurry!"

The three dragons pushed me backwards until I was behind a curtain, while they went to hide themselves behind the scarce furniture in the room.

Mwana had barely hidden her tail when several dragons stormed through the door. "What is going on?" one demanded. I peered around the corner to see a large silver dragon standing where I was moments ago, looking frantically into the orb.

Beside him was Zephyr, his scales gleaming in the aura light like polished brass. "Our guards. They are not at their posts."

"Where are they?" the silver dragon demanded.

"The border is exposed," the other dragons whispered in alarm.

"The wards," the silver dragon said. "They are completely down."

More frantic whispers filled the space. It was strange to watch, but what crossed the expressions of these giant animals looked very much like fear.

"We are no longer safe here," Zephyr said. "We need to evacuate the city."

"No!" the silver dragon barked, triggering several to bow their heads in submission. "This is our home. We stay."

Zephyr remained one of the few who remained upright, staring down the dragon with a steely gaze. "But we are not safe," he challenged. "Let us get out while we can. Whatever is happening will be upon us quickly. You know as much as I do that whatever is out there is strong. If it is fast..."

The silver dragon turned on him. "I am the Great Dragon. I said we stay!"

The room grew silent as everyone took in his words. Something within me began to stir, like a riptide with nowhere to go.

"Drakkar was right," Zephyr pressed. "You are so scared of the unknown, so shackled to this earth, you will allow us to burn in this place."

"Enough. We fight!" the Great Dragon demanded of the others. He circled the room as if daring others to defy his orders. I felt my battlemage crackle at my fingertips, as is if readying myself for something I couldn't yet name.

"You know we can't win against Shadowcasters without the Lightbearers," Zephyr said more calmly now. "We must flee and regroup."

"We will not leave our home."

"What are you afraid of? Think of your brood!"

The Great Dragon's flames flared, licking the air as he drew breath, heat rippling outward as if he meant to turn Zephyr to ash where he stood. A thread within me snapped into place, like a tether from my heart to Zephyr's. His eyes widened, looking towards my hiding spot. He felt it too.

I didn't think—I moved. Stepping out from behind the curtain, I felt the heat wash over my skin as instinct overrode sense.

Zephyr's pupils narrowing to slits. "Miren." His voice cracked with terror. "Get out."

I ignored him. My feet carried me forward as if pulled by invisible strings. My presence drew the Great Dragon's gaze like a hook sinking into flesh. His massive head lowered until his nostrils nearly touched my cheek, hot breath washing over my skin.

Though why I was in front of the Great Dragon, I wasn't sure. It had been instinct.

"Shadowcasters?" I asked finally, forcing my voice not to tremble. "You mean the Shadows—the religious faction? Why would dragons be afraid of them?"

The Great Dragon didn't answer my question. His eyes blazed like molten rocks.

"Why are you in here?" he demanded.

Zephyr attempted to move in front of me, but Mattias slashed a claw across his wing, deep enough that blood dribbled from the wound.

The scream tore out of me raw. The pain that hit me wasn't imagined—it lanced through my skull, burning down my spine, as if the wound had been carved into me.

"Miren, please go." The way he said that gave me pause. It wasn't a command, but a plea.

White flashed around me and all I could feel was rage. Outside, the sky answered with a crack of thunder so loud the walls trembled. Wind slammed into the chamber, scattering loose parchment and rattling stone.

Mattias's eyes widened with surprise. "A stormwielder," he whispered.

Though my eyes were not on him but trained on Zephyr. He watched me with awe as wind began to gust into the room. Despite his injury, his eyes crinkled. *There you are.* He didn't speak it out loud; he didn't need to. I could hear it in my head.

The storm inside me roared outward. Wind whipped the torches from their sconces, scattering sparks across the floor. The Great Dragon recoiled, his silver scales flashing in the sudden lightning that burst through the cracks in the stone ceiling.

Before Mattias could react, Igbo came out from behind his hiding spot. "That was brilliant!" he exclaimed. "Do it again, Miren."

The anger on Mattias's face quickly dissipated as his eyes met Igbo's and then turned to where Ala and Mwana emerged from their hiding places. I stood ready in front of Zephyr, to defend him and the hatchlings if needed.

But Mattias seemed to have the fight drained out of him. Shouts from outside permeated the room. The doorway filled with silhouettes of dragons pressing their heads inside, their wings rustling with agitation.

"They are coming, Great Dragon," one called.

"We saw them ourselves. What shall we do?" another asked with worry.

Mattias looked back at Zephyr and then to his brood. "Retreat."

"What?" a dragon exclaimed. I wasn't sure who said it because all the dragons began to whisper their uncertainty.

"I said retreat," he growled. The others looked at one another, but as the shouts grew louder, they began to file out quickly from the room. Mattias finally turned his eyes to Zephyr. "You must fly."

"How can he fly?" I demanded. "You just injured him!" I said, pointing to the pool of blood.

Mattias turned his head in a way that would have broken a mortal's neck, biting at his shoulder. As he turned back, I flinched. There were bloody scales in his jaws. He moved toward Zephyr.

"Stop!" I called.

"He's healing him," Mwana whispered beside me. "Only The Great Dragon has regenerative magic."

Mattias leaned down and dropped the bloody scales on Zephyr's wounded wing. He lifted his claw, putting it into place. "This should only take a moment," he said.

Zephyr closed his eyes, as if in discomfort. "You are hurting him!" I called.

"I'm fine," Zephyr assured. "It only burns a little. Just give it a moment."

A scream pierced the sky, and I ran to the window. There were hundreds of men dressed in the black regalia and skeletal masks, setting any and everything they could on fire. They had burst through the gates and were now making their way into the castle. These were nothing like the quiet, devout followers I'd seen at the religious gatherings. These men moved with ruthless precision. They carved through the castle dragons at the gates with their battlemages, as if they were made of straw and not hundreds of pounds of flesh and bone.

"We need to move," I said, backing away.

"You won't be able to fly from here. You must go up those stairs," Mattias said, pointing. He turned to Zephyr. "I trust you will keep them safe?"

Them? "Are you not coming with us?"

He turned to me, but instead of answering, he called the hatchlings forward.

"Pawpaw. I'm scared," Mwana said, nuzzling his snout.

Mattias gathered the young dragons in his arms. "What have I told you about your mother? Do you remember?"

"That she was fierce?" Igbo said.

"That she could take down entire armies," Ala chimed in.

Mattias shook his head and looked toward Mwana. "You said she had a kind heart," she said.

Mattias smiled. "That's what I want you to remember of my Seraphina. That she was kind, even to those who did not deserve it. I will not see you for a while, little ones." Their protests came at once, but he hushed them gently. "We don't have much time. You must listen to Zephyr now. He will find your father and Iyla. Promise me you'll be good and mind him until then."

"But what's going to happen to you, Pawpaw? Why can't you come?" Mwana asked, her voice breaking.

Mattias pressed his snout to each of theirs in turn. "I love you more than you will ever know. Make me proud." He held them tightly once more before setting them down.

I had been watching silently, my chest tight with awe. Who would have thought dragons could hold such tenderness, such love?

"Come, little ones," I said softly. They protested at first, but one look from Mattias and they followed me up the stairs. We made it to the roof and Zephyr was able to flex his body, his wing nearly healed. I looked briefly at the carnage below and then shielded the young dragons. "Up you go."

One by one, they scrambled onto Zephyr's back, clinging to him as they would in play—except there was no play in this moment. Once they were settled, I began my own climb.

A deep growl rose from below, joined by the screams of battle. I froze.

"Hurry!" Zephyr shouted.

I had barely swung onto his back before he launched into the sky. My stomach dropped as the land below came into view—once proud and gleaming, now drowned in fire.

My eyes widened as I watched the dragon city go up in flames.

CHAPTER TWENTY

Asha

Nearly five days had passed on the road as we tried to keep Kwasi stable, and I'd spent most of it by his side. When the call finally came that we were nearing Wyrmwood, I felt tension ease from my shoulders. Wyrmwood was unlike any place I had ever imagined. Where Wiyotak built upward, Wyrmwood dug every dwelling into the hillsides as though the people preferred to bury themselves in the dirt.

As we wound down the narrow trails, Drakkar shifted restlessly beside me, his unease mirroring my own as the air grew closer around us as the mountain walls narrowed.

"Who could live in such a place?" Drakkar said.

Heat crept up my spine, settling heavy beneath my ribs. I turned my face away before anyone could see the tension tightening my jaw, fixing my gaze instead on Kwasi. He hadn't stirred. His skin looked stretched too thin over bone, the color leached from it as if something essential had been drained away.

My fingers curled at my sides, nails biting into my palms. I'd begged them to stop, but the shaman had insisted Wyrmwood's healers were his only chance.

We reached a great arch molded into the mountainside, its rim alive with runes glowing deep silver. My stomach twisted. I was not ready to bow before rulers who saw me as nothing more than a woman to bargain with, nor to act obedient while my brother's life ebbed away.

Two guards in obsidian armor stepped forward, spears crossed. The runes pulsed brighter, as if trying to ward off our presence.

"State your purpose," one barked.

"We come under invitation of the Four," Adriel said smoothly.

Both men eyed us suspiciously.

Adriel sighed heavily in the way he did when a Guardian was trying his patience. "I am War Chief Adriel Foxtrail, heir apparent to Wiyotak, and one of the Four. I have Princess Asha in my company."

The guards exchanged glances, trying to determine between themselves if his words were true. Finally, one asked, "Prove it."

Adriel clenched his jaw and appeared ready to unleash his wrath upon them, until I stepped forward. I held my chin high, as I had been taught to by my mother. I looked to Adriel, almost bored, and in my most entitled breath, I said, "Your Majesty, are we quite done? I am ready to rest." I tossed my hair for good measure.

A corner of Adriel's mouth lifted as if to say, you are fooling no one. Instead, he said, "As you can see, this is Princess Asha Osei. Are you satisfied?"

The guards hesitated. "If you keep us waiting any longer, I will ask them to cut you down themselves as a wedding gift," I said.

Whatever they were going to say fled their lips because the next thing out of their mouths was, "Follow us."

The change in them was so abrupt, Adriel and I looked at one another in surprise. The runes died down, and the energy shifted as we passed beneath the arch, the glow washing over me like icy water. The tunnel beyond was broad enough for Drakkar, though low enough that he needed to bow his head. Green fire flickered in sconces carved directly into the stone, lighting our descent. The deeper we went, the heavier and damper the air grew.

At last, the passage opened into a cavernous hall. The palace itself was hewn from the rock. The towers rose like jagged teeth, windows glimmering with crystal light, though where the light came from was a mystery. A carpet of crushed obsidian stretched before us to the towering doors of a room.

The herald's voice boomed as the doors groaned open.

"Presenting the heir apparent, Prince Adriel of Wiyotak, Prince Kadir Firepeak, and their guest, Princess Asha of Ujuima."

My throat tightened. The words felt like chains ready to bind me. But I lifted my chin once more, ready for battle. If they meant to see a pawn, I would force them to see a queen instead.

My eyes roamed until they settled on King Fourie, who leaned forward, his light eyes and bald head catching the firelight. "Your Highness. The rumors have not done your beauty justice. I am honored you grace my lands—and that you have chosen to accept our proposal."

I kept my expression neutral as my gaze locked with King Dija with his grey locs. For a moment I thought I was looking at Atar their features were so similar. His eyes narrowed. "I thought she was blind."

"Sorry to disappoint," I said with a tight smile.

He barely acknowledged me as his eyes flicked to the dragon at my back. Drakkar had that effect.

It was strange seeing these men in the daylight. They appeared dignified and regal, but just days ago, I'd witnessed the debauchery they engaged in when they believed eyes were not upon them.

"I have not accepted," I said, my voice cutting clean through the hall.

The two rulers snapped their gazes first to Adriel and then to Kadir, confusion flashing across their faces.

Adriel did not flinch. "The princess has conditions."

"She requests to meet both suitors before she makes her choice," Kadir added pointedly.

Relief flickered in Dija's expression.

"Naturally," Fourie replied. "After you have rested, we—"

"There will be no negotiations," I said.

The room hushed. Clearly, they weren't used to women directing them. That would change today. "You will either agree to my conditions now, or I leave."

Fourie's smile thinned. He glanced toward the other rulers in the room.

"Who are you to demand anything, prince-killer?" Dija snapped.

Drakkar growled, low and rumbling, baring his teeth. Even the guards who crept from the shadows faltered. Fourie raised a hand sharply, his battlemage flaring, sending earth particles in the air. "This is my court. I was kind enough to allow your dragon to enter for your comfort, Your Highness, but I will not tolerate threats in my home."

"*Stand down,*" I sent down the bond.

I sensed Drakkar's discontent, but he did as I asked and closed his jaws and lowered his head.

"We mean no disrespect, Your Majesty," I assured.

Fourie's gaze shifted from Drakkar and fixed on me. "I suppose that is as much of an apology as I'm going to get." He closed his fist, letting his battlemage settle. "Name your terms."

The shift in the room was immediate—tension gathering like storm clouds. I forced a breath into my lungs before I lost my nerve.

"I have five conditions if I am to enter into this alliance," I began, "the first being that I will choose whom I marry."

A murmur rippled through the men. Fourie lifted a brow. "I believe we can all agree to that—so long as the choice is royal."

I pressed on before the courage wavered. "My brother will be restored to health by your best healers. He is gravely ill."

Fourie's gaze flicked briefly toward Kwasi's cot. He leaned back in his chair, fingers steepled beneath his chin, watching me the way one might watch a game unfold. His mouth twitched, but his face remained unreadable.

"Third," I said, my voice sharpening, "you will not hinder my efforts to seek out Lightbearers needed to fight the Shadows, and you will support that search."

I studied their faces. There was no confusion. If anything, they looked resigned, like they knew the danger. Perhaps they'd known longer than anyone of this existential threat.

Fourie exhaled in interest. "And?"

"There is a man named Cane in the custody of Firepeak. He is to be released immediately."

I'd strategically placed this demand so as not to call too much attention, but by the way Dija stiffened, I knew it had. Fourie did not even glance at him. "And the last?"

I drew a slow, steady breath. "There will be no inspections of my body and none of the customary purity tests. If anyone tries, I am gone."

Dija slammed a fist against his armrest. "This is outrageous! A princess entering a royal union unexamined? How are we to assure she—that she—" I watched him closely. His face had gone ruddy, the flush creeping up his neck, and his eyes darted briefly toward Fourie before snapping back to me. Whatever he'd been about to say, he'd thought better of it.

"Customs exist for a reason. We will not abandon them simply because you demand it," he said. "For all we know, this is a ploy to kill us all."

I tilted my head. "I am an Osei. If I wanted you dead, you already would be."

Fourie rose then, a smooth, placating smile on his lips, his hands lifted in a gesture of peace, though his eyes stayed sharp.

"We have heard your terms, Princess," he said. "But we cannot accept—or decline—until the representative of Entioch, Prince Zaib, arrives. Word has been sent. He should reach Wyrmwood within a day. Once all are assembled, we will reconvene and respond promptly."

Dija scowled, turned on his heel, and stormed from the hall.

"Her brother?" Adriel asked, looking back at his limp body.

Fourie nodded. "I think we can take some liberties while we wait. I will ensure he is cared for."

CHAPTER TWENTY-ONE

Asha

True to his word, the healers descended on Kwasi immediately. There were many theories thrown out about his illness, but no one could yet figure out why he had not awoken. Kitchi and the others tried several times to get me to retire to my room, but I refused to leave until I knew more about what ailed him. He'd grown a beard since I'd seen him last. It aged him, made him look more like our father. My head filled with memories of our childhood, so loud in my mind that I barely registered the sound of footsteps entering the room.

"We have company, Little One."

I didn't need to turn. I could see from Drakkar's gaze that it was Adriel.

"How is he?" Adriel asked.

I shook my head, wrapping my arms around myself. "They don't know what is wrong with him," I breathed. "All they can tell me is it is dark magic. I should have gone to him when he first wrote me. He'd still be here."

Adriel stood quietly by my side. "Or you would have ended up like him."

"You don't know that!"

Adriel did not retreat. He watched me with his steady gaze.

"What would you have me do then?"

His mouth twitched slightly. "Not that you have ever listened to me, but perhaps you should rest. And before you say no," he prefaced, holding up his hand, "your terms have been agreed to, all of them. Prince Zaib has returned, and a banquet is being planned for tomorrow night in your honor."

"I can't go."

"I'm afraid it is a part of the deal. That you engage in all courting activities they have planned."

"Why so fast?"

He shook his head. "They are eager to begin the courtship. The more time that passes, the more likely Elan catches wind of our plan."

"You're right," I whispered, my mouth tensing into a thin line. "I'm not listening to you and I'm not meeting anyone until my brother wakes."

"Then you should go back to the mountains."

"How dare you—" I unleashed my fist in his direction. He caught it with his hand. Drakkar growled in the corner, ready to move. Adriel's eyes did not leave mine though he had to be aware of the threat.

"Save your anger. You will need it soon enough." He dropped my hand before walking out.

I'd just begun loosening the ties to my gown in anticipation of washing when a light knock sounded at the door of my private rooms.

Drakkar stirred from where he'd coiled himself, his golden eye snapping open. I lifted a hand to calm him before he scorched whoever was on the other side.

"Yeah, yeah. Careful, Little One, I know."

Drakkar let out a snort, clearly unamused.

I didn't know who to expect, so to say I was surprised by who was at my door would be an understatement. He was taller than I expected, or perhaps he simply carried himself in a way that made him appear so. His silver hair was pulled back in a loose tie at the nape of his neck, the strands catching the light like polished steel. Where others of rank favored stiff ceremonial dress, he wore layered silks and leather that denoted his royal status.

"Good morning. Pardon the intrusion, Your Highness. I am—"

"Prince Zaib," I finished for him.

"Well—yes." He paused, thrown off by my abruptness and probably the dragon looming above me. To his credit, he seemed to be more curious than fearful. "I wanted to introduce myself before you met all of us this evening. I am sorry I was not here for your arrival." His pale lashes fluttered softly, hiding deep blue eyes.

"You needn't bother with whatever this is. The flattery and flirtations of courting are of no interest to me."

A slow grin unfurled as he asked, "Then what does interest you?"

The question stunned me. Not because of the words, but because he sounded genuinely curious. Not calculating. Not posturing. Just... curious.

Footsteps pounded down the corridor.

Adriel's aura hit me before his voice did. "Asha—" He stopped short when he saw Zaib.

Zaib nodded his head in acknowledgment, though his smile faded slightly. "War Chief."

Adriel's reply was a cold exhale. "You're back early."

"Am I?" Zaib countered pleasantly. "I might have been a day or two slower, as the messenger sent for me never arrived. Had I not had the forethought to have men stationed in Fourie's court to alert me of the princess's arrival, I might still be out looking for her." He tilted his head in innocent curiosity. "Such a... curious failure in communication. You wouldn't happen to know anything about that, would you?"

Adriel's expression remained flat and unreadable. If it were not for his aura darkening, I would have thought he was completely unaffected by the silent accusation. "It is a shame. Fourie should employ better messengers."

The tension increased as the two men stared down one another. I cleared my throat loudly. "Gentlemen." Both men blinked, as if remembering I existed. "It is lovely to see you both, but I must get changed before seeing my brother. Is there any update, Your Highness?" I asked, turning to Adriel.

His eyes peeled back to me. "No. Actually, I came to retrieve you for your dress fitting."

I stilled. "Dress fitting?"

"Yes," he said, voice tight. "For your wedding gown."

I couldn't have been more surprised if he had sprouted wings.

"Surely an attendant could do that," Zaib said skeptically. He turned to me. "I'd be happy to accompany you to this... dress fitting. I'm sure the War Chief has plenty to do."

Something in Adriel shifted at the offer. I could have accepted Zaib's invitation, could have made Adriel stew in the frustration he had earned.

"Thank you for the offer, Zaib, but I can make my own way. I need to be alone in my thoughts, but I look forward to speaking with you further this evening."

Zaib's practiced expression did not falter one bit as his lips graced my knuckles. "As you wish, Your Highness. I very much look forward to our time together."

My gaze flickered briefly toward Adriel.

"If you will both excuse me." I closed the door before they could say more.

"Are you decent?" a voice called through the door.

The attendants had left an absurd selection of dresses. There were silks, chiffons, and a dozen colors fit for a queen, but I'd shoved them aside in favor of the simplest garment I could find. Something I could easily move in.

"Come in, Chato."

Drakkar blew a lazy plume of smoke toward the ceiling just as Chato stepped inside. He immediately choked, smoke waving through the air. "I feel like me and your dragon have gotten off on the wrong foot."

Drakkar opened his jaws, showing off his teeth.

"Drakkar! Stop," I scolded.

"Yes, please," Chato wheezed. "Save that for her actual suitors. I prefer women with a little more—" he gestured to his chest in a circular motion.

I raised an eyebrow.

He grinned unrepentantly. "Someone who could smother me. Though," his grin sharpened, "I would make an exception for you, Your Highness... if it would not result in me losing my balls."

Drakkar growled so loudly the walls rattled.

"Kidding! Joking! Entirely in jest!" He thrust out a hand. "Ready for your dress fitting?"

A giggle escaped me despite myself. "Are we friends? You just made a joke about your balls."

He wrinkled his nose as if only now realizing the implications. "I guess we are. Gods help me. Don't tell Kitchi... or the War Chief."

I shook my head. "We both know you are not taking me to a dress fitting. Where are we going?"

He held a hand to his mouth in mock contrition. "Such distrust. After all we've been through."

I rolled my eyes. "Enough that I definitely don't trust you."

"You wound me." His grin smoothed a bit as he looked at Drakkar. "I will admit, it might be a touch intense for the dressmaker to see your dragon. Might I suggest he stay back for this one?"

"I could do with a meal, but I don't trust this one."

Chato nervously ran his hands through his wavy curls. "I really don't like the way he is looking at me."

"You always know how to make me smile, Chato." I sighed.

"Go eat," I told Drakkar. *"And go easy on Chato. We are friends now."*

"You need better friends."

"I'm going now. You can stay here and wait, but you might be a little stronger if you find a meal while I'm gone."

Drakkar tossed his head in aggravation before expanding his wings to leap out of the open window. Chato held on to the wall as wind filled the room.

"I don't know how you get used to that," he said.

"Where are we going?" I asked as my vision began to fade.

One side of his mouth lifted. "So impatient."

Chapter Twenty-Two

Asha

We were indeed going to the dressmaker.

She arrived not long after, bustling with bolts and fabrics as she fussed over colors and textures. I did not hear a word she said as I fretted over Kwasi. Not even Chato could bring me out of it.

"We could try this beautiful lavender on you. Lavender would look very lovely on your skin. It is very regal. That with a gold lace veil would be perfect, don't you think, Your Highness?"

"Huh?" I asked, realizing I was only half listening. "Oh. I'm sure whatever you choose will be fine."

This was apparently the wrong thing to say, because she said, "Fine? Absolutely not! You must be perfect." I listened as she flipped through her book of swatches. "Give me a moment. I am going to look in the vault. We must do better than fine."

As she departed the room, Chato cleared his throat. "I will just make sure she doesn't get lost," he said before his aura continued after her.

I sat in the room in the silence waiting for them to return. Their absence only made my worries scream louder. I thought about calling Drakkar back but hesitated. He would starve himself for me if I let him. He needed the break. I could rally through this.

An aura entered my periphery, but it was not the dressmaker's, nor Chato's.

"There you are!"

I stood abruptly and turned to the familiar voice. It was unforgettable. "Iná Nayeli?"

"Yes, child. Come so this old woman can lay her eyes on you."

I did not waste another moment as I ran over to embrace her. "I am so glad to be with you again, Nayeli."

"As am I, child."

A throat cleared behind us as Adriel's aura came into view. "Our time is short," he said. "Chato will only be able to stall her for so long."

Nayeli waved her hand at him. "Do not rush us."

"Time for what?" I asked.

"Do not dare let that woman put you in lavender, my dear," she said, patting my hand. "You were born to wear blue. If it can't be Wiyotakin blue, at least the same shade as your pretty hair."

I forced a smile, mostly to keep myself from grimacing. The last thing I wanted to discuss was a wedding I had no intention of rushing toward. "We are still ironing out the terms. There might not even be a wedding."

"There will be," she said with irritating certainty. She touched the necklace Mattias had given me around my throat, turning it to examine the glass pieces.

"Do you like it?" I asked, trying to sound natural.

"I don't think I have seen anything quite like it. Be careful with that," she said. Before I could react, she was already moving on. "Now, come. We must hurry if I'm to assess your brother once more before I leave."

I froze. "I don't understand. Have you seen him?"

"Unofficially, yes. Adriel was able to arrange for the dressmaker to meet us in Kwasi's quarters. We thought it would be believable since you have been so distraught over his condition."

"Why do we have to hide what we're doing at all? If you can help him, why can't you offer your counsel openly?"

"Because Kwasi is the brother of the emperor," Adriel said. He stepped closer, lowering his tone.

"And while you and Elan are enemies, the other rulers do not trust you," he went on. "They trust me even less. I am the newest power at the table. If they discover Nayeli examining Kwasi without permission, they will assume a conspiracy."

"So, you see," Nayeli continued, "I must be quick and unseen. Come, I had the Guardians source a few herbs for us to try."

Adriel led us into Kwasi's room. The moment we crossed the threshold, my breath hitched—his aura had faded even more than before, like a candle whose wax had melted to the stub. "He is getting worse," I whispered.

"Don't panic," Nayeli murmured, though even her voice held a thread of urgency. "I may be old, but I still have a few tricks up my sleeve. Fetch us some hot water, grandson. Asha and I have plotting to do."

The sound of his jaw ticking as his teeth grated against each other filled the space. "Behave, Iná."

"I never have before," she replied. "Why start now?"

He kissed her cheek before he left to do as she requested.

For a few moments, the only sounds were the faint crackle of herbs being crushed and Kwasi's shallow breaths. Nayeli's aura drifted to his bedside, brushing against his like a cautious hand. Finally, I asked what had been gnawing at me since she'd appeared, "Nayeli. Why are you really here?"

"My grandson called me. I'm glad he did."

"But how did you get here so quickly? Wiyotak is easily a fortnight away. You had to have already been here."

"That's right," she said carefully. "Since the war began, I don't often leave Adriel's side. There are too many Guardians to mend for me to sit in an empty palace. Truthfully, I was on a personal errand when he sent for me. He said nothing in the message, but I knew it had to be important to pull me away."

She stirred the concoction with a slow, steady hand. "Imagine my surprise when I found out the patient was your brother. I did not think they were particularly close." A pointed pause. "So, tell me, child—why was Adriel so determined to drag me across kingdoms to save a man he barely knows?"

Heat curled up my neck. "I'm sure it is to get me to cooperate. There is a lot at stake with my alliance."

Nayeli hummed as if unconvinced. "What were you thinking coming back here? After Elan and Enapay, I'd hoped you and Adriel would have run off together."

I stiffened. "Your grandson was a great help to me."

"What happened between the two of you?"

I shook my head. "I don't know what you mean," I lied softly. "I left to search for more Lightbearers, and he... I'm not sure what he did."

"He fought his brother. It was awful seeing what that did to him. He's not the same, my Adriel. I always thought he'd make a better ruler, but there is a darkness that runs through him now."

I mulled over her words. Adriel and I had not spent much time together. I thought it might be resentment, but could it be because of something else?

"Don't dawdle," Nayeli said, interrupting my train of thought. "Help me with my bag."

She placed it in my lap and asked me to organize everything within it while she spent the next agonizing minutes looking over Kwasi from head to toe. I stilled at every sigh and inhalation, hoping desperately that she might have a better plan.

I pulled out the gauze and bandages. I sorted through the ointments. "Could you find my tweezers?" she asked. "They should be in my right pocket."

I rifled through until my hand landed on a small square box. I opened it, running my hand along the contents. "No tweezers. Just this ring."

Nayeli coughed as I held up the box. "Not that one. That is my old wedding ring. The next pocket."

I placed the box back and began moving through the rest of the bag until I found the tweezers she asked for.

"Such a pretty ring," I said. "You no longer wear it?"

"Not since my Bena died. It's a gaudy thing. I didn't have the heart to tell him because he designed it himself. But I always keep it close." She dropped the tweezers on the table. "Come, Asha. I've found something."

"What is it?"

"There is a trace right here," she said, placing my hand under his. "A magic tag. This is very old magic indeed," she noted.

Though she breathed heavily with effort, her aura burned strong and sure. "This is blood magic," she murmured, her voice heavy. "Some kind of memory spell. It clings like tar, feeding on his very breath. Whoever laid it did not wish for death, not yet, just his silence."

"Silence?" My throat tightened. Who would want to silence him and why? "Can you undo it?"

"I am making small cuts along the spell lines," she said calmly. "They will heal. It helps release the hold. And this poultice will counteract the magic—but only for a time. It will return unless there is a counteraction."

My chest constricted. "What kind of counteraction? Like a sacrifice?"

Nayeli's voice softened, though her words did not. "This magic feeds on what remains. It keeps the body alive by stealing strength from what should be healing. If Kwasi is to live, there must be another host. That is how this kind of magic is designed."

Kwasi and I were all each other had. "Will I sleep heavily like he is now?"

That appeared to catch her off guard. "I didn't mean you, dear."

"There is no one else."

"There is always someone else. We will find someone."

I swallowed hard, then reached into my pocket. "I won't let him fade away," I said stubbornly.

"I know," she said, patting my knee. "Don't tell *him* that."

Adriel. "Can we keep this conversation between us?" I asked.

"You want me to lie to my king and allow you to do something foolish?"

"Your grandson, and only as a last resort. Please," I begged. "At least give me time to figure something out."

Nayeli did not have time to respond because the doors opened.

"I have your boiling water," he said.

"Perfect," Nayeli said without missing a beat. "Now, would you be a dear and pour us a pot of tea?"

I'd spent the rest of the afternoon at Kwasi's side. Nayeli had long gone, and Adriel lingered in the room, though we did not speak. I could not trust myself to do so and not tell him everything. I just hoped Nayeli could keep silent long enough for me to save my brother. I was tempted to reverse the memory spell on Kwasi, but if I did so now, the repercussions would be detrimental. I had to secure Cane first and then I wasn't sure what next.

The web I'd spun was getting stickier the longer I waited. I wasn't sure what I was fighting for anymore except for my brother's life.

The only thing that had pushed me from my thoughts was the return of Chato with the dressmaker.

"Where have the two of you been?" Adriel demanded, his disapproval sharp enough to cut glass.

The dressmaker gasped, nearly tripping over her words. "I—I was just leaving, Your Majesty. Please extend my apologies to the princess. I shall return tomorrow."

Before I could tell her the apology was unnecessary, she was gone.

"You were supposed to stall her, not sleep with her!" Adriel chastised.

Chato snorted. "What is the difference? She was lovely."

This seemed to stun Adriel because he did not say more.

"See you this evening," Chato called to me as he whistled on his way out.

Something inside me cracked.

A laugh burst out. It was sharp and wild. Then another. And another. My knees gave way, and I slid to the floor. Laughter twisting into sobs before I could stop it. I put a hand to my mouth as if I could hold it all in. I could not. Would there be anything left of me after everything was said and done?

"Asha—" Adriel said, voice full of concern as he moved toward me.

I pushed his hands away blindly and curled in on myself, the weight of everything crashing down all at once. He didn't try again. He simply stood there, watching me unravel, silent until my shaking finally quieted and exhaustion dragged me under.

Chapter Twenty-Three

She slept heavily against my chest, her breath warm and even, as if the world had finally loosened its grip on her. I held her there, careful not to shift, unwilling to disturb the fragile peace she'd found. Whatever fear or pain had taken hold finally stilled, and for that alone, I was grateful.

But we could not remain like this. I needed to get her back to her room before someone noticed. My eye caught on a sheet of lavender fabric the dressmaker had left behind. It was thick enough that I could drape it over her, and it would look like I was carrying bundles of the fabric.

I laid Asha across my lap and pulled the fabric over her body, arranging it so that anyone glancing our way would see nothing more than a cumbersome bundle of silk. I hesitated before covering her face—an irrational hesitation, but one I couldn't push down.

She'd been holding herself together by sheer will since Kwasi had arrived half-dead. She'd held a brave face, yes—but one that had cracked with every hour that passed. Kwasi did not deserve such devotion for the way he'd abandoned her, but I admired her loyalty all the same. Her loyalty was maddening. Admirable, but maddening.

My gaze drifted, unbidden, to her mouth. Her lips were parted in sleep, soft and unguarded. I remembered the way they would purse when she disagreed with me. It was the same when she pretended not to care or feel. I shouldn't be thinking of touching her. Still, my hand twitched with the urge to brush my thumb across her lower lip, just once, to relearn the shape I'd tried to forget. I forced my hand into a fist, tucked the lavender fabric over her face, and rose to my feet. Time to move.

I was grateful the hall was mostly empty except for the few servants busy pushing carts of food and wine through in preparation for the evening. I tried not to think what it would mean if Asha was unable to attend. One problem at a time. I'd rounded the corner to her room when I heard a honeyed voice at my back.

"Adriel!" the voice called. "Your Majesty, wait."

Celia. Shit. My heart raced as she neared. I felt a tap of her hand on my shoulder and slowly turned around.

"I'm so glad I caught you," she said, twirling a golden ringlet and blinking up at me with those large emerald eyes. Then, her gaze dipped to the lavender bundle in my arms. Her face brightened with curiosity. "Oh—what is this, Your Majesty? Surely the servants can carry that. I'll call for—"

Panic flared within me. "No!"

She startled at my tone.

"I'm sorry," I said. "It's just—I hoped it to be a surprise."

"A surprise?" she asked curiously, staring at the bundle.

I nodded. "Yes. I hope you don't mind. I took the liberty of talking to the dressmaker about fabrics for your dress. I wanted to give my input, but if that is too much…"

"Yes!" she breathed. "I mean, no. I mean, these aren't colors that would complement my skin tone, but, Adriel, may I take such liberties?"

"We are to be married," I reminded her.

"You thought of me." Her voice warmed. "That matters more than the fabric." She looked genuinely touched. A small moment of guilt speared through me.

"Anything for you, Princess."

"May I look at it? Perhaps upon a second inspection, it may appeal to me."

I stepped back as she reached out. "No, you are right. These are not the right colors. I see that now. If you will excuse me, I am going to find the dressmaker so we can match your eyes. They are lovely."

I stepped back slowly.

"Wait!" she said, putting a hand on my arm. I was sweating. One wrong move, and I'd have a lot to explain.

"I must catch her before she leaves."

"I won't keep you. I am touched that you would care about such things. We are going to be a match to be envied. I only wondered…" She paused, and I waited for her to say more. "I wondered if you would accompany me tonight." She hesitated. "Would you?"

Fire and ash, she meant the banquet. Why now?

Her eyes were wide, earnest, and full of expectation. She was beautiful. Young. Entitled. Innocent in all the ways that made this painfully unfair.

I covered Asha's muffled snore with a cough. "Ah—yes. Of course. I will accompany you."

"Are you alright?" she asked.

"Yes, actually, I think I will go lie down. It was a difficult journey here, but rest assured I will accompany you this evening."

Her entire face lit up, and I left on that note, racing to Asha's room before anyone else could see us.

Grateful that Drakkar was not near, I lifted Asha into her bed. I lingered there only long enough to smooth her hair back from her face. "Take care, Asha," I whispered before exiting the room.

"Can you go look in on her?" I asked, fiddling with the clasps around my wrists.

Kitchi batted my hands away impatiently as she took over. "I told you, the attendants said she is not taking visitors."

"That alone gives me cause for alarm," I insisted. "She might refuse me, but she would never turn you away."

She secured the right clasp, then set upon the left. "Her brother lies on the brink of death, her other brother seeks her ruin, she is about to walk into a chamber of kings who want to use her title and last name... and then there is you."

My head snapped up. "What of me?"

Kitchi regarded me for a long, unsparing moment—her lips thinning, her gaze cool, as though weighing whether to speak further. At last, she said, "Nothing of consequence." The lie was as delicate as silk and twice as transparent. She fastened the final clasp with a soft *click*. "You must be on your way. Celia awaits your escort, and don't forget to tell her she looks pretty."

"Kitchi—"

She lifted a hand to stall me. "I will look in on Asha once more," she said, turning toward the door.

As I approached the assembly hall, Celia was adjusting the fingers of an immaculate white glove. When her eyes found mine, she brightened at once and dipped into a graceful curtsy. I offered a measured bow in return.

She was not dressed as I had seen her before. Gone were the youthful frills of her day gowns—the ribbons and the soft, girlish fabrics. Tonight, her bodice was cut lower, the neckline sweeping just above propriety, and the silhouette of her gown traced her form with deliberate intent. Gems glimmered at her throat, meant to draw the eye down. Even her posture had changed; she stood as though she had been waiting her entire life for this moment.

"Your Majesty," she breathed, cheeks warming with a kind of earnest delight. "I had feared you'd changed your mind."

"I wouldn't dare miss this," I said with a tight smile. "You look... pretty."

She put her gloved hands to her cheeks as her face warmed. "You are too kind, Your Majesty. I am glad I could dress up for you."

We looked at each other for a few seconds as I searched for what to say next.

"How are you liking Wyrmwood? We are a simple people; I hope you've enjoyed yourself."

"Yes, your family is very hospitable," I said. "Thank you for the gifts delivered to my room. The jewels must be quite expensive."

"Our mines are famous for them," she assured. "I helped pick out the most beautiful ones."

"You did a brilliant job," I said, reaching out to kiss her hand. "Shall we make our entrance? I'm sure the others are waiting."

The doors to the assembly hall swung open the moment I offered Celia my arm. A hush fell over the room as we stepped inside. King Fourie beamed with satisfaction, seeming to encourage Celia to stand up straighter. King Dija's expression soured instantly, and so did Prince Zaib's as his smile faded into something razor thin. Kadir seemed to be the only one who appeared unbothered.

Celia leaned in closer than necessary, her perfume rising in a sweet cloud as she whispered, "Everyone's watching us."

And they were. Not because we were courting, but because Asha was nowhere in sight.

My jaw tightened. Asha should have been here by now. I looked around the room to see if Kitchi was among the Guardians stationed at the perimeter. I caught sight of Chato, and he shrugged, telling me he had no new information.

They'd fashioned a large round table. I watched as King Fourie and King Dija leaned over in discussion. Zaib appeared to pace impatiently by his seat, and Kadir slouched in his chair.

"When can we eat?" Kadir complained.

Dija shot him an angry look. Kadir turned away in silence.

"Where is she?" Zaib fretted.

"I am told she is still in her apartments," King Fourie said.

"Did anyone look in on her?" I asked.

"The attendants reported that they had to wake her, but that she is dressing," Fourie said. "Your journey here must have tired her out. I am sure she will be along shortly."

"How long must we wait?" Dija grumbled.

A shadow swept over the balcony. All of us turned immediately.

"Look," Celia said beside me.

The rulers followed as we strode to the terrace rail. Above us, Drakkar soared through the night sky as his wings cut the air in massive, thunderous strokes.

"She is magnificent," Zaib breathed.

I stiffened at the words.

"What is she doing?" Dija demanded, stepping back as if the dragon might dive for him.

Fourie's lips curved, entirely too pleased. "Making an entrance."

The air split with the force of Drakkar's descent. He landed on the terrace with a quake that rattled the stone underfoot and sent plates clattering across the council table. A few goblets toppled and shattered. Attendants gasped as guards stumbled, trying to decide if they should stay in place or be ready for a fight.

And then Asha appeared from behind the dragon's wing. She took care sliding down in the gown chosen for her. It was silk and clung to her like molten red cooling against her skin. Her braids tumbled down her back, catching the firelight.

For a breath, we all fell silent as if we needed to learn how to breathe again.

Celia spoke first. "What a beautiful entrance, Your Highness," she gushed, moving toward her. "I hope you love the gown. This was the one I'd hoped you'd choose. You look perfect in it."

Then Fourie stepped forward. "It is a pleasure, Princess. What a wonderful dragon you have here."

She smiled. "You are lucky indeed that he has allowed you to come so close."

I sucked in a breath, but Fourie took her jab well. "You are a wonder. Please," he said, pointing to the table, "join us. Do you know everyone? Let me introduce you."

Fourie gestured grandly toward the table, but Asha did not move. She stood with Drakkar looming just behind her, the dragon's wings folding. Her gaze swept the hall, steady and unflinching.

"I am honored by your invitation," she said at last, her voice calm, edged with steel. "But let us not pretend this feast is for my comfort. We are here to discuss our future."

Zaib let out a short laugh, charmed despite himself. "Spoken like someone who knows her worth."

Dija scowled. "Spoken like someone who does not understand her place," he said just low enough that she couldn't hear.

The tension in the room amplified, taut and ready to snap. Fourie, ever the diplomat, broke it with a clap of his hands. "We will have time for such talk. Tonight is for wine, for music, for celebrating what may yet bind our kingdoms together."

Servants rushed to pour goblets and bring trays of delicacies. The rulers took their seats, motioning Asha to the place of honor at Fourie's side.

I made to move toward her, but Celia's hand clamped down on my arm again, a sweet smile across her face. "Your Highness," she said, "you promised to help me to my seat."

Of course, I was here with Celia, not Asha. To forget that would invite unwelcome questions. I guided Celia, though my gaze strayed, against my will, to Asha as she sat, regal in her crimson gown.

The first course was brought in. Silver trays gleamed with roasted meats, spiced roots, and jewel-colored fruits arranged to impress. Music rose from the far corner, a quartet of strings weaving an elegant melody.

Fourie lifted his goblet. "To unity," he declared, smiling thinly.

The others echoed him, though Dija's voice was flat, and Zaib's eyes never left Asha.

Asha raised her glass last. "To freedom," she said, her tone quiet but carrying easily across the table.

Celia tittered beside me, her hand still looped through mine. "She does love theatrics," she whispered in my ear.

Asha's eyes met mine briefly before she turned to Dija, who asked, "So, Princess, what does freedom mean to an Osei? I'm curious."

The room went silent as if holding its breath. Asha took a sip of her goblet before saying, "I imagine it looks the same for everyone."

"Well said," Zaib murmured.

"No," Dija challenged. "I don't imagine it is the same for an Osei."

"Dija," Fourie warned. "Let's not pester our guest. She has had a long journey."

Dija ignored Fourie's warning, his gaze locked on Asha. "You know what we endured under your father. Comfort for the few, hunger for the many. Do you intend to do the same?"

Asha's eyes swept the room, bored, unimpressed. "I've seen where you live, Dija. You've done fairly well. Especially as my father's closest confidant."

His fist slammed a knife into the table. Drakkar growled low in the corner, the sound rattling the goblets. Slowly, Dija leaned back, but his eyes still burned. "Yes. We lived well—so long as we filled the emperor's coffers. Our people, meanwhile, are starving."

"Which is why we are all here," Fourie interjected. "We want what's best for the Five Kingdoms."

"How do we know that you are not going to be like the rest of them?" Dija challenged. "You have one dragon, maybe more. We'd have no way to stop you if you wanted to rule as your father, and now your brother."

Asha set her goblet down, her voice calm but sharp as glass. "I am not my brother. I am not my father."

"And you are okay with the four of us challenging him, taking him down?"

"I don't intend for you to take him down," she said, and everyone in the room sat on edge. "I intend to do it myself."

Dija crossed his arms and leveled his gaze. To my surprise, the challenge in his eyes had died down.

"Are you satisfied?" I asked briskly.

His eyes flicked briefly to me, then to her. "I have one more item of contention. Asha is here to pick her husband, but it feels the rest of us are at a disadvantage."

"How?" I asked.

"You already know her," he said, leveling his gaze on me. "You might even have a history together for all we know."

I shot up and reached for my sword, only it was not at my waist. Swords weren't allowed in the banquet room. Dija smiled, as if I'd confirmed something for him. I inwardly cursed that he'd been able to get a rise out of me.

"The princess was brought here under the purest of circumstances. To suggest otherwise would be an insult to the crown." I clutched Celia's hands so all could see. "And if you hadn't noticed, I am spoken for."

Dija turned his gaze to Fourie and Zaib. "Of course. What I mean to say is that we are all kings in this room. Zaib will inherit his throne soon enough, and my boy will one day as well. But what are you?" he asked pointedly. "A traitor to your king, who has yet to be found and dealt with."

My jaw tightened. "I am but a man in love." I moved to face Celia and pulled out a ring from my pocket. The room stirred, but all I could hear was the pounding of my own heart.

"Princess Celia Heloc, daughter of the earth and polished stone, would you do me the honor of accepting my hand?"

Her eyes widened as she stared at the ring, one I'd had to source quickly for this very moment. Then she caressed my face and squealed, "Of course!" bending down to give me a chaste kiss on the cheek.

Fourie reached over the table to pat my back. "Well done, son. Drinks, everyone! We must have a toast."

Attendants moved quickly to bring more wine to the table. The entire room was spinning so fast, I was startled by the fist Dija slammed on the table.

"A marriage means nothing if you do not win your war, and even if you do, we do not know if the citizens of your country will accept you knowing that you spilt the blood of your own kin."

"What is your point?" Fourie asked in clear irritation that the moment was being spoiled.

"My point is that until Adriel has secured the throne, he should not have a voice at this table."

"Enapay has no legitimate heirs," Zaib pointed out. "Of course it will pass to him."

"If he wins the crown," Dija corrected.

The silence stretched after Dija's words. The words landed like stones in a still pond, ripples of reaction moving around the table. Zaib smirked, intrigued. Dija leaned back with wolfish satisfaction. Fourie's brows drew together, wary.

Asha's eyes narrowed. She rose, goblet in hand, her crimson gown catching the firelight.

"You speak of my father. My brother. Of crowns, and wars, and thrones. But not one of you has spoken of me. If I am to be courted, it will not begin with being called a whore." Her eyes shifted to Dija, Drakkar stirring behind her. "This arrangement will be on my terms and my terms only."

The hall quieted, measuring her words.

Zaib cleared his throat. "And what would those terms be?"

She turned her gaze to him. "The truth is, I don't need any of you to take down my brother. I have two dragons that fly, and many more that will follow." Her eyes turned to me as if daring me to contradict her. The Great Dragon would never go to war for her, that I knew, but if she found more Lightbearers—who knew how many she had.

"Still, I cannot deny that a marriage would help me unite a fractured nation," she continued. "What I want, I have already stated... I want Lightbearers and your assistance finding them. Whoever provides the strongest plan to locate Lightbearers will win my hand."

A rustle of shock moved through the rulers.

"I'm intrigued," Zaib said. "How long do we have to... procure this plan?"

"One week."

Dija scoffed. "A week? That is absurdly short."

"I cannot remain here any longer," she said. "There is too great a risk that my brother would be upon us."

"I think it is a reasonable request," Zaib offered.

"We must all have time to spend with you, to show you what we have to offer," Dija said, looking toward his son, who seemed lost in his plate. "I will agree if he," his eyes shifted to me, "is not eligible to vote on this or anything else we do."

"You seem hell-bent on undermining my kingdom," I said.

"It is not your kingdom yet," Dija hissed. "That is the problem."

"I will marry whoever has the best proposal," Asha interrupted. My fork clanged on the table as I willed her to stop speaking. "I will entertain a proposal from everyone at this table—that includes Wiyotak."

I dropped my fork, shooting her a warning look. She ignored it.

Celia's jaw fell open. "We are engaged."

Asha gave her a pointed look. "And we are at war?"

Celia froze, hand curling. She turned to me with panic in her voice. "You cannot possibly entertain this."

"We have already agreed!" Fourie barked.

The smart thing would be to reassure Celia. Secure the union, end this chaos. I opened my mouth to do so but stopped as I saw Asha's attention shift subtly toward the servants lined along the wall.

"This is ridiculous," Dija bellowed.

"Adriel, you just proposed to my daughter," Fourie roared in the background, but my gaze remained fixed on the attendants standing in neat little rows until I stopped on a tall male attendant with short, cropped hair.

My blood ran cold. I stood so quickly my chair skidded back. "Ashkii?"

The attendant stepped out of the shadows, bowing with a mock flourish. "At your service, War Chief."

CHAPTER TWENTY-FOUR

All sense of decorum left my body as I watched Ashkii walk toward me. "What are you doing here?" I asked.

He shrugged his muscled shoulders and winked. For just a second, I wondered if the person I'd come to know was still there. "I came to court you. Same as everyone else."

"Who is this? How did you get in here?" Fourie seethed, looking around at the guards in the room who appeared bewildered. "Detain him at once!"

The guards in the room began to close in. Ashkii smiled, lifting a hand in a mock salute before dissolving into shadow.

Gasps erupted around the hall as blades swung at empty air. The rulers jolted to their feet, eyes darting in every direction. Adriel's eyes found mine as sharp, dawning horror widened his gaze. He lunged toward me, but Celia stepped into his path, halting him for a heartbeat too long.

That was all it took before cold metal kissed the hollow of my throat.

Drakkar leapt immediately, mere feet from us as Ashkii held my back to his chest. Heat pulsed through the bond, wild and ready to burn.

"Let her go!" Adriel barked.

"I knew I should have knocked," Ashkii spoke calmly, but the beating of his chest betrayed him. He leaned into my ear and whispered, "This could be bad for both of us. Call them off."

"Let me go and perhaps I will."

He inhaled sharply. "I'd love to, but we both know the moment I let you go, your dragon will have me on a spit."

"If you don't let me go, you will meet the same fate."

Ashkii bent over to peer at my face. "Look who has grown teeth, Princess."

The corner of my mouth lifted. "It appears I'm not the only one who has."

The endearment softened something in his expression. "We were once friends. Do you remember?"

"We were," I said, though I kept my tone carefully unreadable.

"We'll see how much in just a moment," he said as he lowered his knife and stepped away from me.

I felt the dregs of heat sprout from Drakkar's tongue. I held my hand up to stop the stream of fire that licked the air. The other I held up to Adriel.

"No!" My own voice startled me with its force, silencing the room full of kings. "No one moves."

Ashkii held his hands raised in mock surrender, though his smirk didn't quite mask the flicker of fear in his eyes. "Better friends than I thought," he mused.

"That's enough," Adriel snapped, finally free of Celia's grip. His aura burned around him, restrained only by the thin edge of his self-control. "You have no place here."

Ashkii laughed softly, the sound low and maddening. "No place? Then why is it I walked into your banquet, past your guards, your blades, and Asha herself bids me live?" His eyes cut to me. "Perhaps it is you who has no place here."

The rulers murmured among themselves, unsure of what to do. Fourie looked ready to explode, Dija and Kadir had retreated behind their guards, and Zaib studied me with unnerving interest.

"What is it that you want?" Fourie asked.

"I'm here as a representative of the Shadows," he said, though his gaze never left mine.

"So, you did join them?" I asked.

"Yes," he whispered.

"Why? How could you do such a thing?"

I expected him to appear remorseful, but he stared at me instead, as if the answer was obvious. "The Shadows accepted me, all of me."

"We accepted you," Adriel ground out. "We've spent all this time looking for you, and you have joined our enemy."

"Enemy?" Ashkii queried. "What have the Shadows ever done to you?"

I reached for his hand then. "You can come back. Whatever you've done, whatever they have threatened you with, we will protect you."

Ashkii shared a sad smile. "You assume it is they who coerced me, when it was I who begged them to take me in. They could give me what no one else could."

"And what is that?"

"Freedom," he said, dropping to one knee. "I've come to offer you the same."

"You expect me to marry you?"

He shook his head. "No. I hope that you will follow me into the shadows."

"That is enough!" Adriel growled. "Get away from her."

Ashkii continued as if Adriel hadn't spoken. "All of these men want a piece of you. I don't. I want you to remain whole and free. You deserve to be whoever you want to be."

My lips parted. "I will never join the Shadows."

He pulled on my hand in earnest. "Aren't you tired, exhausted, even, of having to bow to and placate men? You would never have to do that with us."

"Come back, Ashkii," I said with one final plea. When he looked down and shook his head, my hand stiffened as I pulled away.

"I'll be nearby if you need me." His battlemage flared, shadows coiling tightly around his form before collapsing inward. In the next breath, he was gone.

A heartbeat passed.

Then one of the guards lunged forward, blade slicing through the space where Ashkii had stood—too late. His sword met nothing but air. A split second later, he gasped and staggered back, clutching his throat as dark veins crept beneath his skin. Whatever power had lingered in the wake of Ashkii's departure struck him like a delayed echo. Blood sprayed across the table, across my dress. The guard collapsed in a gurgling heap at my feet, red pooling the same shade as my shoes.

The hall erupted in chaos. Goblets overturned, attendants screamed, and steel hissed free from sheaths. Drakkar's roar split the chamber, shaking loose dust from the carved stone ceiling.

"Enough!" Fourie bellowed, his voice thundering over the din. He rounded on the guards still standing. "Seal the palace. No one enters, no one leaves until this man is found."

"Seal it?" Dija demanded. "How? He disappeared right in front of us."

Zaib's lips curled into something dangerously close to a grin. "Or ally, depending on what he truly wants. He had the princess's life at his mercy, yet he spared her. That tells us something."

Dija's glare shifted to me, suspicion gleaming in his eyes. "You know him. He called you friend. Perhaps you already have an arrangement."

Adriel surged forward, blue fire licking at his hands. "Watch your tongue, Dija."

"Explain why your men failed to stop him," Dija snapped. "One of ours lies bleeding because you and yours let the Shadows inside our walls."

"Place the blame where it belongs," Zaib countered smoothly, his eyes never leaving me. "On the Shadows themselves. Or on the fact that your halls, Fourie, are not as secure as you boast."

"Does anyone care to know what I think?" I asked, moving toward Drakkar.

The room went silent, waiting.

"I think we need to move up our timeline. The Shadowcasters know where we are, which makes it more likely Elan will too. I will choose my husband in two days' time."

I did not stick around to hear their protests. Without another word, I climbed onto Drakkar, and we flew away.

Seeing Ashkii up close was chilling. The way he looked and moved, the way he seemed grateful to the Shadowcasters, disturbed me greatly.

Drakkar had shown me the temples they'd erected in Wyrmwood. Their devotion thrived here. The laws gave them freedom that Firepeak never had. Even late at night, I had seen lines of people climbing the marble steps, bowing, chanting, and pressing offerings against obsidian altars.

Their loyalty was... staggering.

A sharp knock startled me from my thoughts. The door flew open, and Kitchi marched in without ceremony. "Well, you have certainly caused a commotion. Those men have no idea what to do with themselves."

I leaned against a bedpost. "What are they doing?"

"Scheming," she said, plopping onto my bed. Drakkar cast her a bored look before he stretched on the rug for his morning nap. Kitchi continued as if there wasn't a huge dragon near her. "I can't tell if they intend to impress, frighten, or buy you. I'm supposed to give you this."

She handed me a rolled-up parchment. I broke the seal and read through it. "A courtship schedule?"

"That's what they've been fighting about. Who gets you first, gets you last. It has been a whole debacle. Who is first?"

"There are only three names," I said, looking down the list. "Ashkii is not on here."

"Yeah, I don't think that will stop him."

"He was so different."

"Who knew he was hiding all of that under his armor?"

My face twisted.

"What? It's just us," she said, biting into an apple. "You can admit he's delicious."

"I didn't notice," I lied swiftly. "And I wouldn't think you would either."

"You think because I like women, I can't appreciate a handsome man?" she asked, rolling her eyes.

I turned back to the courtship schedule. "Why is Fourie on here? Is he entering the courtship?"

"He wants to put his thumb on the scales, I think," she explained. "His best shot is to have his daughter marry well, and well... you know the rest."

"Adriel is also not on here."

"Like I said, you know the rest," she said quietly. "Are you disappointed he is not on there?"

I shut the scroll. "Why would I be?"

"Do you want to talk about why you wanted Adriel as a suitor in the first place?"

I threw the parchment onto the bed. "I don't have time for this. Apparently, I need to dress for a picnic."

CHAPTER TWENTY-FIVE

Asha

Zaib waited for me at the bottom of the stairway in one of the main halls. He reached for my hand before I'd even reached the last step, lifting it to his lips with a courtliness so practiced it almost felt like a performance.

I managed a polite smile. "Drakkar is our chaperone today," I warned. "And he doesn't like me to stray too far from him."

Zaib did not hesitate. If anything, he brightened. "Wonderful. I hoped he would join us. There is a lovely spot I'd like to take you to. You don't mind a ride, do you?" he asked.

"I thought we were going to discuss how you will help me find Lightbearers."

A single curl slipped loose from my hair. Zaib caught it delicately between two fingers and tucked it behind my ear. "We will, but what good is a plan without a bit of romance?"

"A well-thought-out one," I answered coolly.

He pressed his lips together as if I had said something amusing, like I was a puzzle he had yet to solve. "I hope you will humor me, Your Highness. Allow me to vie for your heart as well as your alliance."

We locked eyes for a moment as I thought through the proposal. There wasn't any real risk in humoring him. "Very well."

I had no idea what I was in for as a trussed-up floral carriage sat waiting for us outside, draped in pale fabric and threaded with delicate strands of crystal that caught the light. It looked more ceremonial than practical, and I frowned at the narrow seat within. Still, it was open to the air, and I reminded myself that I'd endured far worse.

We climbed in, and soon the carriage rolled forward, wheels crunching softly along the path. This was my first time seeing Wyrmwood in the daylight. Wyrmwood citizens looked up from their plots of land as we passed by, children running after us, their feet slapping against the dirt road. I did not need to see their faces clearly to read what their auras told me as they all had the grey of hunger, and the dull amber of exhaustion as their small bodies could not keep up with the lack of food. Poverty had come for Wyrmwood, as it had for everyone else.

"Do we have any food?" I asked Zaib.

He seemed startled by the question but did not belittle me, or caution me against what I meant to do. He simply pulled on the reins, bringing the carriage to a stop. He helped me down before reaching for one of several picnic baskets stored in the horse's saddle. "What do you want to give them?" he asked. "I have fresh berries, chicken, cheese—"

"Let's give it all," I said, taking out each delicately wrapped plate and handing them one by one to the half dozen children. To his credit, Zaib did not hesitate. We worked side by side, handing out the plates to children with wide eyes and growling stomachs.

One pulled on my skirts. She wore pigtails and a trembling smile. "My family can't afford this ma'am."

I pushed the plate into her hands. "It is for you. There is no charge."

The girl's eyes widened, her mouth revealing a sweet grin, her two front baby teeth missing. "Thank you, ma'am."

"Are you magic?" Another child asked.

Before I could answer, Zaib crouched to his level. "Yes. Yes she is," he said with a smile. Our eyes locked for a moment, before he pulled out another basket, and began handing out the food.

As more children came, my battlemage caught on something that chilled my spine. My eyes settled on a man, watching from the sidelines in a white mask. Over his shoulder, two more assembled behind him.

"We should be on our way," Drakkar cautioned from above.

Zaib watched as Drakkar circled. Taking his cue he swept me back into the carriage. The children cheered, their hands now full with food, auras beaming a bright gold. Zaib pushed the carriage on as we whipped past them.

Soon we were out of the city. Wildflowers blurred past in swaths of color, their scent carried on the breeze. Butterflies rose in startled flurries as we passed. Zaib did most of the talking, telling me about his homeland and how he missed the sea air and the feel of sand between his toes. "You've been there, no?" he asked.

"Yes. A few years ago. I saw the northern lights."

"Ahh, one of our most magnificent attractions. Though I dare say, its beauty does not compare to yours."

I looked away, feeling unnerved.

He was quiet a moment, then almost as an aside, he said, "They are growing bolder."

He didn't need to clarify who he meant; we both knew. "Do you think they've been in Wyrmwood long?" I asked.

"Not so long, by the thinness of those children." His voice was cool and clipped. "The children would have been fed. That is how they recruit, with promises of food, and jobs, and purpose." He paused. "You encroached on their plan."

"Good," I said, my mind wandering to Ashkii.

"The downside is, you fed them enough for a day, while they can feed them for years."

"Are you saying we shouldn't have stopped?" I asked, anger flaring within me.

He looked towards me now with such intensity, I could not look away. "No," he whispered. "I admire your heart. Asha, I don't know what I expected to find in you, but it wasn't this. No one has surprised me more."

My face flamed. I looked in the other direction, needing distance as he seemed to see into my soul. I had no good response, nothing that would remove the unease I felt in my chest.

"Not a fan of compliments? That is curious. Don't tell me you are one of those women who do not know how stunning they are?"

"I spent most of my life unable to see. Looks have never been of great importance."

"I see. So, the care I took in my outfit just to impress you is for naught." He held onto his heart in jest. "You wound me, madam."

I laughed.

"Hmm. A beautiful face, a kind heart, a gorgeous laugh," he said like he was ticking off a list. "What else are you hiding from me?"

I was thankful the carriage stopped so that I could put distance between us. I stepped out as he pointed ahead.

"Look! Our next transport is just up there," he said.

We'd traveled up a hill, and just ahead was a large sailboat. It was painted green with a bright white sail. I looked around. "I don't see any water. Is it stationary?"

"Oh, she sails," he said, patting the hull. "We're taking her out today."

Drakkar snorted so loudly the flowers trembled. *I'm not sure this one is altogether sane,* Drakkar remarked.

"I don't disagree."

"You think I am insane," Zaib said. "Allow me to show you." He interlocked his hands to crack his knuckles, and a light breeze blew through the grass. A cyclone of dragonflies leapt into the air, whipping through my hair and clothes.

"Your battlemage is wind," I said.

He smiled in response, and the wind grew until the wood from the boat began to creak like its weight was shifting. I gasped as the entire vessel lifted several feet off the ground, rocking gently as though on an invisible tide.

"It sails on the wind," Zaib said, sweeping his hair back. He extended his hand. "If I cannot bring you to the sea, Princess, then I will bring the sea to you."

I glanced at Drakkar. He lifted his wings in a helpless shrug. *You will do it anyway.*

"The boat is too small for him, but he can fly next to us," Zaib offered. "I thought he might feel better knowing you are right beside him."

I stared at Zaib's offered hand, considering, before finally placing mine in his. He released the ladder and climbed first, pulling me after him. The deck was wider than it looked from the ground—rigging, pulleys, and a full wheel. Zaib moved with practiced ease, tightening ropes and adjusting the sail.

"Look around," he said. "The view is best at the front. I need only a moment to get us airborne."

He flexed his fingers again. The boat creaked. I grabbed the pole as it rocked dangerously, then steadied. When I dared peek over the side, my stomach dropped. We were sliding forward, straight toward the cliff's edge.

"What are you doing?" I demanded.

Zaib flashed a wicked grin. "Hold on, Princess."

The boat surged as the hill vanished beneath us. We dropped. I opened my mouth to scream, but nothing came out. My body slid backward on the deck, and for one terrible heartbeat, I knew I would fall—

A strong arm wrapped around my waist, yanking me back against him.

"I did say to hold on," he murmured into my hair.

He kept an arm braced around me until the boat leveled, gliding smoothly on a cushion of wind. When he finally let go, he did it slowly, hands hovering as though prepared to catch me again. I swallowed. "More warning would have been better."

"I will remember that next time."

Zaib walked to the front of the boat and took the wheel, seeming at peace, as if he would spend all his time sailing if he could. With his hair whipping behind him, he looked utterly at home—as if the sky were his ocean. When I turned, Drakkar was flying beside us, his wings spread in wide, lazy arcs.

"Would you like to steer?" Zaib asked.

"I don't know how. I might crash us."

"You can fly a dragon," he teased, "but a boat frightens you?"

"That is not what I said."

"I'll guide you. I promise." Zaib rested his hands lightly over mine, positioning them on either side of the wheel. "Just like this. Hold it steady."

He stepped back, letting me feel the weight of the wood beneath my palms. The view was... breathtaking. Rolling hills unfurled beneath us in long green ribbons, caverns cut through the earth like dark veins, and from above it all shimmered the gold of the late afternoon sun. It reminded me of flying with Drakkar—only here, for the first time in a long while, I felt in control.

"Now ease the wheel to the right," Zaib instructed.

I listened, and the entire boat tilted sharply. My breath caught. "Gently," he coaxed, voice warm with patience. "Trust yourself." He unclasped one of my hands, loosening my rigid grip. I adjusted. Tried again. This time, the shift was smooth, the boat gliding as if we were carving paths through the wind. After a few more turns, the rhythm clicked into place. I could feel the wind's push and pull, the subtle balance of weight and direction.

"You are a natural," Zaib called, lounging on a bench with his arms stretched behind his head—as if he'd known all along that I'd find my footing.

My mouth tightened. "You are using your battlemage to steady the boat. I can see it in your aura."

His smile faltered in surprise, as if he had not anticipated my knowing at all.

"It is all right. Drakkar tells me I am a lousy rider all the time, and I should be glad he has such good directional sense."

"If it helps, I'm using very little battlemage," he said apologetically. "Most of this is yours. You'll get the hang of it."

For a moment, I allowed myself the chance to relax, letting my hair blow in the wind as I drank in the view. Wyrmwood was even more beautiful from the sky, I decided.

Zaib patted the seat next to him. "There is somewhere I'd love to take you, and this is the second-best seat in the house."

I left the helm and we sat together and chatted about upbringings. His early childhood was not dissimilar to mine. We were both privately educated and battlemage trained, though he of course made it much further than I. He had a younger cousin, Myrna, that he adored. His mother died in childbirth, and he had very few memories of her. His father was powerful but distant. His health was waning, which put pressure on Zaib to take on more diplomatic duties.

He began to sail us through a series of caverns. The air grew cooler, echoing with the faint rush of wind over rock.

Drakkar groaned as he had to duck lower and lower as we progressed. "How much further?" I asked.

"We are almost there," Zaib assured. "Just a few more turns. It is worth it, I promise."

"There is more room below. We just need to make it around the bend," I said.

"I don't like this," Drakkar warned.

"Perhaps we should turn back."

"Here!" he proclaimed, and, sure enough, around the corner, rays of sunlight filtered through the cave. A wide, clear pool shimmered at its center, reflecting beams of gold. Grass—actual grass—spread in soft patches along the stone floor.

"I've never seen a place like this," I breathed.

"There aren't many," Zaib said, hopping lightly from the boat and offering me his hand. "It took me ages to find this one."

He led me up a gentle slope where the sunlight gathered thickest. From his pack, he unfurled a blanket and spread it over the grass. The care and deliberateness of the gesture startled me.

"I thought we could have lunch," he said, arranging bread, cheese, and fruit with surprising elegance. My eyebrows arched at how far he was taking this courting thing. "I've talked a lot about myself," he said after a swig of wine. "Tell me about you."

I hesitated, still standing as Drakkar's restless tail lashed behind me. Zaib lounged on the blanket like he had all the time in the world, his golden light hovering above us.

"What would you like to know?" I asked cautiously, sitting beside him.

"Anything," he said brightly. "Your favorite memory. Your worst mistake. The first time you fell in love." He waggled his eyebrows. "Pick one."

"None of those sounds appealing."

"Ah," he mused, biting into a strawberry. "So, you have been in love. And had your heart broken, judging by your tone. I'm intrigued."

"Favorite memory," I said firmly, ignoring him.

Zaib gave me a look that said he saw through me but chose not to press. "Go on."

"I have much of my mother, the empress," I said quietly. "She liked to play with Kwasi and me. Not just being present—really playing. Hours of it. She always made us feel like the world wasn't watching."

"She sounds lovely. Everyone always spoke well of Empress Sanaa and her siblings."

I toyed with my hair as I continued. "I never knew her family. She was all we had—and all we needed."

Zaib's gaze softened, the grin fading into something quieter. "I envy that. My mother never played with me a day in her life. Duty made sure of it."

The admission surprised me. I searched his face for mockery but found none.

He leaned back, studying me with a new sort of curiosity. "I hear you enjoy reading. What has captured your interest lately?"

I hesitated, then shrugged. There was no real reason to keep it to myself. "I've been reading about Atim and Oneida."

His brows lifted. "The rulers who founded the Five Kingdoms." A hint of intrigue sparked in his eyes. "Why them?"

"I suppose I wanted to understand how all of this began," I said. "It's strange to think there was ever a time without an emperor."

A faint smile tugged at his mouth. "You're skipping the best part," he said. "Their love story. Atim stole Oneida away from his brother, Melo. Or so the legends say. Some claim she only ever had eyes for Atim."

"I haven't found much written about where Oneida came from," I admitted.

"That's because no one truly knows," Zaib replied. "The stories say Melo found her quite literally in fire."

I frowned. "That doesn't make sense."

"They say he was never the same afterward. That losing her unmade him."

"What became of him?" I asked.

Zaib's gaze drifted, unfocused. "Some say he withdrew from the world. Others believe he ruled in bitterness until the end." He paused. "Either way, betrayal has a way of changing a man."

The silence that followed felt heavier than it should have.

Then he smiled, lightening his tone. "Enough history. Tell me something more interesting." His eyes gleamed. "What is the worst mistake you've ever made?"

"You go first," I encouraged.

"Very well. I saw you that night you disappeared... the night your father died."

My mind reeled back to that night that felt like it had occurred so long ago. That was the night I'd met Seraphina, the night she'd given me an impossible task—to care for her eggs. That was the night I had met Adriel.

"I don't remember you."

"I did not introduce myself, and I kick myself for it every day."

My stomach tightened. "Why didn't you?"

He rolled a grape through his fingers. "I saw you fall; rather, I watched as your brother allowed you to lose balance. I wanted to help but... you know our ways, especially in Ujuima."

I nodded. Any sign of weakness was frowned upon, especially from a royal. From an Osei, it was blasphemy.

"Anyway," he continued. "I hesitated long enough to witness another come to your aid."

"You mean Adriel."

"Hmm," he nodded, throwing the grape into the light waters below. It skittered for a moment before sinking. "Who knows, maybe I could have been your first love if I'd gotten to you first."

I tried to protest, but he jumped to his feet without a glance, with a handful of grapes. "I brought you here for a reason. There is something I want to show you," he said, walking to the edge. He continued to throw grapes into the water, first rolling them into balls of light before chucking them in.

I watched as bubbles rose to the surface. "Is there something in there?"

He grinned. "I heard you liked creatures. I don't have dragons, but I have the next best thing. Come see."

I couldn't help myself; I was intrigued. I walked behind him and gasped as the bubbles grew bigger and began to move toward us fast. When the bubbles nearly touched the shore, a figure jumped in the air, splashing us with water in the process. My jaw dropped. "Are those sea dragons?"

He laughed. "Sea dragons, yes."

"Do they live down here?" I asked, admiring their iridescent scales and flowing leafy tendrils on their backs.

"They shouldn't," Zaib admitted, crouching low as one of the sea dragons nosed toward him, its mane gleaming like threads of emerald and sapphire. Long, leafy tendrils fanned from their backs and tails, fluttering like underwater wings. "They're meant for the coastal pools of Entioch. My people raised them for generations. They are considered the messengers and guardians of the sea. Of course, people smuggle them elsewhere."

"Are you saying King Fourie did so?"

He smirked over his shoulder. "I'm sure he would prefer *rescued*."

The largest of the creatures swam in a lazy circle, glowing faintly as though sunlight clung to its scales. I knelt despite myself, reaching out with careful fingers. The sea dragon leaned forward, brushing its cool, wet muzzle against my palm.

Drakkar's voice rumbled in my mind, low and suspicious. *"Don't be jealous."*

"Those are like the rats of the sea."

"You are jealous."

He grumbled in response.

"Would you like to ride one?" Zaib asked.

"What? You can ride them?"

"Yes. It is safe, I assure you."

I watched the creature sniff Zaib's hand, looking for treats. It wasn't so different from Candy. "Yes."

"Remove your shoes. If you allow me, I can tie up your hair."

I hesitated but nodded. He gently ran his hands along my neck and lifted my hair, seeming to take a moment to take it all in before wrapping it in a loose knot and tying it up with a handkerchief. He took my hand and led me forward until the water was around our ankles.

"Watch me." He tapped the water, and one of the sea dragons reached up with its nose. He caressed its mane, and it bowed as if giving permission for him to approach. Zaib sat on his back and motioned for me to join him. He placed his hand around my waist, and the sea dragon flew through the air.

I gasped as it moved, the water rushing past in glittering streaks as it darted forward, its body undulating beneath me like a current. When it leapt again, sunlight fractured on its scales, casting prisms across the cavern walls.

I laughed, startling myself with a sound I couldn't contain. For an instant, it felt like flying with Drakkar, only softer, smoother, as though the whole world had slowed to let us glide through it.

I gripped Zaib's waist tighter as we moved through the air. Once we stilled and the sea dragon floated in the water, Zaib looked back at me and leaned in. My breath grew shallow as he grew closer.

"I like making you laugh," he murmured.

I looked into his eyes, watching how the green flecks changed in the light, then to his lips.

He reached forward, running his hand through the loose strands of my hair until we were breaths apart. The moment was so intense I barely noticed the splash of water nearby—but the sea dragon did. It bucked beneath us. I was able to hold on, but Zaib went flying into the water.

When I looked to see what had caused the disturbance, I saw Drakkar swimming towards me.

"Dismount the sea rat," he growled.

"Drakkar!" I cried as I frantically searched for Zaib in the water. "Zaib? Are you alright?"

The sea dragon was having none of it as Drakkar moved closer; even as I tried to soothe its aura, it wasn't enough. I went under.

"Now you've really made a mess of things. Zaib!" I called again. No response.

My heart hammered as I imagined him unconscious beneath the surface, sinking. *"Help me!"* I implored Drakkar.

That's when Zaib's brown hair broke through the water. I swam towards him.

"Are you alright?" I asked.

He smiled. "Were you worried about me?"

I moved the hair from his forehead. A bruise was already forming. "It would not bode well if I killed one of my suitors."

He clasped my hand in his, his other arm circling my waist to keep me above water. He brought my captive hand to his lips.

"It would be an honor to die at your hands."

I pulled my hand back, feeling a chill work its way through me. The way he said those words, it almost felt like he meant them.

He glanced toward Drakkar warily. "He doesn't like me much, does he?"

I shook my head, looking to Drakkar. "It is not I you must win over."

Chapter Twenty-Six

Asha

We decided to head back, our clothes soaked through. He found a blanket in the boat to shield me from the wind. Drakkar was quiet on the journey home, no doubt feeling satisfied with his antics.

As we made our way through the castle, still laughing at our adventure, a throat cleared ahead of us. Adriel stood waiting, his expression unreadable, his eyes moving from Zaib to me.

"What is the meaning of this?" Zaib demanded of Adriel.

Adriel tapped his foot impatiently as his eyes met mine. "Kwasi is awake. I thought you should know," he said before walking away.

I did not wait, sprinting across the castle, barely registering Zaib calling after me. Drakkar followed behind.

When we arrived in Kwasi's quarters, Kwasi was sitting up on the bed, awake, while Nayeli tended to him. She gave my hand a brief squeeze before I locked eyes with him. Though his shoulders were slumped in exhaustion, he seemed alert. I reached out to touch him, then held myself back, not wanting to exhaust him. "Kwasi, how do you feel?"

"Like a cart has rolled over me. How long was I out?"

"About a week. I am so sorry I did not heed your first message, but I am here now."

"Message?" he asked, as if something was on the edges of his memory but he couldn't quite grasp it.

Nayeli put a hand on his shoulder. "Too much exertion is unwise at this stage. Whatever you are trying to recall will come back with rest."

"Where are we, Ash?"

"I have much to tell you."

I spent the next hour filling Kwasi in, while Nayeli administered her homemade remedies. Kwasi spat out the orange peel and chrysalis tea when I explained the plan to marry. "You decided to do what? Ash, this is madness."

"What would you have me do?"

"Not marry a stranger! How do you know they won't kill you for the throne?"

"How do they know I won't do the same?"

Kwasi's jaw slackened at my response. Clearly, that was not what he expected. "This is dangerous. Elan could—"

"I am already an enemy of our brother. He will stop at nothing until I am dead. At least this way I will have an army behind me."

His eyes flashed, and he shook his head. "So, finding the Lightbearers has proved unsuccessful?"

"I have found one," I said with indignation. "She is safe in Saeleria."

Kwasi ran his hands over his face. "This marriage talk is giving me a headache. You need more time to think this through."

"I do not, and you know it. I am risking even this time. We should be planning our attack on both fronts, Elan and the Shadowcasters."

He grimaced, touching his head. I took the tea from him.

"I'm sorry to bring this to you, brother. Rest. You need your strength."

He lay back with great effort, sweat forming on his temple. Kwasi fell asleep not long after, which gave me some time to mull over his words. Kwasi was right; this was a risky plan, but what else did I have? I'd allowed myself to be distracted by Zaib today, and I did not have time for it. We did not even have time to discuss his plans for the Lightbearers. I would need to follow up with him, but first I needed to get ready for my next meeting with Kadir.

Not long after, I was summoned for my second outing. I changed out of my muddy clothes and donned a pair of practical trousers to meet with Kadir. I followed his attendants through multiple doors and hallways until we'd made it to one of the lower levels of the palace. Inside, Kadir sat slumped in his chair, chin in hand, in front of a hearth and a roaring fire. When he saw me, his eyes assessed me with apprehension. He stood, nearly knocking the chair he sat in over. The way he moved was unusual. He was arrogant, certainly, but never this clumsy.

"Princess. Thank you for coming to see me." He motioned to a table full of food. "Have you eaten? I heard you are a fan of dates. We have plenty."

"I am still full from lunch."

There was an awkward silence between us as we stared across the room at each other. Kadir spared a few looks at Drakkar, who was making himself comfortable on the marble floor.

"Can I be candid with you, Princess?"

"I like candor."

He leaned his hand on the mantel of the fireplace. "I know we are supposed to be courting, but we are adults. We know what this is." He paused. "Don't get me wrong, you are very pretty, and I think the two of us would get on, but I never planned to rule. That was always my brother."

"I see."

Kadir turned to face me. "I hold no ill will toward you for Atar's death. I have met the emperor and," he shivered, "I understand what he is like. I can only imagine what you have had to endure."

His aura shifted for just a moment, like it was tightening. After a moment it opened once more I into the same guileless warmth. Was it nerves, or had my brother done something truly awful to him?

"What I am trying to say, very badly, is that I would like to be open about what a marriage between us would look like. Our kingdom is very rich, one of the greatest military forces, second only to Elan. As you know, Firepeak and Ujuima have been long allies, and a marriage between us would likely be accepted by the people."

"And how would you rule the people?"

He blinked, genuinely confused by the question. "As we do now. With structure. Efficiency. Though," he added lightly, "I would not hoard food or essentials. A fed population works harder."

"And the Lightbearers?"

"We will use the might of our army to secure them for you, though I believe we can tamp down on these Shadows with a show of force. I have taken the liberty of assembling a special task force that will assist you unless you prefer to choose your own people."

It was strange to think of myself as a queen. I'd spent so much of my life in the dragon pits that the thought of returning to my royal life felt strange. But these rulers seemed to accept it, as my father and brother never could.

"What about those without battlemage?" I asked. "What would you do with them?"

"What do you mean?" He blinked, genuinely confused. "They would be banished, of course."

"Banished," I repeated.

"Yes." He nodded, relieved that he had given a sensible answer. "Those without battlemage have no role in such matters. They would only complicate things."

The silence between us stretched as I thought about his offer. Kadir smiled, oblivious to the alarm bells in my head.

"What if I were to say I wanted them to stay?"

Now he looked confused. "Who?"

"Those without battlemage," I repeated.

He ran his hands over his face and sat across from me as he thought it through. "But why? Why would you want inferior people on our lands?"

"Why does someone have to be able to do something for someone else to be worthy of being part of a kingdom? I'd hoped with the downfall of my brother's rule that this part of the law could change. Would you try to stop me when I pursue this?"

"I think you would get a lot of opposition. May I ask why you care?" Kadir repeated, baffled. "People without battlemage have no place in military affairs. They slow operations. They undermine efficiency. And—"

"And they are *people*," I said with emphasis.

He blinked, as though hearing the word for the first time. "Yes, yes," he said, waving a hand, "people. Of course. But inferior in utility."

I leaned forward. "What I'm asking is if I can count on you not to be among those opposing."

"Of course, I wouldn't stand in the way," he said immediately. "And I would support you if that is what you wanted."

"But you don't agree with me."

"No, I don't," he said honestly. "But I would support you, nonetheless."

"How do I know if these are just words?"

He looked down, as if this turn in our conversation had not been accounted for, as if he could not imagine I would deviate from protocol or efficiency.

I drew in a steadying breath, and my attention snagged on the small book in his hands. "Do you like to read?" I asked.

He seemed startled. "I shouldn't have brought this in. It's childish really."

"Can I see it?"

He seemed hesitant, but eventually he handed it to me. It was a small book that could fit in the palm of my hand. The cover of the book was nothing special, but inside were what appeared to be puzzles and short scriptures. "What is this?"

"It is silly. A game a few of my friends play." He helped me flip through a few more of the pages. "Here is the map we work from, and the goal is to find the next clue, which is presumably here." He pointed to an isolated spot in the mountains.

"Is this Firepeak?"

"This was before the Five Kingdoms were ever conceived. When there was no central government."

"But this is not from a royal library." My brow arched. "This is contraband, then?"

He looked alarmed. "Don't tell my father. It is just a silly game I play sometimes."

Relieved that he was willing to break any rule, I said, "Tell me how to play it."

He gave me a sharp look, as if he was trying to determine if I was serious or not. Then he smiled, and his entire body seemed to relax. I tried to pay attention to what he was telling me about the hidden clues within the texts and how he was using religious texts to decode them. He was close, so very close, but he feared there was a text he did not have in his possession that could help him solve it all.

"What do you get if you solve it?"

He looked surprised, as if he hadn't really thought about it. "I don't know. None of us has solved it. That is what makes it so fun."

"What if it is nothing?"

"Someone went to a lot of trouble to make this. People are playing it throughout the Five Kingdoms. It can't be for nothing."

I closed the book and twirled it in my hand. For the first time, I realized how very painfully young he was. Young enough that he could still find joy in games.

He wet his lips before saying, "I like you. I think we could make each other happy if we tried." He gave a nervous look at Drakkar, who'd been unusually quiet. "Does he?" he asked.

"Does he what?"

"Does your dragon ever allow others near him?"

"I suppose. He is nice to my friends."

"Do you think he would let me ride him?"

"Absolutely not!" Drakkar barked.

Kadir jumped at his growl.

"Maybe not now," I amended.

I looked to Drakkar. *"Be civil!"*

"I don't want to."

"He does like cherries. He is a fiend for them. You might try that if you want to get to know him."

"I might just try that."

"Do you want to be married to me?" I asked suddenly.

His eyes shot open. "Of course I do."

I took his hand. "No, really. Do you want to be married to me, to rule together knowing my passion for finding Lightbearers?"

He swallowed. "Father says I could not do any better, and I agree."

Before I could reply, a knock came to the door. It was Fourie's attendant, there to escort me to my final engagement with him this evening.

"Wait, before you go," Kadir said. "Here." He placed the tiny book back in my hand.

"Don't you need it to solve the puzzle?"

"I have a copy. Take it for good luck."

I nodded before following the attendant out.

Chapter Twenty-Seven

Asha

"Where are we going?"

The attendant turned. "There are parts of the castle that are restricted to His Royal Highness," he said before pulling out a large gold key. "You are very fortunate indeed. I do not remember him bringing anyone back here since his late wife."

As we moved, the rooms changed from ornate to dark and bare. It almost seemed like we were moving in between the walls of the palace, but we were moving up. I could tell that much by the number of staircases and Drakkar's grumbling behind me.

"The late queen died in childbirth, right? She and the child? I remember hearing that."

He nodded. "Indeed. It was a tragedy. His Majesty has never been the same."

I followed him to a large iron door. The attendant rapped once. A peephole opened, and someone peeked through.

"State your business."

"I am here with Princess Asha," the attendant said.

The eyes stared at us a moment longer. "She can come in. His Highness has requested the dragon stay back."

Drakkar protested immediately.

"Drakkar won't allow it," I explained.

The attendant seemed apologetic, inclining his head. "I understand. He will be allowed to view you at the top tower, but he will not be able to enter His Highness's residence."

"Then we are done here," I said, prepared to turn around.

"Wait," the man's voice called after me. "He said if you did that, to tell you that he has information you would find useful in securing the safe release of your friend, Cane. He will part with that information only if you see him this evening. "

I whipped around. "But that was not part of the deal."

"He said to remind you that the deal was to release him, not ensure his safety after doing so."

The threat was clear.

"Should we go or stay?" Drakkar asked.

"You aren't going to fight me on this?"

"It is not safe. I hate that you put yourself in danger, but it is your decision to make."

I shook my head. *"I don't know if I'm ready for this kind of trust between us."*

"You have to be, otherwise you're dead."

"This is for Miren. I am responsible for Cane being taken."

Drakkar leaned in. *"When are you going to learn that not every bad thing in the world is because of something you did?"*

"I will go," I said to the attendant.

"The dragon must leave before I open this gate," the guard said.

I turned to Drakkar. *"I'll see you soon."*

Drakkar groaned before he swept back through the hallway; the attendant trailed after. My vision went dark. "I will need someone to help guide me," I said, leaning on my walking staff.

"No, you won't," he said.

As the door creaked open, I froze. The corridor beyond glowed with light from aura crystals lining the walls and the ceiling above. They were everywhere, giving me faint impressions of the room. "His Highness has taken care of everything," he said, locking the door behind us. "Please, follow me."

I could not describe what I was seeing if I tried. It started off as a hallway but soon led into rooms where the crystals were hung in place of chandeliers and wall sconces. Even the candelabra the guard held in his hand was adorned with them. It brought me back to the garden Adriel had created in Wiyotak.

"This had to have taken years. This could not be for me. When did he do all of this?"

"His Highness is waiting for you."

My head whipped quickly to the side as I heard laughter. My heart leapt at the sound of the voice. Small hands reached for my skirts as I looked down. I saw a figure of a child, no older than six years old.

"You are here," he squealed. "Father has told me so much about you."

"Give her space, Remi," a familiar voice instructed. I whirled around to see a shadow that appeared to be sitting nearby. His aura moved slightly back and forth, like he was in a rocking chair. The faint scent of tobacco wafted through the room.

I dipped into a curtsy. "Good evening, Your Majesty."

"No need for formalities here, my dear," he said. "Take a seat. You have had a long day. I don't envy you this business at all."

The small hand clasped tighter, pulling me down. "Sit here, next to me. I have other friends I want you to meet."

I allowed him to pull me along to a swiveling chair. "Friends?" I asked.

"Yes. They are very eager to meet you." Remi immediately put something soft and furry in my lap.

"It is not alive, is it?" I asked cautiously.

He giggled. "This is my friend PJ. He is a griffin."

I felt around the object until I could make out a mane and wings. I relaxed, realizing this was a stuffed doll.

"Do you like griffins?" I asked.

"Yes! They are my favorites. We have loads of them here. Sometimes Papa lets them visit. I also have Lenox and Falle. They are dragons," he explained, placing them all in my lap. "I've never met a dragon. Papa said you have one!"

"I do," I said, looking at Fourie's aura in the corner.

"Is he nice? Can I meet him?"

I paused, unsure of how to answer that question. "He is nice to me," I said finally, "and anyone I tell him to be nice to."

"He should be in the observation area," Fourie said. "Why don't you go check?"

"Can the princess come with me?"

"We will be along soon. Asha and I need to talk."

"Why don't you take your friends?" I offered.

He scooped them all up, and his silver aura rushed out of sight.

The warmth seemed to drain away with him. Silence settled in its place as Fourie and I faced one another alone. "I was surprised to see you on my itinerary this morning," I said.

The puffing of a pipe filled the quiet. "Don't worry. I could never marry again for any reason."

"I recall meeting your wife, Deidre, once. I was young."

"She was impressed with you," he confirmed. "And worried. She was the first to point out that you were different from your siblings."

"Different how?"

"She said you had a light within you. She sensed that your parents knew and that things would soon go very badly for you... Deidre is never wrong."

"She knew I would end up in the pits?" I asked. "Was she a Lightbearer?"

"No," he said firmly. "At least, she did not have your abilities. But our son, Remi, he is an unseer like yourself."

I swallowed. "No one knows, do they?"

"Only Celia," he said softly. "Remi came into the world too soon. When I lost Deidre, I was certain I would lose him too. He was so frail. But every day he would wake up, I grew more and more hopeful."

"When did he lose his sight?" I asked.

Fourie quieted for a long moment. I thought he would not answer. "He was born an unseer."

I inhaled sharply. "Lightbearers are not born blind."

"I know. You can see why it was much more prudent to claim he had died in childbirth than admit the truth. Your father would have demanded his death." His voice cracked. "I could not."

"So, you designed this space for him," I said, putting the pieces together.

"I sourced the aura crystals from Wiyotak at first until I was able to mine them from our own mountains."

"This place is impressive," I said, looking up.

"I hope I can count on your discretion."

"Of course, although I do think you can count on Adriel as well."

"That is what I've called you up here to discuss," he said. "I imagine you and Adriel grew quite close during your travels. It is only natural between young people."

"Is there a question you would like to ask me?" I asked lightly.

"I would not insult you with such a question," he said. "What I would do is encourage you not to include him in your decision."

"I am looking for the person who can offer me the best plan forward to obtain Lightbearers," I reminded him.

"And if you choose among the other two families, I would be most grateful to you."

"Your gratitude is nice, but it does not solve my problem."

Fourie was quiet, as if he was weighing something. "I will pledge the full might of my own forces to search for other Lightbearers. I'm sure you can imagine I have a vested interest."

"You would do that? But why is it so important that you align with Wiyotak? Unless..." I paused for a long moment. "You want your own source of dracite."

"You are far too clever to have been hidden away for so many years," he said. "Yes. This realignment gives me an opportunity to make sure we are aligned with power. I have no interest in bowing down to Firepeak again, and this would ensure we always have a seat at the table."

"Isn't it a risk to confide in me your plans? What if I choose Kadir?"

"It is a far greater risk to me if you decide to marry Adriel."

"And how do I know you will follow through?" I asked, leaning forward.

"I thought that would be obvious. You now hold a secret that could destroy me."

"What about Cane?"

"Ah. Yes. Cane." His tone shifted, almost regretful. "I'm afraid I don't have good news."

"But you said—"

"That I would tell you enough to ensure his safety," he interrupted gently. "And what I know is this: Cane is not being held by Firepeak. In fact, I don't believe he ever was."

My breath caught. "Then where is he?"

"He is a recruiter," he said quietly. "For the Shadowcasters."

The room seemed to tilt.

Miren.

CHAPTER TWENTY-EIGHT

Miren

"We cannot stay in the woods forever, Miren," Zephyr said with apprehension. "We have already been here too long. He is not here."

The hatchlings were unusually restless and tearful after the invasion, often calling out for Mattias and Asha. When they asked after Mattias, I did not have the heart to tell them that he was probably either captured or worse. We were supposed to be searching for Asha. That was the reason we'd come. But even Zephyr seemed to know the truth I was avoiding—this wasn't about her anymore.

My fingers closed around the locket at my wrist, the one holding the dried apricot pit from our first date. I'd kept it close because it gave me hope for what could be. I put the hood of my cloak up to shield my face.

"Just give me another hour to find him. If I don't see him, we can start looking elsewhere."

"Let me go with you," he insisted.

"Are you insane? Everyone here is terrified of you. They've seen you fly. I must go alone."

"You are not Asha. You are not accustomed to moving without sight."

I tugged on the walking staff he'd fashioned for me at my side. My use of it was clumsy and stilted. Asha made it look easy. "I will manage. I have a plan."

Without another word, I began the trek into the caravan. I'd walked this trail so many times that when my vision began to fade, I did not panic. I knew where I needed to go. I found Mabel's door by memory and knocked. Curtains moved as someone looked out of the window. The series of locks she had on the door began to click as they were unlocked.

"Thank goodness you are okay," Mabel exhaled. "Come in before anyone sees you."

As soon as the door locked behind me, I felt small hands reach for me as Lacey embraced me. She lifted my hood and inhaled sharply. "Miren, your eyes. What is wrong with them?"

Mabel turned me around. "Miren, can you not see?" she asked in alarm. "Did Ada do this to you?"

"Yes, I mean, no," I corrected. "Not exactly. I am told this is temporary and that my sight should return soon."

"Well, thank goodness for small miracles. You'll have to tell us everything. I am so grateful you found your way here."

"I am too. I missed you both."

"Lacey," Mabel began. "Help Miren sit while I boil us a pot of tea."

Lacey took my hand and guided me to the table to sit. "Did you hear about the dragons, Miren? That they can fly? Did you see it?"

"Let her breathe, child," Mabel chastised.

"I did at the Shadows' meeting."

"What did they look like? They must have been so scary. Did they breathe fire?"

I thought back to when Zephyr had found me. He had certainly let out several bursts of flame, but they were directed at anyone who approached us. The way he'd stood over me had scared me. I thought I would die, but looking back, he was directing the flame at anyone who attacked us or approached us with their weapons. He'd been protecting us, I realized. I had been realizing a lot of things since Zephyr and I had bonded.

"I don't remember," I said, taking the hot tea, running my finger along the lip to test the fullness like I'd watched Asha do so many times. "I'm just glad no one got hurt."

"Ada did," Lacey blurted out. "She had scrapes and bruises when she came to see us—"

"Hush!" Mabel said. "I told you not to speak her name. Someone could hear us."

Lacey exhaled impatiently. "I just don't understand why. Ada isn't a part of our group. Why can't we talk about her?"

"Because it is not safe," Mabel warned. "Every soldier in the king's army is looking for her. We don't want them to lay their suspicions on us."

"So, you have not seen her?" I asked.

"Thankfully, not in weeks," Mabel said. "She is a nice girl, but it is too dangerous to get caught up with her. I hope you were able to stay clear."

"Yes, of course," I said. "What about Cane? Has he asked for me?"

Mabel seemed startled. "I thought that was where you had gone. No, I have not seen him since the night you left together."

"Have the Shadows had to go into hiding?"

Mabel was quiet for a moment. "No, they've continued their meetings from what I've heard. They have nearly half the town attending after the dragons were spotted. I know you like them, but I still think they are a strange lot. Why hide behind a mask if what you are doing is good?"

My mouth tightened. "So, there should be a meeting happening right now."

"You can't possibly go," Mabel protested.

"I have to. What if something has happened?" I said, standing to go.

Mabel stood with me. "Miren, where did you go if you weren't with Cane?"

"I was ill."

She put her hand on my shoulder to prevent me from going. "I thought of that, so I checked your rooms and the medical tent. You were nowhere to be found," she said. "You were with her, weren't you?"

My body tensed. She was asking, but the tone in her voice told me that she was already certain. "Stay here, Miren," she pleaded. "We will help you. We help our own. Don't get yourself wrapped up in something that you cannot get out of."

A single tear rolled down my face. "You've been a second mother to me, Mabel. I appreciate your kindness, I do, but I have to go after him."

Mabel wrapped her arms around me. "Don't go," she rasped. "Please."

I returned her embrace, and we stood there for a moment, soaking in the love from each other. Eventually, Lacey ran to embrace us too. She cried against my hip. Though she did not know what was happening exactly, she knew enough that this was a goodbye.

"I must go," I said finally. "The meeting will have already started. I will return if I can."

Mabel straightened my cloak and put the hood over my head once more. "You are always welcome here, my darling, but I do not think you will be back. I hope I am wrong."

I did not know how to respond to that, so I gave Lacey a quick kiss on the cheek before I made my way to the meeting hall.

Making my way through the town without sight was much harder than I could have imagined. I'd already run into a barrel, a gardening hoe, and stubbed my foot countless times. How Asha was able to navigate so effortlessly, I had no idea. Instead of feeling discouraged, I kept Cane's image in my mind and imagined each step was one closer to him.

I tried to move quickly through the streets unnoticed, my hood pulled low. If I caught the attention of the wrong person, I could be turned in. But if I moved too slowly, I risked missing the meeting altogether. Every step was a gamble.

After what felt like hours, the faint hum of singing drifted toward me. My heart wept at the sound, my steps quickening until the music grew into a chorus echoing through the hall. The moment I stepped inside, I was swallowed by the press of bodies. When I bumped into the first person, I was shuffled back, startled when I realized the shuffling was because there were so many people. There was no way I'd find Cane in the crowd that this meeting had brought.

Then, a voice cut through the noise.

"I am so glad to have every single one of you here. How blessed we are to gather tonight!"

It was Cane. Relief flooded through me so quickly it nearly brought me to my knees. I had to get to him. As he began to read from the Book of Shadows, I pushed forward, murmuring apologies as I brushed past strangers. When a hand caught my arm, I froze.

"Are you alright, ma'am? Do you need help?"

"I need to speak to Cane," I said quickly. "Please—let me through."

"I'm afraid I can't allow that. He's our guest speaker."

"I won't bother him. I just need to talk to him after he is done."

"I'm afraid I cannot allow that," he said firmly.

"Well, I don't care what you allow," I snapped. "He'll want to see me."

There was commotion surrounding my presence as more people approached. "You are making too much noise," a female rasped. "If you cannot sit down, we will remove you."

I weighed my options. If I stayed where I was, it was very likely I would not reach him in time and I would be lost in the crowd, and if I didn't, they would likely cart me away. I hated feeling like I had limited options. I did the only thing I knew.

"Cane!" I called, trying to get his attention. "Cane, they won't allow me to speak to you. Please tell them I'm okay."

Hands grabbed me immediately and attempted to drag me away, but I fought them.

"Cane! Help me," I rasped as hands tried to quiet me.

It didn't take long for the Shadows to hold me down. More shouts erupted around me.

"Miren? Is that you?"

"Cane!" I cried.

"Let her go." He kept his voice low, but there was a level of authority that the other Shadows immediately listened to, because they released me without question.

"Miren, are you all right?" he asked, pulling me to my feet.

I clung to him, sobbing into his shirt. He whispered something to the surrounding people before leaning down to say, "Miren, people are watching. I need you to pull yourself together. Can you do that?"

I released him and wiped the tears away. He was right. To cry in Firepeak, even at a Shadow meeting, was not appropriate. Once I fixed my expression back to stoic, he guided me down the steps, away from the murmuring crowd. Only then did he turn me toward him. His fingers lifted my chin, gentle but insistent, as if he needed to be sure I was truly there.

"Why couldn't you have just gone with them? They would have brought me the message."

I was startled that these were the first words out of his mouth, and not *'are you hurt'* or *'I was so worried.'*

"I'm sorry. Today was your sermon. I know how long you've wanted to do that."

"It is no matter. I'm glad you're here," he sighed. "What happened?"

"I heard you'd been detained," I whispered. "I was terrified."

"They did detain me," he said. "They asked a lot of questions about you. And your friend—Ada."

A chill tore down my spine. "What did you tell them?"

"That I barely knew her. And that you couldn't possibly be involved. But..."

"But what?"

"They said you went with her. On the back of a dragon. Is that true, Miren?"

My breath locked. Everything in me screamed to deny it—but how could I lie to him?

"Yes," I said softly. "But it's a long story."

"What happened to your eyes?" he asked suddenly. "Can you not see?"

"Can we go somewhere more private?" I asked finally. "I have much to tell you."

"Of course, but I cannot leave the meeting just yet. I should go finish the sermon. Can you sit here and wait for me?"

"I really don't want to be alone."

He kissed my forehead. "You aren't. I'm right here, and I will be back. Just give me five minutes."

I nodded, not trusting my voice..

I'd found Cane, and he was not imprisoned like I'd feared. I should be relieved, but something in me felt apprehensive. Something was different. Did he always seem distant and unfeeling or was it my mind playing tricks on me? I waited as he asked, hearing occasional claps and shouts of approval from the audience.

"Miren!" I jumped until I realized the voice came from inside my head.

"Zephyr, you know I hate when you do that. Get out of my head."

"They're coming for you, Miren. You need to run now."

"Who is? I need to find Cane. We can leave together right now."

Zephyr was silent for a moment, then my vision flashed, and I could see around me. *"Are you here?"* I asked. He didn't answer.

Once my sight adjusted, I took stock of the room I was in. There was no roof, but there were still walls standing. I was sitting on a concrete bench. I moved quickly to the window to see if I could spot Cane. What I saw caught my breath. There were soldiers, Firepeak soldiers, outside, and Cane was with them. He appeared to be having a tense conversation with a group of them and pointed my way.

My heart began to slowly break as I realized what he was doing. He was turning me in. The bastard was turning me in. I closed my eyes and opened them several times, hoping they were playing tricks on me. But these weren't my eyes; they were Zephyr's.

"I'm sorry, Miren," Zephyr said.

"Don't be," I whispered. *"He's going to be the one who is sorry."* I gripped the locket, clasping it tightly in my hand. *"Zephyr?"*

"Yes?"

"I need you."

He exhaled slowly. *"Who shall I burn, Miren?"*

I looked at him, incredulous. *"You'd really do that?"*

"I am yours."

I looked out the window once more, the locket slipping to the floor, with a soft, final sound. *"I am ready to find Asha. But first,"* I said, pulling on my battlemage. The wind shifted around me. *"Let's burn some shit."*

Chapter
Twenty-Nine

Asha

I sat on my balcony, food untouched beside me as I recounted the day. Zaib had tried to call again, but I couldn't face him. I'd had enough humiliation for the day.

Kwasi was sleeping when I checked back in on him. Nayeli was gone, but Fourie's shamans assured me that he was doing fine and that fatigue was to be expected.

"I still don't understand why you have to pick any of them, Little One," Drakkar bemoaned. *"Especially now that it appears Cane is inconsequential."*

"He won't be inconsequential to Miren." I sighed. *"But they are right. I have much more influence if I marry. I'd have a whole army looking for Lightbearers. It took me two years to find one, and it was by accident."*

"Why do we have to be in such a rush? Mortals are so impatient. Let's leave now and train Miren. By the time she is ready, there will be more."

"I just do not know if we have that kind of time. You saw the mountain in Saeleria; it is losing its magic. Saeleria may not be a safe place for long."

"What about the long-haired one?"

"Adriel? You heard the other rulers. They would not approve, and—he would never agree to it."

"Is it not worth exploring? That is what this time is for, is it not? How can you make a decision without knowing all your options?"

"If he considered us an option, he would have fought harder to be on the courtship schedule."

"And you, are you fighting for it?"

I laughed. *"What exactly am I supposed to be fighting for? And since we are being truthful tonight, what about you?"*

Drakkar arched a brow in confusion. *"What about me?"*

"Those are yours and Seraphina's children, and you barely acknowledge them. You never play with them," I said sharply. *"All they want is their father, and instead they have to cling to me and their Pawpaw because you won't give them the time of day."*

"That is not true."

"Isn't it? I've made every excuse for you, but the truth is, Seraphina would be disappointed. She would never want you to abandon them."

"I have not abandoned them!" he seethed. *"I've been following you on every mission, every whim."*

"Don't blame me because you don't want to be a father."

Drakkar moved then and howled into the sky. A stream of fire struck the branches of a tree and climbed hungrily as the needles curled into ash within seconds.

"You would never understand. You haven't had what I had."

"And what is that?" I shouted.

He swung his great head toward me, eyes blazing like twin suns. *"A love so deep it burns you from the inside."* The bond between us vibrated, raw and unshielded. His voice cracked across our link. *"When she died, I died. Everything I was, everything I built, turned to ash. I swore I would never,"* his claws dug into the balcony railing, shattering stone, *"never let myself feel like that again."*

I staggered back, breath catching at his words.

"You think I don't see them?" he went on, quieter now but no less fierce. *"Every inflection of their voice. Every flicker of light in their eyes. They are hers. They are all I have left of her. And if I get too close—if I let myself love them—when I lose them, it will tear the last of me apart."*

I pressed a hand to my mouth, throat thick with something I couldn't name. *"Drakkar..."*

"Do what you will, Asha," he said before taking flight.

"Drakkar! Wait!"

But he didn't.

I paced along the balcony, wringing my hands. Drakkar seemed so hurt. So fragile after our exchange. I regretted it wholly.

A light step followed by a deep sigh sounded behind me.

"You are the only person I know who can piss off a dragon and live."

I didn't even turn. I wouldn't give him the satisfaction. "What do you want, Ashkii?"

"I just want to talk to you—that's all."

I shook my head. "As you can see, I'm not in the mood for talking."

"Well, it can't be helped. I, unfortunately, seem to have been left off the courtship schedule."

"It has been a long day. I'm certainly not interested in being courted right now."

He fell silent, and for a moment, I thought he might finally walk away. "I know I am not whole, nor was I born into royalty... but I'd hoped."

This time, I did turn. I didn't need to see his face to hear the emotion in his voice. "You know that is not why. I've never cared about your hearing. There are a lot of reasons not to choose you, but that is not one of them."

He inhaled sharply. "And what are they? The reasons."

"For one, you are in a religious cult."

"We worship Yemaya, the goddess, from whom all dragons were originally derived," he said patiently. "Yemaya is loving, and many used to worship her before Idris had their texts burned."

"Second," I continued, "the people would never accept it."

He laughed at that. "They already have, Ash. We have sects in all five kingdoms now. We are growing, unstoppable in numbers."

That made me pause. Curiosity prickled through my annoyance. "Then who is your leader? Who's calling the shots?"

"I am not at liberty to say."

"What do you mean? You are making a marriage proposal, and I can't know who your master is? You know, I'm surprised it is you rising to the top and not Markus. What happened to him?" I asked, remembering the man who had introduced me to the terms Lightbearer and Shadowcaster.

Ashkii frowned. "He failed in bringing you to our side."

"If I remember correctly, you had something to do with that."

His hands intertwined with mine. "You don't understand, Ash. With the Shadows, you never have to be anything other than yourself. You can be exactly as you are. Aren't you tired? Tired of hiding, tired of pretending? I never have to feel that way with them."

I tugged at his hand and turned his palm over. "I never had to pretend with you," I signed on his hand. He sucked in a breath. "With you, I could always be myself; now, I'm not sure anymore. Where is that brilliant boy who wrote poetry and had dreams of being more than a warrior?"

He gripped my wrist and turned over my palm. "I'm still here," he signed.

I used my voice this time. "No, you're not here. That boy is gone, and I want him back." Before I could stop it, a tear escaped my eye, and once it fell, more followed.

He attempted to wipe them away with his thumb. He was so close I felt the heat of his breath on my cheek. "I'm here, Asha, I swear it. Forgive me," he said before he leaned in, his lips grazing mine. I sucked in a sharp breath but couldn't move. My breath caught, sharp and shallow, as if my lungs had forgotten their purpose. The world narrowed to the space between us, to the heat of his body.

A sharp crack sounded behind me. When I turned my head, I could see Adriel's aura blazing like blue fire. "Get. Back."

Ashkii dropped my hands. I felt his aura shift further away. "It's not what you think."

"You know what I think?" Adriel interrupted. "I think you have five seconds to find your way off of this balcony before I kill you."

No one moved. No one even dared breathe. The lethality in his voice made bumps rise along my flesh. "Adriel—" I began.

"I'll leave," Ashkii said abruptly, his robes slapping in the wind. "I will see you soon, Ash." Without another word, his aura was gone.

There was silence between Adriel and me. My tongue felt heavy with all that I needed to say, but I managed, "Adriel, that was not what—"

"I came to check on you when I saw Drakkar leaving the way he did, but it appears that was a wasted effort because you are fine. I bid you goodnight."

He was gone before I could take another breath. And I was too stunned to go after him.

I stood utterly alone on the balcony. My palm tingled. I lifted my hand, feeling where his fingers touched, the moment his lips claimed mine.

Ashkii had signed something against my hand before he'd left. *Trust no one. Especially Adriel.*

My stomach dropped. What could he mean? Adriel had lied to me in the past, so was he lying to me now?

The wind pressed against me as if urging me to move, but I stayed frozen, fingers against my lips, wondering which part should terrify me more—the kiss, the warning, or the man who'd stormed out.

CHAPTER THIRTY

Asha

Kwasi was sitting in his bed eating a bowl of mielie when I arrived the next morning.

"You're here!"

"Well, of course," I said. "I saw you yesterday."

"No, you don't understand," he said, the bowl clanking as he set it down. "I don't have much time before I forget again."

"I don't understand."

"I'm not entirely sure I do either. Everything is muddled."

"The shaman said it was a memory spell."

"I can remember some things," he continued. "But I haven't really been alert until now. I don't know when this sense of clarity will let up, so I need you to just listen."

"You're making me nervous," I said.

"Don't be. What I have discovered is a miracle. You know how I was poring over the histories before the Five Kingdoms came to be? The maps never lined up, so I had to go to the Central Library."

"In Ujuima? Are you insane?"

"I know, but I had some friendly contacts there. It was worth it, trust me."

I shook my head incredulously. "Well, what is it?"

"There is another territory. It is not on any of the maps. It is an island in the Caan Sea."

"Okay, there are new islands being discovered every day."

"But this island was designated specifically for Lightbearers! I cannot find anything that says they ever left. I think they are still there, and there is something else."

My mind was reeling. An island for Lightbearers? How could this be? Surely it was deserted by now. "The Great Dragon told me about lost islands. Isande, maybe."

"The Ifambe Islands."

We both jumped, neither of us realizing Adriel had entered the room.

"Yes!" Kwasi exclaimed. "But that is not the best part. The whole reason I was searching is because of the journal you gave me from Atim. In it, he mentioned a relic that helped him summon," he said. "I thought he meant summon the dragons, but I think it was actually referring to Lightbearers. What if instead of looking for every single Lightbearer, you could summon them?"

I was losing my balance. I found the nearest post to lean against. My legs could not be trusted. "I could call all the Lightbearers."

"We don't know what is on this island," Adriel warned. "It could be deserted, or worse. Do you know where it is?"

Kwasi began to speak, as if to tell us, then stopped. His voice grew distant as he tried to form words.

"Kwasi, who put the charm on you?" I asked.

"What?" he asked.

"I mentioned a memory spell was put on you that made you forget. Who did it?"

"I—I don't know what you are talking about. What spell?" The shift was quick, like a candle that had been blown out. His voice changed, as did his aura. Something was wrong.

"Kwasi?" I asked.

"Ash, it's so good to see you. I feel like we don't see each other enough," he said.

"Do you remember what you were just telling us? About an island?"

His hair rustled as he ran a hand through it. "I couldn't tell you about an island," he said, followed by a yawn. "Man, I'm exhausted. I think I am going to lie down."

I stood to assist him but tripped over Adriel's robes. He gripped my arms before I fell. "I'll find Iná. Give me a moment."

I clutched my hands tightly together, trying to quiet the tremor running through me. Kwasi's shift was as alarming as what he had just shared.

Adriel returned shortly with Nayeli. After some time of her examining him, she tutted.

"What is it?" I asked. "I thought whatever you did had relieved the magic."

"She did what?" Adriel asked with alarm.

"Nayeli?" I asked. "What has happened?"

"Without knowing the specific charm and who cast it, I am unsure. He is fighting the magic; I know that much. Fighting it takes a lot of energy, and that is why he's been so tired."

"What is the cure?" I demanded.

There was a brief silence before she said, "The spell caster has to remove it from him."

"And we don't know who that is. Does that mean he could be this way forever?"

Another pause. Adriel's hand went to my shoulder.

"What aren't you telling me?" I asked. "What are you trying to say?"

"She's trying to say," his voice sounded pained, "that the spell may make him grow weaker."

"No," I said, shaking my head. "He was sitting here talking. He is getting better."

"This magic is very powerful and may not be able to be reversed without the original caster."

"We'll find a way," Adriel assured.

"We have to find this island," I whispered. "The Lightbearers. They must know…"

"We don't know where it is," he said quietly.

"He will be okay for now," Nayeli assured. "Any shaman can whip up a poultice should he need it."

"Any shaman? Are you leaving Nayeli?"

"Yes—but," I could tell she wanted to say more.

I needed to get away. I could not breathe in the room we were in.

"I need air," I said, pulling at the collar of my dress.

"Let me take you outside," Adriel offered.

"No, get away. I can't be next to you right now." I walked away from him and fell to the ground as my knee knocked against an end table.

"Dammit to hell, Asha. Let me help!"

"Don't touch me," I ground out.

"Okay," he relented, a slight edge of worry in his voice. "You can see my aura, right? I'll guide you."

I wanted to tell him off, to yell at him to leave and that I didn't need his assistance. Instead, I pulled myself up and reluctantly followed.

I was grateful that he led me down a hallway that seemed to be free of attendants. I followed him through a series of doors until the nocturnal wind bit my face as we stepped outside. I wrapped my arms around myself, but it did little to still the shivers running through me.

Adriel stayed a pace ahead, his aura flickering faint blue so I could follow. I was thankful. The silence let me breathe, let me steady the chaos that still churned in my chest.

"You don't have to be alone in this," he said at last. His voice was low, gentler than I expected.

I barked a humorless laugh. "I've always been alone. Why stop now?"

He quieted after that and mercifully allowed me to soak in the stillness. There was so much at stake, and yet, did it matter if Kwasi would not live to see it?

"It is unlike Drakkar to leave you unattended," Adriel said, finally breaking the silence. "Maybe you should call him."

"I'm the last person he wants to speak to right now."

"What happened? Drakkar adores you."

"It's none of your concern. Leave it be," I snapped.

"It is if he leaves you unattended," he pushed. "That must be how Ashkii was able to get into your chambers."

I shook my head. "It wasn't what you think."

Now it was his turn to snap. "Are you saying my eyes deceived me, and I did not catch the two of you kissing? What if anyone other than myself had walked in? Do you know what could have happened?"

"You don't know everything."

His fingers popped as he flexed his hands. "Okay, what am I missing then?"

I opened my mouth and then closed it. This was pointless. "Nothing. You missed nothing."

I leaned over the railing, trying to catch my breath and failing. I swallowed hard, the weight of Kwasi's condition pressing heavy on my ribs. "If I lose him…"

Adriel was at my side. "You won't. He will be okay."

But the words did not reassure me. Adriel's fingers ran down the boning of my dress. "You are still struggling to breathe."

I pulled at my corset, trying to find a modicum of give within it.

"I can help you loosen it."

I wanted to tell him to go to hell, to leave me alone, to tell him to stop touching things that weren't his to touch—but all I managed was a choked, "Please."

Adriel worked quickly, meticulously unbuttoning every single button. "Just rip it," I said.

"Asha, I can't—"

"I said rip it!"

"Just give me a moment, and I'll have it."

"No!" I cried as I reached for my collar and pulled down, and pearl buttons clinked to the floor like tiny bones. I pulled on the corset straps, but he swatted my hands away and undid them himself. Air flooded my lungs so fast I nearly stumbled. My chest heaved one final sigh as my breathing resumed its normal rhythm.

"Why can't you let anyone help you?"

"It is just a dress. I will get another."

Suddenly his hands were on me, one on my waist and the other around the back of my head, holding me still. The heat that radiated from him was both overwhelming and familiar. "This isn't about the damned dress," he growled, pulling me closer. He took my hand and intertwined it with his, circling his thumb in my palm before bringing it to his lips.

I didn't fight it. I melted into it, into him, letting myself remember what it felt like to be wanted this way.

"I knew it," he breathed against my ear. "It was you in Firepeak."

My breath stuttered. "You couldn't have," I whispered, remembering that night and how free and unguarded I'd felt.

He pulled back, but his grip around me stayed firm. "I did. But if you doubt me, there is still one more test we could run to prove it, if you like."

I went rigid in his arms, my lips craving his touch. I put a hand between us and pushed him back.

"This is about Ashkii. That is why you are doing this."

"No, this is about why you left that night," he said suddenly. I couldn't see his eyes, but I could feel his aura pressing down on me, demanding that I respond.

My head spun. The shift in conversation hit like the heaviest of stones. I could pretend not to know what he meant. But I did. Of course I did.

"I didn't leave because of you. I left because I had no choice."

"No choice? You disappeared, leaving me wondering if I had imagined it—if I'd imagined us."

My hand pressed against his chest. His heart was beating against it, too fast, too wild, and yet it matched mine. "You think I could stay and live out some fairytale while the world burned around us?"

Adriel's grip on my waist loosened. His thumb brushed a soft, trembling path against my hip before he pulled away entirely, the loss of contact making the night air cooler.

"You should have told me," he said, and the anger was gone now, replaced by something ragged and aching. "You should have let me fight with you."

"I was trying to keep you alive," I snapped. "Ashkii had been taken. Kwasi had been kidnapped and hurt, all because of me."

He exhaled sharply, bowing his forehead to mine but not touching. "Don't you understand? I'm not afraid of dying, Asha. I'm afraid of losing you."

His words sank into the hollow place inside me I tried so hard to ignore.

"Let me go," I whispered.

"You think I haven't tried? You think I haven't spent every waking minute away from you trying to expel you from my mind? And then I see you with Zaib, and then Ashkii, and it all comes back."

My mouth parted slightly. "We can't. I'm getting married. *You're* getting married."

"A marriage won't erase the way I feel about you."

"I think my future husband will care."

For a long moment, all I could hear was our ragged breaths colliding in the small space between us. My pulse thudded in my ears. A thousand memories rose to the surface at once.

Then, I peeled his hands away. "I feel much better now. I am going to go back to my room."

He stood back, but the space that we had just occupied was still charged, raw and unfinished.

CHAPTER THIRTY-ONE

Asha

I was thankful to run into Kitchi on the way back to my rooms. I had no idea how I would have explained myself had someone else seen me with my corset unbuttoned and my dress loose in my hands.

Once we were back in our rooms, she silently removed the corset and replaced it with a fresh one. I'd convinced myself I would slink into bed without having to explain myself when Kitchi rounded on me. "It is none of my business..." she began.

"You are right; it is not."

"But it seems to me," she continued, "that people might have something to say about your leaving Adriel's quarters half-dressed and hair in disarray like you are coming back from a good tumble."

My jaw fell open. "I was in Adriel's quarters?"

"I don't know how he got you in there without being seen. But had I not run into you, that certainly would have changed. Do you two want to be found out? If so, get on with it," she said in exasperation. "And burn it, if you are found out, let it be away from the monarch whose daughter is betrothed to him."

I shook my head. "It was a mistake. My corset was too tight…"

"I'm sure it was, and an engaged man happened to be the one to loosen it for you. Do you understand how insane that sounds?"

"It doesn't matter. I've made my choice of who I will marry, and it is not Adriel."

There was more Kitchi was burning to say, I could feel it, but we were interrupted by a knock on the door. My mouth widened like we'd already been found out. Kitchi calmly walked to the door to answer it. A silver aura shot into the room and embraced me.

"Princess Celia," Kitchi announced.

"Oh, I know I should not barge in here like this, but I am just so excited, and I need another woman to gush over this!"

Ice filled my chest as the air shifted from her hands passing between us.

"You can't see without your dragon, can you? Here," she said, placing my fingers over hers.

The ring was large, so large I wondered how she could lift her finger at all.

"Is this the same ring? It feels different," I said, remembering the one in Nayeli's bag.

"That was the promise ring, do you feel the wedding ring? It is onyx," she said before I could respond. "Isn't it lovely?"

"Two rings. That is really special."

"Isn't Addy romantic?"

"Addy?" I asked, tilting my head.

"Oh, that is my pet name for him. He adores it."

"I'm sure he does," Kitchi said from the door. "If there is nothing else, I will check on the War Chief to make sure he is decent for tonight."

"Tonight?" I asked.

"Oh yes," Celia cut in. "Our engagement party is tonight. You have to come. I did not have time to send invitations, but I would love to have you there for female presence. Will you come?"

"I—my brother isn't well," I began.

"My father's shaman is with him now," she said quickly. "Please, Asha. It would mean so much to me."

I hesitated, knowing resistance would only draw questions. "Of course," I said finally. "But I can't stay too long."

Her face lit up. "That is just wonderful! And there's something else I wanted to ask." She clapped her hands together. "Since you and Adriel are so close, would you consider being part of the ceremony? A kind of attendant. Having you there would mean so much—to him, and to me."

My stomach tightened. "I don't know if that's wise."

"Oh, please," she said, smiling earnestly. "It would make him so happy. And having you there would make everything feel... right."

I forced a smile, guilt blooming sharp and sudden in my chest. "Of course," I said softly. "I'd be honored."

She squealed and wrapped me in a quick hug. "I knew you'd say yes! I'll see you tonight."

As she swept out of the room, the weight of what I'd agreed to settled heavily in my chest. I pressed a hand to my sternum, steadying myself.

I can do this, I told myself. *I have to.*

I dressed very carefully. The need to evoke strength and power was even more important as Drakkar had not returned. Thankfully, Chato had agreed to escort me to the party.

He whistled as I came into the drawing room of my suite. "Black suits you well, though you might want to brighten your mood for the bride. This isn't a funeral." He twirled me around before saying, "Which one of your suitors is this dress for?"

"You are ridiculous," I said, shaking my head. "I can't even see what I have on."

"I love when smart women play dumb. It is what I live for."

I lightly punched his shoulder. "Watch the jokes. Someone could hear you."

"I am only scared of two people, Kitchi and Adriel, and I am only in danger with one of them tonight."

I could tell he wanted me to ask which one, but I did not bother. I needed to focus.

By the time I entered the ballroom, I could see dozens of auras twirling about, alive with curiosity.

King Fourie greeted me first. "I received your message. You've made your decision then?"

"I have."

He lifted my hand to kiss it and leaned in. "I trust we will all be happy with your choice."

"I trust you will," I said noncommittally.

"We will await King Dija and Kadir before making the announcement. Zaib is already here. I bid you enjoy your last free evening, my dear, before then."

I curtsied before Chato took the cue to escort me further into the room. He steered me toward a cluster of chairs along the edge of the ballroom where I could feel the vibration of music and dancing feet and the heat from the crowd just ahead of us. I settled into a chair, and Chato dropped into the one beside me where he conversed happily, noting all the women in the room he admired. "Even your rival Celia looks pretty in white. That is the rival color to black, is it not? Did you plan that?"

"We are not rivals," I reminded him.

"Tell her!" he exclaimed. "Every time Adriel looks this way, she jumps in front of him. Poor thing."

"Don't you have someone you could be dancing with?"

"I'll have you know I have a date later tonight. I want to save my energy for her."

Now he'd piqued my interest. "Who?" I asked.

"Now, now. I know you've always wanted me for my body, but you have enough suitors to last a lifetime."

"Chato," I scoffed, shaking my head. "It is unlike you to be secretive."

He smacked his lips together as if thinking. "Okay, but if I tell you, swear you won't tell Kitchi or Moki."

"I swear," I said with a sweet smile.

"Her name is Viola?"

I searched my memory, trying to place the name. "You don't mean... my dressmaker," I gasped.

"You say it as if it's a curse."

"No, I just... I am impressed you are seeing her again," I said.

He squeezed one of my fingers discreetly. "Thank you. I like her a lot... not as much as you of course, Your Highness," he said. "But close."

"What are you doing with me? I'm here now," I said. "Go find her. Have fun."

"I can't leave you. You'd be a lamb in a den full of wolves."

"Except this lamb has a dragon." It did not seem prudent to bring up that my dragon was nowhere to be found. "Go. I'll be fine."

He hesitated. "If you are sure."

"Go before I change my mind."

He kissed my hand before standing, the chair scraping the floor beside me. I reached out with my battlemage, taking stock of all of the auras around me. I was alone again.

"Is this seat taken?"

Zaib's aura approached. "Not anymore," I said.

"Could I sit with you, or if you'd rather, we could dance?"

"No, I much prefer to sit. You are welcome to do so with me."

The chair creaked as he sat. I felt the heat from his body as he moved in close so that I could hear him over the music. "You look exceptional tonight, Your Highness. I dare say every man has noticed, even the women."

I tucked my loose hair behind my ear. "I have a question for you."

He leaned in closer. "Yes?"

"You never told me your plan for the Lightbearers, how you would find them."

"We were interrupted, weren't we? And you have been understandably occupied with your brother, so I haven't had the chance." He exhaled. "I have to tell you, it excites me that you want to know. I'd heard you'd made your decision and assumed I was out of the running since we had not discussed it."

"So you came over here to change my mind?"

He chuckled. "I like you a lot. I find it endearing you are mostly immune to my charms, for now."

"You have charm?"

"You see what I mean," he said, caressing my knuckles. "When I am around you, I feel... off-center, like you are the only person who can set me straight."

I cleared my throat and pulled my hand away. "I'm listening."

"I already know where hundreds of Lightbearers are. I planned to take you to them."

I inhaled sharply at his words. "Hundreds?"

"Yes."

"That is impossible. I would know of such a place."

"Unless it isn't on any published map."

"You are talking about the Ifambe, aren't you?"

"You know the islands?" he asked with surprise. "Who told you about them?"

"That doesn't matter now. You know where it is?"

"I know every island in the Caan Sea. The Lightbearers reside on the biggest of the Ifambe islands. They call it Orunma."

"Have you been there? Why is it not on any maps?" I asked excitedly.

"Keep your voice down," he said in a hushed tone. "The island is forbidden. It was removed from all maps."

"But wouldn't people still speak of it? There are Lightbearers that live there."

"Not if they want to live. Not even my father wants to speak of it."

I stood suddenly. "Can you take me to it?"

"I would love to," he said, standing beside me. "Only, I think your betrothed would not approve... unless you were planning to choose me. I wouldn't want to be presumptuous."

My lip twitched upward. "I'm sure you wouldn't."

"You have quite a decision to make, Princess. I do not envy it," he whispered in my ear, "but even if it is not me you choose, I'll take you."

My heart clenched at his words. I had no idea if they were true, but if they were false, he was very convincing.

"You would do that?"

"I would."

Before I could respond, Zaib's aura shifted as someone approached. He squeezed my hand briefly.

"Think on what I said," he murmured before melting into the sea of auras.

A sudden hush fell as Fourie's voice cut through the hall. "Honored guests," he declared, "I hate to break up the merriment because it appears everyone is having such a good time. Before we continue, I would like to acknowledge the presence of Princess Asha of Ujuima..."

Polite, if apprehensive, applause erupted. I exhaled slowly, the tenseness in my shoulders increasing.

"We are glad she is here and look forward to her announcement later this evening," Fourie continued. "But first, I would like to take a moment to speak about the joyous union we are all here for between my daughter, Princess Celia, and Prince Adriel, soon to be King of Wiyotak."

Enthusiastic applause followed.

"This would not be a Wyrmwood event if there weren't some surprises in store," he continued.

People in the crowd began to murmur amongst themselves.

"Aren't nuptials supposed to be happy occasions?"

I startled as I saw Ashkii's aura along the wall beside me. "Go away before you are spotted."

"I've been here all night. No one has given me a second glance," he said. "You know you could change your mind about all of this and come with me."

There was something in his voice. It was almost a pity. "You know, I've been thinking. You are not typically caught off guard. It is what has made you such a great spy for the Guardians."

"And?" he asked.

"You knew Adriel was there last night, didn't you?"

"Are you still thinking about our kiss?" He chuckled. "How would our dear War Chief feel about that?"

"What did they do to you?" I asked. "How did you get to be so cruel?"

"It is not cruel to be honest, Ash. It is freedom."

"You're not fooling me. You are not free. You are still doing the bidding of someone else even if you won't admit it."

His aura approached, and I clenched my fists, unsure of what he meant to do. He leaned over and whispered, "Get out while you can. They are coming."

"What?" But when I reached for him, he was no longer there.

Before I could call out, I caught the last of Fourie's speech. "Tonight, there will be a surprise wedding. These love birds just couldn't wait."

I wouldn't have been able to describe what I was feeling if I had tried. I swallowed, but I felt what I had for lunch threatening to come up.

People were clapping and shouting with enthusiasm as Fourie called for the alaga to officiate. I needed to get out of here. I couldn't stay for this. Celia had known when she'd invited me here tonight.

Adriel had to have known as well, and he'd still kissed me. The betrayal made me clench my chest as if I could pick my heart off the floor. I shouldn't care. This should not bother me, but it did.

"Give us a moment, everyone. My daughter needs her veil."

I couldn't stay. I fought my way through the crowd, making little progress, when I heard it. Drakkar's call. The commotion in the room began to quiet as the sound of Drakkar's growls filled the room.

"*They are coming, Little One,*" he said. "*We must go. We must go now.*"

"*Who?*"

"*Elan.*"

CHAPTER THIRTY-TWO

Asha

I thanked every gods-forsaken hour I'd spent memorizing the palace layout. My feet carried me without hesitation straight to Kwasi's chambers. I burst inside, crossed the room in three strides, and gripped his shoulders. "Wake up! Kwasi, please, we are in danger!"

Kwasi moaned as if he was waking from a deep slumber, stretching far too slowly for the moment. "It is good to see you, little sister."

"Yes, you too. Come, we must hurry," I said, shoving his shoes on his feet. "This room has no windows. We need one—help me find the nearest."

"Alright, alright," he yawned. "But I don't know what the fuss is abo—"

"I have Kwasi," I sent down the bond. *"Come get us."*

"I am almost there."

The door flew open before Kwasi and I could emerge from it. I buckled under Kwasi's weight, and I would have tumbled if Adriel's arms had not steadied me.

"It's Elan. He's here."

"I know," he said as if he'd sprinted here. "The alarm has been sounded. We need to leave quickly." Adriel shifted Kwasi's weight onto himself.

"Follow me."

We made our way down the staircase. Auras rushed by as screams and frantic breathing erupted.

I panted, trying to keep up with Adriel, and I wasn't even carrying anyone. We stepped into the hall and immediately I saw a wall of auras ahead. They were solid and unmoving, as if they were blocking the corridor.

The shifting of boots and the clink of armor met my ears. A weapon in front of us was lifted—or lowered—I couldn't tell which.

"No one passes!" a guard barked.

Adriel reached us then; I felt his presence like a flare of heat behind my shoulder.

"Let us pass," he said, voice hard as iron. "I am Prince Adriel. Princess Asha and her brother must be taken to safety. Your king would demand it."

The guards murmured to themselves nervously.

"Your Highness," one of them said, "you and the princess can pass, but we have received direct orders not to allow him to leave."

"Surely that is not a factor now that we are under siege."

"We have not had any updates to our orders. Therefore, the prince must remain here. We will get you and the princess to safety, but Prince Kwasi will have to return to his quarters."

My pulse slammed in my ears as I heard the unmistakable sound of Adriel's blade being drawn.

"No!" I grabbed for his wrist blindly, fingers closing around warm skin, stopping the motion before it could finish. "Not with Kwasi here."

The guards' stance changed as their auras hummed with energy ready to strike. "I will go with you," I told the guard.

"Your Highness," Adriel warned.

"I need assistance," I said, indicating the one who appeared to be in charge.

"Of course," he said. As he reached for me, I touched his aura.

You will let us through. All of us. I pushed the thought from my aura. A hollow space opened beneath my senses, and then images slammed into me.

A raven dropped screaming into a pit. Fire. Screams. Dragons writhing in chains of glowing stone. I gasped as a familiar pair of golden eyes locked with mine—Baquar's—his roar tearing through my skull as pain and fury surged together.

I staggered back, breath ripping from my chest. "Is something wrong, Your Highness?" the guard asked.

I shook my head. "You are a Shadow," I whispered. It wasn't a question.

I did not hear what he said next because more guards approached screaming, "Elan's army has breached the palace! They're inside the east wing!"

Screams followed as footsteps thundered toward us. Metal clashed as swords reached out to strike.

Adriel swore as he pulled me away.

I clutched my shaking hands. "We can't go forward."

"No," he said. "We can't."

CHAPTER THIRTY-THREE

Adriel

"By order of King Fourie, you are to remain here until the danger has passed."

I shifted slightly, putting myself in front of Asha. "Step aside," I said, voice low. "I am not subject to your king's commands."

The most decorated of them, the one who had thoroughly frightened Asha, stepped forward. "We have orders. You'll come with us."

My blood was already running hot. Every instinct screamed at me to cut them down and carve a path forward. It had been a mistake to go after Asha without a few Guardians at my back. My battlemage could wipe them out; I just wasn't certain I could do it without Asha getting hurt in the process.

A tremor shook the castle, dust falling from the beams above. The guards flinched. Their hesitation was all I needed. I shifted Kwasi off my shoulder onto Asha, pulling my blade free when another figure emerged.

"There you are!" Zaib shouted.

He strode toward us, his eyes cutting to Asha. "What is the meaning of this?" he asked the guards before his eyes flickered to me. "If anyone will be in charge of her safety, it is me. Come," he said, offering Asha his hand as though the whole castle weren't crumbling above us. "I've found a way out."

The guards glanced at one another, suddenly uncertain whose orders to follow. Zaib didn't spare them a second look. He had the air of someone used to being obeyed.

"Stop!" one of them called, lunging forward. My battlemage flared—hot, instinctive. I thrust a wall of fire between us, but they leapt through it without hesitation. A sudden gust tore through the corridor, whipping my hair into the flames. Fire roared upward, licking the ceiling as screams echoed behind us.

Zaib caught my eye as he drew his magic back. "Let's go," he said.

I shifted my stance so I could lift Kwasi fully onto my shoulders. "How do we know the way you are taking us is safe?" I asked.

Zaib's smile didn't reach his eyes. "Safe? Nothing is safe, not tonight. But my route is less suicidal than yours, I'd wager. Unless you prefer to fight off more of Fourie's men."

I did not. If I was going to use my battlemage, I needed to save it for the enemy. "Where are you taking us?"

"Through the south wing," Zaib said smoothly. "There's a servant's gate—unguarded, for now. I've secured it."

My jaw clenched. Secured. This all sounded like a trap.

I buckled as dragon fire hit the castle walls. They shuddered, as if the castle would collapse on itself at any moment.

"We don't have time for this," Zaib said. "Are you coming or not?"

Asha answered for us. "Show us, then."

Zaib bowed shallowly. "With pleasure, Princess."

As he led the way, I tightened my hold on my sword. I didn't trust him—not his timing, not his sudden appearance, and not the glint in his eyes when it came to her.

The area he took us to had not yet been breached, as promised. If Zaib wanted to cut me down with my sword arm bearing the weight of another, now was the perfect time to do it.

"We must move quickly then," Zaib said as he loosened a curtain. When he lifted it up, I could see a pathway.

"Do we know where this leads?" I asked.

"It leads to the grotto from yesterday afternoon."

The journey through the castle was long, and we had to stop a couple of times so that Asha could catch her breath.

"They make a cute couple, don't they? She chose well."

I startled at Kwasi's voice. I'd leaned him against the wall to give my shoulders a break.

"I—" My eyes shifted again to Asha.

"Let's move!" Zaib called.

"We should probably keep moving," I finally said. "Can you walk?"

"As much as I enjoy being carried, I appreciate being able to walk."

"Well, we need to run," I clarified. "Let's go."

The area narrowed as we made our way into a cave that the room was carved into.

The further we went, the narrower the path and the lower the oxygen that was available. Water began to collect at our feet as we continued marching deeper and deeper. I pulled on my battlemage to cast a blue ring above us to guide our way. We stopped at a V-shaped crevice that had water trickling out. Zaib pointed. "We will need to pass through and swim up."

"How far?" I asked, trying to gauge it, but all I could see was darkness.

"Fifty meters."

I shook my head. "That is over a minute. How are we going to manage that?"

Zaib shrugged. "We will swim."

I looked at Asha. "Asha and Kwasi are Ujuiman. There is no way they have the training to be underwater for that long."

"I am not certain I can do it," Asha began, "but I am even more worried about Kwasi."

Zaib patted her hand. "We'll have help." He called out into the water, and before I could blink, two sea dragons appeared from the depths.

"How do we know they won't drown us?" I asked.

Zaib frowned. "Because they do as I command. All sea creatures of Entioch obey their rulers. They'll get us up there quickly if I command it."

I breathed heavily and then appealed to Asha. "It is too dangerous. We will find another way."

She shook her head. "There are soldiers behind us. The longer we wait, the more likely they will be upon us. This is our best opportunity."

"Alright," I said, my jaw clenched. "But Asha goes with me."

"Not a chance," Zaib ground out.

"We don't have time for this! Please take care of my brother," Asha pleaded, brushing her hand on his damp forehead dripping with sweat. She turned back to me. "Can I trust you with this?"

I searched her face, and had I not felt the desperation in her voice, I might have refused. "I've got him."

She nodded, her shoulders releasing tension from my words. "Let's hurry," she said.

"I will jump in first," he said. "They must hear my command. You jump right after Asha. The more you delay, the longer I have to hold my breath."

"I understand," she said.

"Alright," he said, pushing his right hand through. He began moving slowly into the crevice until nearly half his body was submerged. He looked toward her. "They are here. Jump in right behind me."

I blinked, and he was gone. Asha moved to follow, but I gripped her hand before she could. "Don't do anything foolish."

She nodded before jumping into the water.

I turned to Kwasi, who appeared barely awake. I lightly slapped his cheeks. "Wake up, Kwasi. You heard her."

He gave a lopsided grin. "My sister can carry a grudge. But I'll be honest, I don't think there is anything you could do that she wouldn't forgive."

My lips tightened into a thin line as I searched for what to say. When I reached and found nothing, I said, "Just make sure you follow right behind me." I put my hand in the water first. It was frigid. Every cell in my body screamed, but I pushed forward until I managed to find the tail. I hoped it was a sea dragon because if it wasn't, we'd have bigger problems to deal with. "I can feel where I'm going. Right behind me," I said, using my free hand to grip his.

"Yes, right behind you," he assured me.

I did not feel assured, but there was nothing I could do but trust. I turned to the water and began to push my way through. There wasn't any light. I had to use my battlemage to be able to see. I was indeed grasping the tail of the sea dragon. Knowing our time was short, I quickly mounted it and looked behind me to wait for Kwasi to come all the way through. He was about half in. I tugged on his hand, but he resisted.

Come on. Come on.

Then I felt a tug from the other way. I nearly lost his hand. Someone was on the other side of him, I realized.

The force with which he was being dragged in the other direction increased. I had one shot, or we were lost. I sent a blast of fire through the crevice, so bright, Kwasi shook, but I was able to pull him through. I wasted no time putting him on the sea dragon. He slumped over and held on as I slapped the dragon to spur him forward. The creature moved immediately through the water. I calmed my body to reserve my energy stores and closed my fingers over Kwasi's nose and mouth. We had seconds. Water had probably already entered his lungs. I slapped the sea dragon again, which it did not like. I counted to ten and began to feel my lungs strain. Attempts to calm my body floundered as the sea dragon's tail whipped me from side to side.

It was trying to throw me off, I realized. ...15...16...17. I waited, ready for us to breach the water, but we were still traveling. ...18...19...20. Kwasi was convulsing underneath me as he struggled for air. We could not wait. I grabbed Kwasi by the waist and used a cool fireball to propel us off the dragon and what I hoped was upward. If I was wrong and we were going the wrong direction, there wouldn't be time to change course. We would be dead. ...28...29...30.

My lungs were screaming but all I could do was lean into my battlemage. Either I was close and would reach it in a few short seconds, or we were dead ... 33...34...35.

CHAPTER THIRTY-FOUR

Asha

The water was frigid, but Zaib's grip was unrelenting. He hauled me upward, slicing through the blackness until we broke the surface. I gasped, shivering as I staggered onto the slick stone at the edge of the grotto. My chest burned from holding my breath for so long.

I sat there for a moment, catching my breath—until I realized something was wrong. I did not see Adriel's aura. Or Kwasi's. "Where are they?" When Zaib did not answer, I reached for him, making contact with his arm. "Where are they?"

"I don't know," he said.

"What do you mean?" I asked frantically. "They should already be here. What could have happened?"

"Perhaps they needed extra time."

I didn't let him finish. I stumbled toward the water's edge. "We have to find them!"

Zaib caught me by the waist and pulled me back. "We can't. The water's too dark to search."

"I should have gone with them. I—"

Before I could finish the sentence, Adriel's aura emerged from beneath the water. He coughed as if his lungs were full of liquid. I looked around eagerly, waiting to see Kwasi's aura emerge as well, but it didn't.

"Adriel, what happened?"

"I have him," he said, pulling something heavy out of the water. Kwasi? I couldn't see his aura. I couldn't see him! "Kwasi!" I yelled.

I bent down beside Adriel and gripped Kwasi. "He's not breathing."

"Get back," Adriel ordered. Then the rhythmic thud of chest compressions filled the cavern, his counting steady despite his own labored breathing.

Seconds blurred. Then Adriel began coughing again, exhausted. "Move aside," Zaib said. "I got him." The chest compressions continued as Zaib took over, then the push of air as he breathed into his lungs with his battlemage. It went on so long, I feared the worst.

My chest tightened until it hurt. "Kwasi," I whispered, reaching for him. His aura flickered faintly beneath my touch, like a dying ember. I tried to grasp it—anything—but it slipped through me, thinning, fading.

"Come on," I begged. "Please."

Zaib's hands stilled.

"Move!" a voice barked from behind us.

I spun. "Who—"

"I've got him." Miren pushed past me, dropping to her knees at his side, which meant...

"I'm here, Little One."

The relief I felt at Drakkar's presence shifted into fear as Miren's aura surged and Kwasi began to gag as if he was drowning on dry land. I reached for her instinctively, panic clawing up my throat. "Stop!"

She shoved me back with surprising force.

"It's all right," Adriel said hoarsely. "She's pulling the water from his lungs."

"She's killing him!"

A loud cough filled the cave as Kwasi's aura blazed. His cough continued, but he was breathing. I watched as Miren's aura continued to drape over him. "Are you okay?"

"I am now," he rasped when Miren eased back.

"There were soldiers on the other side," Adriel said urgently. "We need to go. They may follow us."

***

Smoke clung to my lungs as we exited the cave mouth. The distant sounds of Elan's soldiers still audible from the castle grounds. We moved fast and low, Adriel's hand at my back, Drakkar in the air, keeping his distance but close enough for me to regain sight.

Kwasi was supported by Miren and Zaib. I had no staff. I had no cloak. The night air bit through the thin fabric of my gown and I didn't care.

"This way," Adriel said tersely. We ran for I don't know how long. Long enough that the sounds of soldiers faded behind us, long enough that Kwasi had to stop twice to cough the remaining water from his lungs.

We found Moki first, then Chato. Their clothes were torn, their skin bloodied, but thankfully, the wounds were superficial.

"Kitchi?" I asked immediately.

"Here." Her voice came from somewhere to my left, rough but steady. "I've gone to better parties."

The Guardians had managed to gather several horses from the stables and a few supplies before the attack overtook the palace grounds. Candy was among them, which was the first thing that had gone right all evening. The tents and supply carts had been left at the outskirts of the castle grounds too large to be permitted through the gates. The fighting within the castle meant there was no one on the perimeter to stop the Guardians from retrieving them.

Kwasi was mounted on the first and I on Candy at Adriel's insistence.

We caught up with the Guardians first, and Zaib's men. King Fourie joined us an hour later with his soldiers. Most of them did not have much in their possession, except the weapons and clothes on their back. King Dija and Kadir's absence was chilling.

Princess Celia rushed to Adriel the moment she saw him, wrapping her arms around his neck. He bent instinctively to meet her embrace. I turned away, needing distance from the tenderness of it. It wasn't their fault I felt this way, but that didn't make it easier to watch.

The shamans were upon Kwasi immediately. He had a couple of broken ribs from compressions, but other than that he seemed alright, more lucid than he had been in days.

"What is the plan now that we know Dija has betrayed us?" Adriel asked.

Fourie held up his hands. "We don't know that."

"Actually, we do," Miren said beside me. All eyes shifted to the tall, graceful figure. "I saw the Shadowcasters and Firepeak's army conversing with Elan's men. They are allies."

Fourie turned sharply toward her. "And who are you to make such a claim?"

I turned to Miren, unsure of how to explain her presence. But I needn't worry, because she said, "I am Miren Tolenhail, second Light-bearer, bonded to Zephyr."

All the men startled at her revelation. "The second dragon," Zaib began. "He is yours."

"I am his," she corrected.

The certainty in her voice stole my breath. Only days ago, she had wanted nothing to do with him.

Zaib looked skyward. "And where is this dragon?"

She put her hands on her hips. "He will appear when he is ready, not when you want him to. He is not like the dragons of the Ujuiman court. He has a mind of his own."

I stepped in then. "She is going to lead our army of Lightbearers." I locked eyes with her. "As you can see, we will need more."

"And what will we do about the traitor Dija?" Adriel asked once more. "He knows all of our plans, which means so does Elan, and the Shadowcasters."

"I don't see why our plans must change," Zaib said.

"Of course not," Adriel ground out between clenched teeth. "You now have no competition for your bride."

Zaib looked at me apologetically. "The princess is within her right to refuse any agreement she has entered into, seeing as we are the party that did not hold up the deal. It is her decision."

All eyes fell on me, and I felt closed in. I cleared my throat before saying, "Dija does not know *all* of our plans."

"Of course he does," Fourie said. "Their armies are probably headed to Entioch as we speak to retaliate."

"They will never be able to take us by sea," Zaib said. "If they try it, they will lose."

"So you are all going to live at sea?" Adriel asked.

"Do you have a better idea?" Zaib challenged.

"I do," I said. Again, eyes flickered to me. I stared at Zaib. "Zaib knows where to find more Lightbearers. A whole island full of them."

"Impossible," Adriel said.

Zaib smiled. "Is it? I have promised to take Princess Asha." He looked toward me. "That offer still stands."

"We should go to the island, get reinforcements," I said. "With the help of Lightbearers, we can make a difference. We wouldn't have to run."

"How do we know that this will even work?" Fourie mused. "If we split up, we could gather reinforcements. That seems to be the safer option, especially, when we don't know that Lightbearers could be assembled in time to be of help."

"We have to try," I said. "I have seen them fight. We need their help."

Zaib nodded. "My fleet can take the long route to Entioch and secure ships for the crossing."

"And Fourie's army can hold here," Adriel added. "Buy the rest of us time. My Guardians will take Princess Asha through the mountain passes. It's longer, but safer."

"And why," Zaib asked coolly, "would the princess go with you?"

Adriel met his gaze without flinching. "Because it's the safest route. The passes are warded. Your path by sea will be watched, and your ships will be contested. Mine won't."

"I could accompany them as well," Celia offered. "Adriel and I are practically married already. It would be fun. We can have girl talk," she said to me with a wink.

My stomach twisted.

"No," Adriel said. When Celia looked up at him with a wounded expression he clarified. "We are limited in supplies. There are not enough to support the number of soldiers and Guardians require to protect both princesses."

Fourie looked reluctant but the more I learned about this man, the more I understood that he would do anything for his children. I wondered where his son was right now. Where had he evacuated him to? Fourie and I looked at one another, as if waiting for me to reveal his secret.

"I think it is a good idea for Celia to come," I offered. I turned to Zaib. "And the answer is yes."

Zaib looked at me with confusion. "Yes, you will come with me?"

My chest tightened, realizing what I was about to say. "Yes, I will accept your hand. After you take us to the island, I am yours."

He walked toward me and grasped my hand. "You don't have to. I will take you to the island regardless." He hesitated. "Asha, are you sure?"

Was I? "Yes, unless... you have changed your mind."

He grinned, walking toward me away from the others. It was just enough to make it feel private, despite the audience as he lifted me in his arms. "Never. I plan on making you so happy, Asha."

I couldn't help but return his smile. The giddiness in his expression was sweet. He lowered me slowly until we were only breaths apart.

"Isn't this romantic?" Celia gushed. "Kiss her!"

Zaib leaned in like he might but his lips stopped at my ear instead. "No," he said, looking over my shoulder briefly before meeting my gaze once more. "I haven't earned you yet," he said. "But I will."

"Celia you may go," Fourie said, looking relieved by the turn of events. His eyes flicked to Adriel. "We will part with some of our supplies to go along with our soldiers. I will also loan you a liminal mage. You can make use of his ability to widen tents and carts."

Celia was beaming next to Adriel. "We could have a double wedding."

Adriel tugged on her arm. "Let's give them some privacy. They will want to say their goodbyes," he said, pulling her away. Adriel would not return my gaze.

The world seemed to tilt beneath my feet then, as if something irrevocable had shifted.

What have you done, Little One? Drakkar's voice echoed softly in my mind.

Chapter Thirty-Five

Adriel

I'd disentangled myself from Celia, murmuring some excuse about needing to relieve myself. I raced into the trees and started running, away from Celia, away from my Guardians, away from *her*.

Moving into an unknown forest when Elan's army were just upon us was not my best plan, but the way I was feeling I welcomed the challenge. I needed to break something.

I unsheathed my blade and slashed it in front of me without much thought. My sword met bark with a satisfying *thwack*. It wasn't enough, so I repeated the motion, over and over again, bark crumbling from the tree revealing soft, piney flesh. At some point the tree must have had enough or my blade gave out because the edge of it bounced of with such force it landed several feet over my shoulder.

I leaned over the tree gasping for the air I'd been depriving myself since I'd started swinging. My heart constricted, but no matter how deeply I inhaled, the muscles would not release.

I cursed as the memory of Asha, accepting Zaib's proposal came unbidden into my mind. Of course she had to choose him. Dija had betrayed us, which was no surprise to me. Fourie was playing his own game, and I doubted he ever intended a true courtship. That left Zaib, the man I trusted the least, not because of anything he'd said or done, but precisely because he hadn't done anything. His father, King Musa was misogynistic and arrogant, but so were most royals. Zaib on the other hand was a mystery, which made him dangerous.

A low whistle sounded in the distance. I did not bother being on guard, but instead slid to the ground as Chato came into view. He ran his hands through his auburn hair, as his dark eyes met mine. He crossed his hands over his chest before saying, "Well you are handling this well."

I gathered pebbles in my hand and threw them in his direction. He jumped to the side to avoid them just in time which elicited a low growl from me. "You don't know what you are talking about."

Chato raised an eyebrow. "Clearly."

"Go away, Chato. I need to be alone."

Chato stood quietly for a moment but did not move to leave. "Why don't you just tell h—"

"Why are you here, Chato? What is so important that you cannot give me a moment?"

Chato sighed heavily but relented. "Zaib wanted a word with you. I told him it wasn't a good time, and that you... would be busy making arrangements."

My jaw tightened at his words. "Go on."

"Well he has certain conditions for the princess to travel with us. And Fourie agreed."

I slid my hands over my face leaning my head back on the tree I had taken my frustration out on. "I should have never come here," I said shaking my head. "I could be in Wiyotak, picking our next ruler. That's where I should be, not here."

"Wiyotak would never be safe," Chato offered. "Not with the Shadowcasters growing their ranks. I thought it was bad in Wiyotak, but Firepeak was so much worse. You are doing the right thing... even if it is not easy for you."

He was right of course. I'd contemplated retiring from the Guardians, living out my days alone. I'd even practiced it, spending many nights throwing back spirits just to chase away any emotion I did not like. But in the taverns I'd seen them, the masked men, plying people with promises of food, stable work, and something much more dangerous, a purpose that was not that of building up Wiyotak. The journey I was on was inevitable.

My hand moved the interior pocket of my cloak before I'd made the decision to reach for it, tension easing as my fingers closed around a familiar weight. The true purpose of why I was even here, looking for Asha, I'd had to keep secret, even from Chato. When the time came and she learned what I had done, what I continued to do—she'd hate me again. I would deserve it.

She should accept Zaib's proposal. He wouldn't betray her like I had.

"What does our newly engaged prince want now?" I asked, getting to my feet.

Chato held up a large bundle wrapped in brown paper. "Something Asha is not going to like."

My mouth quirked at the thought.

CHAPTER THIRTY-SIX

Asha

The plan was to camp overnight and move further into the mountains tomorrow to make the long journey to Entioch. I'd said my goodbyes to Zaib.

"I can't wait for my family to meet you," he'd said. "They are going to love you."

Family. That was a foreign word. Other than Kwasi and early memories of my mother, it was a foreign concept. I'd nearly made it to the tent that had been set for me when Miren pulled me from my thoughts. "I know I should let you bask in your newly engaged glow," she whispered furiously, "but we need to talk."

I smiled, grasping her around the shoulders. "We do!" I said. "We should be celebrating. You finally bonded. Where is Zephyr? I am certain he is over the moon."

She licked her lips. "He is..." She looked toward the tent. "But that is not—"

"And don't worry about the disagreement we had before. I know you wouldn't have turned me in. You were just afraid and who wou ldn.'t"

"Actually I..." She grasped my hand and took a deep breath. "Follow me."

It wasn't the words so much as how she said them that gave me pause. I did not have too long to dwell on them as Drakkar rounded the corner, and everything inside me went still.

He lowered his head in a gesture that felt formal, not unlike the deference he showed Mattias. We held each other's gaze for a strained, uneasy moment. "You came back," I finally said.

"Of course I did," he breathed. *"You are mine."*

"What I said before..."

"You were right," he said quickly. *"If you cannot tell those you love the truth, then what you have is... meaningless."*

I ran to him then and wrapped my hands around his neck. *"I never want to fight like that again."*

He huffed. *"That is unlikely with how stubborn you are."* He pulled back. *"As happy as this makes me, there is something you should know."* I turned back to Miren.

"She said the same thing. What is going on, and where is Zephyr?" I asked.

Miren pointed to the tent. Drakkar nodded.

As soon as I entered, I caught sight of Zephyr's copper scales glinting in the sun. He lay on the ground at the foot of the bed, more like a domestic animal than the magnificent creature he was. My smile fell as I saw lumps moving on the bed within the covers.

"Zephyr? What—" A red tail poked out of the sheets, followed by a dark blue nose.

"You're here at last!" Mwana cried.

"Iyla!" Igbo and Ala shouted as all three rushed toward me, demanding to be embraced. I fell to the ground from their weight.

"Okay, one of you start talking," I said breathlessly.

"Gods," a voice whispered. I turned back, catching a glimpse of a surprised Adriel at the tent's entrance. "They are magnificent."

Mwana cocked her head sharply at the unfamiliar voice. "Who is that, Iyla? Is he a friend?"

Adriel stepped closer, his voice thick with awe. "These are them? The eggs?"

"They're not eggs anymore," I said softly. I dipped my head toward the hatchlings. "He is my friend, Adriel," I said, switching to Dragontongue.

Mwana studied him with intense suspicion. "He has long hair like you. Are you sure he is not a girl?"

I laughed. "I'm sure." I reached out my hand to the ground beside me. "Come sit and meet them."

Adriel was hesitant at first, but he eventually crouched next to me and watched them wide-eyed. They looked upon him with wonder, circling like curious cubs at first... until Igbo, bold as ever, leaned forward and brushed his nose against Adriel's cheek. Adriel, to his credit, did not flinch. "What is this on your face? Iyla does not have this."

Adriel cleared his throat. "It is stubble. Males have it."

My eyes widened. He'd learned Dragontongue and was speaking fluently.

Igbo used his front paw to scratch his face. "I don't."

Adriel seemed at a loss for words. "Well..."

"We do not have hair, son. We have barbels." I jumped slightly at Drakkar's voice. In all my time with him, I could count on one hand how often he addressed his brood aloud. His tone changed when he said son, edged with something like pride.

"When will we get them?" Ala asked.

Drakkar chuckled. "When you have completed adolescence. It won't be long now."

"What about me?" Mwana pouted.

Drakkar replied. "Your scales will become more vibrant. They will shine like your mother's did."

Mwana seemed pleased with this answer. She moved toward Adriel and climbed up his back. "How shiny are they now, Adriel?"

"Uhh... they look shiny to me."

She grinned brightly at that and looked over at me. "I like him."

Zephyr cleared his throat, and I noticed Miren leaning against him, a rare smile on her face.

"It's wonderful that you bonded, but I still don't understand how you all are here," I said. "Why are you not in Saeleria?"

"They were scary, Iyla!" Mwana said, crawling under my arm. "I had to close my eyes."

"Who?" I asked. "Who was scary?"

"The Shadowcasters have infiltrated Saeleria," Drakkar said somberly. "The dragons have been compromised."

I stood then, Mwana clinging to me with one talon in my tunic. "Where are they? What happened?"

"We barely made it out," Zephyr said, looking down.

"But Mattias. He would have fought," I protested.

"Mattias was weak," Zephyr continued. "He never heeded my warnings and now..." He paused, looking over at the hatchlings, stopping himself from saying more.

"But where have they gone? Did the dragons flee?"

Drakkar and Zephyr would not meet my gaze. Only Miren was brave enough to say, "We can only hope so."

I rubbed a hand across my face. The image I'd had before when I touched the Shadowcaster. I hadn't had time to stop and ponder what it all meant, but perhaps what I saw was real. They'd captured the dragons of Saeleria. "What are the Shadowcasters planning?" I asked. "We have to go save the dragons."

"No," Drakkar said. "It is not safe for you. And I will not put my hatchlings in danger."

"I hate to say it," Miren began, "but finding this Lightbearer island might be our best move."

Mwana's claws curled in my sleeve.

We talked for what must have been hours because Adriel finally stood, placing a sleeping Igbo and Ala next to Drakkar. "I've been neglecting my duties. I must make sure we are ready to move in the morning." He looked toward me. "You should eat something," he said before walking out.

When I turned around, Miren was watching me curiously. Drakkar and Zephyr also had their eyes trained on me.

"What?"

Drakkar was the first to speak. "Do we hate him today, or is he your ally once more?"

Redness crept into my cheeks. I stood, dusting off dirt from my gown. "I am going to check on Kwasi."

"What is this?" Kwasi said, swinging me around. "I saw you last night, and you act like it's been days," he said, putting me down. "Do you not have a change of clothes?"

I stared into his eyes. "You don't remember then?"

"Remember what?" Before I could respond, his eyes flicked over to Zephyr, then Drakkar. "Are those—" His eyes flicked back to me. "Are these the little dragons?"

He crouched without being asked, head level with Igbo, who hissed a puff of smoke. Kwasi laughed despite himself, coughing as the smoke entered his lungs.

"Igbo!" I called. "This is my brother. Don't be rude."

"Sorry, Iyla," he said with a drooping head.

"What is he saying?" Kwasi asked.

"That you scared him."

To apologize, Igbo offered his front paw.

"What does he want?" Kwasi asked.

"To shake your hand. Just because they are dragons doesn't mean they can't learn good manners."

He tentatively took Igbo's paw and shook it. Kwasi smiled as if he had just won the biggest prize. "Mother would be proud of you, Ash."

I smiled at him, trying to hide my sadness. I'd lost her already. I couldn't lose him too.

I could barely get my gown peeled off my body by the time I entered the tent. Thankfully, someone had left clothes for me.

It was tempting to slip under the covers without a nightgown, but I reluctantly wore it just in case we needed to move quickly. My legs gave out as soon as I pulled back the covers. I snuggled into the soft mattress and brought the luxurious blanket to my neck. This was nice, much too nice for the road. It was almost like someone had planned for me to be here.

As I lay, I began to think about the day's events, the feeling I had when Kwasi nearly died, the knowledge that Saeleria was compromised, the worry I had for the other dragons, and finally, the marriage proposal I'd accepted. I swallowed, reminding myself that I did make the right decision. But no matter how I justified it in my mind, I felt suffocated. I attempted to push back the blankets, but was surprised when they didn't move. I tried to sit up, but the blankets only sat more snugly around my body.

"What is this?" I asked, looking at Drakkar in a moment of panic. I wasn't uncomfortable exactly, but the feeling of being confined was unpleasant. Drakkar attempted to pull the ends of the blanket from my body, but he winced, dropping it from his mouth without making progress.

He ran his tongue over them, scowling. *"There is a spell woven into these covers. I can taste it."*

Footsteps approached outside. Drakkar turned to the door and growled, ready to attack.

Adriel stepped in, hands raised slightly, eyes flicking warily between Drakkar and me. Drakkar roared in warning.

"Oh—right, the blanket," Adriel said, dragging a hand down his face. "I nearly forgot."

"What is this? Get it off me," I snapped.

Adriel momentarily turned his eyes to me. They were filled with a touch of humor. He found this funny.

"I take back everything I said about this man," Drakkar seethed. *"I will burn him where he stands."*

"Don't," I warned.

I turned back to Adriel. "You better start talking. Drakkar is not taking kindly to your antics."

"May I approach?" he asked calmly.

"If it will get me out of here faster?"

He took a tentative step forward, ready to flee at the slightest flicker of smoke.

"There was concern about the chastity of the royal women on this trip," he began.

"You mean Celia and me?" I asked breathlessly. "I told you, no purity tests."

"But you didn't say no binding blankets." He held up a hand before I tore into him. "This does not test your purity in any way, so it doesn't violate the agreement. It is only meant to preserve you as you are."

I struggled against the weight of it. "You bastards. How dare you?"

"Don't be angry with me. It was your fiancé's idea. His and Fourie's."

"Right, and you had nothing to do with it."

He grimaced. "I don't enjoy tying down women unless they ask it of me, no."

My breath caught in my throat as I imagined him with women that did ask it of him.

"The blanket activates at nightfall," he explained pulling me from my thoughts. "But it will release at first light. For what it's worth... Celia isn't pleased either."

So, he'd gone to see her. That was where he'd been. I struggled more furiously, attempting to lift my legs. "This is ridiculous. I could take one of your Guardians to the woods if I wanted to and have my way with him and be back in this bed by nightfall."

Adriel's nose flared. "Is that what you plan to do? I imagine that would displease your betrothed."

"I feel like livestock!"

"Worse," he whispered, stalking forward. "You are the future of this new world we are building."

"I'm never getting in this bed again," I seethed.

"I'm afraid everything has been considered."

My heart quickened as he stood mere inches from the bed. His eyes roamed my form, as if he could see me beneath the blankets.

"If you do not sleep under the blanket, the blanket will find you and force you to lie wherever you are. So," he whispered, "take care it is not in the water or underneath a man."

Adriel watched me for a moment, then looked toward Drakkar. "I love to fight with you, Princess, but truthfully, it has been a long day." He retreated and grabbed a pillow from the chair by the entrance of the tent.

"What are you doing? Get me out of here."

He sat down and used the wooden post to prop the pillow on before laying his head back. "I can't. No one can until morning." He opened one eye slightly. "Don't worry. Whatever gets past me won't get past him."

"Adriel!"

"Sleep, Princess. I will see you in the morning."

"Drakkar!"

Drakkar looked at Adriel and then to me before shaking his head. "This is between you mortals. I am going to tuck in the hatchlings."

"Drakkar!"

"I told you to stay away from men. You never listen," he said before leaving the tent.

The more I struggled against the blanket, the tighter it got until I couldn't move even an inch. Light snores came from the entrance. How could he just sleep right now? Frustrated, I stopped moving, and in no time, sleep claimed me too.

Chapter Thirty-Seven

Asha

I woke up alone the next morning, the cursed blanket slipping from my shoulders as the first light of dawn crept into the tent. Adriel was gone from his post. We did not speak at all. My routine was the same every day. I would spend my mornings with Kwasi, my afternoons training with Moki, and every godforsaken evening, the evil blanket would come for me. It did not matter if I avoided the bed. I would turn around and by nightfall it would be draped around my body, demanding I sleep where I lay. And every night, Adriel would pay me a visit. My resentment of him grew and I learned to say less to him. What was the point?

Later, while I rested beside a narrow stream, Miren spoke softly. "What is that?"

I handed her the book Kadir had given me. "Some game wealthy men play. I'm not sure. Kadir thought it important." I shrugged. "I meant to give it to Kwasi when he wakes."

Her expression shifted as she placed the book on a dry rock, careful to keep it from the water. "I'm very sorry about your brother." The words caught me off guard. Gone was the venom she had for me before. It struck me how different she seemed now—steadier, softer. As though bonding with Zephyr had smoothed her sharpness, or perhaps they had steadied each other.

"There is still hope."

"Really?" she asked, her voice light in a way that made my chest ache.

"He's going to come out of it."

"Of course he is," Drakkar said, giving Zephyr a look.

"Tell me more of what happened to Mattias," I asked, changing the subject. "Did he say where he would go?"

"I think he eventually allowed them to," she said slowly, looking back at the hatchlings. They were at a distance, jumping in the stream. "I am not entirely sure if he survived." She paused. "It felt like he was telling us goodbye."

My heart clenched. Mattias shared that he'd lost all purpose when Seraphina had died and had found it again with her brood. Of course, he would have sacrificed himself to give them more time to escape.

"Perhaps the Lightbearers will know what to do," I said.

"Do you truly believe they are there?" she asked. "Why have they hidden themselves away instead of living in Saeleria?"

"Perhaps it is because they cannot bond with them." That was a theory I'd been floating, anyway. It was as good a guess as any.

"I don't trust it," Miren muttered. "I don't see how going to them is worth it."

"What if they've been waiting for us?" I offered.

"Like we are the chosen ones?" she snorted, turning her head to look back at Zephyr, who was playing hide and seek with Mwana in the shallows. "How do you do it?"

"What?" I asked, bewildered.

"Live without your sight. It is maddening the way it flickers in and out."

"I've been blind longer than I've been able to see. It is like walking from a green room to a blue one. It just... is," I said, shaking my head. "One is not better than the other, and I get some things from one that I don't get from the other and vice versa."

Miren's jaw dropped as she blinked furiously before turning to me. "Oh, I don't believe you at all."

"What?" I asked in confusion.

"You almost had me for a second," she laughed.

I looked to Drakkar, then to Zephyr, trying to piece together what I'd missed. "I don't know what you mean, but I'm serious."

She laughed harder, clutching her chest like she might split apart.

"Am I missing something?" I began—

But then my gaze followed hers, and whatever words were left on my lips dissolved immediately. Adriel stood waist-deep in the creek, shirt thrown aside and tethered to a boulder, water glossing the planes of his chest. His shoulders rippled with the setting sun as he cupped water into his palms and for a second, he looked utterly unguarded as he hurled it at Igbo and Ala. He was not a prince or king here; he was just Adriel.

Something in me wanted to wade through the water to him. I imagined the cool surface of the water and falling into his embrace and allowing him to steady me the way he steadied everything else. I imagined the warmth of his hand as it curled around me, and I allowed it to wander.

Miren nudged my ribs with a knuckle. "I told you," she whispered, grinning like a devil. "Lies."

I blinked away the traitorous images just as Adriel scanned the distance until his eyes found mine. For a heartbeat, they were amused, a slow smile easing the tension in his mouth. He pulled himself out of the stream and stood before us as water cascaded into his trousers. I'd never been so jealous of water before in my life.

I cleared my throat. "Is this where we are making camp tonight?"

He nodded. "We are on the edge of Truin. I thought it best to make our way through the town in the morning. We don't want to draw too much attention," he said, looking to Drakkar and Zephyr.

"Asha was just saying how she wanted to join you—and the hatchlings—in a water fight," Miren said with a smirk.

My eyes widened, but I was thankfully saved as the hatchlings ran to jump in the water. "Fireball!" Igbo yelled, pushing Ala in before jumping in himself. Mwana watched in frustration from the side.

"That's not how you play!" she yelled.

"It looks like you have it covered," I said.

"Adriel!" Celia called from the shore with a warm giggle. She had not bothered to wear traveling leathers the entire trip, preferring her royal gowns with plunging necklines. Today she wore a light shade of pink that matched her lips. Adriel waded through the water to meet her.

"What are you doing?" she cooed. "I have been looking for you all day."

"Duty calls, Your Highness. It is important to me to keep everyone in our party safe."

"Oh, I love how you think of my wellbeing even when we are apart," she sighed. "Will you have supper with me tonight?"

Igbo and Ala jumped into the stream directly in front of me, soaking my tunic. They laughed as I wrung the water from my hair and out of my ears.

Miren sent a water current into the stream, stirring a small wave that thrashed them about. They went under and swam back up.

"Do it again!" Ala called.

When I turned back to Adriel, he was already following Celia back to camp.

It was an unusually quiet afternoon. We had no idea whether Zaib had made it to Entioch, or if Entioch had been invaded. Everyone seemed to be bracing themselves for the final leg of the journey.

The only sounds were the hatchlings running around, talking excitedly of what they would do when they finally got to the ocean. I'd been nervous to have them out in the open. The Guardians gawked but did not dare go near. Drakkar was always nearby, striking fear into anyone who tried.

I did everything I could to stall going to sleep. I'd even requested a late session of training with Moki. I'd shown improvement over my time with him, but not today. Today, he had me flat on my back in seconds. Nothing worked. He was able to deflect and block every advance. As I lay on the ground, breathing hard, I glanced up at the sky. He looked down at me with pity before lying flat next to me.

"You are no warrior princess, that is for sure," Moki said. It was infuriating that he wasn't even breathing hard, like he'd just taken a casual stroll.

"You don't have to rub it in," I moaned. I touched my side tenderly, feeling the bruise that would be visible in the morning.

"Don't get me wrong, if you weren't so distracted you could actually learn something."

"You really know how to flatter a girl," I scoffed.

"What I cannot seem to understand," he began, "is why you prefer getting your ass handed to you over making a decision."

"And what decision is that?"

He turned, his caterpillar eyebrows raised. I'd expected amusement, but all I saw was sternness. "What decision is that?" I asked again.

He turned away and stood before reaching down to pull me up with him. "The decision that has been right in front of you from the moment we crossed paths."

I laughed, trying to break the tension. "I don't know what you are saying."

He blinked. "Yes, you do."

"Who are we talking about?" Chato called from the distance. "Me, I hope."

"No one would bother," Kitchi quipped as she joined us.

I shook my head, smiling despite myself. "We were just talking about you, actually. Did you deliver the food to the family I told you about? How were they?"

Chato's expression darkened as he shifted the bundle on his shoulder. "They weren't there."

My stomach dropped. "What do you mean?"

"They left. The neighbors said they joined the Shadows."

Kitchi put a hand to my shoulder. "It makes sense if you think about it. Now they will have food, shelter…"

I clenched my fists thinking of Jondrey having no other choice then joining the Shadows' ranks. "I hate my brother. I hate what the emperorship has done to its people. No wonder people are leaving for the Shadows."

The group was silent until Chato cleared his throat. "The last few days have been heavy. Perhaps it is time for some fun."

"I'm not in the mood for fun," I said.

"And that is exactly why you will have some. The last time you were like this, a hen night cheered you right up."

I groaned. "Don't remind me. It was right before Enapay dumped me in the woods to be hunted."

"But before that," he grimaced before taking my hand and spinning me around, "you had so much fun. We got to laugh about your dancing skills."

"The War Chief will never approve," Kitchi protested.

"Adriel doesn't have to know. I have it on good authority that he will be occupied tonight."

"So, Celia got her hooks in him," Kitchi said, looking my way.

"They are engaged," Chato said, "which is a boon for us because it means we can treat our newly betrothed friend to a night out! And… I'm tired of this one moping about," he said, pointing to Kitchi.

"It is not safe," Moki said.

"Come now," Chato scoffed. "Don't spoil it. We are just going to go into town. It is a ten-minute walk. We will be back before nightfall," he said with a wink.

Kitchi sighed, shrugging her shoulders before looking to me. "Are you in?"

I looked toward Drakkar who shook his head. *"If I said no, Little One, would you listen?"*

"That's the best part. Viola is from this area and knows where to go."

My thoughts trailed to the late-night supper Adriel would be having with Celia, and the plunging gown she was likely to wear. I pursed my lips, ready to make a decision and leave girlhood crushes where they lay. "Let's do it," I said to the group.

"Where are we going?" Miren asked, rounding the corner.

Chapter Thirty-Eight

Asha

"Why can't Zephyr come with us?" Miren asked.

"The dragons would draw too much attention," Kitchi said. "Adriel would surely notice. We need to be inconspicuous."

I took her hand. "It is going to be fun," I said. "I'll show you."

"Viola swears by this underground tavern," Chato assured. "They make their own spirits, right, darling?"

She giggled. "The very best."

I wasn't sure how he'd convinced her to accompany us, but I now knew why going out tonight was so important to him.

"It should be right here," she said. Leaves rustled underfoot as she moved to find the entrance.

"Oh, you were serious when you said it was in the ground," Kitchi noted.

"Here!" she exclaimed as I heard a wooden door creak open.

The others helped us walk down a series of steep steps. Music greeted us right away. The sound was unlike anything I had ever heard. We were immediately caught up in some kind of line dance.

"Hold on!" Viola squealed.

I laughed as we were tugged along, auras moving and melding together with the rhythm.

"I think I'm going to be sick," Miren murmured.

I pulled her away. "You're still trying to move as if you have sight. You don't—but what you have is in here," I said, tapping her chest. "Feel it in your body, listen to what is happening in the room."

She sighed heavily, but went along with it, her feet tapping to the rhythm. "I hear an akonting," she said.

"What else? What do you smell?"

"Sweat," she groaned. "Dirt, and... ale. Not the piss we had in Firepeak. I think they have some premium ale here, and," she smacked her lips together, "there is definitely a roasted pig somewhere."

"That's it," I said. "Now move with me."

The two of us circled the room, laughing and singing along with the music. As the song changed, the two of us slowed, trying to catch our breath.

"Better?" I asked.

"Yes. I like your friends," she said finally. "I can see why you were so disconnected when we lived together. You already had important people in your life."

"I was never disconnected. You hated me."

"I did not!" she protested. "Well, maybe a little, but you hated me too."

I mumbled, "Only when you brought Cane around. Speaking of which—" I paused. "You told me you saw him. You never said what happened."

She sniffed. "I didn't, and I wish never to speak of him again."

I wanted to pry more, but Kitchi and Moki came to join us with clinking glasses of ale.

"Where are Chato and Viola?" I questioned.

"Do you have to ask?" Moki groaned. "It is really unfortunate I chose to bunk with him. They are not quiet."

"That is disgusting," Kitchi gagged.

"You don't have to hear it," he reminded her.

"Can we change the subject?" Kitchi said, taking a big sip. "Do you want to play darts, Miren?"

"And how am I going to do that without killing someone?"

Kitchi slapped her back. "I do it all the time. Let me teach you my ways, and then you can show Moki how it is done."

"I don't play darts anymore," Moki protested.

"We know! The last time you did, I wiped the floor with you."

"Don't listen to her, Miren," he said. "Her form is as bad with a dart as it is on the battlefield."

Kitchi cackled. "Let's see what you got."

I made to follow but paused. I thought I saw a flicker of something familiar. "I forgot my ale," I said, though they were too busy comparing egos to notice as I pulled away.

I moved closer to the bright cherry aura. Of all the people I'd ever known, only one carried that unmistakable glow. "Tazbah?" I whispered.

The aura halted. "Tazbah, it is Asha." When she did not respond, I said, "You can pretend all you want but I know it is you," touching her aura. I felt a chill run through me as I felt the depths of her fear. She was panicked. "Don't worry. Kitchi would have said something if she'd seen you."

"She's here?" Her voice was hoarse, almost unrecognizable.

"Yes. Are you alright? Why are you in Wyrmwood? Kitchi has been sick over you."

"I—tell her I am sorry I did not write. I couldn't."

"What do you mean you couldn't? It is simple. You put a quill in your hand, and take a piece of paper, and you write."

"Asha, I wish I could tell you—that is, I must leave now, before anyone sees me."

I grasped her hand as she began to move away. "But you haven't told me why you are here. Do you live here now?"

"I—was supposed to meet someone, but they never showed."

"Who?" I asked.

She hesitated, then. "Your brother."

Now I was really confused. "You know Kwasi? Why would he be meeting you here?"

"It doesn't matter now. Asha, I need you to take this to him," she said, shoving a small book into my hand. "Do you know where he is?"

"He is back at the camp, but none of this makes sense."

"I know," she said, squeezing my hands. "Promise you will give this to him and don't let anyone else see it, especially Adriel."

"Tazbah—"

"Please. This is important."

"Alright. I promise," I said, putting it in my pocket.

"Good. I must make my exit now. Please don't tell Kitchi you saw me."

As her aura moved through the crowd, I fought the urge to go after her, to demand more answers. I was so deep in thought I barely registered the tap on my shoulder. "I'm coming," I said, expecting Moki, but every muscle in my body froze as the familiar aura pressed against mine. The one I'd grown up beside. The one who had been my most loyal friend… and who had betrayed me to save my brother Elan. "Asha?"

"Ekon?" I breathed, taking a step back.

"Asha," he said as if he'd rehearsed this moment many times in his head. "You don't know how long we've been looking for you."

"Stay away from me," I breathed. I bumped into someone behind me. "Help me! This man is dangerous," I said.

"Should I help her, Dragonlord Ekon?"

My stomach dropped at the familiar rank, the one Ekon had so coveted. I reached for his aura and immediately regretted it as I felt the calcified bond between us. There was no love between us anymore and that terrified me.

"I think you should," Ekon said. "Do not pull any of your tricks, Asha, or I will have men kill the Guardians you came in with. They are just waiting for my order."

I stilled, the sounds of the tavern floating away as my racing heart drowned out the sound.

"Good girl," he said, brushing a curl from my face.

I flinched. "Fuck you."

"You've gotten sassy," he said. "Take her."

Two pairs of hands lifted me off the ground by my arms and moved me through the tavern until the sounds around me quieted. No one questioned it. No one protested a woman being dragged out of a tavern.

I had to get away. Going back to Elan meant certain death. Ekon had to know that. We'd grown up together. He knew exactly what he was returning me to. I'd sooner die if it came to it.

"Are you really going to let him kill me, Ekon? Are you going to watch me die?"

"If you'd just gone with me back in the woods…"

"What?" I asked. We were out of the tavern—I could tell by the quiet and the sounds of the sleeping town. "What would have happened, Ekon?"

"And you made a fool of me."

I leaned in then. "You could have never been anything more than a friend to me," I whispered. "And now you are not even that."

His hand came down and struck me so hard I fell to the ground. I did not see it coming, not because of my lack of sight, but because despite everything Ekon had done to me, I still held a glimmer of hope that he still cared. That hope had just withered away.

I didn't even think as I reached for his aura. I felt the emotions of power and lust. I twisted until he felt physical pain and whimpered.

"Dragonlord?" the others called in concern. As Ekon fell, I whipped around and ran.

"Get her!" Ekon called. "Do not let her escape."

"Drakkar!" I called. *"I need you!"*

"For fuck's sake!" Drakkar cried.

Moving in an unfamiliar setting with men running after me was not ideal. I just needed to hide long enough for Drakkar to find me. I moved faster, using every bit of training from Moki that I could to get away. I could hear their footsteps fading, and that gave me hope. Unfortunately, that hope was short-lived as something snapped around me until I fell on the ground. I tried to move, but the material clung to me tighter and tighter.

My heart pounded as I recalled the words Adriel had said. If you don't sleep under the blanket, the blanket will find you. Burn it! This blanket would be the death of me.

"What's this?" one of the men asked breathlessly. "What is that thing?"

"A lifeline," said another. "Let's grab her and go."

They lifted me, between them, like I was a perfectly wrapped gift. The more I struggled, the tighter the blanket became.

"I'd put her down if I were you." I wasn't able to turn but I knew immediately that it was Adriel making the threat.

"Who are you? Get out of our way," one of my captors said.

"Have it your way, but it is not me you will be answering to."

The men dropped me to the ground unceremoniously so they could draw their swords. "There is only one of you. We should be able to take you fairly quickly."

"You think so?" he asked.

"Draw your sword!"

"Oh, I have no intention of fighting you," he replied. "But these two…"

Drakkar and Zephyr crashed into view, wings beating and fire building at their throats.

"*RUN!*" Drakkar roared.

The men fled, screaming, Drakkar and Zephyr descending on them.

Adriel knelt beside me.

"Adriel, I—"

"Don't speak," he said, lifting me into his arms. "I don't trust myself not to throttle you."

I stayed silent as he carried me back to camp as screams and burned flesh filled the night. I should have felt bad for Ekon, but I felt nothing.

CHAPTER THIRTY-NINE

Asha

"You are supposed to be my most loyal, and here you are risking our entire future. She could have been taken, and then what?"

All I could do was listen as Adriel barked at his Guardians.

"Chato," he said. "You are now first lieutenant."

Everyone in the tent gasped.

"But War Chief…" he protested. "It was my idea to go."

"And yet," he said, looking down at Kitchi, "you were not in charge of my army."

Kitchi's lips pursed. "Am I to be relieved from duty, War Chief?"

"I haven't decided yet," he growled. "Get out of my sight. Especially you."

I watched as Kitchi exited, head down. I wished I could have left too, but I was confined under the blanket still.

"You were a little hard on her, don't you think?" I said finally.

Adriel said nothing. He reached for my face, inspecting my injury. "He nearly broke your nose," he said quietly, pulling a chair next to the bed.

Drakkar stirred restlessly with the hatchlings in the corner.

"He says you are waking the hatchlings."

"I'm angriest with you," he said in Dragontongue. "You are supposed to protect her, and you failed."

"Tell the mortal he can be breakfast if he likes."

"Hush. It's been a long night," I said through the bond.

"Why did you do that to Kitchi?" I asked him once more.

He put his head in his hands. "We are not kids anymore. I know she's been lost ever since that girl but..."

"Tazbah," I murmured, feeling the book burn in my pocket. She'd made me promise her not to show him, but why?

"Yes. Ever since she left, Kitchi has been reckless, and I cannot have it. I am to be the king, and every decision is a reflection of me. Truthfully, she is my best warrior and most loyal friend, but she has never been suited for the role. I've known for a long time that Chato should lead it."

"Because he's a man?" I asked in disgust.

"No. It is because Kitchi is my truest friend, and as king, I should be able to reprimand and with her, I cannot bring myself to."

My heart softened a bit, finally realizing the hard position our actions put him in. It wasn't just him on the line anymore; it was his whole kingdom.

"We need to do something about this blanket."

He stood. "I agree," he said, walking out of the tent without another word.

"Ash, don't go."

The voice drifted through the fog of my mind. Somehow the sound wasn't right. It was too close, too real. I turned and Ashkii stood behind me, though I had not heard footsteps or felt him arrive. He simply appeared, carved out of shadow and moonlight.

"Ashkii?" My voice felt thick, underwater. "What are you doing here? Can I get no peace?"

He didn't answer. His eyes, bright and still, held mine.

"It's dangerous," he said finally, though the words trembled like the tremors of a quake. "You should turn back. Find somewhere safe to hide."

"There is nowhere safe." My voice echoed strangely, as if the air swallowed the ends of my words. "Your people invaded Saeleria. There is nowhere else for me to go."

"Then hide." His figure flickered, as if a breeze passed through him. "Go back to being a nameless person in a nameless town."

"That would go well with a dragon," I said, but the humor fell flat. Even the ground beneath my feet felt uncertain.

Ashkii turned sharply, like his body moved before he decided to. "You are not hearing me." His voice split. "Whatever terrible thing you imagine awaits you, multiply it. It will be worse. So much worse. They will not kill you," he whispered, "but you will wish they had."

A chill swept through me, though there was no wind.

"Why do you care?" I asked. My voice sounded distant, as if spoken by someone else. "Weren't you praising them? Weren't you begging for me to join them with you?"

He didn't turn. His shape blurred at the edges, bleeding into the darkness.

"Don't go, Asha," he murmured.

Then he stepped backward and fell away like ash on the wind.

I startled awake. Light was shining through the tent. I threw the blanket off me as if to shed the dream.

Chato poked his head in. "You're finally awake." He paused. "Are you okay?"

I must have looked shaken. "I'm fine, just a bad dream."

"Well, you better get moving," he said solemnly. "The War Chief is on a rampage."

The camp hummed with energy as we prepared to leave—dragons stretching, soldiers loading supplies, the entire company on edge. Yet beneath it all was a current of fury. Adriel's current. He moved through the camp like a storm, his orders clipped and wooden.

I'd checked on Kwasi, but he was fast asleep. I had so many questions for him that only he could answer, and his sleeping spells were getting longer and longer. Though I'd stayed hidden, Kitchi eventually came to get me when it was time to make the last of the journey.

"Do you want to talk about it?" I asked.

She blinked and turned away. "Not really."

The guilt I felt having seen Tazbah and not saying anything gutted me, but I feared revealing what I knew would hurt her even more. I couldn't do that to her. Not today.

"Are you sure you're ready for this?" Kitchi asked quietly.

I was surprised she wanted to talk at all. "Ready for what?"

"Another engagement. Another marriage."

"What choice do I have?"

She turned to me, her face serious. "You have a lot of them. I don't care what those men tell you. You are the one with the cards, not them."

"Cards only work if there is no one rigging the game."

Kitchi sighed. "Then find a way to win. I'm betting on you," she whispered. "Don't let me down."

"I had a dream last night," I admitted. "A dream about Ashkii."

That stirred her out of her melancholy. "Ah," she said, her eyes trailing to Adriel as if she was putting things together. "A sex dream?"

"No," I said quickly. "It felt so real. He was warning me. He told me not to go to Entioch."

"Have you told Adriel?"

"No, he wouldn't give me the chance. He won't even look at me."

"We should still tell him."

"It won't change anything," I said. "It's not like Ashkii was actually talking to me. It was my brain reacting to last night."

"Maybe," she said.

"Do you think we are going to find Entioch under siege?" I asked.

Kitchi shook her head. "I don't know. But if it were, that might solve one of your problems." She paused. "So, you and Adriel are not—sorry, it's none of my business," she amended.

I looked around to see if anyone was nearby. Thankfully, we were out of earshot. "It definitely is not anyone's business."

"I only meant that this whole agreement is null if you and Adriel have already—lit that fire. And if you haven't," she paused, "but you want to get out of your engagement, perhaps you should."

My cheeks stung as I tried to find words.

Kitchi laughed. "Okay, clearly you haven't, or you wouldn't look like that."

"How would these rulers even know?"

"I'm afraid there is magic for everything," she groaned. "As much as it feels like we have progressed, this is something that has not changed. Rulers want virgin wives. It's disgusting."

"What if I want a virgin man?" I challenged.

"Then you might as well turn around. No need to go to Entioch."

"Surely, what I have to offer—the keys to the Five Kingdoms—is greater than who I have lain with."

"It is, but if they even get a whiff of impropriety, they may come down on Adriel. I suspect that is what they've wanted all along, although Dija's betrayal certainly helps him more than it hurts."

We continued the grueling journey through the hills. It was not well traveled, which meant brush and trees tore at my blouse. For most of the day, we couldn't travel by horse because the ground was too narrow. I'd spent the afternoon near Celia, who went on and on about wedding plans.

"Of course, I will wear the finest pearls from the vault. I am just not sure if I should wear traditional green, or a bold color like coral. Are you listening, Asha?"

"I'm sure you will look beautiful in whatever you wear."

"Well, have you given your own gown more thought? Did you like the lavender?"

"What? No, I'm sure whatever is chosen will be suitable."

"Surely you have an opinion on color. White, then?"

"No, I should like to be in blue, I suppose. It is what my mother wore for her wedding."

"Blue is Adriel's favorite color," she noted with pride. "I've learned all about him. You've known him for a long time. Is there more you can tell me?"

My eyes widened. "Like what?"

"His likes, dislikes. What his type is," she said, twirling her hair around her fingers. "Perhaps you've known women he has been involved with. What do they look like?"

"I—I wouldn't know. I haven't known Adriel long, but he does not strike me as someone who has casual dalliances."

"Don't be silly," she giggled. "All men do. I prefer to know who my competition is. His female lieutenant, for instance. Do you think they could be together?"

"Kitchi?" I tried to suppress a laugh, but it came out anyway..

"I don't see what is funny. She spends a lot of time with him."

"They've known each other a long time, since they were children. I highly doubt it."

"Well, that is a relief. And you? Were you and he..."

I spat the water I'd been drinking. "The man who sold me to his lunatic brother? You're asking me if I have feelings for him?"

She let out a startled laugh, then caught herself. "Sorry. That isn't funny. I don't know why I asked."

"He likes to read," I said finally. "Especially about dragons and the histories of the Five Kingdoms."

She made a sound of disgust. "I was hoping he enjoyed something more fun, like throwing parties or traveling."

Before I could respond, a tremor rolled through the ground beneath us.

"Was that—" Celia began.

Another rumble. Louder. Then a shout pierced the air. One of the Guardians ran past us.

"Down! Everyone down!"

"What's happening?" Celia asked.

I took her arm and brought her low to the ground.

"Drakkar, what do you see?" I ground out. He was already in flight.

"The Guardians are running toward us from the bottom of the hill. It appears to be Elan's colors."

"They found us," I whispered. "I need to find my brother."

The next instant, an explosion ripped through the ground. I lay instinctively as debris and flame tore through the air.

"Get down!" Adriel roared, tackling us both before something hit the ground beside us.

"Is that an arrow?" Celia gasped.

"Get into formation!" Adriel cried. "Steer clear of open areas."

The roar outside was deafening now—horses, dragons, the clash of metal, the screaming of men and battlemages colliding.

"I thought you said they wouldn't come this way," I said.

"It looks like they knew we were in the area," he said, meeting my gaze.

This was my fault, I realized. They'd found us because we weren't being careful.

"It is half the size that I would expect," he continued. "But we are in a vulnerable position. When I give the signal, you both need to run."

"Kwasi?"

"Moki is with him. They are further ahead. Keep down. I will tell you when to move."

A flash—white, then blue—split through my vision, like someone had slammed a fist across the sky and then peeled it away. For a heartbeat, I was somewhere else, the cool rock of Drakkar's flank beneath my palms, the thunder of wind through his scales. Then I was on the dirt, breathless.

A plume of smoke bloomed at a distance behind us. *"Drakkar, are you there?"* I called, voice raw and small against the roar.

"Yes. We are. They have you pinned. I will draw them away to make a path forward. Be ready to run when I call."

I closed my eyes and tasted ash and cold wind. Every muscle in me screamed. "Do it," I whispered.

"Do what?" Adriel asked with eyes full of concern.

"Drakkar. He is clearing a path for us. He said to be ready."

Moments later, the sky tore open with fire as Zephyr roared. All eyes went to him, giving Drakkar the perfect opening to sweep in from behind and tear through the army with fire. Yells and agonizing screams filled my ears.

Adriel squeezed my hand. "Now!" he yelled. We followed the other Guardians through the narrow ravine to escape. No one tried to stop us as we pushed through.

Adriel signaled for Celia and me to keep moving while he stayed behind to make sure the men and the rest of the horses made it through.

Below, in the smoke and ruin, I saw figures—men, injured horses, and Elan's dragons unleashing streams of fire in Drakkar's direction. Grounded by dracite, the could not follow him into the air, allowing him to maneuver around them easily. I turned around to keep going, pulling Celia along with me. She stared at the two dragons in awe. "Magnificent," she whispered.

"Come on. We have to keep going."

I turned back to see a plume of smoke at a distance behind us. *"Drakkar. Are you okay?"*

"Yes, Little One. Right behind you."

I turned to let Adriel know, Drakkar had eliminated the threat and was coming back. I wouldn't get the chance because he was locked in battle, fighting against two men. I meant to nod in assurance and turn away, but as much as I tried I couldn't look away. After he cut them down with relative ease, he turned to lock eyes with me, as if he knew mine were upon him.

A shiver ran through me at the intensity of his gaze. I did not have a chance to examine it because my eyes widened as a ball of fire leapt over him, slamming into the rock above. The hillside shuddered. By the time Adriel looked up, it was too late, the ground was already shifting beneath him. I watched in horror as the rocks from the hillside tumbled down, Adriel leaping over the edge of the cliff, and there was nothing below but smoke and ruin.

"Where did he go?" Celia cried. "Where is he?"

I was already running. *"Drakkar?"* I called. I needn't call for Drakkar because he felt the devastation within me before he saw it. I threw myself onto his back and we scoured the hillside, his wings beating hard through the smoke.

"Adriel!" I called.

Only dirt and rock answered.

"We have company," Drakkar warned.

Below, six dragons lined up in formation, their dragonlords mounted, they're dracite canes whipping at their scales until they burned. They were readying them for their next kill—us. They meant to take us down.

The men motioned to each other, each chanting "Hasira! Hasira!"

"Let's go!" I cried, but Drakkar was already climbing higher, just as the flames released. We nearly missed their assault, the heat licking my skin like the door of a furnace thrown open. From this vantage, I could see the army in its totality. It wasn't big, not near the full size of the Ujuima army, every soldier positioned in just the right place, to cause maximum damage, almost like they'd been waiting for us.

"Shall we retreat, Little One?" Drakkar asked.

Below, the army pressed forward across the broken bodies of Guardians who'd been caught up in the landslide. Men and women I knew, faces I'd eaten beside, trained beside, were being trampled. Adriel could be down there. He could already be dead, the mere thought of which affected me in ways I could never explain.

"Not a chance," I said.

"As you wish," Drakkar answered with unbridled pride.

The dragons below had not had time to recover, still weakened by dracite in their hides, from their last release.

"Hasira!" I cried and Drakkar unleashed his fire on the group below before sweeping back in the air to avoid the arrows shooting our way. The dragons panicked and rolled on the ground to put the fire out, some of them smothering their dragonlords in the process.

Men on horseback scattered, retreating from the blaze. *"Stop them,"* I said.

Drakkar whipped around, a second stream of fire hit the ground in a wide circle, a wall of flame the retreating soldiers could not pass. The horses reared, unseating their riders, who now had no means of escape. I sat atop Drakkar, admiring the havoc we'd created, men running in all directions trying to find a way out of the circle of death.

Then one dragon caught my eye. She was one of the few that wasn't running. She knelt by her rider, pushing his cracked head with her snout as if to wake him from sleep. Her bright eyes and teal scales, a shade I had yet to see anywhere else in the world, caught in the firelight. My throat tightened.

"Nira?" I whispered.

Memories of the two of us singing to each other as we lived out the life neither of us chose for ourselves flashed into my mind. Two years since I'd lived in the pits when the world around us tightened like a fist. I watched as the other dragons limped away from the fires, that were growing larger by the second. Now, the entire army was retreating from the blaze.

"What do you command, Little One?"

I closed my eyes, remembering Adriel's wide brown eyes as he'd fallen, the reason I was even here. I glanced back at the wreckage of rock and stone, my heart grappling with the thought that he had not made it.

"Little One?"

I swallowed. *"Give me a moment."*

I closed my eyes, Searched inward until I honed in on the familiar thread, the thread that had hummed me to sleep in the darkest of nights.

"Nira—it's me."

The teal dragon paused her ministrations and looked around in alarm. *"Blind one?"* she called, her voice raw and exhausted from carrying sorrow for a very long time.

"Asha— yes, I am the blind one," I said.

"This was you?" She asked looking up from her deceased rider. *"You have killed my master?"*

I was quiet a moment, taking stock in the devastation I had caused. The dozen or so dead men, and the injured dragons limping around listless without their riders. The fires still eating the dry grass in slow, methodical bites.

"Yes," I whispered.

Nira's thread quieted a moment, as if she was taking it all in. She looked up and our eyes met through the smoke. They were gray and fierce and full of something, I could not name. It was like she'd known we'd meet again, that she had always known it would be like this.

"Good," she said.

My eyes widened. I couldn't have been more shocked if she had lifted from the ground and flown.

"Good? You're not upset I killed your dragonlord?"

"He was cruel," she said shaking her snout as if ridding herself of a long-held weight. *"Cruel, and so, so heavy."*

"I miss you," I said surprising myself. She, Akimba, Morin and the other dragons had been my family, when mine had abandoned me. They'd been all I had.

"I miss you too blind one," she said. *"But you should run along now. There will be reinforcements not far behind."*

I looked into the distance, and there were indeed more troops barreling forward. They'd be on us in a few minutes.

"Will you be alright," I asked watching the fires catch on new patches of grass.

"I will be fine, but you won't if you stay. Run, I will stall them."

"I can't leave!" I said frantically. *"I'm looking for someone."*

Her eyes swiveled towards the pile of rocks, her eyes pausing on a tree with limbs that were leaning to the right from the amount of debris. Her nose wrinkled. *"There,"* she said. *"You'll find him there. He smells of you."*

My heart lurched as I first spotted a hand, then a shoulder, then Adriel pulling himself upward. *"How did you—"*

"Blind one?" Nira interrupted.

"Yes?" I asked, locking eyes with her once more.

"Thank you," she said softly. *"Thank you for seeing me, seeing us. Those were some of the happiest days of my life."*

I did not have time to respond. She raised her head and roared into the sky. Around her, the other dragons stopped. Every one of them turned toward her, then fell into line behind her, moving as a single body toward the approaching army, placing themselves in between us and Elan's dragonlords.

"Time to go!" Drakkar said. My eyes stayed on Nira and the other dragons, until I was forced to look away.

Adriel's eyes found mine as he waved from below, covered in dirt, but otherwise whole. Before we could sweep down, I caught sight of a horse with a woman with lovely, sand colored skin and delicate tendrils framing her petite face racing toward him. Her guards trailed behind her.

"Adriel!" she called jumping from her horse, and leaping to embrace him. His eyes ripped from me and went to her.

I closed mine in turn. Adriel was not mine to save, not anymore.

I rode on Drakkar back to the Guardians who had regrouped miles away, relieved to see there were minimal casualties. Kwasi, was awake, but barely lucid, which further bruised my battered heart. My only solace was that Kitchi, Chato, and the others were unhurt, though they fussed over me sensing that something was amiss.

We traveled at full speed without breaks until there was no daylight left, and we were a few miles from Entioch. I could almost taste the sea air in my throat.

By then, my feet were so sore I could hardly move them. The effort I'd exerted was akin to ten of Moki's grueling training sessions. I'd called out to Drakkar, but he'd assured me he'd be there in the morning. He needed to calm his nerves and take to the sky.

Fewer items were unpacked for my tent, a precaution I was told, in case we needed to leave at a moment's notice. They really needn't bother. I wasn't sleeping on that cursed bed. They couldn't make me. I sat outside with Moki, leaning against the posts until I finally nodded off in exhaustion.

Chapter Forty

Asha

I stirred slightly as I realized I was being carried into the tent.

"Won't Celia mind your always being in my tent alone—especially tonight when she almost lost you?" I asked groggily. When he didn't respond, I stirred awake. "Perhaps I'll go ask her myself."

He offered nothing, just sat me on the bed and began to remove my shoes. I stood, pushing him away to move toward the door.

"Stop!" he called.

I turned sharply, folding my arms. "Why should I?"

"I don't understand why you're angry with me."

I let out a bitter laugh. "Perhaps because you are okay with me being restrained to a bed," I fumed.

I don't know if it was being awoken from sleep or the adrenaline from the attack earlier, or the way he'd held Celia, but words began to leave my mouth unbidden. "Or perhaps because only days ago you nearly kissed me."

His breath faltered.

"You reached for me," I continued, stepping closer, forcing down the hurt I'd buried, "and then you stood hours later to marry Celia."

Silence stretched between us.

"I am now forced into a marriage to save my own life and others like me. And you dare ask why I'm angry."

He stepped toward me, and I refused to retreat. I held my ground, my glare steady.

"For someone who despises marriage so fiercely, you've done very little to resist it."

"What do you expect me to do?" I shot back. "Bend the rulers to my will? Break everything at once? You act as if I've done nothing—but I'm still standing here, facing you."

"It never ceases to amaze me that you doubt yourself. You're clever enough to find a way out if this is not what you want. Look at what you accomplished today," he said in pointed frustration. "The only one in your way is you."

My pulse hammered, remembering Kitchi's similar words from the morning. "You don't get to lecture me about freedom while you're the one tightening the shackles."

He moved closer, and I stepped back until the bed touched my legs behind me. "That would be your fiancé. Take it up with him."

My body braced, but my voice didn't waver. "Get out."

His voice tightened. "No."

I pointed a finger at his chest. "You don't get to decide. Not anymore."

He exhaled slowly with an intensity that unsettled me more than his words ever could. "And yet you endure it. Chains. Alliances. Every decision made for you. You wear them as if they're unbreakable. You know what I think?"

"No," I snapped. "I don't care what you—"

"I think," he cut in smoothly, heat rolling off him as he leaned close, "you like to be tied down."

My heart hammered in my chest as my mouth fell open. Whether from rage or something else, I could not say.

The clink of his belt being unfastened broke the silence between us.

Finally, I forced the word past my lips, though it was not as steady as before. "Leave."

"Only if it is what you want and not what is expected of you." He leaned in, so close I could feel the edges of his aura.

Leather hissed free as he slipped the belt from his trousers.

"What are you doing?" I asked as the belt pulled free. "If you think you will force me into this bed again, you are in for a rude awakening."

"I promised you long ago that I would never force you. Not into a bed. Not into a vow. Not even to stay by my side."

The words sliced deeper than I expected, my hand pressing to my chest as if I could hold my heart in place.

I bit my lips. "Then what do you intend?"

He reached for me, his hands firm on my hips. I didn't stop him. His touch sent a delicious tremor through me as he lifted me to sit on the edge of the bed. My breath tangled with his, sharp and uneven. He caught my hand, kissed my palm, and I bit back a sound low in my throat. Then, gently, he guided my fingers around something hard... and cold, before releasing me.

I blinked, closing my hand on the handle of the short sword now in my grasp.

"What?" I asked, bewildered.

"Someone has to keep the agreement," he said, settling heavily into the bed beside me. "The enchantment demands a body in it each night, but it doesn't care who. I trust that you will watch over me while I am incapacitated."

"You do realize word will get out that you're sleeping in here."

Adriel groaned as he burrowed into the lavish bed. "And how will anyone enter past a fire-breathing dragon?"

I tightened my grip on the sword, fighting the urge to fling it at his smug head. Burn it to hell. "Can I at least get a pillow?"

"No," he said sleepily.

I startled awake, rubbing my hands over my face and trying to shake Ashkii's voice from my ears. Another warning. *Don't go to Entioch.*

It was not quite light outside, and Adriel was still beside me. I blinked, testing my sight. Drakkar was likely somewhere beyond the tent, keeping his silent watch.

I listened to the rhythm of Adriel's breathing, like it was part of some familiar song. Images of his half-naked body flashed in my mind, only this time, I did not blush. It was a relief to have this moment of quiet to myself after yesterday. He could have died yesterday, and that would have affected me. It was a painful admission, but not as painful as the memory of him running into the arms of another woman. It did not matter that this woman was a princess, that she was beautiful and cunning, exactly what he needed.

It was clear he'd moved on and if I weren't such a glutton for punishment, I would have as well. Now he was committed to another. Had he kissed her? Had they done more?

Today, I would enter my fiancé's kingdom. The dread was immediate and terrifying. I just wanted to hold on to this blissful moment with him a few moments longer.

I traced the lines of his face, gently, so gently he would not notice, pausing only to assure myself that he was still asleep. When his steady breathing continued, I grew bolder. Even with the barrier between us, I could feel how solid he was. My fingers craved more, like a dessert so delectable I could not put it down until I'd licked the bowl clean.

My fingers tensed, wanting to memorize him, to prove to myself that he was real and not another dream I'd lose at sunrise. The thought frightened me more than anything I'd ever faced. I drew my hand back and placed it over my own heart instead, feeling its uneven rhythm try to match his.

For a moment, the world outside didn't exist—no armies, no alliances, no promises I couldn't keep. There was only the quiet rise and fall of his chest, the warmth between us, and the unbearable truth that I was never meant to want this much.

"Why did you stop?" he asked. His voice was husky but alert, like he'd been awake for a long time.

"You know why," I whispered, dropping any pretense I had prepared.

"I don't," he breathed. "Keep going."

"It is wrong," I said firmly.

"I can't even touch you," he murmured, flexing in the blanket to make a point. "Do you see?"

I almost smiled. "I don't."

My hands found him again before I could talk myself out of it. Slow. Curious. Familiar in a way that frightened me. His breath turned uneven as I traced around his hips, and he shivered. "Gods!" he growled. My hands continued to his thighs, which tensed as my fingers explored. Then they traveled back up to find the hardness between them. Then I felt inspired. I moved before I could change my mind and straddled him. I felt myself clench as I sat on top.

"What are you doing to me?" he gasped.

I rocked my ass on top of him. "Whatever I want."

The next series of events happened so fast I could hardly breathe. He sat up, one hand pulling my dress up to my thighs, the other cupping my cheek. Then his lips were on me. Soft and demanding, it was like no time had passed between us since our last kiss. His tongue pushed my mouth open and consumed me. I could barely catch my breath before he rolled me over onto my back.

"I thought—" I said, coming up for air. I pushed at his chest. "What happened to the blanket?"

He gave the slightest pause, so slight I almost missed it. "Hmm?" he murmured, unsnapping my stockings and pulling them free.

"The blanket? It is not holding you down."

"It must be daybreak."

I turned my head, waiting for the sunlight to filter through from the sun flap, but my skin remained cool. "No. It is not," I said firmly.

His head touched mine. "I'm ashamed to say."

"Wait, were you lying to me?" I said, pulling back.

"Just a little." A pause, then a glint of humor was etched in his voice. "There is a way to...disable the blanket."

I punched him then. Hard. "You mean, you could have done so this whole time and chose not to?"

"Yes," he admitted, his mouth twitching upward on my skin. "I'd apologize, but it wouldn't be sincere."

He rocked into my body, leaning in to claim my mouth once more, but I turned at the last second. "Don't pull away," he breathed.

"I don't know whether to be angry with you or not."

"I vote not."

I untangled myself slowly, and he rolled off me but did not let go.

"I don't know what came over me," I managed. "One second I'm dreaming and the next..."

Adriel caressed my cheek patiently. "Hmm. Good dreams, I hope. Were you dreaming of me, Princess?"

"No." I stilled, remembering the contents and the warning I'd been given. "It was of Ashkii. It felt so real."

Adriel's hand on my cheek stilled before he rolled away from me completely. "Can't get him out of your head, can you?"

I pushed up on one elbow. "Adriel—"

He was already gone, the bed lifting from the absence of his weight. The space between us felt instantly colder, as if the air itself had retreated.

I laughed. "I can't believe this. You have been locking me up at night..."

"It was not me," he said through clenched teeth.

"But you could have removed it the entire time."

"Not without consequences." He laughed softly, but there was no humor in it. "I'm such a fool. You dream of *him*, then wake and reach for me. Tell me, Princess—what am I supposed to make of that?"

I opened my mouth, then closed it again, unsure of what to say.

"It is better this way," he said, his words slightly muffled as he tugged on his tunic. "You will be married soon, as will I. Maybe I should go share a bed with Celia. She'd be more than willing."

His words hit their mark, like a blade so sharp I almost didn't feel the cut at first. Celia. Of course, sweet Celia, who'd never make him question himself. I should have stayed silent, let him leave. That is what the old Asha would do. Instead, the words tumbled out before I could stop them.

"Is that supposed to make me jealous?" I bit out. "I couldn't care less who you lie with. You aren't my priority. I thought I'd made that clear."

The silence after my words felt like something had died between us—worse because I could still feel him on my skin, still taste the apology I wouldn't give. I wanted to scream that the dream wasn't what he thought—that Ashkii's face had come to me with a warning, not a want. But what difference would it make? The moment was already shattered.

"Better get dressed, Princess. You want to look nice for your future kingdom," he said before leaving the tent.

I pressed a hand to my chest, feeling the uneven rhythm beneath my palm. Every beat felt like a betrayal. I had let him close—again—and the gods had reminded me why we could never be.

CHAPTER FORTY-ONE

Asha

I was relieved to see that Entioch was not under siege. Instead, the moment we arrived, the villagers leading to the capital spilled into the streets to watch us pass. People moved toward me with flowers and small trinkets clutched in their hands. Many wore threadbare clothing, their faces drawn thin by long winters and lean harvests. It did not feel right to take anything from them.

Eventually, I climbed on Drakkar's back to avoid the swarm. It was sad to hear their well wishes, as if my marriage would somehow bring prosperity. They yelled their congratulations and remarked on my beauty. Once I climbed onto Drakkar, I could barely hear them, but they kept their distance. The hatchlings were captivated by the crowds, and the people were captivated in return.

In this lifetime, no one had seen creatures such as them and here were three. They bobbed their heads in delight, small tails swaying as they happily chewed on the sweets and sugared candies thrown in our path.

As we grew closer, more and more people assembled. My mind raced to the brief time Adriel and I had spent here. It was crowded then too, but they'd come for a festival, not to see me. It was strange, people paying me attention. Growing up in the pits, I never imagined I'd be in a position to be watched and bowed to again.

My gaze slid to Adriel, riding beside Celia. She appeared genuinely delighted, basking in the attention, at times slipping her hand into his. He let her lift their joined hands, and the crowd responded with swoons and cheers.

The palace was magnificent, made of crystal and light. It glittered, catching the sun until it was almost painful to look at. Light shimmered across the towers like water, refracting in hues of sea green and pale gold. Even Drakkar seemed awed, his wings beating slower as we approached.

The moment we arrived in the outer courtyard, a crowd surged forward—royal attendants, guards, courtiers draped in translucent silk garments that matched the crystal of the palace. I slid from Drakkar's back, my legs trembling with more than exhaustion. The air smelled of incense and crushed blossoms, sweet enough to sting.

A man in robes of deep green stepped forward, bowing low. "Princess Asha," he announced, voice carrying over the murmuring crowd. "Welcome to Entioch, beacon of the east."

Adriel dismounted and spoke to another attendant, his expression carved from stone. He didn't look at me, not once.

"Your arrival is most auspicious," the attendant continued. "His Majesty awaits you inside. Preparations for your union have begun."

The word union made my stomach tighten.

"We have an area for your dragons to rest..."

"My dragons stay with me," I said. "I require rooms that will accommodate them."

"As you wish, Your Highness. However, the king has declared that dragons are not allowed in the sitting room, where you will be introduced to His Majesty. They may wait just outside."

I exchanged glances with Drakkar, then Miren and Zephyr.

"Very well. Show us the way."

We followed him into the palace. It was almost too bright for the eyes. The only reprieve was the tropical trees that provided a bit of shade inside. Birds flew above us, calling to one another and singing. We stepped over pools of water that seemed to connect directly to the ocean below. Fish occasionally jumped to the surface, disturbing lily pads as big as my foot. Drakkar barked at the hatchlings to stay away from the pools.

The attendant stopped and pointed to a contraption that moved between the levels. "The dragons must halt here."

"I require my confidante, Miren, to come with me."

The attendant wanted to say no. I could see it forming on his lips, but he didn't get the chance.

"We will also accompany Her Highness."

It took everything in me not to react as I turned to meet his eyes. Adriel met mine briefly before turning them back to the attendant.

"We will accompany them both," he said, gesturing to Celia at his side and to Kitchi and Chato, who flanked him. "Do you have a problem with that?"

The attendant swallowed. I almost felt sorry for him. Almost. "Of course not. Follow me."

I looked back at Drakkar and the other dragons. *"Don't—"* he began.

"Die," I finished for him. *"I'm learning."*

"You'll never learn," Drakkar said.

The door to the room closed, and everything went dark.

CHAPTER FORTY-TWO

Adriel

The structure lurched violently, yanking my stomach into my throat. Ropes creaked overhead as the platform swayed, jerking upward and then dropping without warning. I braced myself against the rough wooden slats, fingers digging in as the world tilted beneath my feet. I loosened my grip only when I noticed the attendants remained unfazed.

Asha lost her balance. She reached for something to steady herself and found me. Instinct took over. My hands closed around her waist, steadying her before she could fall. Her palms landed against my chest. She kept them there, not quite long enough to be improper but long enough that it could be noticed. Chato cleared his throat beside me. Thankfully, Celia was too caught up in all the sights outside to notice.

The sound snapped me back to myself, and I stepped away at once, releasing her. "Steady," I said, guiding her hand to the railing.

Once the doors opened, we all walked out like we'd found land for the first time. As I looked around the room, I realized we were underwater. While the entrance was all light and airy, this was moody and dark. I watched as fish and narwhals swam by. But what took my attention was the gold chair in the center of the room that held King Musa, who slumped in it, a gray beard trailing down from his chin to the floor in several intricate braids.

Zaib stood tall behind him.

His eyes narrowed at me, then at Asha as we walked to the main floor. The women also curtsied as would be expected of another royal.

Zaib stalked toward Asha and embraced her, running his hands down her body as if to check for wounds. "Are you okay, my dearest? Father, come meet my betrothed. Isn't she splendid?"

Asha smiled politely but seemed to be lost for words. I spoke first.

"Your Majesty," I began. "Thank you for your warm welcome. I am Adriel Foxtrail, the future King of Wiyotak, and my fiancée Princess Celia of Wyrmwood."

"I am honored, Your Majesty," Celia said. "You have a beautiful kingdom."

Zaib smiled, though the expression didn't reach his eyes. "It was built by Lightbearers long before either of our kingdoms existed. A symbol of peace."

"Or vanity," Kitchi muttered under her breath.

My head snapped toward her.

"Peace," King Musa repeated, voice brittle but commanding. "A word the young toss around as if they invented it." His face was drawn, his skin pale against the gleam of his crown.

"We appreciate the invitation, Your Majesty," I said.

"Does she not speak?" he said, pointing at Asha. "I thought she was blind. Is she mute as well?"

Before I could intervene again, she stepped out of Zaib's shadow. "I can speak, and I am also very glad to meet you and honored to be able to join your family."

Musa peered at her, assessing her from head to toe in a way that made my blood boil. "She's not as pretty as her mother. What was her name, Sanaa?" He paused, looking briefly to Zaib. "But her hips are comely enough. Is she pure?"

"Your Majesty," I said evenly, though every word burned. "Perhaps you forget you are talking to the next ruler of this house."

Musa laughed. "That title will belong to my son. But I suppose you're right. Forgive me, I forget myself—such scandalous talk isn't fit for a lady's ears."

"Such talk does not offend me," Asha said carefully.

Musa frowned, taking a sip of his wine. "You all traveled far together. I assume she had the binding blanket at night?"

I fought the urge to grimace as I reached for my satchel. One of the attendants took it from my hands, passing it to the others dressed in white robes. They inspected it in silence, the king's gaze never leaving us.

Zaib said nothing.

At last, one of the attendants leaned in and whispered something to him. The king gave a small nod.

"It appears you are a man of your word, Adriel," he said. "Thank you for ensuring her virtue remained intact."

I exchanged a brief glance with Chato. He had managed to switch Celia's blanket with Asha's before we arrived. A quiet miracle.

I could only hope Fourie wouldn't insist on examining the other one and if he did, that he wouldn't care whose warmth it truly held. In the end, our silence served us all.

"Am I to get the same accolades?" Asha asked. "Or is that reserved for the men in the room?"

"You have fire," Musa said with appreciation. "You are going to need it for what is ahead. I hope you will be pleased that I have set your wedding to commence immediately, so you will not have to wait to wed my son."

Her lips tensed as she caught Zaib's gaze. "I'm afraid your son and I have a different arrangement in mind," she said. "I would like to visit the Lightbearers before the nuptials."

Zaib stirred. He cleared his throat. "There is something you should know, my love," he said gently. "We were attacked on the journey here. We lost a quarter of my regiment."

The room shifted. "Yes, we were also attacked," I said. Zaib did not even spare me a glance, but kept his gaze locked on Asha. He cupped her cheek just as I had earlier this morning.

"You were?" Zaib said. "It is a miracle you are alive."

"Tell me why we cannot visit the island," she pressed.

Zaib's expression shifted, becoming harder. "Because our ships are deployed," he said. "They are the only barrier between Entioch and Ujuima's fleet. Without them, this city would already be burning. That is why Elan diverted to Wyrmwood."

I stepped forward before I could stop myself, unable to stay silent. "Why is Elan toppling his allies? Everyone was told to be discreet. How did he discover us?"

Zaib's jaw ticked. "Someone obviously tipped him off. Perhaps you were correct in your assertion that it is the same someone who was absent from the attack in Wyrmwood." He dropped his hand from Asha's cheek. "It is all right. He would have figured it out, eventually. But now we must unite the kingdoms with this wedding. We can go to the island when it is safer."

Asha stood so still I could not tell if she was breathing. "No. I don't care how you do it. We are going to the Ifambe Islands."

"No?" Musa repeated. "What do you mean, no? You ungrateful..."

"Careful—" she said, cutting him off. "My presence here is a courtesy. I could turn around right now, and you would lose me as an ally forever."

"You wouldn't—"

"I would. There are a few things I won't tolerate. Betrayal, followed closely by lying, scheming men."

All that could be heard in the chamber was the sound of King Musa's furious breaths. Everyone else waited. If it came to a fight, we were dead. This chamber was sealed tight.

King Musa nodded. "You've got your work cut out for you, son."

"Very well," Zaib said. "It is a risk, but if it will make you more comfortable with our alliance, then I will take you. My only request is that we get married straight after. Right on the ship."

Asha swallowed. "I accept these terms."

Musa clapped his hands. "Splendid!" He gingerly stood up from his chair. "I am only sorry I won't be able to accompany you. My bones are much too old for such a journey, but we will have a celebration fitting for a new king and queen upon your return and then the real work begins. Taking back Ujuima. The ships will be ready at dawn."

Asha's brow wrinkled as she nodded to Musa. "That is very kind, but I would like to set sail today."

Before Musa could reveal his wrath, Zaib took her hand. "Eager to get married? Me too, my love. You are right. We will set sail immediately."

There was a struggle in the negotiations over whether the Guardians would join the journey. Zaib's men claimed there was not enough room because of the wedding arrangements, but once I spoke to Celia and discussed my plan with her, she was able to charm our way on board.

"You would deny my happiness of a romantic voyage with my betrothed? And to miss your wedding! It would break my heart," she'd said.

Zaib's face had been murderous, and I did very little to contain the smirk on my face. I turned away before my satisfaction could betray me further, toward the harbor where Entioch's fleet awaited.

Entioch was known for its naval ships. They gleamed in the sunset. Their hulls were carved from pale driftwood, polished and smoothed by weeks out at sea. Each was etched with runes that warned off nefarious creatures lurking in the ocean. Mahogany rails curved into the shapes of sea dragons and serpents, the sigils of Entioch. I did not care about the craftsmanship so much as the battlemage that made it a war vessel. I took note of every battlemage and stitch of machinery. One day, Wiyotak's ships would rival Entioch's.

I caught a glimpse of Asha, helping Kwasi board the ship. They were followed by Igbo and Ala. Mwana had taken a liking to me and was content following behind me. My Dragontongue was minimal but that did not stop me from attempting to explain to her how ships worked.

These did not have oars but were fitted with a series of metal arms that were controlled and powered by several mages. She seemed enamored by what I showed her.

"You were always so fascinated with contraptions," Kitchi said. "I remember when you were barely ten, asking for a book on the sanitation system in Wiyotak." She chuckled.

"I'm glad you are amused, seeing as you insulted the future royal of this house."

Her smile faded but she did not apologize. "Would you like me to leave?"

I looked down and sighed deeply. "What am I going to do with you?"

"Kill me, probably." She shrugged. "Do you really think Zaib knows where this island is?"

I looked out at the railing, watching the anchor being pulled into the boat. "There is not a chance in hell, but for Asha's sake," I said, softening, "I hope so."

"If he doesn't," she said, feeding Mwana a dried cherry, "what is he going to do when she figures that out?"

"That's why we need to determine what he is after."

"So, you are allowing her to sail into danger?"

"Don't worry, I have a plan."

CHAPTER FORTY-THREE

Asha

I'd rarely been at sea, and this time it got to my stomach. I could barely eat, but Zaib was attentive, checking on me throughout the day and giving me updates on where we were on the map. Drakkar did not like being at sea much either. He often took the hatchlings flying with him on his back, though he remained close to the ship. The soldiers on board had been horrified by the exotic fish that Zephyr plopped on deck to devour. It was endearing to watch them teach the young dragons to fish.

As joyous as the scene in front of me was, there was one person's absence that I felt keenly. Adriel had not made an appearance. When I'd asked after him, the attendants said that he was busy, or attending to other things.

I placed my hand in my pocket, where the book Tazbah had given me lay. I'd tried to read it, but it was in a language I was unfamiliar with. I'd attempted to share it with Kwasi, but he was much too sedated to read it. I settled for leaving it by his bedside, hoping he could give me some insight once he was awake, whenever that was. The book itself was baffling, hastily sketched drawings, no real structure. I wasn't sure what I was meant to glean from it.

"How is your stomach today?" Miren asked.

"Better than yesterday. Zaib brought me a broth that helped."

Miren arched an eyebrow. "You aren't actually going through with this wedding, are you?"

Gods, not her too. I looked around to make sure we were alone. "I don't see why not. He is kind, intelligent, literally born to rule. I couldn't ask for better."

Miren shook her head as if I'd lost my mind. "I am hopeful that what he says is true, but what if these Lightbearers aren't what we imagine?"

"What do you mean?"

"I mean, what if they are assholes?"

"This again?" I sighed. "They can't be. They were the original rulers before there were Five Kingdoms."

"Exactly. How many rulers do you know that aren't assholes? I am just saying...," she said, watching Zaib approach. "Be careful."

"How are we doing today, ladies?"

Miren bowed low. "Excellent, Your Highness. You have taken such good care of our princess. She is looking much better today thanks to you."

I gave Miren a look to turn down the faux flattery, but Zaib didn't seem to mind. In fact, he seemed to thrive on it.

His chest puffed out as he said, "It was my pleasure, really."

"Really?" Miren continued. "The princess was just telling me it made all the difference."

"Well," he said, turning to me, "it was my honor."

"I should leave you two lovebirds alone," she said with a wink before leaving to join the dragons. I could wring her neck.

"So, you do talk about me when I'm not around," he said, taking my hand to kiss it. "I can't tell you how happy that makes me."

I smiled demurely at him before taking my hand back. "I am grateful for your attention, Your Highness."

"Asha," he began, leaning on the railing beside me. "I am no fool. I know you don't love me."

I startled at his words. "I—"

"It is okay. I know it will come with time. It is the way for those like us, born into power," he said. "We are expected to make a match, although I have to admit, I am glad it is with you."

I averted my gaze, feeling slightly embarrassed. "What more could I ask for in a suitor?"

His smile widened as he took my hands again in his. "Love will come for both of us in time. Until then, we can take the relationship at the pace you prefer." I felt the tightness in my chest lessen a bit until he said, "I had your wedding dress unpacked. The dressmaker has it now. She mentioned that she would love to start fitting it on you this evening."

"Isn't that getting ahead? Bad luck and all. We'll be at least a week out at sea."

"My darling, we have been sailing for five days. We will be there in a day or two. I thought we could have dinner together the next two evenings before we land, and you could start preparing for our wedding. Celia has been so eager to help you plan."

"I did not realize she was on board. I have not seen her."

"She has been on the other ship. That is where the wedding will take place. It will be beautiful when she's done, but I've had it arranged for her to join us for the rest of the journey."

"I think that sounds lovely," I said. "Thank you for thinking of it."

"I am always thinking of you."

"It is a bit loose," I said as Viola worked on attaching lace that felt like bits of seaweed to my skirt. We hadn't spoken at all since the underground tavern. Every time I tried, she'd quickly excuse herself from the conversation. "Is it supposed to feel this way?" I asked.

"Oh yes," Celia said. "Entioch fashion dictates it must. Have you never been to an Entioch wedding?"

"No. I didn't get out much," I said.

"The fabrics are light and loose because after you kiss your husband, you are to make your first leap together into the waters you are sworn to protect together. Heavier gowns were worn at one time, but brides would sink to the bottom. Thank goodness we've moved to more practical fabrics."

My eyes widened. Thank goodness indeed.

"How do you like it, Your Highness?" Viola whispered.

The question was clearly meant for me, but Celia answered for both of us. "I think the sea foam green was the right choice, but what are we going to put in her hair? Pearls? Flowers? Perhaps aquamarine gemstones?"

"I like my hair simple," I said.

"Oh, you couldn't possibly wear your hair unadorned. You are going to be a queen after all. We need you to look the part." She giggled before saying, "It is kind of romantic that you cannot see the dress. The prince will see it even before you do."

Something I could never explain to anyone—except perhaps Miren—was that I did see the dress. Just not in the way they did. The gauzy texture between my fingers, the delicate lattice of lace, and the coarse pearls sewn into the seams... all of it told a story deeper and truer than any color ever could. "I will wear my hair unadorned," I said. "I wouldn't want it to compete with the dress."

"You are right, Asha," Celia amended. "You are beautiful enough. You should not hide behind it, but surely you will wear a veil."

"I don't know. I hadn't thought about it."

"This one is crafted in the Ujuima fashion," Viola offered. "I thought it would be nice to have a piece of home. Would you like to at least try it and see if it feels right?"

"Yes, of course."

Viola got to work pinning the fabric into my hair. As her hands worked, my mind flashed unbidden to the moment in my tent when Adriel had his hands in my hair.

"Are you in love?" Celia asked.

I startled at the question. "What?"

"You smiled just now. I saw it," she said curiously. "Have you finally warmed toward Zaib? He'd be so pleased to know, I'm sure."

I was suddenly very grateful my warming face was hidden behind the veil. "I am very lucky," I said, though it sounded flat to my ears.

"I knew it! I saw the two of you talking today and I am the one who encouraged him to ask you to dine with him this evening." She swooned. "It is just like Adriel and me. I swear he almost kissed me today."

My head shot up so fast Viola nearly swore. "No sudden movements, Your Highness. You will rip the veil."

"Sorry. What were you saying, Celia?" My chest tightened.

"We spent the day together," she continued. "He showed me several of his books. You are right; that did get him talking. One moment, we were talking about the ship's battlemage system, the next—well, I will leave that to your imagination."

I felt sick, like I was going to lose the little contents I'd managed to keep down.

"All done," Viola said excitedly. "I think this might be my best work yet. What do you think?"

"I—I think I need a moment alone," I said.

"Oh," she said with disappointment, "I can help you out of the dress."

"No!" I said a little louder than I meant to. "I just need a minute to settle my stomach before I have dinner tonight. I can manage on my own."

"You're anxious about the wedding," Celia said. "Don't worry. You make a beautiful bride. Zaib will be pleased."

I rubbed my hands, trying to prevent them from shaking. "I thank you, Celia. I will see you soon. I don't want to be late."

"Of course! Enjoy your time together. Don't forget to finish your broth. It'll settle the stomach."

When the door finally clicked shut, I collapsed to the floor. Piles of gauze hiked up against me like a cloud. I wanted to scream, but I knew if I did, I would alert Drakkar and everyone else on board. This felt real, too real.

I stayed on the floor, palms pressed to the cool boards, veil pooling like fog around my knees. The room still smelled of rosewater and pins. I could feel the tiny pricks they'd left in my scalp, each one a reminder that I was being fastened to a future, this time of my own making. Unlike the time I was betrothed to Enapay or the champion of the Fire Challenge in Ujuima, this time I had chosen my husband, and yet my decision felt confining.

I tried to breathe past the ache in my throat. *It's nothing. It's nerves and the dress. It's the veil.* Lies, all of them. What had disturbed me was the picture Celia painted so easily—Adriel in a quiet room, head bent over his books, lifting his face at her voice.

The ship sighed around me, ropes creaking as I pressed my forehead to my knees and told myself I would stand momentarily.

A faint scrape on the outer wall startled me out of my pity. I caught the sound of cloth brushing wood and the hiss of a line sliding along a hook.

I froze. Another sound—too deliberate to be the wind. Someone jostled the shutter; it lifted the width of a breath, then slipped back into place. There was a brief pause. *Someone was breaking in*, I realized much too late.

Then, with the same kind of caution, someone tried again. I did not have a weapon near me, and I worried that whatever the threat was, Drakkar would not get to me in time.

The shutter tipped open, and a figure eased through the gap, all shadow and careful breath. Fear spiked; I was already rising when light gathered around him like a tide.

I let out the breath I'd been strangling. "Adriel."

CHAPTER FORTY-FOUR

Adriel

Moving on the ship had been an arduous affair. I was watched every second of the day and accompanied by Celia the rest of the time. Though my mind remained focused on the mission, I had to admit I had softened somewhat toward her. Every interaction, though trying, gave me a glimpse of what being married to her would be like. I had no doubt that she would not mind if she did not take part in ruling Wiyotak. She talked excitedly about our upcoming wedding, and the desire to blend traditions and honor my parents, who were no longer alive to attend. I realized, over time, Celia had endeared herself, even if being around her was tedious at times.

"Are you ready, War Chief?" Moki asked.

I nodded. "Good luck," I said.

He grinned. "Won't need it," he said as he took the lamp I'd filled with blue fire.

I waited a few moments, looking skyward. Then I heard glass crack as the lantern broke. "Fire!" Moki cried. The blaze loomed bright, to a height of ten feet. I could see it even though I was at the very back of the ship.

"Fire!" others yelled. "Get water! Go! Go!"

Water would not help them. The only thing that would work was sand, and the Guardians lay in wait in the wings to offer such a suggestion if it did not occur to them on their own.

I looked up again. We had only a small window of time before others would notice a dragon boarding a ship. "Come on, Miren," I whispered.

As if the gods had heard me, she appeared near the lower deck on Zephyr. It was incredible how quickly she'd mastered riding. Then again, Asha learned fast too, like it was instinct.

"You had me waiting long enough," I called out.

She grinned. "You know you could always take your chances and swim."

I grumbled before jumping from the deck onto Zephyr's back. He growled at my intrusion but waited patiently for me to get a better grip.

"I've never helped someone wreck an engagement before," she said.

"That is not what I am doing."

She turned, arching her brow. "I am sneaking you into the room of a woman who is engaged to another man. What would you call it?"

"I am trying to protect her. We don't know what Zaib has planned," I said, though I wondered who I was trying to convince.

"She has a dragon. Why does she need you? She can protect herself, if you ask me."

"I wasn't," I huffed.

Zephyr was able to get me close enough to jump onto the railing. "Are you sure this is her room?" I asked.

She grinned. "You'll know soon enough, won't you?" she said before soaring off.

I clung to the rail and peered through the narrow pane. The moon and dim candles were the only sources of light that allowed me to look into the room. A figure lay pooled on the floor in a cloud of chiffon and white, the veil so long it nearly consumed the small cabin. She was in her wedding dress, I realized. The sight of her in a dress—this dress—did something to me I hadn't prepared for. All the words I'd rehearsed lodged in my throat and would not move.

For a breath, I questioned everything. I shouldn't be here. Not now. Not like this. I'd resigned myself to calling Miren back, but then the faint cries reached my ears. I listened to them as they clawed at my heart. I took a deep breath before tapping once on the frame. I lifted the latch and eased the shutter inward on its tired hinges.

She turned her red-rimmed eyes to me. She was beautiful; it was like I was truly seeing her for the first time. I wanted to tell her so, but my mouth wouldn't cooperate. She hid behind her hands, her veil falling forward.

"Let me help you," I said.

I grabbed the edges of the soft fabric and lifted it. Though the tears still streaked her face, her expression had hardened, her lips pulled tight in a thin line.

"You shouldn't be here," she said.

"I know."

"Then why are you?"

I searched my memory, trying to recall what had possessed me to enter her room at night, when we were both betrothed to other people. "I don't know—I was worried."

"You needn't worry. Zaib has made sure to take care of my every need." My fists clenched at my side as I imagined his greedy little hands on her body. "I imagine you have been busy doing the same with Celia."

That caught me off guard. "No."

She turned away. "No need to lie to me. She was in here moments ago telling me how well you've gotten on. Honestly, I'm relieved to hear it, that we've both moved on."

I swallowed. "Have you moved on?"

She blinked and gestured toward her attire. "You haven't noticed?"

I watched as the fabric clung to her curves, accentuating every part of her.

"I always notice." I paused. "When it is you."

She shrugged her shoulders. "Well, now you know that I'm well, so you can go before you are found out. Celia will be missing you."

I shook my head. "It'll take some time for her to be escorted back to the other ship."

"Other ship?" I watched as something clicked. "You are not on this one."

"No," I sighed. "And I am sure that is how Zaib wanted it."

"Perhaps, but it has allowed me to get to know him. Zaib and I..." She paused. "We could be content together if I gave it a chance."

Alarm bells hammered behind my eyes. My mind was screaming at me to hold my tongue. "Is that why I've found you in your wedding dress in tears?"

"I am happy," she said, desperation hanging from every word. "These are happy tears."

I clenched my jaw and stepped forward to wipe the tears from her cheeks. "Don't marry him."

That startled her so much her mouth fell open. "Isn't this what you want—what everyone wants?"

I smoothed back the veil until the comb fell from her hair and her curls fell free. "I've been very consistent in what I want."

"You are promised," she reminded me.

"I should hate you for leaving," I breathed into her ear.

Still, disbelief trailed her face. "But I left. We missed our chance."

My hands went to her sides tentatively. I waited for her to tense or pull away. When she didn't, I grew bolder, slowly lifting the delicate silk to her waist. The fabric was formal. Pristine.

"This is beautiful," I murmured, my thumb brushing one tiny button until it came undone. Then another. This continued until the dress barely clung to her frame. I leaned closer, enough that she could feel my breath.

"What would the man you belong to say," I asked quietly, "if I were to free you from it?"

Her breath caught.

I paused. "Tell me to stop," I said quietly. "And I will."

She stepped back, and I fought the instinct to follow, to reach for her.

Her hand went to her collar, then slowly down the line of buttons. I followed every movement like a man dying of thirst, and she was the last drop of water. When she reached the last one, she paused. "I belong to no one," she said as she undid the last one and the gown slid down to her waist.

I grabbed her, claimed her, pressing her back into the wall before lifting her thigh. I kissed the top of her breast, and she rewarded me with a delicious moan.

I stilled, my forehead resting against hers, our breaths tangled. "I belong to you."

Her whimper found my name, and I kissed her—careful, asking—and she answered, fingers at my collar, pulling me closer. The world narrowed to the rasp of fabric, the thud of my pulse, the way her shoulders loosened under my hands as if a weight finally slid free.

"Nothing," I began, kissing my way down her body, "can satisfy me but you."

The last part I said with a feral grin before burying my face under the layers of silk until I found the barest layer of lace over her core. She clung to my shoulders, her fingers digging into me as I breathed against her. I pulled her undergarments to the side and allowed my tongue to explore until she shivered, melting against me, before I couldn't take it anymore and ripped the lace free. I pressed her more firmly against the wall, and my tongue satisfied that craving—that part of myself that had died when she had left..

"Adriel!" she whimpered. The sound of my name on her lips did something to me, and it took all that I had not to take her fully, right then. Instead, I pulled back to insert a finger and watched as she arched her body against me. With each thrust, I went a little deeper, a little faster, and I was rewarded by a sound I had not yet heard from her. Just when she'd adjusted, I slipped another finger in and began to pump more intensely until she cried out and writhed against me.

"More!" she moaned. I stood, answering her cry with a kiss, opening my mouth so that she could taste herself on my tongue. She wrapped her hands around my neck and rode my hand, arching her back as her whole body convulsed under my attention.

I reveled in how my touch brought her such pleasure, that I could give her this when so many had only taken from her. She was holding back, trying to rein in her bliss, but the effort trembled through her like a held breath on the verge of breaking.

I pushed my knee between her legs to widen her stance, giving me more access. "Come for me, Asha," I coaxed. "Give me what I want."

Asha's eyes flashed wide as she shuddered against me, surrendering to my demands. She cried out, and I held one hand gently against her mouth to quiet her, the other still inside her as she rode wave after wave of pleasure, and I watched every single one until her breathing slowed. Asha's knees buckled as I helped steady her on her feet, removing my now slick fingers.

I'm not sure what came over me, but the smallest tinge of worry seeped in. I'd wanted this, she'd wanted this, and yet we'd been here before with the same passion—and she'd walked away.

"Asha, I—" I faltered, searching for words I didn't have. I wasn't sorry, not in the slightest. "I saw you there, and I lost control."

I swallowed.

Her brow arched. "Liar."

That caught me off guard. "I—what?"

Asha pushed off the wall and stalked toward me. The remnants of her skirt pooled around her until they dropped to the floor, leaving only her torn undergarments behind. Heat climbed my spine; whatever composure I had completely abandoned me.

"I'm tired of everyone treating me like I'm this fragile thing," she murmured.

"I didn't mean— "

She stopped me. "Yes—yes, you did. You think you did something to me." She pointed a finger at my chest. "Not that I allowed you to."

I was speechless. She was right. I inhaled sharply. "And what will you allow me to do to you next?"

She bit her bottom lip before closing the distance between us. Just when I thought she was going to kiss me, she pressed a hand to my chest until I fell into a chair behind me.

"Asha, what are you doing?" I asked, trying to get my balance.

She dropped slowly to her knees, her hand exploring my chest until it dipped to my stomach, and she touched me. I gasped as she used both hands to grip the laces at the top of my trousers until they loosened. She placed her hands inside to pull me free.

I waited patiently until she held me, her expression changing as she explored my length. By then, every whisper of her fingertips was sending me further and further over the edge until I placed my hand over hers.

"We can stop—"

She slapped my hands away, and before I could protest further, she swirled her tongue over the tip of me. I hissed between clenched teeth as she took me fully into her mouth. She pulled away, and I nearly cried in agony.

"We don't stop unless I say," she said before taking me again in her mouth. She sucked and moved her hands, trying to find her rhythm. I hummed in pleasure that she would even think to desire me in this way.

When I tried to reciprocate, she pulled her body away, taking me in her mouth once more. This time, all the way to the hilt. I relented, my head falling back. My lips parted as my breathing came in short, shallow pants. She pulled back, catching her breath. "Is this alright?"

I scooped her hair in my hands to pull it from her face. "You literally cannot do it wrong." This seemed to give her more confidence because her mouth steadied when she took me again, her hands locking into a rhythm. It took everything within me to hold my hips still and not thrust. This was about her taking pleasure from me, not me taking my pleasure from her, though I wanted to. Gods, I wanted to bury myself inside her.

Her mouth moved faster, and her breaths grew unsteady as she struggled to take all of me. I watched her move with rapt attention until my eye caught her naked backside and the tattoo I'd placed there. She'd kept it all this time. She could have removed it, but she hadn't. The sight was my final undoing. I was at my limit. I leaned down and lifted her into my arms. As she clung to me, I thrust myself into the crease of her ass until my body released.

"Asha!" I cried, holding her tight as her fingers clawed into my back. The aftershocks of pleasure had me sinking to the floor, and I reached for her, cradling her in my arms as a final tremor ran through both of us.

"I've got you," I whispered, forehead to hers, counting our breaths until they stopped snagging. Her heartbeat slowed against my chest.

"Don't move," she murmured, as if the ship itself might shake us apart.

"Never."

CHAPTER FORTY-FIVE

Asha

I reveled in the way Adriel held me, the way he used his thumb to rub circles on my back. I'd spent so many nights dreaming of this, wishing for him to take me in his arms. I snuggled closer, wanting to snuff out the rest of the world and pretend for just a moment that it was just us. That we were all that mattered.

He seemed to be waking from his own dazed state, twirling the necklace at my throat. "This is pretty," he murmured.

I pulled his hand away and onto my hip as I snuggled into him. "From Mattias," I said.

His shoulders seemed to relax at my words.

"What now?" I whispered.

"Hmmm. We can go again if you like?" he said, turning me so my belly lay flat on his.

I propped up my chin and traced his beard. "I meant our engagements. What do we do about them?"

"We end them," he said as if the answer was obvious.

"End them?" I said with a pause. "We can't, or at least I can't. I made a promise. Any day now, Zaib is about to uphold his end. I must uphold mine."

Adriel's hands dropped to his sides. "You're still going to marry him then?"

"Yes, and you should feel free to marry Celia or... whoever you want."

He was silent for a moment, and I immediately regretted my words. Why did I have to ruin the moment of peace we'd found in each other?

"I see," he said quietly.

"You do?"

He used his hands to move me to his side so that he could sit up. I sat up with him.

"I do," he said. "You think I can marry Celia after what we just did?"

"It is not as if you are not experienced. She will not care."

"You think she won't care that I just had the future Queen of Entioch on my tongue?" he asked carefully. I flinched, but he grabbed my hand, refusing to let me retreat from his words.

"Stop," I said breathlessly.

He released me and stood.

"What are you doing?" I asked.

"Getting dressed," he said. "You should too."

"You really expect me to go back on my word to Zaib?"

"Your word to Zaib?" he asked incredulously. "What about your word to me?"

"I've never promised you anything."

He pounded something hard, probably the wall. "To never hear my voice, feel my touch, taste my lips. Did you mean that when you said it?"

I startled at his recollection. "I—"

"Did you mean them?" he demanded through gritted teeth.

"So much time has passed. Our circumstances have changed."

He let out a long sigh. "You forgot to mention there was a time limit for your affection. You might want to mention that to Zaib before you say I do."

How had this gone so wrong? "This was a mistake," I said, going to my chest to retrieve clothes.

He was silent as I dressed. I could not be sure, but I had a distinct feeling that he was watching my movements. I fumbled with the buttons of my dress and finally whirled on him. "What? Just say it!"

His boots shifted, causing the wooden floor beneath us to creak. "I've never seen anything like it. I've never seen someone so eager to climb back in the cage she just escaped from."

Before I could speak, the cabin door burst open. I covered my chest and turned, but not before catching a glimpse of Kwasi's unmistakable inky aura.

I quickly fastened the top of my dress as Adriel stepped in front of me. "What are you doing here? You should be resting."

"I think I should be asking you that," Kwasi said.

"Kwasi, it's not what you think."

"Sister, I do not care who is in your sheets; in fact, I never want to speak of whatever this is again. That is not why I am here."

"What is it?" I asked in concern. "Are you feeling worse?"

He grasped my hand and placed the book Tazbah had given me in it. "I remember. I know how to find the Ifambe islands, and we are nowhere near them."

CHAPTER FORTY-SIX

Asha

"Zaib said we were less than a day away. Where are we going if he is not taking us there?" I cried frantically.

"I don't know," Kwasi said. His eyes were fixed on the book. "But the journal you left with me—it helped me remember something. Adriel, use your battlemage. Burn it."

Adriel hesitated. "You want me to set it on fire?"

"Yes." Kwasi didn't look up. "All of it."

The flame bloomed across the page—cool against my skin, wrong in every way.

"More," Kwasi said sharply.

Adriel inhaled, his aura shifting as he pushed his battlemage. The energy flared, spreading through the air in a controlled blaze.

Kwasi's breath caught. "That's it. That's exactly how I remember."

"Wait until it cools," Adriel warned, but Kwasi was already turning the pages.

The paper crinkled beneath his fingers, fragile as dried leaves.

"Ash," he said urgently. "Put your hand here."

I brushed my palm over the page and felt it—raised lines beneath the surface. "Elliarb!" I said, trying to understand. "But it is a game, the message. It is nonsensical. What does it have to do with the island?"

"This is not a game. It is a map," he said, flipping through the pages. "This!"

"What is it?" Adriel asked.

"This is a map to the island."

"It looks like nothing to me," Adriel said.

"It is so brilliant. This is not just Elliarb," he said. "These are coordinates."

"How can you be sure?" Adriel asked.

"Yes, please tell us."

I froze.

That voice—familiar enough to pull the air from my lungs.

"You!" Adriel said, his rage reduced to a single word.

I whipped around. "Marlon!" The name tasted bitter, heavy with a memory I hoped never to relive again. He stepped through the doorway with unsettling calm, and my heart dropped further when I saw the faint shimmer of Ashkii's yellow aura behind him.

"Ashkii..." I breathed, barely audible.

The sound of Adriel's sword sliced through the air.

"We don't want violence, Adriel," Marlon said smoothly. "Not while I am in possession of these sweet little dragons."

My heart clenched as Ala and Mwana cried out.

"Drakkar!" I called down the bond.

"Give them to me!" I said frantically.

He pulled them away. "Now, now. They are sleeping."

The entire ship shuddered as Drakkar's growl ripped through the hull. I staggered, but Adriel caught my arm with his free hand.

"Isn't this sweet, the two of you? Although, I don't imagine Zaib would be pleased."

"What do you want?" Adriel demanded.

"It is not what *I* want. It is what the Shadowcasters demand. They want Asha."

"Why?" he demanded.

Marlon chuckled. "All will be revealed soon enough, but I do need you to call off your dragon, Asha, before he burns the ship and all of us with it."

Ala suddenly let out a strangled cry, his tiny throat constricting as if invisible hands were tightening around it.

"What are you doing? Stop!" I cried.

"I would love to," Marlon said lightly. "As soon as you call off your dragon."

Ala gasped wildly for air.

"Calm yourself," I said through the bond. *"They will hurt them if you don't."*

The rumbling ceased. Drakkar pulled up sharply outside, circling the ship with blistering rage, his fury condensing into a tight, ominous volcano.

Ala sucked in breaths, like his neck had been released. "Good," Marlon said. "We're all being reasonable."

A tear slipped down my cheek. "I loathe you."

"Well, that's unfortunate," he sighed. "But your affection isn't required for your cooperation."

"What do the Shadowcasters want with me?" My voice shook despite myself.

"You're the key, Asha. Look," he gestured to the journal in Adriel's hands. "Already you've pieced together something we've worked on for decades."

"Decades? You haven't been with the Shadows that long."

"No. But the plan predates all of us. Long before we were born."

"You're not taking her," Adriel said, voice like drawn steel.

"She doesn't have to come with me," Marlon said sharply. "But the dragons will." He adjusted his grip on the hatchlings. "We'll be waiting above deck. You can come of your own accord, Asha... or I take the dragons instead. Either way, I'm not leaving empty-handed."

He paused in the doorway.

"I'd decide quickly, though. Elan's army is nearly upon you."

Then he was gone.

The door had barely shut before Adriel seized my hand. "We need to get off this ship," he said urgently.

"The Guardians," I said frantically. "We have to warn them. We have to warn everyone. We can't leave. We can't leave the hatchlings."

Adriel placed a hand firmly on my shoulder. "Listen to me. Asha, listen. I don't know what the Shadowcasters have planned for you, but they are going to great lengths. You are important to them, which means you cannot fall into their hands."

"I'm not leaving the dragons."

"We will get them back. I promise."

"No! We aren't leaving them," I said firmly.

He didn't have a chance to respond, because the ship lurched and we all went flying, surrounded by the sound of splintering wood. Something had slammed into the hull and now the whole ship ceased its movement.

"*Asha,*" Drakkar called.

"*I'm alright. I'm coming up.*"

"We have to get above deck!" Kwasi shouted.

Adriel grabbed my hand, and we ran up the flight of stairs. The sound of soldiers waking up from sleep echoed as chaos filled the deck.

Another crack sounded as wind and cold sea water sprayed over our bodies. I'd been separated.

"Adriel!" I called, but I could not hear anything over the shouts of men yelling around me.

Chapter Forty-Seven

Drakkar

The voyage had been too long.

The sea was wrong. It rolled beneath my claws, never still, never solid, the deck rising and falling like a wounded thing that refused to die. Salt burned my nostrils. Rot and kelp fouled the air. This endless rocking offended every instinct in me. Dragons were not meant to be trapped on water.

If not for the hatchlings, I would have taken to the sky and remained there. But their wings were still soft, untested. Zephyr was newly risen, his strength unproven for long carry. So, I endured, remaining grounded on this floating piece of wood that groaned with my every step.

Asha was occupied, and while I'd begun to hate the mortal less and less, I wanted nothing to do with their mating rituals. Mortal emotions were unnecessarily complex and confusing.

It was nights like this that I missed Seraphina the most. She'd have found a way to laugh about Asha's love life. She would have teased me about our own love story, how she'd changed course to fall in my path. I was nearly asleep when I heard a desperate call from Asha.

I jolted upright as my wings spread instinctively. Igbo lay by my side blinking slowly. "Where are your brother and sister?" I demanded as Asha's warning rang in my ears. Igbo looked sleepily around him.

"I don't know," he yawned.

I growled, moving frantically on deck in search of them and Asha. That is when Zephyr appeared in the sky with Miren. "Ships with the Emperor's sigil are coming!" he warned. "We need to get Asha and the hatchlings off the ship."

I paused for a second, listening for Asha. I whipped my head around. "They have the hatchlings!"

Zephyr's eyes flickered with fear. "Who? Where?"

"I do not know!" I yelled, scrambling, flames licking in all directions. The soldiers on board retreated from me. I was seconds away from burning the ship to ashes until Asha's voice cut through everything. *"STOP!"* she warned.

I could not go below deck. The space was too small. I paced, waiting for her to give me word. I would break every nail and board on this ship to get to them.

I waited until I felt the first blast of the assault. There was indeed a fleet of ships sailing perilously close to ours. Dragons chained to the deck held cannon balls in their mouths and, on command, began to shoot the fiery weapons in our direction. They meant to sink us!

"Asha! You need to get above deck now!"

I turned to Igbo. "Stay hidden. I will be right back for you."

"Papa, I'm scared."

Weeks ago, one of my hatchlings referring to me like that would have terrified me, but tonight I was filled with the determination to protect him. "I'll come back. I need to buy Asha some time. Can you be brave for me?"

He nodded. Another fiery cannonball hit the side of the ship, and I had no more time. I lifted into the air and signaled to Zephyr to flank me. As we neared Elan's ships, I began to realize that we were vastly outnumbered. We had three ships, and they easily had forty all stocked with dragons. I ducked as another cannonball shot off into the water. The impact sent enough water onboard to extinguish the existing fire and blow the ship off course. Zephyr let out a stream of fire, setting the sails of two ships ablaze. I worked to stop the cannons, but there were too many.

Finally, we decided to set the sails of the first line of ships on fire. We trailed the water, coming from opposite directions, until we met in the middle. There was more that we could do, but I needed to get Asha and the hatchlings to safety. When I returned to deck, Igbo was not where I left him, which set my heart racing. The deck had holes from where the cannons had met their mark. Several mortals lay on the ground, unmoving. I just hoped none would be Asha.

"Asha. Where are you?" I called.

"Here!" But it was not the voice I'd expected. It was Adriel.

He was bent over with Asha's crumpled body in his arms. He gathered up her skirt, now splattered with blood, and headed in my direction. Kwasi came to his aid to help hold her up.

"Zephyr!" I called.

He was there in an instant. Before Adriel could speak, I bared my teeth.

To his credit, he did not look scared, just determined. "I can't understand you," he said in mangled Dragontongue, "but Asha is hurt, and the Shadowcasters have Mwana and Ala."

Riders or hatchlings—my mind tore in two.

"We don't have time, brother," Zephyr snapped. "I'll take Kwasi. You take Adriel and Asha. We'll keep searching for the brood."

Sense. I clung to it. Adriel swung up as I crouched just as Zaib lunged toward us.

"You can't take her!" he shouted. "Adriel, she is not yours!"

Adriel didn't miss a beat. I surged skyward, leaving Zaib's screams behind. "Asha," I called down the bond, but she did not respond.

I circled around the ship, frantically calling for them. The ship was nearly consumed in fire when I finally heard a scream. "Papa!"

I turned. It was Igbo. I moved closer, calling for him, following his voice. "Son! Where are you?"

Then I saw him. He was on a fiery deck. There was nowhere for him to go. He turned in all directions, trying to find a way out. Each time I tried to move toward the flames, they licked higher. Normally, that would not be an issue, but with Asha on my back, the flames could kill her. Adriel began coughing, covering Asha's face with his cloak.

I had seconds to get Igbo. There was no other choice. When I circled back, Igbo was no longer looking at me. His gaze was locked onto something else. I turned to look in the direction and found that he was looking at Ashkii.

"Get away from him!" I growled.

Ashkii froze, his gaze remaining on Igbo. Then Igbo did something strange. He leaped into the air.

"Stay right there!" I said. "I'm coming to get you!"

But before I could make my descent, Igbo successfully leaped above the flame. No—*leap* was not the right word. He *flew*! His wings flapped in unison.

"Igbo!" I called, but he did not turn in my direction. He remained fixed on Ashkii, whose eyes were a molten gold. *No, it couldn't be.*

Ashkii opened his hands just as Igbo flew to him, landing just inches away. Ashkii reached out to touch his face.

The deck cracked as I landed, and this time Ashkii stumbled, taking Igbo with him.

"Let my son go!"

Fire rose in my throat, and I was ready to burn him to ash.

"Drakkar!" I paused at Asha's scratchy voice. *"No! Don't you see? They have bonded. Ashkii is... a Lightbearer."*

Lightbearer.

The word dropped into me like lava into water—hiss, steam, a hurt I couldn't name. My flame rose to my tongue anyway.

"Igbo has claimed him." Asha's voice cut clean through the bond. Within my soul lay the pain and certainty of it all.

I swallowed the fire so hard it scalded. The air tasted of pitch and salt and ash.

Across the gap, Ashkii's eyes burned. He didn't look at me; he looked only at Igbo, who clung to his forearm with new, clumsy wings, shivering from that first impossible flight.

"He is too young," I whispered.

"Drakkar, we must go!" Zephyr called.

"I can't leave Mwana and Ala."

"They aren't on the ship," Asha said. *"We must get in the air before we're all lost."*

I sighed deeply before flapping my wings. My talons clenched the collar of Ashkii's cloak. He yelled, but I did not take heed as we rose—right before the ship collapsed into itself.

Chapter Forty-Eight

Asha

Igbo moaned below, as Ashkii lay motionless in Drakkar's claws. I'd called Igbo to join us on Drakkar's back, but he had refused. He continued to lament, crying that Ashkii was not well.

We had traveled all night. Drakkar was unable to speak. I'd attempted several times, trying to reach him within the bond, but he'd remained quiet. Even after I told him that Marlon had them, and that was their best chance at survival, it did not faze him. We needed to locate Marlon, but without the Lightbearers, we didn't stand a chance. I'd never forgive myself if anything happened to Ala and Mwana.

"How much further, Kwasi?" Miren asked.

Kwasi held the book, studying the maps within. He shook his head. "This says we are already there. I'm not sure where we went wrong."

"We have to be here," he added in frustration.

"Let me see it," Miren said. "Perhaps you need fresh eyes."

"I've studied maps all my life," he grumbled as he handed the book to her. "I know what I'm looking at."

"We are missing something," she sighed, looking toward me. "Asha, that book Kadir gave you. Do you still have it?"

I reached into my pockets and was surprised to see it was still there. "I do, but what does this—"

"Hand it over," she said. As I reached over Drakkar to hand it to her, she said, "Have you thought about how similar these two books look? I mean, nearly identical, except one we can easily read, and one we cannot."

"Kadir said it is some silly game he plays."

"Morozco," Miren corrected. "It's a coding game. None of the riddles are what they seem. You have to decipher them using a rubric." She hesitated, then added, "What if—*and this is a big if*—that's the point? What if this isn't a map at all, but a code?"

Kwasi stared at her, awe softening his frustration. "It's mad... but maybe."

They bent over the books together, Miren copying symbols while Kwasi translated aloud.

"Do you think," Adriel whispered beside me, "it matters that Igbo bonded with Ashkii?"

I frowned. "What do you mean?"

"Isn't Ashkii a Shadowcaster?"

"I don't know. I thought dragons could only bond with Lightbearers. Isn't that right, Zephyr?"

Zephyr was quiet for a long moment. "You and Miren are the only Lightbearers I've ever known," he said at last, not meeting my gaze. He shifted in the air, glancing toward Drakkar. "Whatever we do, we need to do it quickly. We've never flown this long and no offense, but you're all heavy."

We continued circling the same stretch of sky. Igbo's cries cut deeper with every pass, and Drakkar's silence was worse.

Then Miren straightened. "I know where it is."

"What?" Kwasi said. "Where?"

"Just sit back and relax, map expert."

Zephyr dipped, and I motioned for Drakkar to follow. We circled an area of ocean a few times before Adriel yelled, "There is nothing here."

"Exactly!" Miren said.

She pointed. "See the swell? There are two of them, one from the open ocean, one... bending. Waves don't bend like that unless they're refracting around something solid. And the wind—feel it? It drops in a clean circle. That's a wind shadow."

I held my breath and felt it too, a hush in the air, a soft hollow where the wind should have been. Subtle and not quite right. "I feel it," I said.

"Weather has signatures, a pattern that it follows, even when it is disrupted by a barrier like an island."

"Why can't we see it?" Adriel asked.

"That, I do not know."

"So are you suggesting that we land in the water?" I asked.

"I think we should land," she confirmed, "but I don't think it is water."

"Those waves are big," Kwasi noted. "We could be taken out?"

"Only if I'm wrong," Miren said. "And I am not wrong."

"Are we all in agreement?" I asked. Everyone nodded except Drakkar.

"Won't you climb up, Igbo?"

He shook his head.

I sighed.

"We will go first," Miren said.

Zephyr tipped into a slow descent. We followed, salt spray needling our faces as swells reared and folded, each wave climbing the back of the next. Drakkar hovered just above, and Adriel leaned over in case we needed to carry out a rescue mission.

They seemed to be landing just fine, and then I blinked. They were gone. I blinked again. "Where did they go?" I asked frantically.

Suddenly a wave burst above us. A wall of spray burst over us, and Drakkar wasn't fast enough to clear it. The wave slapped us sideways and down. We fell, all of us, and I braced for cold weight and drowning, but I hit slick, wet ground instead. I thrashed, gulping air, waiting for the water to close over my head.

It didn't.

My palms skidded on something that felt like glass slicked with rain. Salt stung my tongue; the air was thin and dry. I thrashed around, waiting for the water to overtake me, for me to have to swim for air, but I was breathing just fine. Only my sight was gone.

"Drakkar!" I called, but the bond was silent. "Adriel!"

"Drakkar. Can you see me? Why can't I see you?" Drakkar was always the constant being that I could see no matter what, but this time, I couldn't see him at all.

"We are here," Miren said somewhere to my left. "Kwasi and I are alright, but we cannot see you."

Her aura burned nearby like a bright flame. Kwasi's pulsed close behind it. "It is like being bonded all over again," she whispered.

"Can you hear Adriel or Ashkii?" I asked. "I don't see either of their auras."

"No. It is just us so far," Kwasi said.

"Adriel?" I called. I stood, not daring to go too far but searching for him. After ten paces, I nearly tripped over him. "Are you all right?" I asked.

"Halt!" a voice called in the distance.

I felt the tip of a sword at my throat before I noticed the auras closing around us.

"Don't touch her," Adriel growled.

"I don't think you are in a position to be making threats," the voice said.

I held up my hands slowly. "We don't mean any harm."

"Why are you here?"

"What business is it of yours?" Adriel snapped.

The blade moved from my throat momentarily. "This one wants to die first."

"No!" I cried. "We are Lightbearers. We are in search of an island that carries more."

Something shifted because suddenly all the movement around us stilled. The crowd grew eerily silent. "What did you say?" the voice asked.

I swallowed. "We are Lightbearers, and we have dragons. They will not be happy if we are hurt."

The woman seemed unimpressed. "Dragons are not allowed here, and you cannot be Lightbearers. Who are you? What is your name?"

"Don't," Adriel warned, but it was too late.

"I am Princess Asha Osei. I am the only daughter of Idris, the late emperor."

Voices murmured. "He's dead?" someone whispered.

"Finally!" another exclaimed.

"Quiet!" the woman said, and to my surprise, they all listened. "How do we know what you say is true?"

I held out my hands. "I can show you if you would take my hand."

"What is your battlemage?" the woman said with interest.

"I read auras."

"You... what?" Now I knew something was wrong.

"Auras. It is how I can see you moving about."

"And you were born with this?"

The line of questioning was growing more confusing by the second. "Yes, of course."

"And once you find these Lightbearers, what do you intend for them?"

I had thought about the answer to this question so many times. I wanted everything. I'd pinned my entire future on finding them. "I just want to talk. The world is falling apart between the new emperor and the return of the Shadowcasters."

There was a collective exclamation. People began to talk in earnest now until I finally asked, "Is this the first you are hearing of Shadowcasters?"

The woman moved closer. "You must go. All of you. We do not want to get involved."

"We?" I paused, daring not to hope. "Are you Lightbearers? Did we find you?"

The knife was back at my neck. "I said, leave!"

"Have we met before?" Adriel asked. That seemed to take the woman off guard because I was able to reach out and grab her aura.

I gasped. "Odina."

CHAPTER FORTY-NINE

Asha

"No one has said that name since I stepped onto this island," she warned. "Who are you?"

"I tell the truth," I said, lifting my chin. "I am Asha, Princess of Ujuima."

"Ujuimans are not welcome here," another voice cried. Others rallied in affirmation.

I turned to Adriel's aura. It was electric, like his emotions were spinning faster than he could contain. "What would you like me to call you, Odi?" he breathed.

The spear clattered in front of me, discarded, suddenly meaningless, as Odi's aura approached Adriel. "It can't be," she whispered. "How did you find me?"

"I didn't know you were alive to be found," he said quietly. "If I had, I would have started searching long ago. I thought you were dead."

The emotion in both of their voices was so raw, I felt wrong being witness to it.

Odi's aura pulsed—shades of deep crimson mixed with gold. "You should have left me buried," she said quietly. "You risk much coming here." There was grief there, swathed in disbelief.

"Where are we?" he asked. "And why can we not see?"

"I will explain everything, Adriel," she said. "But first, we must escort you to the citadel. It will be unpleasant, but it is our way."

"What do you mean—" He choked mid-word, collapsing to his knees.

"What are you doing to him?" I cried.

"Do not resist," Odi said sharply. "It will only make it worse."

A burst of energy struck me before I could. My body convulsed as I fell on my back and tried to run from it, but there was no running. I could hear the others screaming in the background. I was slipping under, nearly unconscious, until I heard Odi's voice.

"Let go," she whispered. "Don't fight it."

I stopped, but only because I had nothing left to give. As soon as I relented, so did the current.

I was hoisted upright, my feet dragging through air that felt thick as honey. My body was weightless but heavy all at once, my chest rising in shallow, trembling breaths.

"Where are you taking us?" I whispered, though the words barely reached my own ears.

"The Iroko to meet the Ori Mothers," Odina said, her voice distant now. "You'll understand soon."

The auras around me shifted. I could feel eyes upon me, studying, sliding across my body like a curious hand. Then, a burst of sound, a single, low gong that rippled through the air and opened the space before us.

The current that held me began to move. It wasn't walking, not really, more like being drawn forward, as if invisible hands had hooked beneath my skin and were pulling me through an unseen tide. The others had quieted; the only clue that they were near was their auras.

The hums of wherever they were taking us grew louder, layers upon layers of sound and whispers. We were in a procession, I realized. And others were gathering to watch us as we paraded through like the spoils of war. As we continued to move, no one spoke to us. They just watched with hushed whispers.

The procession was long. It was terrifying to be taken somewhere that I did not know and had no means of escape. It did not appear that even Odi was willing to save us.

When at last our captors halted and lowered me to the ground with unexpected care, my palms pressed against something cool and slick. I reached out, mapping the world through touch. Thick roots twisted around each other like serpents, damp earth breathing beneath my fingers. Trees, perhaps. The ground was wet, and when I crawled forward, my hand slipped into water that rippled at my touch.

"Be careful," Kwasi warned. His voice came from somewhere on my left. "There's water ahead. We don't know how deep."

So forward was no escape. Backward, perhaps, but I already knew we wouldn't get far.

A cool hand found mine. Adriel.

"Are you alright?" I asked. I was one of the few who knew Odi's story. The thought of what he must be feeling, discovering his sister alive after all this time, made my chest ache.

"I should be asking you that," he answered softly.

"Asha?"

My head snapped toward Ashkii's aura. He'd finally awakened, his energy fluttering wildly.

"What is happening? I can't see anything."

"Don't talk to her," Adriel barked.

"It is okay," I said.

"Who was talking to me?" Ashkii asked, panic weaving through his voice. "There was someone before... a voice in my head. It was so clear."

I frowned. Where were the dragons?

"It seems he has bonded with a hatchling," an elderly voice said, cutting in from the darkness. "That is unfortunate."

"I know we have come to your island uninvited," I said quickly. Urgency tightened my voice. "We traveled with three dragons. We need to find them."

"Dragons are not allowed in Lumira," the elder said.

The voice came from directly ahead, still and unmoving. It pressed against me like a weight.

"Is this not the Ifambe Islands?" Kwasi asked.

The elder voice bristled. "Only your people call it that. By all that live here, this island is called Lumira."

Adriel stood—or tried to. He seemed to stumble a bit on the uneven ground.

The woman chuckled softly. "You might as well sit, young man. You are not accustomed to our land, and it may take some time to adjust."

Adriel's voice sharpened. "What do you want with us?"

"Shouldn't we be the ones asking that?" came another voice, also old, but deeper. "What do you want with us?" he demanded.

"We are here to find other Lightbearers," Miren said. "Like Asha and me. We had heard of this island, and we'd hoped..."

"Yes?" the deeper voice asked.

"We hoped to find more like ourselves," I finished.

Silence followed. The stillness from the first voice sharpened, displeased.

"And yet, you bring one of them here?" the first voice said.

"What do you mean?" I asked.

"A Shadowcaster stands among you. Their presence alone raises grave questions about why you have come."

"But they found this island all on their own, sisters." This was yet another voice. How many were there? "That has to count for something."

Her tone was gentler, but it carried weight. Whoever these women were, I sensed they held authority. "Perhaps we should introduce ourselves," the gentler voice said. "I am Ireti."

The woman ahead of me spoke next. "Dara."

And the deeper voice, circling somewhere nearby, "Tayo."

A murmur rippled through the group of onlookers. Even without sight, I sensed the deference in their voices.

Adriel's aura flared. "If you are who you claim, then you know what we say is true."

"That is not what is in dispute," Dara said coolly. "The problem is that you have not been invited to Lumira, and when you came, you brought our enemy."

"He's bonded, like Miren and me," I argued. "What makes him different from us?"

There were whispers moving around us, and the bits I could catch were not in agreement.

"You know nothing, child," Dara said. "That you do not know the history of your own kind is disappointing."

"What history?" Kwasi asked.

"The history of our people and how we came to be."

Tayo chimed in. "It is no wonder you know nothing. That ignorance perpetuates the Shadows."

"But the Shadowcasters have only just returned," I argued.

"You are dense if you believe that," Dara hissed. "They have been present for some time, waiting for the perfect opportunity to return in full force. They are the answer to our light. As long as we do not come into our full power, neither do they."

"Is that why you all are hiding here?" Miren asked with a tinge of judgement in her voice.

"We are here for our preservation," she replied.

"Is there a reason you have taken our sight? When will it return?" Adriel asked.

There was a deep breath. "It won't, not while on this island, anyway," Ireti answered.

"Why?" Ashkii finally spoke.

Whispers circled at his voice, and they were not pleased.

"Because Lumira is ours and we prefer to inhabit it as we are, not as others want it to be," Dara said.

"Now it is your turn to answer questions," Tayo interjected. "We want to know about the Shadowcasters and their movements."

"Our first sighting of them was at the base of the Saelerian Mountains," Adriel said. "During the conflict with the new emperor."

"New emperor?" Tayo asked. "So, Idris has finally perished?" There was no sadness in her voice, only curiosity.

"Yes," he said.

"I hope it was a lengthy, painful death," she said finally.

My father was not beloved, so I'm not sure why I was surprised. Perhaps because of the level of disdain in her voice, it was more than most.

"Go on," Dara encouraged.

"They took us down quickly," Adriel continued. "We barely made it out with our lives. Some of us, like Ashkii, were captured. That was over two years ago."

"And what have they been up to since?" Ireti asked.

This time, Ashkii answered. "The Shadows provide social programs, and word and scripture that fuel their souls."

Pages of a book flipped in someone's hand. "Yes, I have your book," Ireti said.

"Then you know we mean to bring peace and prosperity to the land. Nothing more."

"I think we have spoken enough," Ireti said. "The Shadowcaster will remain. The rest of you will see the memory mage to have your memories wiped before you go on your way. We do not wish for you to return."

I stood then. "No. We will not leave until we've said our piece. The world is collapsing, and if you are what is left of the Lightbearers, we need your help."

Ireti's aura approached, close enough that I could smell the coconut in her hair. "My word is final."

I reached out then, desperate to get answers. I just needed a moment, one touch, and I could get some of the answers to my questions. However, when I touched her, I was met with fire. I stepped back, cradling my burned hand. "We are not leaving until we get what we came for," I said.

I heard the sound of lips pursing followed by a disappointed sigh. "I judged you wrong. You have Sanaa's fire after all."

My mind screamed at her words. These were not the casual words of someone who did not know her, or who only spoke of my mother's beauty. "What do you know of my mother?"

"Much, I'm afraid. I was saddened to hear of her passing," she said regretfully. There was a tense silence, long enough that there were low murmurs in the background. "Alright, you may stay. You will be shown to private rooms, and we will treat you as guests. This should be interesting as we have not had this many in a decade."

The conversation was apparently over because we were shuffled once more out of the room. Adriel grasped my hand, and Kwasi, my other. I was the only one who could navigate this world out of the five of us, I realized. Before we left the area, I turned back and saw Ashkii was not following us.

"Where are you taking him?" I asked.

"To a cell," Ireti said, before we were forced away.

CHAPTER FIFTY

Asha

"When can I speak with my sister?" Adriel asked.

The attendant guiding us through the grounds did not sound moved by his urgency. "I suppose when she is ready to be spoken to." Her tone was clipped, businesslike. "My name is Gloia. I am here as a temporary guide to prevent you from wandering into a ravine or drowning in one of our pools."

"What kind of magic is affecting our sight?" Kwasi asked. "Is this battlemage?"

"I am not authorized to answer your questions," she said briskly. "Only to help you navigate Etherie Court, the Gardens, and the Citadel."

I heard the faint clatter of wood as she passed something to each of us. "You now have walking staffs. Once you grow familiar with the grounds, you won't need them. For now, hold the staff out and tap in front of you. Listen."

She demonstrated. The sound shifted—stone... grass... gravel.

"Notice the texture and tone of each," she continued. "All of our pools have a ring of gravel around them. Just know if you notice that sound, you are headed into water. Our pools are very deep, and it can be very disorienting to swim if you have never done so without sight."

"So, we won't be swimming while here," Miren grumbled.

"Stone is good. It means you are on one of our designated paths. Our stones are all the same size, so you can count your steps for wherever you need to go," she said. "Again, this will be less necessary the more acclimated you get."

"There are rails and bannisters with Elliarb," Gloia continued. "Reach out to them if you get lost. They will tell you where you are and give directions to the next location. If you feel grass, most of the time it is alright, but do not venture too far off the designated paths. We have untouched rainforests that allow the island to thrive. If you venture too far, it is unlikely the Ori Mothers will authorize a search party, and you will be on your own," she warned. "There are many beasts within those trees."

"What about all the water I hear?" Kwasi asked.

"The island has hundreds of bodies of water. We have utilized them in different parts of the Citadel to assist with direction. The louder they are, the closer you are to the Citadel. You know you are within the court when they reach a mid-level sound. Flowers are another resource. Within the court you will smell anthuriums; further out, we have ginger lilies and orchids."

A bell chimed, three clear tones rolling across the grounds.

"That signals tea," Gloia said. "Would you like it in your rooms, or will you join the others?"

"Who are the others?" Miren asked.

"Those on the high courts that make the laws, our esteemed judges, and the Ori Mothers if they choose."

"We will take it into our room if that is alright," I said.

"Very well."

The first thing I did once I was alone was familiarize myself with the space. It was quite large, with several rooms. To my surprise, there was a terrace and a balcony, though I couldn't be certain how high off the ground it was. I continued to call for Drakkar, but my connection to him was eerily silent. I hoped he was alright.

The bed was calling to me. It had been a long journey at sea and then a full twenty-four hours without sleep, but a bath felt necessary seeing as I hadn't had one in days and was beginning to smell like it.

Warm spring water circulated through a small pool in the bathroom. This pool was surrounded by etched stone, not gravel, so I assumed it was shallow. As I stripped down, I sighed in contentment as I experienced a level of luxury I hadn't experienced while being on the road for so many years. There were soaps lining the pool that I took full advantage of. I had no idea if there were clean clothes anywhere in the room, but I would figure that out later. Right now, I was content just lying there, letting my bones relax.

My mind wandered to Ashkii, who was undoubtedly locked away somewhere that would be difficult to reach. I needed to convince them somehow to let him go. I did not know what would happen to Igbo if his bonded were to be imprisoned forever, or worse, killed. And then there was Odi. I still could not believe she was really here. Questions swirled about how she had managed to survive the fire.

Though I had questions, they did not seem pressing, whether because of tiredness or something else. This place had to be disconcerting to Kwasi and the others, but for me it was peaceful. I defaulted to skills I had already mastered, and I did not have to hide here, or pretend I wasn't an unseer. The word didn't even exist here. I could just be.

I hummed along with the bells that sounded outside my window, laying my head back to get a good lather.

"Do you need any assistance?"

I startled, water sloshing against the edge of the pool. I hadn't heard the door open.

"Adriel?"

"I knocked." His voice sounded sheepish. "It took me a while to realize I was at the wrong door. A woman named Hanbi was nice enough to guide me here."

"You shouldn't be in here."

I watched his aura hesitate on the threshold. "It is not as if I can see you."

I realized I'd dipped under the water and was clasping my hands around my bits, but he was right. He couldn't see me. I let my hands fall to my side. Neither of us said it aloud, but the memory hovered between us. We'd already crossed that threshold not even a day before.

"I thought you might have fallen asleep."

"I nearly did," I said, my voice soft with exhaustion. "But I'm fine."

He didn't move closer, yet the air felt alive between us. We had yet to revisit our last conversation. Truthfully, I wasn't ready to, at least not with words. My body on the other hand betrayed me whenever he was near.

"I can wait outside," he offered. "Or," a pause, "I could join you, if you want."

"I'm finished," I said, quickly reaching for a towel.

I turned away, as if he could see me, before wrapping the towel around me. "What are you doing here?"

He inhaled deeply. "I do not trust the people here. I wanted to make sure you were alright."

"I am," I said. "It should be me looking after you."

"Would you like me to retreat to my own bath so that you can?" he said with amusement.

"No," I said quickly, trying not to imagine him naked. I moved past him into the bedroom and pulled a brush from the vanity. I hadn't prepped my hair, which meant the knots were going to be awful. "Now that you know there is nothing wrong, can you leave me to dress in peace?"

He walked carefully into the bedroom. Something metal clattered on stone. His aura shifted to the ground, his hands gliding over the floor. Whatever it was skittered away. His quiet exhale sounded as he contemplated whether to go after it.

"Leave it," I sighed.

"Is that what you want?"

"Of course. You'll spend all day looking for it."

Silence followed. "I meant are you certain you want me to go?"

"Why would I say it if I didn't want it?" I snapped.

He paused long enough that I turned to face his aura, expectantly. "I notice you have a tendency to say yes to things that you don't actually want," he murmured. "Here, give me the brush. I can hear you pulling out your roots."

"How do you know anything about hair?" I asked.

He put his hand over mine searching for the brush. "A few hours without sight and you've already forgotten my own luscious locks."

No, I could never forget those.

"Nayeli taught me," he shared. "She starts at the ends and uses her fingers to break the knots if needed. Did your mother teach you?" he asked.

"She tried. I was too impatient and by the time it mattered, well, she was no longer here."

He knelt behind me, careful to orient himself. He touched my shoulder, then my neck, before pulling back my curls from my face. I felt the air shift between us as his fingers combed gently through the wet strands, separating each one. His breath on my neck was intoxicating, like my personal bottle of pleasure.

"We shouldn't," I murmured.

"I know."

My insides quivered at the way he ran his fingers through my hair, carefully, so carefully. My heart pounded, and I suddenly found it very hard to breathe. I needed to break the silence somehow.

"And Odi? Has she spoken to you?"

His hands momentarily stilled. "No, not yet," he said. "She will come to me when she is ready."

"I don't know why but now that I'm here... it feels so strangely comforting."

"I'm sure. You can be yourself here. You don't have to fear for your life, at least not for your sight."

"The Ori Mothers seemed alarmed by the spread of Shadowcasters. Do you think they will help us?"

"I hope so. I fear dealing with them and Elan's army," he said.

A tear ran down my cheek. "Do you think Mwana and Ala are okay? They must be so scared."

"I do not think they care to hurt dragons, especially hatchlings. We will get them back, I promise."

I sniffled. "You can't promise. Everything has fallen apart. Saeleria is no more, Wyrmwood was attacked, and we don't know what has happened to Zaib."

He stilled the brush, laying it down. "Turn toward me," he said.

As I did, he ran his hands through my curls, checking for snags. "It looks bleak now. It has to because that is the only way we appreciate the light. It will all work out. We will win this."

"How do you know?" I asked breathlessly.

"Because as long as you are safe, I can handle anything else that comes our way."

I swallowed hard. The words sat heavy between us.

His hands lingered at the ends of my hair, twisting a single curl between his fingers. The gentleness touched me more than any promise could have. The space between us held all the things neither of us dared to name. I could feel the warmth even without touch. Then, a knock sounded at the door.

Both of us jumped. "Hold on. I'm dressing."

The door opened anyway, and Adriel stilled, blending into the space.

"What is the meaning of this?" I demanded. "I'm dressing."

"Forgive me, Your Highness," came the familiar voice. "It's Dela—Odina. I've come to inform you that Mother Ireti has requested your and Kwasi's presence for dinner in the Observatory."

"Just the two of us?" I asked.

"It is not my place to question an Ori Mother's wishes," she said with a casual shrug.

"Thank you for the message," I replied. "Now, if you please, I'd like to change in peace."

"Of course." Her aura retreated toward the door, but she paused on the threshold. "And brother, since you are here, I'd like to invite you on a stroll this evening after dinner."

My cheeks flamed, but before I could muster up an excuse, she was gone.

Chapter Fifty-One

Adriel

I grimaced as my knee came into contact with stone for the tenth time today. I couldn't fathom how Asha was able to spend her life this way. It gave me an appreciation for how graceful she was in any room without visibly counting or needing assistance. I, on the other hand, stumbled into everything. I wouldn't dare admit it had taken me over an hour to find her room. I'd mistakenly walked in on Kwasi and Miren talking on my way back. Kwasi seemed to have newfound strength since being here. I hadn't expected him to be growing so close to Miren.

Miren and I ate in the dining hall together. This was another unexpected challenge. The food rolled around—at times I grabbed bites that were too large, at others the fork was empty when I put it to my mouth.

"Clockwise," Miren offered as I cursed under my breath. "Move around your plate starting at the top and eat to the right."

She gushed over all the food, but I could barely taste it as I worried for Asha. She was too comfortable here, and we had no idea if we could trust the Lightbearers.

"Have you tried using your battlemage here yet?" Miren asked.

"No, I haven't needed to."

"I haven't been able to summon a lightning strike, not even a few drops of rain. Do you think they have something blocking battlemages?"

I flicked my wrist, but nothing happened. I tried a few more times, pulling deep until I felt a cool fire sputter. "Something is definitely affecting it," I said. "All the reason not to stay on this island for long."

"Tell the Oseis that. They act as if this is their new home," she sighed. "You should have heard Kwasi go on and on about the technology of the fountains and how they coordinate with the lunar month."

I leaned forward and whispered, "We should keep our ears to the ground. There has to be a way to leave this place, with or without the Lightbearers' help."

"I'm no spy, but I'm up for the challenge," she said.

"Good. See what you can find out."

"What does Adriel need to find out?"

I did my best to hide the surprise in my voice as Odi walked from behind us.

Miren recovered faster. "We wanted to know more about the island."

"Is that so? Well, I'd be happy to be your guide any time," she said, though her tone told me she did not believe us for a second. "Are you ready for that walk, Adriel?"

"Are you okay alone, Miren?" I asked, reaching for my walking staff.

She tapped my hand. "Go! I have the whole grounds to keep me occupied."

I squelched a sigh. She couldn't be more obvious.

Odi took my arm, and as we walked, I tried to recall the thoughts I'd prepared to say. For some reason, none of them came out. I sensed from the way her arm tensed in mine that she was feeling the same. So we just walked in silence for a time. I had no idea where we were, only that we were leaving the bustling sounds of the court.

The first words out of my mouth were not what I expected. "You missed Mother and Father's funeral," I said, then inwardly cursed because that was not how I wanted to begin things.

"Yes, I got word that they had passed," she whispered.

"Dragonfever took many that year," I said. "I just never thought we would lose them at the same time."

"I thought of you often," she said. "Even before I'd heard of their deaths, there wasn't a day that went by that I didn't miss the life we had."

"Then why did you leave?" I asked suddenly. There it was—the words I'd held onto since the moment I'd learned she was alive. "You couldn't come back for the funerals at least? Do you know what it was like to see the home that you were supposedly in collapse in a fiery blaze?"

I pulled away from her then, needing the space. Only two women in my life could make me lose the tightly wound control I had over my emotions, and one of them was standing right next to me.

"I am sorry," she whispered. "I did not know you would be there. I—it's not how I planned it at all."

"Why are you here, Odi? What was so important that you needed to abandon your family?"

She sighed. "I am Dela now. I didn't want you to spend any time coming after me. I wanted you to move on."

"Why?" I asked angrily. "Do you know what your death did to me, to all of us? We buried you."

She was quiet again, but continued walking. "I'm a Lightbearer. I mean, you probably guessed that now, but I had no words at the time to explain it. And Mesof offered me a way out."

"So Mesof is a Lightbearer?"

"There are many of us, brother. Asha is not the only one, but she certainly would be the highest ranking we know of."

"But why wouldn't you tell me?" I insisted. "Why wouldn't you tell our parents?"

"It was easier then putting you all in a position to choose me or the kingdom. That is not fair to any of you and even if I told you I was leaving, I wouldn't be able to tell you why."

I scoffed. "We would have chosen you...Dela. Kingdom be damned."

"Then there'd be a civil war. Father would have been compromised and you all would be in danger. No, it was better to leave and allow you all to grieve in peace. I'd hoped you and Enapay would lean on each other, become closer."

"Well, that didn't happen." The bitterness was thick on my tongue.

"Is he ruling Wiyotak?"

I caught her up on the current state of events and the war we'd been fighting the last couple of years.

"And where is he now?" she asked.

I deflected the question. "It doesn't matter. He will be dealt with soon enough."

"You are going to kill our brother?"

"Would you rather he rot in a prison or I give him to his enemies?"

"I don't know," she sighed. "I wish it hadn't come to this. Why are you not ruling from Wiyotak?"

I ground my teeth, unsure of how to answer.

"It is because of her, isn't it?" she asked gently.

"Who?"

She paused. "In some ways you have changed a lot, brother, but in others—not at all."

I chuckled. "Is that a compliment or an insult?"

"Both."

And for just a moment, it felt like we were back home when things were simple. That moment quickly ended when she asked, "I want to know why you have come."

"Isn't it obvious? We want your help in the fight."

"Have you considered just sheltering here? The Shadowcasters cannot touch us on this island. The magic prevents it."

"And what happens if that battlemage fails? If it can fail for the dragons in Saeleria, it can fail here."

"It won't fail here," she said with unwavering confidence. "This has been a safe haven for Lightbearers since we came into the world. Atim and Oneida built it themselves."

I nodded, realizing she had confirmed something I'd already guessed at. "Atim Wiyotak, the architect of our kingdom? I've been reading his histories. Are you saying that they were Lightbearers?"

She inhaled proudly. "I am saying they were the first. The very ground we walk on, they built to protect us from the Shadows."

"Why do Lightbearers need such a place?"

"You see how the world treats us. Here, we can be ourselves. Even if you don't want to stay, have you thought that Asha might? Maybe you could be happy here—with me."

"I can't leave our people, Odi—Dela. They're counting on me, on us, to bring the Lightbearers into the fight. Why won't you help us?"

"Because it's a battle we cannot win."

"How can you say that when we haven't even tried?" I asked.

Her voice softened, almost pitying. "Their power mirrors ours, Adriel. And they draw others to their side with ease. I saw the man you brought—your newly born Shadowcaster. His mind is already lost."

"He's not lost," I said, surprising myself. I'd had very complicated feelings about Ashkii's return, but I hadn't given up on him entirely. "He's struggling, yes, but I believe he'll find his way back."

"I've never known anyone who has," she said, and there was a weight in her voice that chilled me.

"No one?" I pressed. "Surely someone, some record, some legend—"

"Never."

The way she said it was final and absolute. "Why could you not at least visit us? It would have been hard but preferable to thinking you were dead."

"We are told that once we commit to residing here," she said, "we cannot go back, or risk never being allowed back in. The Ori Mothers forbid it."

"I thought this was supposed to be an oasis you were running to. What kind of place encourages you to run away and cut ties with your family, but one wrong step and you are exiled from it forever? These people don't care about you, Dela, if they can cast you aside so easily."

"You know nothing."

"Don't patronize me," I said. "You chose exile over family. We mourned you while you found comfort here among strangers. These are not your people."

"They are," she whispered. "They are Asha's too. You'll see. When a Lightbearer sets foot on this island, the bond calls to them."

"You never lost your sight," I noted.

Her silence stretched, heavy with indecision. "I did," she said at last. "You just never noticed. My battlemage allowed me to manage my sight, but it was temporary—days, sometimes weeks. I finally decided it was time I stopped being ashamed of who I am. That night, I asked you to come because I couldn't see in the dark. I was afraid I'd lose my sight completely on the road."

"I was there," I said, voice breaking. "I was right there when the building collapsed."

"I know," she whispered. "And I'll never forgive myself for letting you see that. I don't want to lose you again, Adriel."

The anger released from my body like wasted energy. I didn't think. I just reached for her, pulling her into an embrace that felt both foreign and familiar.

"Never," I said, my voice rough. "I will never lose you again."

CHAPTER FIFTY-TWO

Elan

"Bring him in," I said.

The palace doors creaked open, and Dragonlord Ekon entered, though with far less confidence than before. He knelt at once at my feet.

"Your Holiness."

I steepled my fingers, my battlemage simmering below the surface with wavering restraint. "I asked you to deliver my sister to me," I said calmly, "and you have failed for the third time."

He kept his head bowed. "I am sorry I have failed you."

"Do you know why I asked you to find her?"

He hesitated, then answered carefully. "She betrayed you. Defied your emperorship by running off to Wiyotak."

I laughed softly. "Is that what you think?" I said, leaning forward. "Let me tell you a secret."

His shoulders stiffened.

"She betrayed me the moment she was born," I said quietly. "I was raised to be the light—to carry it, to embody it, to lead with it. And then she arrived, and my birthright was stolen from me."

Ekon looked up at me, confusion flickering across his face, but he did not speak.

"The Lightbearers called it balance," I continued. "I called it theft. Everything I had been taught about my purpose, my right as the sovereign, fractured the instant she drew breath. From that moment on, I was no longer the future, she was."

I turned over the stand next to me and Ekon had to move to avoid it. "She never earned what was given to her." I regarded him coolly. "The only reason you are not in chains right now is because you once saved my life. That mercy will buy you only a swift death."

His eyes widened in panic. "Please, Your Holiness. I can find her this time. I know it!"

My battlemage crackled between my fingers. "I do not believe you."

I channeled the magic into his skin. The smell of burning flesh curled through the chamber, and I sighed, savoring it.

"Wait!" he screamed. "The dragon!"

"The Shadowcasters have the hatchlings, not us," I snapped. "Another failure." I increased the voltage.

"No, the dragon she is bonded to," he gasped. "She will come to us."

My battlemage cut off instantly.

Ekon clutched his arm where melted armor had sealed to his skin as he wheezed in pain.

"What did you say?"

"We have *her* dragon," he said again, barely conscious.

CHAPTER FIFTY-THREE

Asha

I had expected to have to dine with all the Ori Mothers but was pleasantly surprised that it was truly just Ireti, Kwasi, and me. The intimacy of it eased my nerves. Instead of sitting at a table, she invited me to walk with her through her gardens as we dined. We ate and talked among the flowers, plucking our meal straight from the vine. Each delicacy was impossibly fresh, like the gods prepared it. It felt less like eating and more like partaking in something sacred.

"I imagine this is old hat to you, moving around our citadel," she said. "Most who come take several months before they grow comfortable."

"I'm not sure how to feel about it," I said honestly. "I suppose I feel like myself for the first time ever."

"I like that," she said. "I will have to use it on anyone new who comes through."

"Do you get a lot of new Lightbearers to the island?"

"Not anymore," she said. She didn't elaborate immediately, and something in her tone suggested the story behind those two words was longer than this walk. "Once this was a place of refuge, but eventually it became a place of necessity and survival. We received a lot of new people back when Idris took the throne,; now it is a slow trickle. Dela is still one of our newest recruits and she has been here for six years, I think."

"You are speaking of Odi?" I asked.

"That name no longer belongs to her," Ireti said. "She is Dela now. You can change your names too."

"How does one change one's name?" I asked.

"You may either choose one yourself or undergo a naming ceremony and let the community choose one for you."

"Which did Dela choose?"

"She wanted the whole experience, so she had the naming ceremony." A pause. "It was a good one. The community spent three days with her before they chose."

"Can I ask how long you have been here?"

Ireti seemed to move in a way that made people follow. It was no wonder she was one of their leaders. "I am one of the few who were born here. All Ori Mothers are."

"People are born here?" Kwasi asked.

"Of course. Lightbearers do not typically leave the island unless on a mission to seek out other Lightbearers, and Lumira has been closed off for some time."

"Are there healing properties on this island?" he asked.

"Yes," she said. "Haven't you noticed the extra energy in your body?"

He paused.

"Are you saying the island is healing him?" I asked.

"From the moment he set foot on our lands, yes," she said with humor in her voice. "I am surprised it worked so quickly. The charm on you is powerful."

"I am grateful to you," he said earnestly. He inhaled deeply. "Ah, I feel like I could explore the world and nothing would hurt."

Ireti's aura dimmed slightly. "Those are the healing properties of the island. Wonderful, aren't they? If you were to leave, the magic would revert back, and depending on its progression, it might even kill you."

That took us both off guard. "He can't leave?" I asked.

"Unless there is someone to absorb it, no."

"Never," Kwasi said firmly.

"It is vessel bound," she said. "It must pass to another or kill the host."

"Could anyone be a host?" I asked.

"Don't even think it, Asha," Kwasi said. "This is my burden to bear."

"But you may never leave."

He exhaled. "This is paradise," he said bitterly. "I can think of worse fates."

"You seem displeased," Ireti observed. "You both would be very welcome here, for as long as you need."

"It is just a lot to think about," I said carefully. "We have come here to see if you will join us in the fight against the Shadowcasters. They are consuming the world, and Elan, my brother, is driving them into their arms. Their numbers are growing."

"We do not leave the island, child. Once you are here, you are expected to stay here. There are rare exceptions that recruit new Lightbearers, but no more."

"But this is why we came. To get you to join us and help identify more in the world."

"If you find a Lightbearer, you should direct them here," she said sternly. "We can keep them safe."

"What about the rest of us?" I asked.

"You mean the rest of *them*?" she said. "You and Kwasi are one of us."

"I am no Lightbearer," Kwasi said quickly.

"Not yet," she said with amusement.

"What makes you think he is?" I asked.

"Your bloodline," she said as if it were obvious. "Your mother was a Lightbearer."

I could not describe the heaviness in my chest that lifted at her words. It was as if my whole life began to make sense. "How do you know?"

"Because Sanaa was my sister."

CHAPTER FIFTY-FOUR

Asha

"She was a Lightbearer, Kwasi. Just like us," I marveled.

"Or like you," he said, poring over a map in Elliarb. "I don't know if she is correct in our lineage. I have never felt anything different about my battlemage."

"But Miren didn't either until her dragon found her. Perhaps it is the same for you."

"Perhaps. But that also means that Elan is a Lightbearer as well."

"No, he couldn't be."

"He is if bloodline is the way one becomes a Lightbearer. But he hasn't bonded with a dragon either."

I shivered. It was a terrifying thought that he could. "Would that mean he could come here?"

"I don't care how much of an oasis this place has been; it is not safe. Nowhere is. I'm starting to believe that we are being recruited instead of the other way around."

"You mean they want us to stay?" I asked.

"Yes, Ireti has said as much, but I'm sensing they want us to stay very badly. I want to know why."

"Well, we can't," I said. "It has already been several hours. Drakkar must be worried sick about us. We will just have to try harder to convince Ireti that stopping the Shadowcasters is in all our interest."

"Auntie Ireti," Kwasi corrected.

"She must have so many stories about Mother. Do you think she would share them?"

"I hope so. Maybe we give this place another day," he said, stretching. "I certainly feel better when I am here."

I was relieved to hear him say so. "Yes. One more day."

One more day turned into several. Things just felt so peaceful and right on the island. I had never slept so well. Even Adriel and I had found a comfort in each other's presence, more than we had in a long time. Ireti dined with Kwasi and me every evening. She was so open in sharing. I learned all about how Mother grew up, her love for adventure and all things nature.

"There was a flower Mother always wore in her hair," Kwasi recalled.

"Cintears," Ireti answered. "She enjoyed the ones that smelled like honey. We called her that sometimes."

"I'd like to gather some for my room," I said. "Where can I find them?"

"Oh, they are in the Papillion grove. You don't want to go there. It is far from the path. I will have them sent to your rooms."

An arrangement of cintears was in my room in hours set out for me. I did so happily, tending to every stem. I was so transfixed I did not even jump when Adriel entered unannounced.

He leaned over my shoulder to smell them. "Smells lovely," he said.

My heart warmed. "Don't they? Ireti said she would have them sent to my room every day if I wanted. They were Mother's favorite. I'd love to visit the grove where they are from."

"Perhaps we can go there today," he offered.

I frowned. "Ireti warned it is far off the path. I'd hate to get lost."

"How could we with you as our guide?"

I thought about it for a moment. He was right. If anyone could get us there, it was me. "I think that would be alright. Let me just tell the others."

"I took the liberty of letting everyone know. Ireti is aware that you will be a little late to dinner."

"Are you sure she is alright with it?"

"Of course. You could tell her yourself, but I worry we will lose daylight if we try to track her down."

There was something in the way he spoke that made me wonder. I quickly shook it off. Things were good here and he was right. No one would miss us.

The path curved away from the hum of the Citadel, and before long, the air began to change. The further we walked, the quieter everything became. Even the waterfalls sounded distant, muffled by thick mist. I filled Adriel in on all I had learned so far from Ireti. He listened with intense interest, flicking his battlemage. I could feel the change in temperature as the blaze grew taller in his hands.

"It is curious that she never reached out when your mother died, don't you think?" he asked.

"Not really," I said. "She was here, and certainly she did not want Father to know about this place."

"Not even to have a relationship with her nephews and niece?"

That was odd, but surely it was done for the safety of all involved. "I am just glad that I am in contact with her now. She is so kind and brilliant."

"Mmm. Yes, everyone says that."

"Why do you keep playing with your battlemage? I've never known you to do that," I said.

He was quiet for a moment. "What is the saying, power resents being ignored?"

"Well stop," I said, "it is sweltering."

"As you wish, Princess," he said with an air of mockery.

I rolled my eyes. I could just imagine the grin on his face. "You don't seem to like Ireti very much. And you don't share much about Dela."

His whole aura tensed at the mention of his sister. "I like your aunt just fine. I just have a lot of unanswered questions. I don't get to spend as much time with her as you do. Actually, with Odina, I mean, Dela, I've been spending a great deal of time accompanying her on her healing rounds. With Miren and Kwasi being so occupied with each other, I either spend my time with her or alone."

"Why would Miren and Kwasi be spending so much time together?" I asked.

Adriel paused, dropping his walking staff. "Really? Oh, I wish I could see your face." He laughed. "Do I really know something about two people that you do not?"

I sighed. "What are you talking about? Kwasi hasn't said two words about Miren since we arrived."

Adriel laughed out loud. "I don't even want to spoil it for you. That is the thing. What to do?"

"Just tell me," I demanded.

"I will, but only if you promise to take a quick detour with me."

"Where?"

"I'll tell you when we get there, but first, promise."

"Fine," I said, planting my feet stubbornly. "But only if you tell me now."

He leaned down to whisper in my ear, which made my spine tingle. "I heard them kissing in the gardens the other night."

I pulled back. "What? That can't be. You must be mistaken. Your senses are off."

"I know what I heard. It was... passionate, to say the least."

"But my brother doesn't... I've never seen him take an interest in anyone."

He ran a hand down the length of my hair. "Perhaps he hadn't found the right woman to take an interest in until now."

My chest felt heavy as our breaths mingled. "Perhaps."

"What do you have against Miren?" he asked curiously.

"Nothing. She's great; I just never imagined..."

Adriel cupped my cheek. "That Kwasi could be happy."

"I don't know." I stepped back to allow my mind to settle. "Where are you taking me? We have to hurry if we are going to make it back in time for dinner."

"Yes, Princess. I wouldn't want you to be late for your dinner. Come with me."

Adriel moved me onto several winding paths with ease. He'd clearly made the trek several times.

"Can you tell me where we are going?"

"Not just yet. But soon."

It grew cooler the farther we walked, and I began to notice how different the sound of our steps had become. The gentle sound of fountains faded, replaced by the faint scent of ginger and a deeper, hollow echo of uneven stone beneath our feet.

"Adriel," I said, pausing. "This doesn't feel like we are on any of the main paths."

"It is just over here," he replied easily.

Something about his tone made me hesitate—it was light, teasing, but there was an edge to it. Still, I followed. The path curved sharply, and I felt him guide me down a narrow incline.

"Are we underground? You've taken me beneath the island, haven't you?"

"Something like that."

The humor in his voice didn't land fully. He was tense. I reached out, brushing the wall beside me; it was damp and cold. My stomach tightened. I stopped in my tracks.

"Adriel... where are we?"

"We're almost there. Just around this corner."

There was a metallic creak, iron perhaps, and the smell of salt and rust filled the air. I took a small step back. "Adriel!"

He stopped then, exhaled slowly. "You said you wanted to see more of this place."

"I meant the grove. Not wherever this is."

He didn't answer. Instead, he reached forward, and the air shifted as a door, no, a gate opened. A faint moan of wind, or maybe something else, slid through the corridor.

Then I heard it.

A voice, weak but familiar. "Adriel?"

My blood turned cold.

The world tilted. I froze, heart pounding. "Ashkii? You brought me to the prisoner cells." My voice broke on the word.

Adriel didn't deny it. He just stepped aside, the faint glow from Ashkii's aura spilling past him.

"Why are we here?"

"You've begged me to hear Ashkii out, to allow him to come back to us, and we get here, and you completely forget about him. It is strange, Asha."

"He is a Shadowcaster. The Lightbearers say he cannot be saved."

"And what exactly is a Shadowcaster?" Adriel demanded. "No one has been able to answer that question for me. I'm starting to think they are Lightbearers that the Ori Mothers disagree with."

"You've seen their power, the way they work. How could you say the Lightbearers are like them?"

"Because they are," Ashkii said.

I turned toward him. "I don't believe you. I don't believe anything you say."

"Hear him out," Adriel said. "We've been talking and— "

"I don't need to hear him out!" I yelled. "He is the reason Ala and Mwana are in danger." My heart raced. Ala, Mwana, Igbo, Drakkar. I hadn't thought about them for days.

"You're noticing it too," Adriel said. "The flood of memories. The longer we stay here, the more we forget why we came here in the first place. You are in the court playing house as if you have no intention of leaving."

I tried to turn away, but he gripped my shoulders. "I felt it too until Miren discovered where Ashkii was being held, and it all came back."

"Do you think it is a battlemage? Is that why we are forgetting?" I asked. Even as I said it, I felt the edges of it— the way that the last few weeks had felt like a never-ending dream. How easy it has been to stay.

"I don't know, but whatever it is, it is not happening to Ashkii, which makes me wonder if it is intentional. They wouldn't waste a battlemage on a prisoner."

"Surely Ireti has no clue this is happening," I said.

Adriel did not answer right away. Finally, he said, "Hear what Ashkii has to say. Maybe it'll put some pieces together."

Ashkii's voice faltered slightly. "We made a blood oath never to share what we learned from the Shadows. I fear they will come for me."

"We won't let them," Adriel assured.

Ashkii laughed, but there was no humor in it. "A blood oath cannot be stopped, especially if turning Shadow is a result of a cruel act or malice. But the moment I bonded with Igbo—that is his name?"

"Yes," I confirmed.

"He spoke to me, in my mind. Is that how it is for you?"

"It is necessary for the bond."

"Well, once he claimed me, or I claimed him, I was finally able to see Marlon for what he is." He took a deep breath. "The first few months of my capture, I was tortured. Marlon has a particular affinity for mind games, and I spent weeks on end wondering if what I saw was reality or not. He excels at finding the thing that scares you before exploiting it. He is a terrible man, and I had fooled myself into believing otherwise. And I've helped fool a lot of people. For that, I can never forgive myself."

"All you've told me is that you hold your meetings to invite people to learn about your cause. Feeding starving people is admirable," I admitted.

"Giving people a glimpse of happiness and what they could have is the gateway. It is all a lie. But once you are in it, it is too late."

"What are the Shadowcasters after?" I asked.

"You."

The words sat in the air between us all. Somehow, I knew it was true; it was the only thing that made sense. My mind reeled. "What do you mean? They can certainly take on Elan and rule over the Five Kingdoms without me."

"Yes, but without you, there will always be a threat to their power. At any moment, Lightbearers could rise up against them. It has happened time and time again."

"Why would I be able to stop the Lightbearers from rising up?" I asked.

"I don't know exactly, but it is very important that you not marry. That is why I came. To make sure that never happened."

My head spun with this new information.

"What would marrying have to do with anything?" Adriel asked.

"I'm not certain. Whatever it is, I am not privy to it. But it is their greatest wish that you join them."

I thought of Zaib, of the terms I had accepted and how neatly it had all fallen into place.

"Who leads the Shadowcasters?" I asked. "Marlon?"

"No, Marlon is the face, but there is someone else pulling the strings. They call him the Nightborne."

"So the Shadowcasters are being led by someone they have never seen with a name like Nightborne?"

"They do not have to see him. His words are passed to them through his works, through his book. We learn to know him and worship sight unseen."

"Like an emperor?" I asked.

"No, like a god," Adriel said.

"Yes," Ashkii confirmed. "We worship him like a god."

"Why take the hatchlings?" I asked.

"To control you," he said as if it were obvious.

"And Elan. Does he play any part in this?"

"We have been coordinating with him. His ego prevents him from seeing the truth, but he is not the one holding the power."

"Dija? It would have to be him," I said.

"That would explain how Elan knew where to attack us at Wyrm-wood," Adriel agreed.

"There is more," Ashkii continued. "We have been told to be on the lookout for something. A relic or maybe a place."

"What is it?"

"It is supposed to hold both light and darkness. I don't know what it does exactly, other than whoever holds it, holds the power of both the Shadowcasters and the Lightbearers. Whatever it is will hold a lot of magic." The bars creaked under Ashkii's weight. He must've been leaning on them. "There is one name I overheard. Melo Wiyotak."

My heart jumped. "Melo... the historian? The scholar who chron-icled the Dragon Wars?"

"He was no simple scholar," Adriel said. "He was a king. I know this story well. The Dragon Wars began because of Oneida, the wife his brother Atim stole from him. It was said they had a great love."

Those names again. There had to be a connection. "She must have been something if a war was started on her behalf," I said. I thought of what I would burn down for the people I loved. The list was never ending. "How did dragons get mixed up in it?"

"The details of that are murky, but it seemed to me that Atim and Oneida were allied with them, and that caused Melo to form the Five Kingdoms to create a united front against them, the dragons."

"That is when dracite was more heavily used," I said, remembering my history lessons with Kwasi. "What happened to them, Oneida and Atim?"

Adriel shrugged. "All assumed they perished in battle, but no one really knows."

"I think—" Ashkii began.

He wasn't able to finish because the heavy footsteps of guards began to approach. "You have to go!" he whispered. "Their guards check in every couple of hours. I believe there is an exit to your left. Hurry."

"We need to get you out first," I said frantically, pulling on the bars.

"We will do that later," Adriel whispered. "We can't be found here, or they may move him."

"Who's there?" a man called, maybe twenty paces away. "We can hear you!"

I gripped Ashkii's hand and caught one last bit of information in his aura before I pulled away. I saw, and he knew that I saw. Neither of us said anything out loud.

Adriel pushed me forward, and as footsteps drew closer, we moved into a sprint.

Adriel's hand pressed into my back as we tore down the narrow corridor. The stone floor was slick beneath our steps. The moisture in the air clung to my skin, followed by the sound of voices behind us.

"This way," he hissed, tugging me left. The tunnel narrowed sharply, and the sound of rushing water grew louder—first a trickle, then a roar.

"Adriel, this is a dead end!"

"It's not," he said, pulling at vegetation until he found a chamber door. He groaned as he tried to pull it open. "Help me open this."

I dropped my staff and gripped the circular handle, and we both pulled. It groaned as if it had been sealed for many years, but eventually the door opened just enough for us to fit through. As we burst into the chamber, mist billowed into the room, cool and wet against my skin. The sound was unmistakable.

"You can't be serious. You want us to jump into a waterfall?"

He took my hand. "You trust me, don't you?"

"I haven't decided yet!"

He used the other hand to caress my cheek, and before I could react, his lips were on mine hard and fast. I blinked, and it was over.

"Then decide fast," he whispered.

Boots thundered somewhere behind us. They were closer now as shouts filled the halls. I squeezed the hand he was holding. Without another word, Adriel wrapped his other arm around me and stepped into the mist.

CHAPTER FIFTY-FIVE

Asha

The world dropped out from under us. My body stretched awkwardly, as if my bones were pulling outward as if remembering something. Fear took over and I continued to fall.

The waterfall swallowed our screams, freezing and blinding all at once. My body spun, water pounding against me, stealing air and sound until all that existed was the rush of the current. Then suddenly his grip tightened, and we slammed through the surface into calmer water below.

I flailed, and he tried to keep me near, but the current took me.

"Dammit!" he yelled, but it was nearly lost in the sound of the falls.

I plunged under the water, coughing and spitting every time I came to the surface. I gripped the surrounding stones, but they were slick with moss. My limbs were growing numb as the temperature of the water grew cooler. One more plunge and I would be lost, my strength waning as my limbs grew heavy.

A powerful current broke through the water, my fingers tingling with it by the time Adriel's arms wrapped around me once more. "Tell me where to grip," he gasped. "Do you know where the shore is? I can get us there."

I didn't. I couldn't see anything, and I was so disoriented and frozen that I couldn't respond. Sensing my panic, he hugged me tighter, somehow keeping us both above water. "We are not dying today. You hear me? Fight, Asha!"

I searched again, looking frantically, but all around us was darkness, until—

I gasped at what I was able to discern. I did not have the power to see the shore, but I could sense auras, and there were lots of them on either side of us. Animals. Beasts. Spirits—I had no idea. I could only pray they wouldn't harm us. "There!" I choked out. "Just ahead to the right. Hurry."

He released one hand and began to swim with me in tow. I kicked to give us more momentum until we broke through together. Adriel lifted me onto the shore. He had to be exhausted. Once I was on land I turned and gripped his hand. He was able to maneuver on the rock with me. We just lay there on our backs, gasping for air. The night was cold; the water was moving quickly with the current. I coughed and sputtered as the sound of the falls continued to thunder, an endless wall of sound that drowned everything else out.

"Are you alright?" he asked, brushing hair from my face.

I swallowed hard. "We are not alone," I whispered, watching the auras creep closer.

Adriel sat up quickly. "What is it?"

"I don't know," I said, sitting up with him. We stilled, waiting as they moved closer. There had to be hundreds of them. Whatever they were, we would not succeed in fighting our way out. One of them brushed against my cheek. I inhaled sharply.

"Asha, are you okay?"

I reached out blindly, palms open. One of the fluttering creatures skimmed my fingers. Its wings were feather-soft, trembling like laughter against my skin. Suddenly, I was laughing hard, helplessly, until my sides ached and I fell back onto the damp rock.

"I'm trying to decide if we're safe or about to be eaten alive," Adriel said warily.

"They're... Papillions," I managed.

"Like butterflies?" he asked, confused.

"Oh, they do not like you calling them that." The air filled with a rush of movement as the Papillions swooped past him in protest. Adriel ducked, covering me protectively until they finally drifted upward again, their hum fading into the trees.

When the last of the Papillions drifted upward, their auras shimmered over us like a thousand tiny stars. The air smelled faintly of fresh rain and sweet moss.

Adriel still hovered above me, his breath ragged, his hair dripping water onto my neck. For a moment, neither of us moved. The only sounds were the waterfall's steady roar and the soft hum of wings fading into the trees.

"I think they are gone now," I whispered, though my voice came out softer than I meant it to.

"Yes." His aura flickered, pulsing with heat. "Are you certain they are harmless?"

"Yes—unless you plan to insult them again."

His hand lifted, and his fingertips traced a hesitant path from my forehead down to my chin, mapping me the way only he could.

"You're shaking," he murmured.

"It's cold," I said, though it was only a half-truth.

There was a flicker. His breathing grew heavy as he struggled to call his battlemage, but eventually he was successful. He used his fire to warm my arms, gliding it over my fingertips before moving to my neck, then my torso. He held it there for a moment as my chest heaved.

"Adriel," I breathed.

"Yes?"

The warmth stilled, hovering.

"I can't find the words."

"Try," he said, sitting still.

I licked my lips, knowing that once I spoke the words, I could never pull them back. "I want you to make love to me."

He swallowed hard, his thumb finding my lips, tracing them as though deciding whether to believe me.

"I want you. I want you right now," I whispered, catching his thumb gently between my lips.

He exhaled sharply. "Not here, not like this. We should find our way back," he said, though his hand didn't move.

"I want you," I repeated, guiding his hand down my neck and to my chest. "And I think you want me."

His breath hitched as he traced his fingers along my collarbone before pulling away reluctantly. "I told you before, I want all of you. I don't want to be your stand-in for Zaib, or an alternative to Ashkii. I want you, your mind, and your heart." He said the last with his hand flat on my chest where my heart lay. It beat wildly for him.

"I want you to laugh only at my jokes and smile only for me as I do for you. Oh, that smile," he gasped. "It makes me want to rip your clothes off every time I see it."

His other hand slid to my waist, fingers curling as if fighting himself. "I want you never to leave me again," he whispered. "I want... I want—"

His voice broke, raw with everything he had not said. "What do you want?" I asked mere inches from his lips.

He continued, his hands trembling slightly. "I want to be the one who touches you and never has to let go. I want to be your husband, Asha. No titles, no thrones—just us."

I should have been shocked; I should have been terrified at such a confession. But I wasn't. I had been waiting for someone to want exactly this—not the princess, not the political alliance, not even the Lightbearer. Just me.

My heart somersaulted. "You have me."

He stilled, then lifted a hand to keep space between us. "I mean it. Asha Osei, I want you as my wife—bound to me, body and soul."

This time, I didn't hesitate. I found his face, traced the line of his jaw, and kissed him until his words faltered.

"Yes," I whispered against his lips.

He drew back just enough to cradle my face, his thumb brushing the corner of my mouth. "Say it again," he breathed, his lips grazing mine. "I want to hear you say it."

"I will never leave you again. Adriel, I am yours."

He exhaled sharply, then gathered me into his arms, as I clung to him desperately. Carrying me towards higher ground, he rubbed his cheek against my hair. He moved like someone who'd been an unseer all his life, carefully lowering me into a field that met my back with the softness of grass and the faint scent of honey in the air. The spray from the falls misted over us, cool against my skin, but I hardly noticed. I was lost.

Our mouths collided as he settled on top of me, one hand on my ass to bring me to his hips. Our lips met again—not soft this time, but desperate. I reached for the fastenings of my dress, but his hand covered mine.

"Let me," he said, his voice low, rough. He moved, untying the laces at an infuriating pace.

"This is taking too long," I complained.

"Always so impatient," he teased, giving a playful nip on my lower lip.

I groaned as I leaned back and let him loosen every strap until I wore nothing. I let him explore, each movement careful, discovering, as though his hands were his eyes and I was something sacred he'd been waiting to find. He dipped to my stomach, and then between my legs. I could feel his smile as he leaned down and kissed me. I wasn't just wet for him; I was drowning with need. He moved to insert his fingers, but I rolled over on top of him.

"My turn." Unlike him, I was an expert at undressing without sight. I released his belt with one hand and hauled at his shirt with the other. The fabric resisted, plastered to him, cold and slick as I tore it away. I reached into his trousers and inhaled sharply. It was one thing to have him in my hands and entirely different thinking about him between my legs.

My hands wrapped around him, stroking slowly from base to tip. He groaned in response to the sensation. "You are going to be the death of me."

He shifted beneath me, gripping my ass firmly and positioning me directly above him. "We should wait until you are...."

"I'm not waiting anymore," I breathed. The tantalizing friction as our bodies rubbed together was nearly unbearable.

He complied, gripping himself and guiding the tip along the slick folds of my core until it brushed against me. My whole body shook with anticipation, and then he stopped.

"What's wrong? Why did you stop?" I panted.

He rose up to curl his hands tightly in my hair. "I wish I could see you. I love your little expressions."

"I have something better," I breathed.

"What?" he asked curiously.

I gripped the tie of his braid until his thick, coarse hair loosened into my hands, and then I tapped into his aura. I had never done anything so intimate. I'd been close when we were on the ship years ago and he'd allowed me into his memory, but this was not a memory. This was happening now.

We couldn't see exactly, rather it felt as if our souls were tethered to one another. Our auras brightened, and suddenly I could see heat, longing and his surprise as clearly as if we had sight.

His presence surged closer, surrounding me in warmth. My breath hitched as the connection deepened, drawing us together in a way that made my bones melt. Aura met aura, heat folding into heat, and the world narrowed until there was nothing left but him and the energy between us.

"There you are," he whispered, ripping the last of my undergarments away before entering me slowly. Both of us reeled in ecstasy as he filled me just an inch. I panted. "More," I demanded.

He ran his finger across my face, pulling my hand to grip himself at my entrance. He placed his hands over mine. "You control how deep." The words came tight and controlled, as if his composure were something he was actively holding together.

I pressed down, testing, and his cock pushed in another delicious inch. This time I felt pain.

"It's okay. It can hurt the first time. We'll go slow," he said, though I could hear the strain.

Before I could change my mind, I settled down all the way until he filled me.

He sat up, pulling me to him, burying his face in my neck as he groaned. "Fuck!" My own fingers clawed at his back as I adjusted to him. When his breathing slowed, he pulled back to bring my forehead to his. "Are you alright?"

I wasn't sure. I felt like I'd been stretched fully and I couldn't imagine being stretched any further. "I—I think so."

"You stubborn woman," he groaned against my lips. "Why did you do that?"

"I've waited long enough."

He smiled against me. "So have I. Since the moment we met," he said gripping my hips in his hands, "I've wanted you like this." He lifted me slightly before setting me back down on top of him, taking a breath before doing it again. I cried out as I felt every ridge as he pushed inside and then released me. I whimpered as he held my hips still, moving in and out with complete control. Soon the tenderness in my core began to dissipate at his slow, deliberate thrusts. His movements made my body hum with pleasure, and soon I took over until I found one seamless rhythm. "That's it," he breathed.

I moaned, surrendering to the feelings as my breathing grew frantic. "I'm close."

"Let me help you," he urged, his hips powering into mine, his fingers swirling in just the right spot and his teeth grazing my nipple. He drove into me, his cheek against my chest as my entire body pulsed like it was on fire, like at any moment I'd burst into flame.

"I'm so close," I whimpered.

"Come for me," he demanded, pushing his fingers inside me with more vigor.

"Adriel!" I called as if he could stop the knot of pleasure that unraveled inside me. He caught my scream in a kiss and rolled us over until my back was on the ground. As I was drowning in pleasure, he thrust into me. Beads of sweat dotted my brow as the wave of pleasure began to ebb.

"Oh no you don't," he said, bending my knee, giving him more access. I held onto him, meeting him thrust for thrust. This is what I wanted from him the moment he'd caught me in that ballroom—to possess him, to climb his magnificent body.

"I'm going to come again," I whispered.

"You better," he said.

"I love you," I said. The words came out between breaths, unplanned, unstoppable. Words he'd carried patiently for years, and ones I could finally give without fear. He went still, just for a heartbeat, his rhythm faltered as the last of his control dissipated. He plunged into me once more, driving toward his own release.

"Asha!" he gasped with a hint of delicious agony.

Everything in my core tightened, waiting, losing my mind somewhere along the way. A feral animal sound of ecstasy escaped his lips as his release tore through him. He exhaled hard and fell back, pulling me with him until I was sprawled across his chest. I rested my head against his shoulder, both of us catching our breath.

Only then did the enormity of what I had done begin to wash over me. The choice I'd made, the want, the trust I'd put in him, but more importantly, myself. For the first time in a long while, I didn't feel like I was breaking apart—I felt like I was coming into myself.

After a long, quiet moment, he murmured, "Is this still okay?"

I lifted my chin, grinning. "You're telling me I've been missing out on that this entire time? We're doing it again."

We spent the night wrapped around each other beneath the flutter of papillons, their auras drifting overhead. It was a wonder we slept at all—but at some point, exhaustion claimed us.

I moaned when he eventually coaxed me awake. I lay limp against him. "Again?" I asked.

"As much as I'd like that, I imagine we need to find a way back before they realize we've gone."

I groaned into his chest. "Can't we just stay here?"

"I fear the longer we do, the more we forget about the dragons, my Guardians, your empire."

"I don't care about the empire."

He kissed the top of my head. "No, you care about people. That is why I love you."

I'd heard the words before but somehow, they meant even more now.

As much as I wanted this moment to last, I knew he was right. There was something about this place that made one forget about the atrocities of the world. The allure was strong, but we needed to resist it.

It took a while before I was able to get us back on a path. The morning bell rang as we entered court hand in hand.

As we reached my door, Adriel pulled me in for a kiss. "It was real, wasn't it? Last night?"

Something in his voice made my chest tighten. Whatever my answer was, it mattered.

"It was real," I said quietly. More real than anything I have let myself have in a very long time.

Relief softened his aura. He kissed me once more—slowly, like a promise—then released me.

I closed the door behind me and froze. "Ireti? What are you doing here?"

She exhaled, the sound weary, disappointed. "Trying to stop you from making the same mistakes your mother did," she said. "Sit."

CHAPTER FIFTY-SIX

Asha

"Where have you been all night?" The tone of her voice was unnerving. I'd never heard her speak to me with such sharp disapproval. "Don't lie to me, girl."

My eyebrow arched. "I didn't realize you were so interested in my whereabouts. Why do you care?"

"Because you are my blood!"

"So you've claimed," I said, taking the seat across from her. "And yet, you allowed me to waste away in the dragon pits when my mother died. You share very little of our family unless I pry and even then, it's vague."

"I see that man has already planted seeds of doubt in your heart," she bristled. "You were with the War Chief, weren't you? Adriel."

I crossed my arms. "And if I were? I had no idea you had such animosity toward him."

"Do you love him?" The way she asked it was cold, like the question itself offended her.

"He has asked me to marry him," I said carefully.

"And?" She slammed her hand on the table.

I leaned in. "I've accepted," I said it with such certainty it rocked even me; I could not imagine what it was doing to Ireti.

Her chair scraped as she surged to her feet. "You're a fool, just as Sanaa was."

The words hit harder than I expected. "You speak of her as if she were a curse," I said quietly. "She was my mother. Your sister."

"She was reckless," Ireti snapped. "Sanaa was supposed to charm Idris. She wasn't supposed to fall in love with him. You are repeating her mistakes."

My brows knit. "You're saying you didn't approve of their union?"

"Of course not. Idris was a monster. She was meant to remain here, among the Lightbearers." Ireti's voice sharpened. "Idris was meant to be our ally, not her husband. They both betrayed us." The way she said the last word held so much pain.

I frowned. "What betrayal?"

Her tone hardened. "The risk of your mother having a Lightbearer was high," Ireti said. "So a ritual was performed at your parents' union. Her womb was blessed to bear only sons."

The words slid past me at first—ritual, union, blessing—none of them landing.

"Sons," she continued, "are far less likely to be born Lightbearers."

My fingers curled against the arm of the chair.

"Then she had me," I said.

Ireti nodded once.

"She defied us. She defied the ritual. And Idris never forgave her—because you were the one born with light. You were the Light-bearer of the three."

The room seemed to tilt. I pressed my palm flat to the table, grounding myself in the cool grain of the wood. Suddenly so much made sense—the way my father looked at me, the hatred that clung to his every word.

"He hated me," I whispered. The truth of it opened in my chest like an old wound. "Kwasi never drew that kind of fury. But me?" I swallowed. "I was hated from the beginning."

"Your light threatened Elan's claim to the throne," Ireti said.

"Then why not use it?" My voice sounded thin to my own ears. "Why not train me?"

Ireti's silence stretched. "Because a boy with that power can rule," she said at last. "A girl must be married off."

My breath caught. "He could have left me in the dragon pits," I said. "No one would have known."

"You would have begun changing," she replied. "People would have noticed."

My hand drifted to my throat as memory rearranged itself—my father's sudden tenderness, the strange pride in his voice that night.

"The only way to retain his power," Ireti said, "was not to marry you off—but to end your life."

The room went very quiet.

"That was his plan," she finished, "after the first night of the Fire Festival."

"No," I breathed.

The word barely made it out.

"We killed Idris," she said. "And you should be glad of it."

My pulse roared in my ears. They meant me to be seen. The realization landed with sickening clarity.

"He planned to kill me," I said.

"Yes."

The simplicity of the answer hollowed me out. "That is why they wanted me to be seen that night." My hand lay flat on the table, trying to comprehend. It had been strange after all those years for father to take an interest in me. "He planned to kill me."

"Unbound and unclaimed, you would be a force; once married, your light would not be your own. It could be twisted and used to control others like your mother's was. You cannot marry Adriel. You cannot marry anyone."

"I don't understand. You are saying that if I marry Adriel, he will have access to my blindness?"

She pursed her lips. "You speak as if that is not coveted. Do you understand that your power, if properly honed, could level cities? We can teach you. Believe it or not, your light has already shown itself, once with Miren. And now—one Shadowcaster."

"Ashkii," I breathed. "Because with every Lightbearer, there is a Shadowcaster to counteract."

"That is right."

"But he turned later. I had nothing to do with Ashkii turning Shadowcaster."

Ireti did not falter. "Who was he with before he was taken?" she asked.

I thought back to my conflict with Elan. "Me," I finally conceded.

Ireti put a hand on my shoulder. "And Miren? Did you know her before she turned?"

I closed my eyes. It couldn't be true. It felt true.

"Asha," she whispered, placing a hand on my shoulder, "your light changes those around you. It draws them. Corrupts them. Saves them. You are born of two forces. That is what the prophecy speaks of."

My pulse hammered.

"Her soul burns with the fire of dragons..." The old words clawed their way back, words Marlon once spoke.

"Stop," I whispered.

"You are the reason Adriel is so close. Here, the change will not complete, but out there... out there he will become a Shadowcaster if he remains by your side. And he will dull your light whether you want him to or not," she said. "For those already standing on the precipice, one act of darkness is all it takes. He may be already there."

"But I've seen an army of Shadowcasters—at the battle with the Guardians, and Miren saw them near Saeleria. I could not have done that."

"They have limited power without dragons. Let's hope Ashkii is the only one," Ireti said. "All the more reason to stay here, Asha. Yes, Shadowcasters are awakening, and they can be a menace, but you have no idea the power they hold the moment they bond with a dragon."

"No." My voice trembled. "You're wrong."

"Asha, I feel it. Adriel is closer to darkness than you realize."

"I don't believe you."

"You should," she said softly. "Your mother ended her life to contain the power Idris wielded. Had she lived, his reign would have been even more oppressive. He would have had unbounded power. I'm sure Idris was devastated once he lost that."

My stomach twisted. "If I stay here... would it be the end of bonded Shadowcasters?"

"It would stop them from growing their numbers," Ireti said. "They have already tried to bring you to their side, haven't they? They won't stop. You are the key to their survival."

"And if I leave? If I marry?"

"At best, your light will become your husband's. At worst, if the Shadowcasters got ahold of you, they would be unstoppable."

This was the last piece of the puzzle, the reason the Shadows wanted me.

"And Drakkar?" My voice cracked.

"Separated from you, he dies," she answered without hesitation. "Your bond will wither."

My pulse hammered painfully.

"So if I stay, Drakkar dies. And if I leave... Adriel turns."

"There is no path that lets you keep them both."

My knees went weak. I stood anyway. "No," I said. "I refuse this."

"You cannot defy who you are," she warned.

"I can try," I said, retreating into the room.

"And Adriel has nearly turned Shadowcaster himself. If you leave, you will cement that fact."

"You can't know that."

"I can feel it. You must have felt it too. He is almost there. If you leave, he will surely turn."

"Liar," I hissed, even when I knew she was right. Ashkii had already shown me when I touched his aura. Adriel belonged to them, the Shadows.

"I may have withheld things from you, Asha," she said, "but I have never lied. I don't need to. If you want to leave the island, never come back."

CHAPTER FIFTY-SEVEN

Asha

After Ireti's departure, I crawled into bed and did not leave it. Adriel's aura had entered the room filled with light and happiness, but I could not speak, could not bear to tell him what I knew. If I did, all of it would become real, and I desperately needed it not to be.

"Asha, what has happened?"

"Please go," I begged. "Please."

The earnestness in my voice must have convinced him because he did. Soon Kwasi was in my room, and then Miren. I said nothing, just lay there, allowing my heart to break little by little. Morning turned to evening. Soon nothing would force Adriel out of the room. He climbed into the bed next to me and rubbed my back. I could tell he wanted to curl up next to me, but he mercifully didn't. I did not know what I would have done if he had.

I don't know what time it was when I decided to let the melancholy rest and I stood from the bed. "Asha?" he asked.

"I need a bath," I said, moving from the bed. I paused. "Will you join me?"

He seemed hesitant at first, but took my hand and followed behind me without protest. I stripped down and sank into the warm water. He did the same and settled in across from me. As I pulled my hair free to wash, he said, "Allow me."

I was patient as he struggled to open the sweet smelling concoction. He rubbed the liquid in my hair before he carefully massaged my scalp, then down the strands. I should be enjoying this. Having a man wash my hair suddenly felt more intimate than anything we had ever done together. My muscles coiled as Ireti's words played again in my head. *"There is no path that lets you keep them both,"* she'd said.

I was grateful when Adriel instructed me to lay on his lap so he could rinse. The warm water gave me something to focus on other than the silent tears streaming down my face.

Once he was done, and before I could change my mind I said, "Now, you."

He turned his body in the tub, and I pulled him back towards my body, hugging him, burying my face in his hair. His heart beat rapidly against my fingers as he submerged his hair into the water.

I uncorked the vial from around my throat, gripping the bottle tightly until my hands shook. My lungs constricted, and my breaths roared over the sound of the trickling water from the spout. I can't do it, I realized closing the vial. I couldn't use the sleeping draught Mattias had given me, even if it saved Adriel.

My voice softened. "No, it wasn't. That is not what is wrong."

His hands interlocked mine over his heart. "Tell me what is wrong, Asha. It is not too late." He lifted our encircled hands to his lips and kissed them. "I can help."

How could I? How could I tell him any of it? That he was in danger because of me. That I could choose a life with him here in exchange for the life of my dragon. That we'd have to leave our friends behind if we chose each other.

I tipped up his chin and kissed him instead, my hands roaming his body hungrily. He met my kisses fiercely at first, but then slowly pulled away, lifting himself out of the water leaving a coolness behind before retreating to the bedroom.

I sat in the bath, confused, waiting for his return. When he didn't, I found a towel and wrapped it around myself. "Adriel?" I called after him.

His aura was by the window, still as night. When I circled my hands around his waist, I was disappointed to see he had already dressed. He turned around, disentangling himself. "No," he said. "You are not going to do this to me again."

"What?" I asked, confused.

"You want to have sex so that you feel less guilty about leaving. Tell me I'm wrong," he challenged.

I was stunned, not that he'd figured it out but that it sounded so callous when said aloud. "I—I didn't mean..."

"You just decided to play with my heart—to leave again. Will I see you again in two more years? Five? Maybe a decade this time?"

I felt untethered, like I'd float away any moment, despite my attempts to stay grounded. "You don't understand."

"Tell me then, Asha. You don't have to deal with any of this alone. You have others who can bear the weight. Tell me. I can take it."

"I can't marry you," I blurted out.

The room fell silent. I waited for him to lose his temper, but instead he drew in a slow breath. "Why not?"

My mind searched for a plausible excuse, something he might believe. "Because I made a promise to marry Zaib."

"Don't you think that promise is in the fiery pits of hell at the moment?"

It was a loathsome thought that if I told him the truth—that staying beside him would doom the entire Five Kingdoms to the Shadowcasters. I knew with him having that information he would still choose me anyway. I couldn't allow that. Better he hated me.

"I don't love you." The lie nearly strangled me. I continued as his aura recoiled. "I care for you deeply, but that is not enough."

"And you love Zaib?"

"Yes." The word felt like acid on my tongue but I couldn't relent.

"And you want to go back to him," he said without emotion.

"Yes, as soon as possible."

"What aren't you telling me, Asha?"

"I've told you, I'm not in love with you. Why can't you accept that?"

"Because it is not true," he said simply. "You forget I know you. If you told me you wanted to marry Zaib because you felt it was your duty, I could accept that. But you said you didn't love me... I know you are lying. There is something you are keeping from me, and I need to know what it is."

"I can't say!" I cried, a tear falling onto my cheek.

He put his hands on my shoulders, soothing me as he said, "Alright. What can you say?"

I sucked in a breath. "I need to get off this island, and I need you to stay here. I can't explain why."

Adriel was quiet as if regarding me carefully. "What is your plan?" he asked.

My breath hitched. "Really?"

He moved to the floor, pressing the side of his face to my stomach. "I serve you. That has not changed." His lips grazed my navel. "Just promise me you won't disappear in the night. Promise that whatever you decide, you will let me in."

I ran my fingers through the wet strands of his hair, before leaning down to kiss the top of his head. "I promise," I whispered.

His grip tightened. "Thank you," he said with shaking breath as if I'd given him the most precious of gifts.

Two words. That was all it took for the last of my defenses to fall in shambles around me. I opened my mouth to tell him everything, but the words never left my lips as the whole world around us shook. I heard it first, the loud crack, like the world had split open, before I felt the floor beneath us shake. I would have lost balance if it weren't for Adriel's hands around me keeping me from falling. We stood still for a moment as shouts from the distance sounded around us.

"That sounded like cannon fire," I gasped. "But who?" I asked, though both of us knew immediately.

"Get dressed," he said hurriedly. "I'm going to find out what is going on." He cursed as he crashed into the bedpost before finding his way out the door.

I'd barely strapped on my last boot when he'd returned with Miren and Kwasi.

"We are under attack," Miren said.

My stomach dropped. "The Ori Mothers?"

"No," Adriel's voice was flat and final. "We can't trust them. We have to leave."

"We can't leave these people. They don't know what Elan is capable of," I said. "Ireti. She will help us."

CHAPTER FIFTY-EIGHT

As we traveled through the halls, we'd heard a series of more blasts, along with screams as people ran past us. It felt like the attack in Wyrmwood all over again.

The stone around us groaned in protest as if struggling to stay soundly in place. When we arrived at Ireti's quarters, Dara and Tayo were already with her, along with several other auras that I could not place.

"Ireti," I called. "What's happening?"

Another blast sounded as the ground shook beneath us. Some kind of pot vase fell to the floor and shattered.

"You should be seeking cover," Ireti said. "Everyone will be headed in that direction."

"Why should she be safe in our mountains? They're the reason the emperor is on our doorstep," Tayo hissed.

"Elan?" I asked. "Are we sure?"

Tayo scoffed loudly. "Do you know of anyone else who would bring hundreds of ships to an island that doesn't exist on any map? You did this! I know it."

Adriel cleared his throat, in the way he did when he demanded his Guardians listen. "You assured us that Lumira was safe, that no one can get in."

"That only works if they don't know where it is," Dara interjected. "Somehow, they know exactly where we are and the only way for that to be is if one of you said something."

Adriel squeezed my hand, and I knew what he was trying to tell me because I'd already thought it. Ashkii. He'd told us as much and we hadn't listened.

"But they won't be able to enter the island without invitation," Dela said coming from behind us. I hadn't noticed her aura before. She moved in front of us to the mothers. "We have to invite them in... right?"

The Ori Mothers were silent. Whispers grew around us as unease settled in the room.

"It can't be," Kwasi said from beside us. "If so, Ashkii would have never been allowed here, just like the dragons. You can't control who comes in or out of here. You can only control whether they can see the island."

Now the people around us were speaking in a frenzied pitch. Dela said, "It can't be," over and over again, like something precious had been broken. Trust. "Why tell us this lie?" she asked.

Ireti moved forward raising her voice so that we all listened. "To protect you, all of you."

"But they found us," someone called in the distance.

"What are we going to do?" another said.

This time Miren spoke. "We fight," she said. "We have the advantage. They are on fragile ships, we are on land. All of us have battlemages. We fight."

"If," Adriel interjected. "The suppressor you've put on all of us can be removed."

"That won't be necessary," Ireti said.

I gasped in surprise. "Why?"

"Because you all are the only ones with the suppressors."

Though I'd known our battlemages were affected by being on the island, Kwasi had said as much, but I'd convinced myself the effect was limited, especially since I could still see and manipulate auras. I felt a wave of disappointment that the Ori Mothers had direct involvement in making it so. It was irrational and if it was my island I'd likely do the same. Still it was a reminder that this wasn't my home, no matter how much I wished it to be.

"Shouldn't you remove them for this?" Adriel asked.

"You won't need them. None of us will. The barrier will hold. It has never fallen."

Another blast sounded above us, this time something from the ceiling shattered.

"The barrier will fall," Adriel said with certainty. Those in the room gasped, though whether it was from his words or that he dared challenge Ireti, I was not sure. "Release our battlemages. We still have time to fight back. Allow me to lead. I have experience fighting against Elan."

Dara's laugh was humorless. "As if we would trust you, any of you. We should put you all in the dungeon like the other one."

"I'd like to see you try," Miren bit back.

"No one," Ireti cut in, "will be doing any of that. We retreat. That is the final word of the mothers. Go!"

The finality of her voice was deflating. "Cowards," I whispered.

"I beg your pardon?" Tayo seethed.

"Cowards!" I said loud enough for all to hear. "You don't know the man at your gates, I do."

I lifted my tunic, Adriel releasing me. I gripped Ireti's hand. "Touch it. Right there." Ireti touched my back reluctantly but when she did her voice caught and a moan escaped her.

"Asha, what is this?"

"This is what my brother calls mercy," I said. "He will show none to you. If he can do this to his own sister, what do you think he will do to you if the island is taken?"

The room grew quiet once more; the sounds of bombs exploding were the only thing breaking the silence. Adriel's warm hand at my back was my only tether.

Dela's aura moved towards me. "What would you have us do?"

"Fight. We must fight for this place, your home...my mother's home."

She took a deep breath before saying, "I will follow you."

"Dela!" Ireti yelled. "What are you doing?"

"She is right. You know it, and she is the only one who has not lied to me. I will follow her, and I will round up others who want to fight."

"But you know what this means," Dara asked, stepping forward. "By going against a mother."

"Death," she breathed, "will come either way if we don't fight. I will take the just death of a mother over the painful one of an enemy any day."

Dara gasped in shock.

I stepped towards Ireti. "So what will it be? Will you kill us all now, or will you stand down, and allow us to fight?"

"You shall have your battlemages, but leave this place and do not return," Ireti gritted out, her aura turning away. The shift was immediate, as I could feel Adriel's aura burn more brightly as his blue fire came to life.

The last words I heard Ireti utter as she retreated were, "Foolish like your mother."

CHAPTER FIFTY-NINE

Adriel

"Dela, slow down," I called, groaning as I ran into something, probably a pillar in the hallway. "We need to strategize. We need to keep the shields up as long as possible. How do we do that?"

"Our shieldwielders will be near the Iroko keeping the attacks at bay."

"The Iroko?" Miren asked.

"The tree where you were introduced to the Ori Mothers. It is the source of the power that runs the island."

"Good," I said. "That will be our stronghold. We will stagger anyone willing to fight around the perimeter. Miren, go get Ashkii, and bring him to us. I have questions for him."

"I got it," Miren said, the glee in her voice evident. She was loving this.

"Where are the weapons stored?" I asked.

I could feel Dela's hesitation. "You've gone this far," I reminded her. "If you are going to be treasonous, you might as well go all in."

"It's not that," she sighed. "The Ori Mothers have always insisted this place is a stronghold, that we don't need weapons."

"You have no weapons?" Kwasi asked.

"I didn't say that," Dela clarified. "They are beneath us in the crypt. It is going to take several people to get the doors open."

More explosions sounded above us, the succession of them growing louder and more frequent.

"They will have weapons. We have to get them. Kwasi and I will gather them if you show us where to go."

"And I will rally anyone willing to fight."

"Who will tell the shieldwielders we are coming with reinforcements?" she asked.

"We can tell them after we get the weapons," I pushed back.

"We can't risk them breaking," she said. "If they yield before we get there, all of this will be for nothing. I will go."

My teeth ground against one another as I fought every instinct to link my arms around her possessively. I did not want her out of my reach for one second, but she was right, and she was capable. She could do this, I just didn't want her to.

"Good luck," I said squeezing her hand.

She sighed in relief that I wasn't going to fight her.

"Asha," I said. I wanted to tell her to stay with me, to not go. That I would tie her up and carry her over my shoulder if it would keep her from going off alone. "Promise me," was all I could manage.

There was a lot I was communicating with those two words. I could breathe easy if she didn't do anything reckless, if we were in this fight together as one.

"I promise," she said.

I knew better than to take her word, and I also knew I had no other choice but to do so. Loving her meant trusting that she would do what was best. I just hoped what was best wouldn't hurt us both in the process.

CHAPTER SIXTY

Asha

The eight shieldwielders were easy enough to convince, as they'd had no official orders from the Ori Mother and seemed grateful to hear from someone. Their murmurs of agreement held a weariness that told me they were already feeling the strain. "We can hold it," one of them said firmly, even as the assault from above became more frequent and intense.

I wanted to ask how long was feasible for them to hold the shield but I resisted. I did not want to be the cause of them underestimating their limits. Instead I used my battlemage to infiltrate the tight coils in their mind, the parts of their mind that needed to ease in order to continue. Several were concerned about their families, one had a pet fox they'd left in its kennel, another worried he'd not said how he really felt to the one he fancied. I did my best to soothe all of it. I could help with fear and even mental strain, but I could do nothing for them physically. As the silence stretched I began to count the explosions overhead, as if keeping count could help us in some way. I waited for what seemed like hours but it could only have been minutes when

Dela arrived with warriors, all with weapons in hand. Kwasi and Adriel were not far behind.

I did not even get a moment before he began giving orders. He'd mapped out the whole island, I realized. While I'd been reconnecting with Ireti and entertaining ridiculous dreams of family and living my life out here, his mind had always been on the threats in front of us. He was born for this. I sadly was a disgrace, easily manipulated by someone who claimed to care about me. None of my bloodline had ever had my best interests at heart but Kwasi. I should have seen it.

"Are you okay?"

I snapped my head up realizing Kwasi had asked me a question and I'd missed it.

"Huh? Sorry, what did you say?"

Kwasi was quiet a moment before reaching out to touch my shoulder. "I'm disappointed too," he said knowingly.

He was trying to be understanding. I knew it was coming from a good place but it felt like acid on my tongue.

"Let's get through this," was all I could manage.

"Adriel sent me to find you. He wants you closer."

"I'm fine right here. We need the shieldwielders to last as long as possible. I can't fight, but I can help with this," I said.

"He won't like it, but I suppose you know that."

"Tell him that I'm useful here. Tell him—" I stopped, taking a breath. "I cannot be tucked away. I am a queen. Let me be one."

Silence again before Kwasi let out a deep sigh. "You are, and I've never been more proud of you," he said. "Let me go break the news to your boyfriend. Expect him down here shortly to change your mind." He left without another word but I could feel the dread his aura left behind. I stood there for a moment, the grove quiet around me. It was the quiet you feel when you know something terrible is about to happen.

I needed to check on the shieldwielders once more. They'd moved further into the grove. I walked toward them but before I made it very far, a familiar aura caught the side of my vision.

"Ashkii? Is Miren here?"

"No," he said. "I had to move out of her reach as soon as I could."

He was using his battlemage. I was the only one who could see him.

"You did this, didn't you?"

He didn't try to deny it. "I did, though they would have found this place whether I helped or not. I told you once you join their ranks, you cannot leave."

My thoughts flickered to Adriel. Would it be the same for him? I pushed the thought away. There was no room for it right now.

"What do you want? Why haven't you tried to leave already?"

He was quiet a moment before saying, "The shields must fall."

Alarm surged through me. "Absolutely not. We need time to plan an offensive. Why would you say such a thing?"

"Because we both need to get to their ships," he said.

"And why in the world would I do that?"

"Because they have the dragons."

The ground felt unsteady beneath me. I reached down the bond immediately, searching like you would if you were told a limb was missing. Nothing.

"All of them?" I shook my head in disbelief. "No. Drakkar wouldn't have allowed that. He would have burned them alive."

"Not if it risked the hatchlings."

Worry speared through me as I paced. After a moment I stopped in front of him. "Let me see," I said forcefully. "Now!"

Ashkii acquiesced, guiding my hand to cup his cheek and reach for his aura. I gasped as images flashed in my mind, but these images weren't through Drakkar's eyes. They were through another, someone with blue scales and long talons, and a birthmark under his chin. It was Igbo.

I saw the reflection of fear in his eyes and my breath stopped. The face looking back at me was obstructed except for his eyes. I'd seen those eyes before.

Then the vision shifted and I wished it hadn't.

Igbo was pinned, his body trembling against hands that pressed down with practiced cruelty. A large knife caught the light as it approached one of his claws. He screamed, and the sound of it traveled through the bond like something tearing, setting off the other dragons in a chain of agony that knocked the breath from my chest. The hatchlings. They were all there. All of them.

"Come to me, Asha..." a voice whispered. "And this could be over. No one else need get hurt."

I pulled back; my hand dropped, trembling from Ashkii's face.

"The shields have to come down," he said again. "It is the only way we can get to them."

I needed to protect them, needed to help them, but if I did, I would expose everyone on this island. Elan would not let them go. I swallowed turning to view Adriel's aura at a distance. I'd promised not to leave minutes ago. I'd sworn. But I had to. I could only hope he'd understand.

"I have a plan," I told Ashkii, hardening myself for what I must do. "As soon as the shields fall, Adriel's vision will likely return. We will have to move fast."

I left his side to walk towards the shieldwielders. The walk was painful, not because of distance but because I had to force myself to turn away from Adriel. If I allowed myself to gaze at his aura, I would not be able to do this.

One of them pushed out a sigh of relief as I approached which made what I had to do feel even worse. This had to be done with precision. It was easier now that they trusted me.

"I could use another dose of whatever battlemage you have left," he said. "This is hard work."

I stood there for a moment with their auras in my awareness. These people had trusted me, had felt relief when I soothed their fears just moments ago. And now I was going to use that trust against them. There was no version of this that wasn't a betrayal, and I had no choice.

"I know," I said. "You've been working so hard. It's time to rest."

"Wh—what do you mean? Is this part of the War Chief's strategy?" he asked doubtfully.

"No," I whispered. "It is mine."

I held his and the others' auras in my palm. I'd done this a handful of times but only with one person. This many at once was different. I could already feel the pull behind my eyes, like a thread of energy stretched too thin. If I failed, the others would run and I'd never get another opportunity. That couldn't happen.

I squeezed the auras until their colors collided into a rainbow coalescing, then pulled until the light was snuffed out. The shieldwielder fell to the ground, the others folding one by one.

The thread of energy frayed, and my world began to tilt. Ashkii caught me before I fell, holding me up as my knees buckled.

"What has happened?" the man gasped.

"I'm sorry," I whispered. "Tell Adriel I'm sorry."

CHAPTER SIXTY-ONE

Adriel

Regaining sight after so much time was disorienting, so much so that it brought me to my knees before I ever realized I was falling. The onslaught of color, texture and light overwhelmed my senses. Kwasi retched beside me as his own sight returned. After a few moments, I staggered to my feet trying to make sense of what happened. The shields fell, but why? My eyes immediately shifted to where Asha stood, only she was no longer there. I looked where she had been; my mind kept trying to correct itself, kept insisting she was there and I was looking in the wrong place. She wasn't there.

"Where. Is. She?"

I did not await an answer. My feet carried me towards the Iroko as if of their own accord.

The shieldwielders were on the ground, debilitated. I moved to the closest one. "What happened?"

The man struggled to speak. "Water," I called. Kwasi handed me his water pouch and I poured a small dribble into his mouth. He coughed, but was able to move his lips.

"Tell me," I demanded.

"She betrayed us," he rasped.

"That is impossible," Kwasi said.

"She brought down the shields," the man confirmed.

"But why?" I asked.

My breathing accelerated. No. She promised.

I stood and leapt to my feet that carried me across the island as if I knew where I was going. As I predicted we were not far from shore. Unfortunately, the path I'd taken led me to a cliff. I saw Asha and Ashkii standing on the shore looking out to the rows of ships.

I knew what she was going to do before she did it. Someone had gotten to her. It was the only reason she'd take the risk.

"Asha!" I shouted. "Asha!"

Her body stiffened. Whether she heard me or not I was not sure, but it was no use. She jumped into the sea.

"Asha!" I called.

I looked beneath the cliff, determined to get to her, even if it result-ed in broken bones.

"Adriel!" Miren called.

I looked to the sky. Miren was in the air, Kwasi seated behind her. "Get Asha!" I yelled pointing.

"We're getting you first!"

Zephyr circled above before making a smooth landing to the ground. I ran to them and climbed up behind Kwasi.

Zephyr appeared to grumble with the extra weight. Miren patted him gently before looking back.

"Hang on. Zephyr says they have cannons. We will have to sneak up on them."

"Whatever gets us there fastest."

Without another word, Zephyr took flight. I'd long gotten used to flying on the backs of dragons. I just hoped I wasn't too late.

CHAPTER SIXTY-TWO

Asha

The water was cold and jarring to the senses. I immediately wanted to stand and retreat back to shore but I knew if I hesitated or let go of Ashkii, he would leave me behind. I'd known our plan was idiotic the moment I could not channel Drakkar's sight when the shields in Lumira fell. Our only saving grace, and the only reason I'd not turned back, was because Ashkii had access to Igbo's. My fate was in his hands while we were in the water, and I would not let go.

We moved through the sea the best we could. The water weighed me down like I was made of iron. Ashkii eventually put me on his back as I was slowing him down. At one point he dove deeper into the water without warning. I closed my mouth but it was too late. I climbed back up gasping for air that felt like shards of glass.

"Who is there?" someone called.

Hands seized my arm before I could react. "It is her!" someone called.

"This is the woman we've been chasing along the Five Kingdoms?" another asked. "She doesn't look like much."

I was still coughing when they brought me to my feet. I clung to my sides, shivering.

Ashkii's aura sat beside me. "This is Princess Asha Osei," he said evenly as if he hadn't just swam half a mile with me on his back. "I've brought her to the emperor as requested."

The soldiers peered at me like I'd grown fins. "Is it true you seduced King Musa so that he would give you safe passage?" one of them asked.

"I heard she overthrew the Wiyotakin king, and now she has her sights on the other rulers of the Five Kingdoms."

"Does she really bleed gold?" said another. "Should we test it?"

"Enough," a voice commanded, sharp enough to quiet the deck. "She is to remain unharmed."

Feet stirred as the surrounding people began to scatter to other parts of the ship. I watched as Ekon's aura turned towards Ashkii. "Welcome back, Shadow. You did well. He will be pleased."

That stung. I'd known this was the plan, Ashkii had told me as much but still the thought of a man I'd once called a friend handing me over was unfathomable.

My chest seized. "So this is it? All those years I let myself believe you cared... what a fool I was." Whether I was speaking to Ashkii or Ekon, it didn't really matter.

Ekon answered. "You made your choice," he said. "What's done is your own fault."

"Don't worry, Ekon," I said quietly. "You've already done the worst thing you could ever do to me."

"Bring her," was all he said in answer.

My wrists were cinched so tightly behind me I could feel my pulse throbbing under the bindings. As we walked, I heard the groan of wood as they forced me forward. My boot slipped on something wet.

A soldier yanked me upright before I could fall. That's when I smelled it, copper. I'd slipped on fresh blood.

"Careful," Ashkii muttered. "The emperor wants her intact."

The air stopped moving after that. The last time I'd seen my brother, he'd attempted to beat information out of me. This time he would certainly kill me.

Ekon's voice cut through the darkness. "Straight ahead." His footsteps moved beside me, close enough that I felt the watchful shift of his aura. "So quiet now," he said. "Not so brave without your dragon, are you?"

I tilted my chin toward his voice. "I'm listening. That's all," I said.

"For what?"

"For the sound of your heart. I want to know what it sounds like before I kill you."

He paused. I felt—actually felt—the jolt of surprise ripple off him. "You've changed. To think I ever loved you," he muttered in disgust. "Bring her," he said. The soldiers bound my wrists against my back and pushed me to walk.

A door creaked open and our footsteps echoed like we were in a large room as we marched forward. This had to be the main cabin, though cabin wasn't a good word to communicate the size. This was like having a castle on a boat.

The familiar sound of crackling battlemage reached my ears as we approached.

"And you, sir. Do you swear to cast away your oath to your faux king and swear allegiance to me?"

"Eat dragon shit," a man said firmly.

A crack sounded that rattled the back of my teeth. My eyes widened seeing the familiar aura of a man I'd traveled with for weeks as he fell to the ground ravaged by battlemage. *Chato.*

"I was hoping you'd say that," another said gleefully. "But wait. What is this?" Elan asked, narrowing his gaze on me. "Bring her forward."

The soldiers forced me onto my knees. The floor was cold through the thin fabric of my clothes.

The bond flickered before me, tentative at first, like flame, catching wet wood before sight rushed back in. I almost gasped with the relief of it. Drakkar was here, though he was not himself. I searched for him, my gaze settling on the auras of other Guardians, many of them familiar to me, until I locked in on Kitchi and Moki's auras. Their energy matched how I felt. We were in danger.

My gaze settled on the inky black aura of the man who'd tortured me from childhood.

"I must say, sister," Elan drawled, "You've made quite the entrance."

"*Drakkar,*" I called down the bond. This time I felt a weak stirring.

"Your dragon?" he said lightly. "Is that who you are looking for?" There was a pop of his snapped fingers which signaled the soldiers to move to another side of the room. Whatever barrier was in place had been removed because I gasped at the sight of Mwana and Ala who were several feet away confined in a cage of dracite. They looked weary and frightened, clamoring to get out of their poison coated prison. Igbo was nowhere in sight. Drakkar was chained, his limbs rubbed raw by the metal. They'd even put the dracite around his head and snout. His eyes were faced out of the window, towards the shore where I'd been. They were open, but vacant. He did not turn towards me like he normally would.

"*Drakkar,*" I whispered, tears flaring in my eyes. He did not acknowledge me. It was as if he didn't feel my presence at all. The dragon who had found me deep in the woods at night, who had come for me over mountains and through fire, could not feel me standing a short distance away. The grief of it almost took me down. I could not afford it in this moment. Not now.

"Beautiful, aren't they?" Elan said softly. "Such power wasted on you."

"What have you done to him?"

Elan shrugged. "What all the dragons in our possession have had done to them. We've wrapped them in dracite until they are docile and obedient. It is good for them, what they were made for."

"You're hurting them."

"Now, now. They are here to help you behave," he chided. "This is nothing. You should see what I did to their leader."

My head swiveled. "Mattias? You have him."

"It wasn't difficult. They basically begged us to invade them."

"Where is he?" I growled.

"All in due time," he said, his battlemage crackling in his hands. My body tensed as the visions of the cruelty his magic inflicted over the years seared through me.

I did my best not to give him the reaction he wanted.

The heat of his power as he neared was intense, causing sweat to prickle my brows and run down my back. "Such a pretty thing. I am so glad we don't have to hide your scars anymore. I have plans for this face."

"Don't touch her," Chato warned, his voice hoarse with pain. "Or you will die a painful death."

"Says the man on the floor." He laughed. "Look around, you've been beaten. Your Guardians are soon to be executed. I have her dragon and his offspring. I have the great Lightbearer. What do they call you? The Anointed One? How exactly are you going to beat me?"

Chato's chains rattled as he attempted to move. I say attempted because they rattled to the ground almost as soon as he stood.

"How did you do it?" I asked, trying to shift his attention. "How did you convince Dija to join you?"

"You forget, sister, that they were already mine. You really think these rulers wanted to marry you?" he chuckled. "You're not even royal."

I licked my lips. The longer I could keep him talking, the better. "I am the daughter of the late Emperor Idris Osei."

A bitter laugh escaped him "That is a sweet thought," he said. "That whore of a mother certainly convinced my father of that." He paused. "She was good at that."

I pursed my lips, sensing there was something more he wanted to say. "What are you talking about?" But I already knew. I'd sensed it from my last conversation with Ireti, what she wouldn't say aloud.

His mouth curled cruelly. "You really think you have the blood of Idris Osei? You are an abomination."

The room grew so quiet that the thoughts in my head seemed to scream at me. I should be shocked, but I wasn't. "Who then is my father?"

"My father never said, and I've spent a great deal of assets to find out. But all that matters is that you can never rule the Five Kingdoms, because they do not belong to you."

"And the Shadowcasters. Do they belong to *you*, or do you bend the knee to them?" I taunted.

The crackle of his battlemage quieted, and my body chilled at the thought of what he was planning.

"Bring it in," he said.

Soldiers' steps moved across the wooden floor, as the scraping of heavy doors opening filled the space. The room was deathly silent as wheels squeaked along the stone. Something large was being moved towards me. Whatever it was caused Drakkar to stir, and my vision to more fully return.

Igbo lay at the bottom of a cage similar to Ala and Mwana, his tail wrapped around him like it was the only thing keeping him together. He didn't look frightened like the others, but resigned, as if he was ready to die. The image of his toe being removed flashed into my head as I saw the blood droplets that were smeared over his blue coat. Igbo's eyes flashed as he saw me, no not me. It was Ashkii. He attempted to stand but curled his bleeding appendage beneath him once more.

Ashkii ran to his side. "Your Holiness," he said. "I request that you release him to me. I have done what you've asked. I brought her to you."

Elan looked down upon him with indifference. For the first time, I could see the scars of our last encounter. Half of his face drooped like melted rock, unmoving as he took the claw and ran it across his chin, then circled back to his eyes.

His eyes were on Ashkii. "You can see," was all he said. "That's too bad. You're going to hate what I must do to him. But our Anointed One is responsible."

My jaw clenched. I had to stop this. Only I could stop this.

"You're spineless!" I said between clenched teeth. "You're going to attack a defenseless dragon, when I am the one that ruined your face." I spit in his direction.

Many in the room shuffled nervously, anticipating what the emperor would do. I was counting on him doing something—and he did.

"You think this is the best time to hurl insults?" he asked.

"I think I should do the other side, so you can match."

Before I could blink, tiny pricks formed against my cheek. It felt like he was taking a nail and rubbing it against my skin. It quickly intensified until I was on the ground. I bit down on my tongue, refusing to scream. Blood coated my lips, warm and metallic.

Drakkar growled behind me, but the chains around his limbs and snout kept him from moving. *"Let her go!"* he said. *"Let her go!"*

There was a scuffle nearby, and relief as the intensity of the pain ceased. Chato, now free from his chains, thanks to Ashkii, seized in front of me as he took the brunt of the fire. I screamed, not because of the pain, but because I knew what was happening as Chato's eyes rolled back. He was dying, for me. He had done this for me.

"Chato," I cried reaching for him. I held on for a short time until I could smell my skin burning. I let go, and the shocks increased. Shouts erupted around me and a figure moved in the doorway. For a heartbeat, I thought it was another soldier. Then a voice cut through the hall, raw and stunned.

"What are you doing?" the man asked, gripping me before I fell. He cut through my bindings with a short sword.

It was Zaib.

"Asha!" he called. "Asha!"

"Nightborne," I whispered, the remnants of Ashkii's vision finally coming together. He had been who I'd seen, the one who had cut Igbo to lure us here. "I know who you are."

Every interaction with Zaib rearranged itself as I said the words. "You're their leader," I said remembering Ashkii's words.

Zaib went to speak but stopped himself, examining my wounds instead. "That is going to leave a scar," he said gravely.

I flinched at his touch, not from pain, but from the memory of those same hands, steering mine at the wheel of his flying boat. The way he complimented me, knowing the way it made me blush. The memory of our engagement when he'd held back, seemingly our of respect. The wedding on the ship he'd so cleverly arranged. Every kindness rearranged itself into something else entirely, each one a door opening just wide enough to keep me walking forward. He had known all along that every smile, every careful moment between us would allow him in, to put him just within reach.

"Why? Why are you doing this?"

He didn't answer right away, looking at my wounds as if his answer were somewhere in the damage. He was patient, I realized. The kind of patience a spider has in its web, certain in the inevitability of what comes next, like he had always known exactly how this would end.

Before he could reply the ship groaned as if it were being weighed down. The soldiers around us readied their swords and battlemage for whatever was coming through that door.

"Shall we wait?" Zaib grinned looking towards the door. "I'd love to meet you both properly."

After a few moments of scuffle, Adriel burst through the door, Miren and Kwasi behind him. His eyes found mine immediately, then locked in on Zaib's hands around my body.

"Get your hands off her," he demanded, "now."

CHAPTER SIXTY-THREE

Adriel

My heart twisted so much as I watched Chato's lifeless body ravaged by Elan's battlemage that I barely registered the tens of swords turned in our direction.

Kitchi strained against her chains reaching for him, her face grief stricken. My heart pounded wildly as I met Kitchi's gaze. She looked to be in shock. Moki turned to me in horror, like he was seeing ghosts. I'd failed them, failed all of them by leaving them behind. Chato's blood was on my hands, and I'd never be able to wipe them clean.

I caught sight of a silent Drakkar. He was pinned by a lattice of steel dracite, wings dragged wide and confining. Ala and Mwana were huddled in their own cage, crying from the effects of the dracite surrounding them. Their small chests thrummed with terrified moans.

Igbo let out a wounded, keening sound I had never heard from him.

Ashkii reached out awkwardly to stroke Igbo's snout. "Easy," he whispered, voice cracking. "I know. I know." Igbo pressed into him, shaking.

But my attention once again fell on Zaib as he held onto Asha possessively.

Elan loomed over Chato's body in distaste but his face cracked with a cruel smile at the sight. My mind and body wanted to grieve but I couldn't let it. I needed to keep my head clear. Whatever happened, I needed to get Asha out.

"Ah, welcome War Chief," Elan said. "We've been waiting for you."

I loosened my grip on my sword just enough to call my battlemage, heat flickering along my skin. "I've always wondered," I said evenly. "What about Asha threatens you so much? Third in line and a woman. In Ujuima that doesn't seem like much of a threat to you and yet there is something about her..." my gaze moved from her to him "that scares you."

Something in Elan ignited as his nostrils flared and his battlemage rippled through his skin. "You know nothing."

"Oh, I know enough," I said, forcing my voice steady. "I know fear when I see it. You hide it behind your cruelty, but she terrifies you. A woman who can bond with dragons."

He strode toward me, the air around him crackling. "You think she's powerful because of what she can do. You're wrong. She was born an abomination!"

"What am I missing?" I asked circling him.

He smirked, but there was something uneasy in it. "You'll see soon enough," he said looking towards Zaib. "*He* will show you."

"So you do fear *him*, Zaib," I said quietly. "He told you to keep what she is a secret didn't he? And like a good little boy, you di—"

I clenched my jaw as he struck. The pain of his battlemage was all consuming, but somehow I managed to keep on my feet. I channeled my battlemage and let it shroud my body in blue energy like a shield. It gave me just enough relief to barrel towards him. Hands reached for me but they fell away realizing they could not touch me without being burned. Elan's gaze flared as he realized this. He tripped on the stairs and I managed to put my foot on his hand. He screamed in agony. I relished it, pushing down harder. "Get him!" he screamed.

"Stand back, or your emperor dies," I warned.

I pressed my boot harder into Elan's hand until his skin sizzled with blue fire. The guards froze, uncertain. The air stank of burned flesh and fear. Elan writhed beneath me, fury twisting his drooping face.

"You think you can kill me, War Chief?" he rasped.

"I don't think," I growled turning back towards him. "I know."

He reached up and bit my hand.

My battlemage faltered, the fire in my palm wavering. Elan felt it and took his chance, his free hand shot up, and a surge of shadow flared between us. The blast hurled me backward. My head hit the stone with a crack, the light sputtering out of my grip.

I groaned, forcing myself upright in time to see Elan stumble to his feet. Blood streaked down his temple, his smile triumphant.

"Kill him!" he spat pointing to me.

The guards stepped forward, battlemages ready—but just as quickly they stopped.

Not because of me. They were looking at *him*. Zaib.

"Did you not hear me?" Elan barked. "I said kill him!"

No one moved, only Zaib. "Stand down," he said quietly to the soldiers.

The men obeyed. Just like that.

Elan turned, his expression curdling into disbelief. He met my eyes as if he could not accept what was coming to pass. He turned back to Zaib. "What are you doing?"

Zaib's gaze was fixed. "I should be asking you the same."

"I am taking care of both of them like you requested."

"You hurt her!" Zaib snapped, the calm gone from his voice. "That wasn't part of the agreement."

I pushed myself to my knees, my breath ragged. "Agreement?" I spat.

Zaib didn't even acknowledge me. His wrath was solely focused on Elan.

Elan backed away toward the steps. "You forget yourself," he hissed. "You think they'll follow you instead of me? I am their Emperor!"

Zaib smiled like a predator honing in on his prey. "He's all yours, Asha. My first wedding present to you. You may do with him what you wish."

I turned to Asha, confused at what was happening. Elan was too. I was missing something. "What is she going to do?" he asked skeptically.

"He killed your friend—attempted to kill your lover. Most would do so for less Asha."

Elan turned to the top of the stairs, his battlemage releasing until it set off a flare. I shielded my eyes as light exploded in the cabin. Seconds later the sound of cannon fire filled the room. Asha's eyes fell as they turned to the window. The army was attacking the island, an island whose shields had fallen.

"No!" she cried. "You have me. Let the Lightbearers go!" she said, looking to Elan, then to Zaib. "Stop this!"

Zaib looked resolved. "The damage is done," he said motioning to soldiers who left the room. "By the time they are able to stop the cannon fire, much of the island will be destroyed... because of him. I cannot undo the damage," he said, handing her a blade, "but you could end him—the one who has harmed so many."

She hesitated, her eyes flicking back to the fire filling the windows.

"You want to kill him, I know you do," he whispered closing her fingers over the blade. "Here is your chance."

Asha hesitated before taking the blade Zaib offered her and approached Elan.

Elan's eyes grew wide. "You think you can take me down, little sister. Little blind bitch! Never could measure up to anyone. I should have killed you in your crib for trying to steal my birthright. I'll take great pleasure in making you watch your boyfriend die at my hands."

She leapt then. "Asha, no!" I said, but she was already on him. Her hand ripped the necklace from her throat, releasing the contents from the gem. Elan withered in her grasp, until he grew rigid and seemingly unable to move his mangled hands. His eyes rolled to the back of his head, and I could see the life force leaving his body.

"You can't let this happen!" My eyes flicked to Drakkar, whose pain-filled eyes were finally on us. He looked as if he wanted to intervene, but it wasn't he who commanded my attention. It was Mwana.

"You must stop her," she said.

I went completely still, my jaw open, mesmerized by her sweet voice. It was clear as if we'd always been able to communicate in this way.

"Father says, this will destroy her."

I blinked. A dragon, I was listening to a dragon. I'm not sure how long I stood there when she said, *"Move, Adriel!"*

I abandoned any attempt to understand and moved quickly to Asha's side. My hand fell to the blade.

"Asha," I whispered. "Let go."

"He's sent his men to kill the Lightbearers. He killed Chato," she said between clenched teeth.

The tip of the knife pricked Elan's skin and he looked genuinely terrified, as if he never imagined this turn of events.

"You of all people deserve this vengeance. I don't want to deny you that, but if you go through with this, he wins. You will relive this moment for the rest of your life. No matter how justified you feel right now, I can promise you it will not erase the guilt."

Her eyes tear streaked, turned to me. "How do you know?"

I closed my eyes and gave her my free hand. She took it and tapped into the one memory I'd managed to keep from her. The one thing I could not take back.

"You're going to wear down your boots walking back and forward like that," Enapay gurgled. He'd been hurt badly in the last battle, the last of his men handing him over to save themselves. I'd killed them all. But now I was faced with a choice, an awful one, something I could never come back from.

"If you are going to kill me," he coughed. "Get on with it."

"Suppose I don't," I offered. "Suppose I let you rot in here."

He flashed a grin in my direction, his front two teeth gone. "We both know you can't do that, your reign would never be legitimate."

I stared at him, trying to find another option and coming up empty.

"You are really wrestling with this," he said in surprise. "I would have killed you immediately, without hesitation."

"I am not you," I said quietly clenching my fists.

He tilted his face, showing off the mangled mess of his neck and shoulders. "You are right," he said. "I am not the one who has killed a sibling. That is your department."

"It wasn't my fault," I said. "I'm past all of that."

Enapay shrugged. "If you say so, but you know what I think?"

"No," I said stone faced.

"I think," he continued as if I hadn't spoken, "you enjoy killing. I think it is in your blood. I think our little Odi was your first taste of it and you haven't been able to stop."

"Be quiet," I said walking into his cell, my battlemage hot in my hands.

"And where is the girl? The one you stole from me? Did you kill her too?"

I gripped his collar and pulled him forward. "You don't know what you are talking about."

He laughed cruelly. "Don't worry, I know you don't have her, because we found her first."

My shoulders dropped at his words searching his eyes to see if what he said was true.

"You lie!"

"Pretty little thing. I made sure she had a good night with soldiers before I slit her throat."

"Fuck you!" I yelled hitting him in the face, the satisfying sound of cartilage filling the cell.

He tried to speak once more. "All this for a tight little cunt. It's not worth all this trouble."

My mind went quiet, dead quiet. I couldn't say what came over me. It wasn't anger. Anger was too small a word to encapsulate the rage that coursed through me. I didn't even register that I was smashing his face in until his body slumped. As he lay limp in my hands, I bowed my head.

I could feel in my bones she was still alive. And yet, the words spilling from this man could never be reconciled. I'd never be able to forgive their utterance. Blue fire crackled in my hand and I watched his eyes spring open in fear as it traveled toward him.

"No!" a voice said in my mind.

I turned my head and saw a face I had longed to see. "Asha?"

"Adriel! Come back."

If I let her do this, kill Elan, she would never come back from it. I would not let her carry what I had carried.

She gasped as she pulled back. I waited for the look of horror and disgust on her face but it never came. All I saw was sadness and understanding. She out of all people knew what it meant to be betrayed by someone who shared your blood, who was supposed to love and defend you.

Her eyes flicked to Moki and Kitchi, whose chains fell to the ground. Igbo was at their feet, somehow freed from his cage. This was their plan, I now realized—to have Ashkii free everyone they could. It was a good plan for what it was. It served my purposes now.

I took the moment of distraction, while her eyes were on the drag-ons, now being freed, to push down on the blade myself and puncture Elan's neck. He choked, his face contorting first with rage, then with the sick, stunned realization that this was the end before he crumpled to the floor.

"No!" Asha screamed. "He wasn't yours to kill!"

I met her eyes and knew—if she crossed this line, Zaib would own her forever. A single tear rolled down my cheek. "I couldn't let you do it."

Out of the corner of my eye, I saw Kwasi fall to the ground, Miren grasping him asking what was wrong. We were out of time. Kwasi would be free, and I would soon take his place.

Zaib laughed maniacally in the background. "This is too good!"

I kneeled then, grasping at my chest. Asha looked at me alarmed. "What's happening?"

The world tilted. Pain lanced through my chest. My body felt—wrong. "He's changing," Zaib said. "He embraced the shadows. He is one of us—because of you. You have awakened us!"

CHAPTER SIXTY-FOUR

Asha

I watched in horror as Adriel's veins appeared silver against his skin, like all the warmth was leaching out of him.

"Adriel," I cried, reaching for him. His face was frozen. "Adriel, come back to me. Come back. I didn't mean it. I swear I didn't mean it. I love you, don't leave me!"

When he didn't respond, I attempted to tap into his aura, but I was only met with fire. I pushed through, but all I could hear were the screams of Enapay.

"Adriel!" I cried, tears running down my face.

Hands grabbed me from behind. It was Kitchi, I think, but I couldn't be sure. "Stop, Asha. Your hand. You have to stop."

"We can't leave him. We can't leave him here."

"We'll take him with us," Moki promised.

"You can't take him, Asha," Zaib said. I stood tall, meeting his gaze.

"You will not stop me," I said. "You will not take him from me."

I was stunned because his gaze was not filled with anger, as I'd anticipated, but pity. "I did not say I would stop you from taking him. I said you cannot take him. He belongs to the shadows."

Confusion speared through me, but I ignored it. "Watch me," I said.

Kitchi and Moki carried Adriel between them. We had to get back to the island. We had to stop Elan's forces. I started towards Drakkar. Only I stumbled across a figure that lay dead on the ground. My heart broke as I recognized the chilled cheeks and auburn hair. "Chato," I whispered, using my fingers to close his eyes. I leaned down and kissed his cool forehead.

I turned around and glared at Zaib, forcing away every tear I felt. "You will send his body back to Wiyotak. He will be buried with honor."

Zaib's face was blank. "As you wish it."

"I will make sure he is sent to his family," Ashkii said from behind me.

"You are staying then," I said. It wasn't a question but he answered anyway.

"I am of the shadows. I will always return. So will Adriel."

I whipped around unable to accept that Adriel would return. He wouldn't leave. He wouldn't leave me. I made it over to Drakkar, who was nearly free from his bindings. *"Little One."*

The sound of his voice warmed my heart for the briefest of moments.

"Don't try to talk," I said. *"Can you make it to the island? We will need your help getting to land."*

"Yes, I can."

With me at the head, we walked out of the room, passing the emperor and the blood pooling across the throne room floor.

I moved quickly, getting Mwana and Ala onto Drakkar's back and signaling Kwasi and Miren to make room for Moki and Kitchi on Zephyr. Ashkii waited beside Igbo, whose injury needed wrapping but would have to wait until we reached Lumira. Every minute we stayed was a minute for Zaib to change his mind.

Adriel had not moved from where I had left him. His skin was cool when I took his hand, cooler than it had been even minutes ago, the silver now reaching his neck. The morning sun was just beginning to push over the edges of the clouds and I was grateful for it. He needed the warmth more than any of us.

"Don't leave," he gasped. I stopped, turning to him. He looked terrible, spidery veins now covered his entire body.

"Never," I said. "I'm right here."

He smiled, though it cost him as he flinched in pain. "We are a pair, aren't we?"

"Adriel, I'm sorry. I never meant—"

"Hush," he whispered. "We don't have much time."

Tears streaked down my face. I wasn't sure what he meant except that somehow I was losing him. "There is something in my pocket," he gasped. "It is weighing me down. Can you remove it?"

I rifled through his cloak until I found a small blue pouch with a dragon emblem on it. It was light in my hand. I wasn't sure why he needed me to take it off him.

I opened the pouch and gasped at what I saw. A ring. The moment I touched it, recognition struck. White gold shaped into a dragon's head, a sapphire set into the curve of its back, smaller stones tracing the sweep of its tail.

"I've seen this before," I whispered. "This was Nayeli's."

"I had her reset it," he said. "With a sapphire. To match your hair. Do you like it?"

"You did this... for me?"

"When you were at Empira Castle," he admitted.

My breath hitched. "That long?"

"It's been in my pocket a long time. I only found the courage to change the stone recently. For the day I had enough nerve to ask you to be my wife."

I tried to speak. I couldn't.

"I need you to wear it," he said.

"Of course," I said softly. "Every day."

He shook his head. He tried to speak but his throat was swelling.

"It's okay. You don't have to say anything more."

"Tazbah," he breathed. "Memory mage."

My heart stuttered as I tried to understand.

"Wear it," he said faintly. "When you're ready."

"I don't understand."

"Find Tazbah. She'll explain everything."

His fingers brushed my cheek—the uninjured one. "I'm fading," he whispered. "I can feel myself forgetting. It won't be long now."

"No," I said fiercely. "Whatever this is, we can fix it."

He wiped my tears away—and then, impossibly, sat upright. Color returned to his face as the silver faded from his skin. "Come here."

I climbed up beside him on Drakkar's back, wrapping my arms around him. He held me just as tightly.

"Wear it," he murmured. "So I'll come back to you. So I'll remember this. Remember you."

"I don't understand," I sobbed. "You can't leave me."

"His change is nearly complete," Ashkii said quietly. "He'll feel the pull back to the Shadows."

"But does he say he is forgetting?" I asked. "What does that mean?"

Ashkii looked as lost as I felt. "Memory loss is not a part of the transition."

"He can't leave," I whispered.

"He has to." Drakkar's voice was heavy. Ala watched us with sad eyes. "They both do."

"No!" Mwana cried realizing he meant Igbo too.

"They'll die without each other," Drakkar said softly.

"I'll be fine, Papa," Igbo said bravely, pressing his snout to him.

Drakkar stroked him gently. "I know you will." He looked to Ashkii. "Take care of him."

"I will," Igbo promised.

Adriel's grip changed in my hands—uncertain now, unfamiliar. When I met his eyes, he was looking at me the way you look at someone you almost remember.

"Adriel?" I whispered.

"Yes," he said politely. "That's my name. How did you know?"

"You're... well known on this ship," I managed.

He studied me, puzzled. "I don't know how I ended up on this creature, but I should be going."

"Where?" I asked desperately.

"I'm sorry," he said. "I don't know you well enough to say."

He noticed my tears and offered me a handkerchief. "Don't cry. Whoever caused tears isn't worth it."

That broke me.

He seemed to take in his surroundings for the first time, noting the dragon beneath him. He slid carefully down from Drakkar's back and onto the ship, flexing his ankles as if to gain his bearings. "Do you think you could show me around?"

"Of course," I whispered. "Ashkii... could you assist?"

"Yes." Ashkii nodded. "Come. I'll take you to the mess hall if you're hungry."

Adriel's stomach rumbled in answer. "I am," he said bewildered.

"It is part of the change," Ashkii said knowingly. "Follow me."

He began to turn but stopped, locking eyes with me. I returned his gaze for as long as he would allow.

"I know you," he said finally.

The words hit me more deeply than I was prepared for. I couldn't speak, couldn't breathe. I stood there holding the pieces of myself together by a thread.

"Yes," I said, my voice breaking.

"Come," Ashkii coaxed. "Let's get you fed. Come Igbo."

Igbo looked to Ashkii, and back to me and Drakkar.

"Don't worry. I'll watch over them."

I embraced him tightly. "You take care of yourself," I said, voice breaking.

"I will."

Igbo leapt onto the deck, following behind them.

Drakkar and Zephyr took off into the sky. If Adriel looked back, I never saw it. I turned away as we disappeared into the sunrise.

Some goodbyes were too painful to watch.

EPILOGUE

If your heart is shattered, keep reading...

I walked across the once-peaceful island, now destroyed. What had been a sanctuary—the one place where I could exist without sight and still be whole—was nothing but ruin. The fountains that once sang softly at every crossing stood shattered, their basins split and dry. The stone-brick ground beneath my feet was darkened, slick in places, stained with blood that had seeped into the mortar. Buildings that had once curved gently with the land lay toppled and torn open, their walls collapsed inward as if the island itself had folded under the weight of violence.

And now that the magic was stripped and I could see it fully, the devastation was even more painful to witness. Seeing it only confirmed what grief I already knew; the island had been broken, and something in me with it. I had done this, I had sacrificed this island for my dragons.

Miren and the Guardians moved through the wreckage, searching carefully, calling out to one another. "There are survivors," Miren assured me. "All is not lost."

But they were wrong. Everything had been lost.

"Ireti?" I asked.

Miren looked down before saying, "We haven't found her."

I took a step back before I realized I was moving, and a sharp clink rang against the stone at my feet. My breath caught. I reached into my pocket—my fingers brushed empty fabric, a hole torn straight through.

"No," I whispered, frantic. "No, no—"

"What is wrong?" Drakkar's voice slid into my mind as he approached.

"The ring!"

Kwasi stepped to my side. "Calm yourself, Sister."

"I found it," Mwana called, nudging at a small and gleaming object with her snout.

Relief buckled my knees. I scooped the ring into my hands, holding it to my chest as my body convulsed with silent sobs.

"Let's give her space," Kwasi murmured. The Guardians cleared away.

I cradled the ring—his ring—turning it in the light.

I slid it onto my finger and wiped my tears, letting the sunlight catch the sapphire's surface. A perfect fit, of course it was.

For a moment, its glow warmed my skin.

Then the world tilted. A sharp jolt shot through my skull, and the island dissolved.

When my eyes opened, I was no longer in Lumira.

I stood inside a vast library—towering shelves, scattered scrolls, and maps pinned haphazardly to the walls. A single lantern burned low.

At a table in the center, Tazbah hunched over a microscope, muttering to herself. She looked frantic—dark circles under her eyes, pink hair tangled, as though she hadn't slept or bathed in days.

Suddenly, the door burst open.

Adriel and Kwasi walked in. "Did you find it?" Adriel asked.

"I think so," Tazbah breathed, still bent over the table.

"Do you realize what we have?" Kwasi asked, excitement trembling in his voice.

"Show us," Adriel demanded gently, stepping closer.

Tazbah pushed the map toward them. "There is an island. It was once called Lumira. It's been erased from all known charts—but I found this old one hidden between the pages of an atlas."

Adriel leaned in. "And the Phoenix of Tears? You said you traced it."

"We've been assuming it was a pit of fire or a body of water," Tazbah said. "But it's not."

"It's not?" Adriel asked.

She shook her head, eyes wide. "No. It's a flower that grows near water. Look here—the structure is built into the side of these hills. And here... these markings."

Kwasi squinted. "Are those butterflies?"

"I thought so too," she said, almost giddy as she pulled out another text. "But they shouldn't exist anymore. These..." she tapped the illustration, "...are papillions."

I tore myself out of the memory with a gasp. I stood there on the ruined ground of Lumira, breathing hard. He had done this before I had given him a single reason to, after I had left him, after I had shattered both of our hearts. He had decided after my betrayal that if there was a price to pay, he would be the one to pay it. That was who he was, who he had always been. I'd spent years running from this man and he had been running towards me the whole time.

Then I ran.

I didn't know where I was going, only that my body remembered what my mind did not.

Past the square where Lightbearers once laughed. Past the bell tower that marked our days. Past the cells where Ashkii had been held.

I kept running until the cliffs opened before me—the edge of Lumira, and the waterfall roaring below.

Adriel's voice echoed in my mind, soft but firm. *"We must not recall this information until it is time. If it fell into the wrong hands, the result would be devastating."*

"Each of us will have a piece of it. Tazbah will carry the map, Kwasi the ability to read it, and I will carry the location of the Phoenix of Tears."

"Where will you put that memory?" Tazbah asked.

He pulled out a ring from his pocket. "Here."

"Are you sure?" Kwasi asked.

"Yes."

"But a memory charm that powerful could wipe our memories forever," Tazbah warned. "It is not worth it."

There was a prick of the fingers and an exchange of blood as Tazbah's battlemage had bound the memory. "If there is a price, I will pay it," he said.

"You can't be weakened," Kwasi argued. "I'll carry it until the spell is done."

Adriel leaned into Tazbah. "And then it will pass to me. That is the deal or I'm not doing this."

They nodded. "We cannot allow this information to fall into the wrong hands," he said.

I stood at the edge of the cliff, the waterfall, thundering below, the mist rising, and clouds that caught the light. And there on the water's edge, growing from the rock face, were Cintears, my mother's favorite, in clusters. I had been amid the Phoenix of Tears all this time. I understood then what I was. Not just a Lightbearer. Not just a woman who could bond with dragons. Something older than that.

Adriel's face appeared in my head, his fingers entwined with mine.

Do you trust me?

I did. I always had.

I thought of Drakkar, who had found me in the dark when I was nothing. Of Adriel, pressing the ring into my hands with fingers that no longer knew my name. Of every person in the Five Kingdoms who had tried to break me and failed. I thought of my mother, who defied a ritual to bring me into this world, who had ended her life to contain what loving the wrong man had cost. I would not concern myself with whether I was making the same mistakes. But I would honor what she gave me.

I didn't leap so much as surrender, allowing myself to fall forward into the roar and the mist and the not-knowing what was next.

The water hit me like a stone wall. It was cold, then not, a pressure that pulled, as if the waterfall itself was reaching itself around me. It felt like I'd unlocked something without even realizing it.

My skin ignited first. The pain wasn't immediate, rather it felt like I was moving against a current that pulled at my bones that lengthened with every wave. As bones lengthened and shifted, I opened my mouth to scream, but what came out was not a scream. It was something else.

I didn't know how long it lasted because time was irrelevant here. The only thing that mattered, the only truth that could be gleaned was that I'd had this feeling my entire life, and I'd run from it. No longer.

Instead of falling, I rose—pulled upward by a force older than the time itself. I was becoming what I had always been meant to be. Wings unfurled in the sun. Wings, I had wings and silver scales. When I emerged from the water, I threw my head back and roared into the sky.

I will free you, my love. I will force the shadows to bow at my feet.

ABOUT THE AUTHOR

Dr. Iman has been in love with love ever since she picked up her first Babysitter's Club romance. Since then her fascination has blossomed into a lifelong passion for stories with battling kingdoms, moody dragons, and the kind of magic that only comes from love. Today, she writes sweeping romantasy novels that center characters who rarely get the spotlight—heroes and heroines whose voices deserve to be heard and celebrated. When she's not weaving worlds filled with epic adventures and forbidden love, Iman is living out her own love story with her husband, chasing after their two adorable children, and sharing her home with a cat she's wildly allergic to, but far too attached to ever give up.

Check for updates on the final book in the Lightbearer Series by signing up for the newsletter or visiting imanchristians.com . You can find Dr. Iman posting daily on her socials. TikTok/Instagram/Threads: @drimanauthor